OXFORD WORLD'S CLASSICS

═══

THOMAS CARLYLE

Sartor Resartus

═══

Edited with an Introduction and Notes by
KERRY McSWEENEY
and
PETER SABOR

OXFORD
UNIVERSITY PRESS

OXFORD
UNIVERSITY PRESS

Great Clarendon Street, Oxford OX2 6DP

Oxford University Press is a department of the University of Oxford.
It furthers the University's objective of excellence in research, scholarship,
and education by publishing worldwide in

Oxford New York

Athens Auckland Bangkok Bogotá Buenos Aires Cape Town
Chennai Dar es Salaam Delhi Florence Hong Kong Istanbul Karachi
Kolkata Kuala Lumpur Madrid Melbourne Mexico City Mumbai Nairobi
Paris São Paulo Shanghai Singapore Taipei Tokyo Toronto Warsaw

with associated companies in Berlin Ibadan

Oxford is a registered trade mark of Oxford University Press
in the UK and in certain other countries

Published in the United States
by Oxford University Press Inc., New York

British Library Cataloguing in Publication Data

Data available

Library of Congress Cataloging in Publication Data

Carlyle, Thomas, 1795–1881.
Sartor resartus
(Oxford world's classics)
Bibliography: p.
I. McSweeney, Kerry, 1941– .
II. Sabor, Peter.
III. Title.
PR4429.A2M37 1987 824'.8 87–5753

ISBN–13: 978–0–19–283673–1
ISBN–10: 0–19–283673–0

6

Printed in Great Britain by
Clays Ltd, St Ives plc

SARTOR RESARTUS

THOMAS CARLYLE was born in 1795 at Ecclefechan, a small market village in Dumfriesshire. He studied for the ministry, enrolled in law classes, and taught briefly before deciding on a career as a writer. During the 1820s, his essays and translations helped to introduce German literature and thought to a British audience. *Sartor Resartus*, his one full-scale work of imaginative fiction, was first published periodically in 1833–4. In 1826 Carlyle had married Jane Welsh. In 1834 they moved from Scotland to London and settled at Cheyne Row, Chelsea. It was here that Carlyle wrote the works that confirmed his position as the most influential of the Victorian cultural prophets: *The French Revolution* (1837), *On Heroes and Hero-Worship* (1841), *Past and Present* (1843), *Latter-Day Pamphlets* (1850), and the six-volume history of *Frederick the Great* (1858–65). His *Reminiscences* were published shortly after his death, in 1881.

KERRY MCSWEENEY is Molson Professor at McGill University in Montreal. His publications include the World's Classics edition of Elizabeth Barrett Browning's *Aurora Leigh*, *Tennyson and Swinburne as Romantic Naturalists*, *Four Contemporary Novelists*, *Moby Dick: Ishmael's Mighty Book*, *George Eliot: A Literary Life*, *The Language of the Senses: Sensory-Perceptual Dynamics in Wordsworth, Coleridge, Thoreau, Whitman, and Dickinson*, and *Supreme Attachments: Studies in Victorian Love Poetry*.

PETER SABOR is Professor of English at Laval University, Quebec. His other editions for Oxford World's Classics are Burney's *Cecilia* (with Margaret Anne Doody) and *The Wanderer* (with Doody and Robert Mack), and Cleland's *Memoirs of a Woman of Pleasure*. He has also edited Richardson's *Pamela*, Sarah Fielding's *David Simple* and *Remarks on Clarissa*, and Burney's *Complete Plays*, and published two books on Horace Walpole: *Horace Walpole: A Reference Guide*, and *Horace Walpole: The Critical Heritage*.

OXFORD WORLD'S CLASSICS

*For over 100 years Oxford World's Classics have brought
readers closer to the world's great literature. Now with over 700
titles—from the 4,000-year-old myths of Mesopotamia to the
twentieth century's greatest novels—the series makes available
lesser-known as well as celebrated writing.*

*The pocket-sized hardbacks of the early years contained
introductions by Virginia Woolf, T. S. Eliot, Graham Greene,
and other literary figures which enriched the experience of reading.
Today the series is recognized for its fine scholarship and
reliability in texts that span world literature, drama and poetry,
religion, philosophy and politics. Each edition includes perceptive
commentary and essential background information to meet the
changing needs of readers.*

CONTENTS

INTRODUCTION

[1]

Sartor Resartus has long been recognized as a work of the foremost literary historical importance. For one thing, it marks the transition from the Romantic to the Victorian periods as sharply as the Preface to *Lyrical Ballads* marks that between the eighteenth century and the Romantic period. And unlike Wordsworth's manifesto, Carlyle's book enacts within itself the dislocations of the passage. For another, *Sartor Resartus*, which was first published in book form in Boston in 1836 with an enthusiastic preface by Ralph Waldo Emerson, was an important stimulus to the great mid-nineteenth-century flowering of American literature. Poe may have loathed the book, as he did everything of Carlyle's; but it was a key influence, both thematic and formal, on two of the master-works of the American Renaissance—Melville's *Moby-Dick* and Whitman's *Song of Myself*.

Most importantly, *Sartor Resartus* is the seminal expression of the thought of the most influential of the Victorian cultural prophets. The fundamental Carlylean doctrines are all articulated, or at least adumbrated, here: the horrors of Utilitarianism; the religious basis of society; the pattern of conversion—from the Everlasting No, through the Centre of Indifference to the Everlasting Yea—which showed that, in the words of Thomas Henry Huxley, 'a deep sense of religion was compatible with the entire absence of theology';[1] the importance of vocation—of an individual's finding his 'maximum of Capability'; the superiority of renunciation to the pursuit of happiness; the moral imperatives of work, duty, and reverence; the need for heroes; and the social vision that saw contemporary Britain divided into the two nations of rich and poor. As such, *Sartor Resartus* is of quintessential importance for understanding the literature and the moral and intellectual culture of Victorian Britain. 'For there is hardly a superior or active mind of this

[1] *Life and Letters of T. H. Huxley* (New York, 1900), i. 237.

generation', George Eliot observed in 1855, 'that has not been modified by Carlyle's writings . . . The character of his influence is best seen in the fact that many of the men who have the least agreement with his opinions are those to whom the reading of *Sartor Resartus* was an epoch in the history of their minds.'[2]

Of course, literary historical importance does not of itself make a literary work intrinsically interesting, let alone a major achievement. In the case of *Sartor Resartus*, its extrinsic importance and tract-for-the-times aspects can even become serious obstacles to seeing the work for what it actually is—so serious that a process of defamiliarization may be necessary before Carlyle's text can recover its freshness. 'Custom', as the central personage of *Sartor Resartus* says, 'doth make dotards of us all.' One of the first things overlooked by customary readings of the text as a secular scripture for the Victorians is the exuberant play of mind and trenchant insight. There is, for example, this *en passant* encapsulation of a complex process of historical change: 'He who first shortened the labour of Copyists by device of *Movable Types* was disbanding hired Armies, and cashiering most Kings and Senates, and creating a whole new Democratic world; he had invented the Art of Printing.' Or consider the chilling prediction concerning the 'two Sects which . . . divide the more unsettled portion of the British People; and agitate that ever-vexed country'. The roots of these sects 'extend through the entire structure of Society . . . striving to separate and isolate it into two contradictory, uncommunicating masses', which 'it seems probable . . . will one day part England between them; each recruiting itself from the intermediate ranks, till there be none left to enlist on either side'.

But the most important part of the process of recovery would involve the recognition that *Sartor Resartus* is essentially a work of imaginative fiction that demands a more sensitive and complex response than that in which its formal and stylistic husks are stripped away to reveal the doctrinal kernels. Carlyle would have seen the attempt to turn him into a literary artist, let alone a writer of imaginative fiction, as an impertinence. But this is exactly what must be done in the late twentieth century if *Sartor Resartus*, his one sustained and fully realized

[2] *Essays of George Eliot*, ed. T. Pinney (London, 1963), 213-14.

piece of imaginative fiction, is again to be recognized as one of
the master-works of nineteenth-century English literature.
When so considered, *Sartor* can be seen as a work that has less in
common with such classic Victorian prose-of-thought texts as
Newman's *Apologia pro Vita Sua*, Arnold's *Culture and Anarchy*,
Ruskin's *Unto this Last*, or even Carlyle's own *Past and Present*
and *On Heroes and Hero-Worship* than it does with such
problematic fictions as Emily Brontë's *Wuthering Heights* (in
both works the informing Romantic content is severely quali-
fied by the narratorial form through which it is presented to the
reader); Melville's *Moby-Dick* (both works employ uncertain,
self-conscious narrators who are energetically and sometimes
comically attempting to discover coherence and meaning in
their material and to say something important about ultimate
issues); Dostoevsky's *Notes from Underground* (both works use
an alienated anti-hero to launch attacks on Utilitarian beliefs
and values); and even Nietzsche's *Thus Spake Zarathustra* (the
prophet figures of both works are rebellious and isolated,
oscillate between constructive and destructive impulses towards society, and speak in a 'hyperbolic hortatory voice'[3]).

[2]

The 'Getting Under Way' chapter in Book II of *Sartor Resartus*
contains some shrewd observations concerning the problem of
vocation in the nineteenth century: 'To each is given a certain
inward Talent, a certain outward Environment of Fortune; to
each, by wisest combination of these two, a certain maximum
of Capability. But the hardest problem were ever this first: To
find by study of yourself, and of the ground you stand on, what
your combined inward and outward Capability specially is.'
By 1821, when he was 26, Thomas Carlyle, after much anxious
reflection, had discovered his vocation. He would not be a
clergyman, a lawyer or a teacher; he would be a writer: he
'must live by Literature, at all hazards'.[4] But there is a
considerable difference between identifying a vocation and

---

[3] A. J. LaValley, *Carlyle and the Idea of the Modern* (New Haven, 1968), 110.
[4] *Collected Letters of Thomas and Jane Welsh Carlyle*, ed. C. R. Sanders *et al.*
(Durham, North Carolina, 1970–   ), i. 336.

becoming launched in it; to quote again from *Sartor*: 'Between vague wavering Capability and fixed indubitable Performance, what a difference!' Large questions remained: what would Carlyle write about and in what way? What would be his subjects, his style, and his form of expression?

One possibility that Carlyle began to explore was prose fiction. His father, a strict Calvinist, would not tolerate anything fictitious in books and had forbidden his children to read imaginative literature. But when young Thomas was sent away to school, he boarded with a family whose lending library included novels and romances; during the next years he read through Smollett, Defoe, Fielding, Sterne, and Swift; and he later read Walter Scott's novels as they appeared. By the time he decided on a career as a writer, Carlyle's ambition was to write prose fiction, which (partly owing to his reading of Goethe and Schiller) he considered superior to history for the revelation of truth.

Carlyle's first known attempt at fiction was 'Cruthers and Johnson', a tale of friendship set in the eighteenth century and recalling that century's fiction in its narrative method and mood. The story was written early in 1822. In December of the same year, in a letter to Jane Welsh, Carlyle described his plans for a far more ambitious fiction, an epistolary novel in the mode of Wertherian romance. The hero of the projected novel would speak forth his sufferings—'not in the puling Lake-style—but with a tongue of fire—sharp, sarcastic, apparently unfeeling' yet at the same time revealing 'a mind of lofty thoughts and generous affections smarting under the torment of its own overnobleness, and ready to break in pieces by the force of its own energies'. It would be evident that the hero 'cannot long exist in this to him most blasted, waste and lonely world'. Carlyle proposed to Jane that he would supply the hero's letters while she would indite those of his female interlocutor. But the scheme never got off the ground. One reason was circumstantial: Carlyle found that he and Jane needed to consult together every day, which they were unable to do. The other reason was subjective: 'I grew affrighted and chilled at the aspect of the Public.'[5]

[5] *Collected Letters*, ii. 230.

Carlyle's next fictional project involved no incapacitating premonitions of the Public's disapprobation: during 1823–4 he worked on a translation of Goethe's *Wilhelm Meister's Apprenticeship*. The process of translating the novel proved laborious and irksome: 'There are touches of the very highest most etherial genius in it; but diluted with floods of insipidity, which even *I* would not have written for the world.' 'There is poetry in the book, and prose, prose forever. When I read of players and libidinous actresses and their sorry pasteboard apparatus for beautifying and enlivening the "moral world", I render it into grammatical English—with a feeling mild and charitable as that of a starving hyaena. . . . [I] could sometimes fall down and worship [Goethe]; at other times I could kick him out of the room.'[6] Both these comments suggest how uncongenial Carlyle found Goethe's patient accumulation of realistic detail. As Henry James was to note in his 1865 review of a reissue of Carlyle's translation: 'In few other works is so profound a meaning enveloped in so common a form. The slow, irresistible action of this latent significance is an almost awful phenomenon.'[7]

That Carlyle was impatient with Goethe's realistic method is clear from *Wotton Reinfred*, which novel he began writing in autumn 1826. The subject is similar to Goethe's—a young hero's search for transcendent wisdom—but the means are very different. Carlyle's unfinished work is a didactic, fabular novel of ideas which eschews realistic modes of narrative and characterization in its impatience to air thematic issues of overriding import. It is not surprising that Carlyle broke off composition of *Wotton* and that another story ('Illudo Chartis') begun around this time, which has a Wertherian hero and employs the device of an editor as a frame for the narrative, was also abandoned. By the end of the 1820s Carlyle was having growing doubts about the status and efficacy of fiction, and thinking hard about alternative means through which to realize himself as a writer.

These doubts had hardened into dicta by 1832, when Carlyle

[6] Ibid. 434, 437.
[7] *Literary Criticism: French Writers; Other European Writers; The Prefaces to the New York Edition*, ed. L. Edel (New York, 1984), 944.

wrote his essay, 'Biography'. Even in the highest works of art, he argued, one's interest was apt to be 'strongly or even mainly of a Biographic sort'. The same was true 'through the whole range of what is called Literature'. The entire thrust of history, for example, was biographic, and when one came to consider 'the whole class of Fictitious Narratives, from the highest category of epic or dramatic Poetry, in Shakespeare and Homer, down to the lowest of froth Prose in the Fashionable Novel', one found that all these were 'but so many mimic Biographies'. The problem with fiction was that it inevitably partook 'of the nature of *lying*'; and therefore inevitably possessed an 'in some degree, unsatisfactory character'. What was important and significant was '*Reality*'. Even if 'the *probable* be well adhered to' in works of fiction, the evil, while 'much mended, [was] nowise completely cured'. Here and there, 'a *Tom Jones*, a *Meister*, a *Crusoe*, will yield no little solacement to the minds of men; though still immeasurably less than a *Reality* would'. As for the varieties of literature, including the 'Ship-loads of Fashionable Novels': they were 'the foam of penny-beer' because 'there is no *Reality* in them'. One had to realize 'how impressive the smallest historical *fact* may become, as contrasted with the grandest *fictitious event*; what an incalculable force lies for us in this consideration: The Thing which I here hold imaged in my mind did actually occur.'[8]

Carlyle had begun to think about historical subject-matter as the outlet for his literary talents as early as 1822 when he had read Milton and histories of the English Civil War in the hope of finding a subject to write upon. But it was not until 1833, after almost a decade of attempting to write fiction, that he became fully convinced that the (mainly biographical) subject-matter of the French Revolution could furnish material for a historical work that might become a masterpiece, perhaps even 'the grand Poem of our Time'.[9] The 'Biography' essay, how-ever, itself suggests that it was not so easy for Carlyle to escape contamination by fiction as he seemed to think. For in the

[8] *Works of Thomas Carlyle*, Centenary Edition, ed. H. D. Traill (London, 1896–9), xxviii. 45, 46, 47–8, 49, 51–2, 58, 54.

[9] *Collected Letters*, vi. 446.

middle of his essay Carlyle had introduced a fictional device, a book by a non-existent German professor—Doctor Gottfried Sauerteig's *Aesthetische Springwurzeln*—and inserted into a long quotation from the Professor's work his argument concerning the mendacious character of all fiction. This was the very same fictional device that Carlyle had used two years previously in *Sartor Resartus*, which opens as a review article of a learned book on clothes—*Die Kleider, ihr Werden und Wirken*—by a non-existent German professor named Diogenes Teufelsdröckh. It was in *Sartor Resartus*, which is simultaneously his one full-length work of imaginative fiction and his farewell to fiction, that Carlyle finally found a way to record the story of his earlier life, including its Wertherian anxieties, to express the social and religious vision he had been forging during the preceding decade, and pre-emptively to dramatize his affrighted premonition of 'the aspect of the Public'.

[3]

The first reference to what became *Sartor Resartus* appears in Carlyle's journal for September 1830: 'I am going to write— Nonsense. It is on "Clothes." Heaven be my comforter!' A month later he wrote to his brother John: 'For myself here [in Craigenputtock] I am leading the stillest life. . . . What I am writing at is the strangest of all things: begun as an Article for *Fraser*; then found to be too long (except it were divided into two); now sometimes looking almost, as if it would swell into a Book. A very singular piece, I assure you! It glances from Heaven to Earth & back again in a strange satirical frenzy whether *fine* or not remains to be seen.' The piece was called *Teufelsdreck* (*Devil's Shit*) after its principal character. Early in November this 'singular piece' was sent to *Fraser's Magazine*. To its author's great disappointment his bizarre submission was rejected. When the manuscript was back in his hands Carlyle determined to expand it into a book. He outlined his plans in a letter to John of January 1831: 'I have taken a notion that I can make rather a good *Book* of it, and one above all likely to produce some desirable impression on the world even now . . . I can devise some more Biography for Teufelsdreck; give a second deeper part, in the same vein, leading thro' Religion and the nature of Society, and Lord knows what.' Carlyle worked on his book from January to late July 1831, when it was finished. The original two-part article had become Book I of the completed work; the biography of Teufelsdröckh formed Book II; and the 'deeper part, in the same vein', concerning 'Religion and the nature of Society', became Book III. At long last, more than a decade after determining that the vocation of writer was the means of realizing his powers to the full, Carlyle had succeeded in writing a book. But he now had to endure the frustration of being unable to find a publisher. Eventually, he had to return to *Fraser's Magazine*, and offer to 'slit' his manuscript 'up into stripes, and send it forth in the Periodical way'. The work was accepted for serial publication and finally appeared in print under the title *Sartor Resartus* (*The Tailor Retailored*) between November 1833 and August 1834.[10]

Between its original conception as *Teufelsdreck* and its eventual publication as *Sartor Resartus*, Carlyle considered a third title for his work, 'Thoughts on Clothes; or Life and Opinions of Herr. D. Teufelsdröckh D.U.J.',[11] and in the 'Editorial Difficulties' chapter of Book I the Editor characterizes his book as 'properly a "Life and Opinions of Herr Teufelsdröckh" '. The allusion is to an eighteenth-century precursor of *Sartor Resartus*, Sterne's *The Life and Opinions of Tristram Shandy* (1760–7), one of Carlyle's favourite fictional works. A more direct reference follows in the 'Adamitism' chapter of Book I, which concludes with a quotation from 'Yorick Sterne's' novel. Both *Tristram Shandy* and *Sartor* are fictions concerned with the making of biographies; both are steeped in the tradition of learned wit, deriving from Rabelais and Cervantes; and both provide dazzling displays of linguistic inventiveness, making frequent use of neologisms and borrowings from a variety of languages. Both are, at least in part, playful works, like Carlyle's earlier, abandoned fiction 'Illudo Chartis' ('I play on paper'). C. F. Harrold rightly noted over fifty years ago that

[10] Ibid. v. 164, 175, 215; vi. 395. The name of the hero had been changed from *Teufelsdreck* to the less vulgar *Teufelsdröckh* (Devil's excrement) by February 1833.

[11] Ibid. vi. 395. 'D.U.J.' could be expanded to 'Doctor of Universal Jurisprudence'.

while Carlyle's ideas are profoundly indebted to those of German thinkers, his formal debts are primarily to English experimentalists such as Sterne, whom Carlyle termed our 'best, our finest, if not our strongest' humorist.[12]

A still more important influence on Carlyle was Swift, whose *A Tale of a Tub* (1704) provides the seminal idea for Carlyle's book about clothes and their symbolic and religious meanings. Central to Teufelsdröckh's theories is the idea expressed in the 'Prospective' chapter concluding Book I that 'the whole external Universe and what it holds is but Clothing; and the essence of all Science lies in the PHILOSOPHY OF CLOTHES', just as the editor had enquired in the second section of *A Tale of a Tub*, 'what is Man himself but a *Micro-Coat*, or rather a compleat Suit of Cloaths with all its Trimmings?' In the 'Tailors' chapter of Book III, Carlyle acknowledges his debt when Teufelsdröckh expounds 'the doctrine, which Swift, with the keen forecast of genius, dimly anticipated . . . that the Tailor is not only a Man, but something of a Creator or Divinity'. As Teufelsdröckh's 'dimly anticipated' suggests, however, Carlyle makes profounder use of the clothes metaphor than had his predecessor. In *A Tale of a Tub*, the fit suit of clothes is that worn by moderate Anglicans, in contrast to the excessive gaudiness of Catholics and the fanatical plainness of Dissenters. But in *Sartor Resartus*, the clothing fashioned by society and by religious institutions must be removed and replaced entirely; Carlyle thus resembles Jack, the persona for dissent in *A Tale of a Tub*, more closely than Martin, Swift's Anglican representative.

Despite this obvious contrast between the descendentalist Swift and the transcendentalist Carlyle, *Sartor Resartus* is imbued with the spirit of various Swiftian writings. Teufelsdröckh's observation in the 'Pedagogy' chapter of Book II on man's 'omnipotent or rather omni-patient Talent of being Gulled' clearly derives from Swift's famous definition of 'Felicity' in the ninth section of *A Tale of a Tub* as '*the Possession of being well deceived*'. *Gulliver's Travels* (1726), another favourite of Carlyle's, is also a recurring presence in *Sartor Resartus*;

[12] *Carlyle and German Thought: 1819–1834* (New York, 1934), 6; Carlyle, 'Jean Paul Friedrich Richter' (1827), in *Works*, xxvi. 17.

the Laputians' 'Bladders with dried Peas' appear in the 'Pure Reason' chapter of Book I, while Teufelsdröckh's acerbic reflections on warfare in the 'Centre of Indifference', Book II, are surely influenced by Gulliver's grimly ironic account to the King of Brobdingnag of human beings killing one another. More Swiftian overtones are heard in the project for shooting, salting, and barrelling paupers described in the 'Helotage' chapter of Book III, a savage piece of irony deriving from the scheme to kill, dress, and export children of the Irish poor in Swift's *A Modest Proposal* (1729). And in the earlier definition of man as 'a forked straddling animal with bandy legs', in 'The World Out of Clothes' chapter of Book I, Carlyle is quoting directly from the eleventh chapter of *The Memoirs of Martinus Scriblerus* (1741), a collaborative production of Swift and his fellow Scriblerians. Allusions such as this, as well as ones to Pope and Gay's *Memoirs of P. P. Clerk of this Parish* in the 'Prospective' chapter of Book I and to *The Adventures of Ferdinand Count Fathom* (1753) by 'English Smollett', in the 'Centre of Indifference' chapter of Book II, demonstrate Carlyle's immersion in the satirical, non-realistic fiction of the eighteenth century that prepared the way for the constantly shifting ironies and mordant satire of *Sartor Resartus*.

Other important influences on *Sartor* are found in Carlyle's own writings of the previous decade. A number of passages from *Wotton Reinfred*, for example, were worked into the story of Teufelsdröckh's spiritual development in Book II. Of much greater importance is the influence of the periodical essays that Carlyle had been writing. Generically speaking, *Sartor Resartus* is a distinctly mixed work; but it is before anything else a fictitious review essay in which Carlyle makes brilliant imaginative use of the conventions of the form that he had himself helped to develop during the previous decade. In 1823 he had written the first of a series of essays and review articles that were to play a significant role in introducing German literature and thought to a wide British audience. The basic method of these pieces was to combine biographical accounts of the lives of their subjects with descriptions and appreciations of their work. At the same time, the review essay format more and more became a vehicle for the expression of Carlyle's own emerging ideas and sense of the times. In fact, by the end of the decade his review essays were being superseded by pieces such as 'Signs of the Times' and 'Characteristics' that show Carlyle emerging *in propria persona* as a social critic and cultural prophet.

One of Carlyle's review essays, his first for the *Edinburgh Review*, was on Jean Paul Richter, the German humorist whose 'fantastic, many-coloured, far-grasping, everyway perplexed and extraordinary' mode of writing was an appreciable influence on *Sartor Resartus*—a point indirectly acknowledged in the fourth chapter of Book I when the Editor/narrator recalls that the only time he ever saw Teufelsdröckh laugh was during a conversation with Jean Paul, the one writer of all those mentioned in the text who appears in person. Jean Paul's works, Carlyle wrote in this 1827 review essay, were 'no less multifarious than extensive', and while his chief productions were novels, 'the name Novelist, as we in England must understand it, would ill describe so vast and discursive a genius.' The most striking feature of Jean Paul's method was his sporting with the text, the two principal manifestations of which were his disruptive editorial and narratorial commentary and his style. Concerning the former, Carlyle noted that 'every work, be it fiction or serious treatise, is embaled in some fantastic wrappage, some mad narrative accounting for its appearance, and connecting it with the author, who generally becomes a person in the drama himself, before all is over'. As for the style, it was deliberately outlandish: Jean Paul

deals with astonishing liberality in parentheses, dashes, and subsidiary clauses; invents hundreds of new words, alters old ones, or by hyphen chains and pairs and packs them together into most jarring combination; in short, produces sentences of the most heterogeneous, lumbering, interminable kind. Figures without limit; indeed the whole is one tissue of metaphors, and similes, and allusions to all the provinces of Earth, Sea and Air; interlaced with epigrammatic breaks, vehement bursts, or sardonic turns, interjections, quips, puns, and even oaths! A perfect Indian jungle it seems; a boundless, unparalleled imbroglio.[13]

Given its generic miscellaneousness, and the variety of

---

[13] Ibid. 5, 9, 12.

literary influences upon it, it is hardly surprising that *Sartor Resartus* has very little in common with the dominant mode of nineteenth-century prose fiction—the realistic novel. *Sartor* lacks a narrative skeleton, and while it is full of vivid concrete details, this solidity of specification is not used to give a sense of verisimilitude or create a representational illusion. Nor is such a sense given by its hyperbolic, metaphorical and densely allusive style, which is essentially an expressive and rhetorical medium unsuited to narrative or representational effects. But the most significant way in which Carlyle's fiction differs from the tradition of the realistic novel is found in its attitude to character and to ordinary human experience. The author of *Sartor* is uninterested in either, and gives no evidence of the human sympathy that seems an essential feature of the realistic novel.

In Book I, the narrator suggests that a key reason for the 'short-comings, over-shootings, and multiform perversities' of Teufelsdröckh's book on clothes has to do with the 'strange impartiality [and] strange scientific freedom' with which he looks 'in men's faces': he seems 'like a man dropped thither from the Moon'. *Mutatis mutandis*, the same thing may be said about Carlyle's attitude to his characters. Even in Book II, the story of Teufelsdröckh's development from childhood to the threshold of adult life, which is in essence modelled on Carlyle's own early years, there is a *cordon sanitaire* between the implied author and the central character; no suggestion of intimacy is permitted. In the 'Romance' chapter, for example, the narrator remarks that 'psychological readers' will naturally be interested in knowing the details of Teufelsdröckh's first love affair. But Blumine's station in life, her 'parentage, fortune, aspect', her behaviour when she met her lover, and even her real name—in fact, all the details with which readers of realistic novels expect to be supplied—are withheld. Even the emotions of Teufelsdröckh himself are described in a hyperbolic and distanced way that suggests an implicitly dismissive, even anti-humanist authorial attitude to an important phase in the development of the personality.

While *Sartor Resartus* has little in common with the realistic tradition of verisimilar representation of human situations in their social and moral contexts, it does have affinities with another fictional tradition, one that has been well described by Robert Alter. This tradition includes the kind of prose fiction that 'expresses its seriousness through playfulness, that is acutely aware of itself as a mere structure of words even as it tries to discover ways of going beyond words to the experiences words seek to indicate'. A fully self-conscious novel is 'one in which from beginning to end, through the style, the handling of narrative viewpoint, the names and words imposed on the characters, the patterning of the narration, the nature of the characters and what befalls them, there is a consistent effort to convey to us a sense of the fictional world as an authorial construct set up against a background of literary tradition and convention'.[14] For Alter, prime examples of fully achieved self-conscious novels include Cervantes' *Don Quixote*, Fielding's *Tom Jones*, Diderot's *Jacques the Fatalist*, Sterne's *Tristram Shandy*, and Nabokov's *Pale Fire*; and others would want to add works like Melville's *Moby-Dick* to the list.

Associating *Sartor Resartus* with the tradition of self-conscious fiction helps bring into focus its reflexive features, as well as the way in which the text is continually challenging the reader's expectations and competence. The key feature of Carlyle's *modus operandi* is that the text is about both itself and the experience of reading it. *Sartor* contains its own commentary and has within itself a fully developed model of a reader grappling with a difficult text. The description of Professor Diogenes Teufelsdröckh's strange book on clothes given by the Editor in the 'Characteristics' chapter of Book I is at the same time a pointed description of the very book that the reader of *Sartor Resartus* holds in his hands. Throughout the text the Editor continues to be the reader's surrogate as he struggles to make sense of Teufelsdröckh's book and the six bags of miscellaneous and randomly arranged autobiographical documents. On behalf of the reader, the Editor attempts to find useful meanings in materials that fascinate him and compel his attention even while he suspects their authenticity, doubts the intentions and sincerity of their author, and comes to realize that none of his doubts can ever be settled with certainty.

[14] *Partial Magic: The Novel as a Self-Conscious Genre* (Berkeley, 1975), ix, xi.

[4]

In Book I of *Sartor Resartus*, the narrator, an English reviewer whom we come to know as the Editor, describes a new German book by Professor Teufelsdröckh of Weissnichtwo that he has undertaken to introduce to the British public. *Die Kleider, ihr Werden und Wirken* (*Clothes, their Origin and Influence*) is divided into a Descriptive-Historical portion and a Speculative-Philosophical portion; while the Editor is clearly more comfortable with the former, he senses that there is something in the latter that may prove useful to 'us English', whose 'mercantile greatness, and invaluable Constitution' are examples of the 'practical tendency' of English culture and endeavour, which has perhaps cramped 'the free flight of Thought' and impeded the growth of 'pure Science, especially pure moral Science'. It is 'direct value' and 'inference of a practical nature' that the Editor wants to draw from Teufelsdröckh's book. In doing so, however, he is repeatedly hindered by his own literal-mindedness and inexperience with the free flight of thought, by genuine difficulties in the text, and by its gratuitously rebarbative features, chief among them 'an almost total want of arrangement', that makes *Die Kleider* seem 'like some mad banquet, wherein all courses had been confounded, and fish and flesh, soup and solid, oyster-sauce, lettuces, Rhine-wine and French mustard, were hurled into one huge tureen or trough'. From this 'German printed and written Chaos'—*Die Kleider* and the supplementary autobiographical documents in six paper bags—the English Editor endeavours to 'evolve printed Creation'.

In understanding Teufelsdröckh's thought, and in building a bridge between it and the British public, the Editor is keenly aware of the value of biography. The professor's radically original thought and peculiar mode of expression must reflect his life-experience, and to know his ideas 'without something of his personality' is likely to ensure 'entire misapprehension'. Since the Editor has visited Weissnichtwo he is able to supply some vivid descriptive details of Teufelsdröckh in later life: his standing up in a crowded coffee-house to propose a toast to the Cause of the Poor; his physical appearance ('loose, ill-brushed, threadbare habiliments', thick locks overlapping a grave face; eyes 'deep under their shaggy brows', in which are seen 'gleams of an ethereal or else a diabolic fire'); and his watch-tower, an attic room in the tallest house in the Wahngasse, from which he looks out on the living flood of humanity below while sitting in Byronic isolation 'alone with the Stars'.

These brief outside glimpses of the older Teufelsdröckh are supplemented in Book II by the much more extended inside views of his earlier years, which make up a spiritual biography charting his inner development from childhood to when his 'spiritual majority . . . commences'; that is, to the threshold of adult life, the point at which *Bildungsromane* normally conclude. Essentially, Book II offers a highly stylized and schematic account of the development of a certain kind of Romantic hero. Most of its stages will come as no surprise to readers familiar with Wertherian and Byronic heroes, and with *Wilhelm Meister*. The 'Idyllic' chapter of Book II describes the 'happy season of Childhood' before the shades of the prison house begin to close. During this season the perceptual given is all-sufficient and existence is 'a bright, soft element of Joy'. A sense of reverence and obedience is instilled in the child through his parents and their 'simple version of the Christian Faith'. The limitation of this stage of development, however, is that the child remains in a state of passivity with his 'Active Power' still dormant. The birth pangs of this power come around the time of puberty when the 'happy season of Childhood' gives way to the 'fervid season of youth'. The death of Teufelsdröckh's father and the revelation that his father and mother were only foster parents bring the realization that '*I was like no other*'; this self-conscious awareness dissolves the childhood sense of oneness with what surrounds him.

During the course of his higher education, Teufelsdröckh lays the foundation of a literary life; but his intellectual development at a 'Rational University' leaves him susceptible to the infection of religious doubt which soon develops into 'the nightmare, Unbelief' and causes a bifurcation between head and heart, between the doubting intelligence and emotional values and needs deeply rooted in the religious culture of childhood. The problem of vocation, of realizing one's 'maximum of Capability', is closely related to this incapacitating split; to find one's vocation means to find work that fosters an harmonious and mutually supportive development of all one's faculties.

First love is a dangerous time in late adolescence because it seems to offer a way to transcend psychic divisions and recover the transporting joy of childhood. The beloved other seems to hold in her hand 'the invisible Jacob's-ladder, whereby man might mount into very Heaven'. During Teufelsdröckh's romance with Blumine, 'Pale Doubt fled away to the distance; Life bloomed up with happiness and hope.' But when 'the gay silk Montgolfier' balloon loses its air, Teufelsdröckh is plunged into the depths of an extravagantly exaggerated world-sorrow. Like Byron (in Arnold's phrase), he carries across Europe the pageant of his bleeding heart. At one point during the 'Sorrows of Teufelsdröckh' chapter, he is found in the mountains gazing at silent and solitary peaks bathed in the evening sunlight. In their presence he begins to experience one of those moments of expanded consciousness and sense of oneness with the visible world that are the *raison d'être* of Romantic reverie. But this momentary renewal proves a false dawn because it is bathed in the light of the ego as well as of the setting sun. It is meant to be contrasted with the mature reintegration with the natural and human worlds that Teufelsdröckh experiences in the 'Everlasting Yea' chapter after he has gone through the three stages of the conversion experience that are the climax of his spiritual development.

The 'Everlasting No' chapter describes Teufelsdröckh's spiritual nadir. The universe has become 'all void of Life, of Purpose, of Volition, even of Hostility: it was one huge, dead, immeasurable Steam-engine, rolling on, in its dead indifference, to grind me limb from limb'. The turning-point in this dark night is described rather than enacted; it comes in the *Rue Saint Thomas de l'Enfer* in Paris when 'my whole ME' stands up and says NO to negation: '*I* am not thine, but Free, and for ever hate thee!' The peal of the Everlasting No is followed by the 'Centre of Indifference' chapter in which Teufelsdröckh's attention is shown to be shifting away from his own sorrows to the world outside him—to towns and cities, the battlefield of Wagram, the lives of great men.

Finally comes the 'Everlasting Yea', the advent of which is neither described nor enacted. Teufelsdröckh simply says that 'the heavy dreams rolled gradually away, and I awoke to a new Heaven and a new Earth'. The enabling condition of this culminating phase of spiritual development, 'the first preliminary moral Act', is said to be 'Annihilation of Self'. Its hallmarks are a '*Divine Depth of Sorrow*', the renunciation of happiness in favour of doing '*the Duty which lies nearest thee*', and recognizing that the ideal is not out there or up there, but 'in thyself': 'America is here or nowhere.' 'Love not Pleasure; love God', urges Teufelsdröckh: 'This is the EVERLASTING YEA, wherein all contradiction is solved.' The God he describes is a presence 'felt in my own Heart'. Such a feeling 'is Belief; all else is Opinion'. Thus the antagonism between head and heart is resolved through the demotion of the former: 'all Speculation is by nature endless, formless, a vortex amid vortices: only, by a felt indubitable certainty of Experience' does the human personality 'find any centre to revolve round'. And thus, too, is the importance of spiritual biography underlined; for truth is grounded not in any universal axioms of reason, but in personal subjective experience authenticated by the feeling self.

In Book III the Editor returns to expounding the thought of *Die Kleider*, especially the key concepts of symbols, Helotage, organic filaments, and Natural Supernaturalism. There is clearly a close parallel between Teufelsdröckh's predictions of social regeneration and the process of his individual regeneration described in Book II. As Carlyle had put it in his letter of 1831 to his brother John, the material in the two books is 'in the same vein'. But this means that his social diagnosis and prescription are subjective in origin and can no more be intellectually justified or perhaps even understood than can the personal beliefs of Book II. They, too, must be felt in the heart. For this reason, it is especially important in Book III to notice the reactions of the Editor, who is the reader's surrogate. Will the empirically minded English Editor, who respects the 'Institutions of our Ancestors', come to a felt acceptance of the radical social views of the German Philosopher?

During the course of *Sartor Resartus*, it is noticeable that the Editor becomes increasingly involved with the material on

which he is working. In Book I he had admitted that great
efforts, 'partly of intellect, partly of imagination', had to be
made if Teufelsdröckh's life and work were to be sympatheti-
cally understood and 'a firm bridge' constructed for the British
reader. In the first two books, the Editor experienced repeated
difficulties in becoming habituated to Teufelsdröckh's idiom
and ideas. But by Book III, one notices a certain degree of
convergence of Editor and subject. At the opening of the book,
for example, the Editor admits that he has adopted his subject's
method of proceeding 'leap by leap' rather than 'straightforward, step by step'; and he subsequently admits that Teufelsdröckh's mode of utterance has, unhappily, somewhat affected
his own. He also affirms that after 'long painful meditation' he
has found the cornerstone of Teufelsdröckh's thought, the
'stupendous Section, headed *Natural Supernaturalism*', not unintelligible, 'but on the contrary to grow clear, nay radiant, and
all-illuminating'.

At the same time, however, residual doubts and uncertainties
continue to plague the Editor throughout his labours. 'Up to this
hour', he exclaims in Book I, 'we have never fully satisfied
ourselves' whether there is in *Die Kleider* 'a tone and hum of
real Humour, which we reckon among the very highest
qualities of Genius, or some remote echo of mere Insanity and
Inanity'. At the end of Book II he confesses to a painful
suspicion that the autobiographical documents on which he has
relied for Teufelsdröckh's life history are partly a deliberate
mystification. Near the end of Book III he repeats once again
that with Teufelsdröckh 'there ever hovers some shade of
doubt' concerning his sincerity and his intentions. And while
the Editor does feel that he has been successful in constructing a
bridge between the German philosopher and the British Public,
he has to admit that it is 'no firm arch, overspanning the
Impassable with paved highway', but only a 'zigzag series of
rafts floating tumultuously thereon'.

[5]

Is the reader of *Sartor Resartus* meant to share the Editor's
doubts, or to regard them as examples of the Editor's imperfect

comprehension of his subject? The question is crucially important in connection with the reader's reception of the text. In
considering the question, it is important to realize that Teufelsdröckh's philosophical beliefs are essentially a simplified version of the leading themes of German Idealist philosophy,
especially as it contrasts with an equally simplified version of
eighteenth-century British empirical philosophy, the nineteenth-century name for which was Utilitarianism. The fundamental premise of Teufelsdröckh's thought is the epistemologi-
cal distinction between the understanding (*Verstand*) and
Reason (*Vernunft*). The former mental faculty is essentially
passive, containing impressions ultimately derived from sense
experience. Such empirical knowledge is strictly bounded by
the containers of space and time, by 'WHERE, with its brother,
WHEN', as Teufelsdröckh puts it, and can supply knowledge
only of the appearances of things, never of things in themselves.
Such knowledge can be objective and accurate, even scientific;
and it can certainly be useful; but it can never tell one anything
about things-in-themselves or about noumenal (as opposed to
phenomenal) objects of thought. The existence of God, an
after-life, or the soul can never be established by the empirical
understanding.

Noumenal knowledge is supplied by the intuitive faculty of
the Reason (or the Fantasy, as Teufelsdröckh sometimes calls
it). Reason, the organ of spiritual and imaginative insight, can
reveal to man supersensible realities undetectable by the understanding. 'To the eye of vulgar Logic', asks Teufelsdröckh,
'what is man? An omnivorous Biped that wears Breeches. To
the eye of Pure Reason what is he? A Soul, a Spirit, and divine
Apparition.' 'Not our Logical, Mensurative faculty, but our
Imaginative one is King over us,' he insists in another place.
'The Understanding is indeed thy window, too clear thou canst
not make it; but Fantasy is thy eye, with its colour-giving
retina.' Space and Time are no barriers for the Reason, for both
are modes of the understanding, and as such 'superficial
terrestrial adhesions to thought'. Reason can pierce through
Where and When to the 'celestial EVERYWHERE and FOREVER',
to 'the universal HERE' and 'the everlasting NOW'.

According to Teufelsdröckh, the progress of science, that is, the increasing power and dominance of the faculty of the understanding, has led to the destruction of wonder and its replacement by mensuration and numeration. The more this power waxes, the more the intuitive power of the Reason wanes. In the wintry light of the understanding, soul has become synonymous with stomach, and happiness has become the aim of man, who, in the hedonistic calculus of the Utilitarians (the 'Motive-Millwrights'), has become 'a dead Iron-Balance for weighing Pains and Pleasures on'. What is needed is a restoration to its rightful kingly place in the human personality of Reason, Fantasy, Intuition, and Wonder. Love, Duty, and a sense of the sacred nature of social bonds can only flourish in the light of the Reason, which can give man a saving sense of the infinite within the finite, of the religious nature of human life, and of the miraculous potential of any aspect of creation.

As such, Teufelsdröckh's thought closely answers to M. H. Abrams's description of 'the central enterprise common to many post-Kantian German philosophers and poets, as well as to Coleridge and Wordsworth[:] to join together the "subject" and "object" that modern intellection had put asunder, and thus to revivify a dead nature, restore its concreteness, significance, and human values, and re-domiciliate man in a world which had become alien to him'.[15] One can go even further and place Teufelsdröckh's thought in the larger context of a perennially recurrent human effort to restore a sacred and transcendent dimension to human existence. In *Living and Dying*, for example, Robert Jay Lifton has spoken of the importance of a 'symbolizing process' that can provide 'forms and images adequate to guide behaviour and render it meaningful'.[16] Like Teufelsdröckh, Lifton has analysed the profound psychological and psycho-historical dislocations that cause systems of symbols (clothes) to lose their power to generate a sustaining sense of what he calls symbolic immortality. One might further point out that Teufelsdröckh's chief concern in his book is the same as that of Mircea Eliade in *The Sacred and*

---

[15] 'Structure and Style in the Greater Romantic Lyric', in his *The Correspondent Breeze: Essays on English Romanticism* (New York, 1984), 96.

[16] Robert Jay Lifton and Eric Olson, *Living and Dying* (New York, 1974), 31.

the Profane: to convey a sense of what the total experience of life is like for someone living through symbols in a sacred universe, in comparison with the impoverished experience of those living without religious feeling in a completely 'profane world', a wholly 'desacralized cosmos'.[17]

It would be misleading, however, to leave the subject of Teufelsdröckh's thought without remarking on certain features of it that will give careful readers pause. One of them concerns the extraordinary number of Christian and biblical allusions embedded in his utterances. Keeping the connotations while changing the denotations of Christian images and concepts is a common aspect of Romantic rhetoric. But this feature of *Sartor* is so insistently present in the text as to suggest a deliberate attempt to blur the differences between traditional Christian beliefs and the subjectivity of Romantic regeneration. A second trouble spot is Teufelsdröckh's insistence on the moral imperative of duty: '*Do the Duty which lies nearest thee.*' Such an imperative, as he says, cannot be grounded in 'Speculation', only in 'felt . . . Experience'. But in the highly schematized and rhetorical account of Teufelsdröckh's conversion experience in Book II, one is only told about, never convincingly shown, his inner transformation. As a result, the reader cannot feel with Teufelsdröckh. At best he can give only notional assent to the professor's moral injunctions; at worst he may come to find them factitious. An overemphasis on moral conduct, triggered by the breakdown of traditional religious beliefs, was a leading feature of the Victorian temper. The syndrome was memorably encapsulated in George Eliot's solemn observation that while God was inconceivable and immortality unbelievable, Duty was 'peremptory and absolute'.[18] What Nietzsche said apropos of George Eliot in *Twilight of the Idols* could be equally well applied to Teufelsdröckh: 'They are rid of the Christian God and now believe all the more firmly that they must cling to Christian morality . . . We others hold otherwise. When one gives up the Christian faith, one pulls the right to Christian morality out from under one's feet. This morality is

[17] *The Sacred and the Profane: The Nature of Religion*, trans. W. Trask (New York, 1959), 13.

[18] F. W. H. Myers, *Essays Classical and Modern* (London, 1921), 495.

by no means self-evident . . . it stands and falls with faith in God.'[19]

There are other aspects of Teufelsdröckh's thinking that seem less perennial than distinctively Victorian. One of them is instanced in the climactic passage of the climactic chapter of *Sartor*. Teufelsdröckh's exposition of 'Natural Supernaturalism' culminates in an attempt to finesse the question that was to become of pre-eminent concern to many Victorian writers: the question of immortality, of a life after death. 'Is the white Tomb of our Loved One', he asks, but a 'pale spectral Illusion! Is the lost Friend still mysteriously Here, even as we are Here mysteriously, with God!' The answer is that only the 'Time-shadows' have perished and that 'the real Being of whatever was, and whatever is, and whatever will be, *is* even now and for ever . . . believe it thou must; understand it thou canst not'. It is hard not to regard this passage as rhetoric in the pejorative sense of the term, and as an attempt to substitute the wish for the deed. Why must we believe? Not because one is assured of a life after death; but precisely because one is not. One must believe because it is too demoralizing not to. 'Better an ignis fatuus / Than no illume at all', as Emily Dickinson wryly remarked in her little poem on the breakdown of traditional Christian beliefs during the nineteenth century. In this passage, as in other utterances of Teufelsdröckh, one is once again reminded of *Twilight of the Idols*, this time of what Nietzsche said about Teufelsdröckh's creator:

Carlyle: a man of strong words and attitudes, a rhetor from *need*, constantly lured by the craving for a strong faith and the feeling of his incapacity for it (in this respect, a typical romantic!). The craving for a strong faith is no proof of a strong faith, but quite the contrary. If one has such a faith, then one can afford the beautiful luxury of scepticism: one is sure enough, firm enough, has ties enough for that . . . [Carlyle] *requires* noise. A constant passionate dishonesty against himself—that is his *proprium*; in this respect he is and remains interesting. Of course, in England he is admired precisely for his honesty. Well, that is English . . . At bottom, Carlyle is an English atheist who makes it a point of honour not to be one.[20]

[19] *Twilight of the Idols*, in *The Portable Nietzsche*, ed. and trans. W. Kaufmann (New York, 1954), 515–16.
[20] Ibid., 521.

[6]

There is really no need to go outside the pages of *Sartor Resartus*
to call attention to a factitious strain in Teufelsdröckh. Carlyle
has placed within his text a number of features designed to do
just that—chief among them the ever-doubting Editor. In the
last chapter of *Sartor*, the Editor asks a blunt question: 'How
could a man occasionally of keen insight, not without keen
sense of propriety, who had real Thoughts to communicate,
resolve to emit them in a shape bordering so closely on the
absurd?' On the literal level, the question concerns Teufelsdröckh and the strange book, an 'enormous, amorphous
Plumpudding, more like a Scottish Haggis', he has 'kneaded
for his fellow mortals'. But it is also apparent that through the
Editor, the Scottish author of *Sartor Resartus* is challenging the
reader to think about his experience of the text and to seek
satisfactory answers to the question.

Traditional readers of *Sartor Resartus* have had no difficulty
in providing answers that presuppose a constructive and communicative authorial intention. C. F. Harrold, for example,
argued that Carlyle's method was of great value for several
practical reasons: it 'permitted him to indulge the wayward,
boisterously ironic freedom of his genius'; it enabled him to
present the unpopular and misunderstood subject of German
transcendentalism 'without the formidable apparatus and the
appearance of metaphysical inquiry'; and it united 'the didactic
aim of the philosophic discourse with the human interest of the
biographical novel'.[21] Others have argued that *Sartor*'s extravagant style, the 'rich, idiomatic diction, picturesque allusions,
fiery poetic emphasis, [and] quaint tricksy turns', is the appropriate linguistic vehicle for a thematic tenor concerned with the
need for a revolution of consciousness, in which Fantasy would
overthrow the tyranny of rational modes of thought and
discourse. It has also been urged that the hoax aspect of *Sartor*
and its other bizarre features do not destroy the serious import
of Carlyle's message, but make it more effective 'for the very
simple reason that it is not a bleakly expressed, dull, moralizing

---

[21] *Sartor Resartus*, ed. C. F. Harrold (New York, 1937), xxx.

statement'.[22] Similarly, the 'humorous' tone of the book has been said persistently to defeat 'any potential movement toward despair. The humor, the essentially friendly and sympathetic rather than satiric laughter that Teufelsdröckh and his Editor inspire, keeps the reader constantly in mind of the fact that the ultimate aim of the book is not Denial but Affirmation.'[23]

The strategies of reconstruction and recuperation, which might be called examples of the husk-and-kernel approach to *Sartor Resartus*, are more positive answers to the question posed by the Editor than the one he himself goes on to posit. Why did Teufelsdröckh resolve to emit his thoughts 'in a shape bordering so closely on the absurd'?

Our conjecture has sometimes been that perhaps Necessity as well as Choice was concerned in it. Seems it not conceivable that, in a Life like our Professor's, where so much bountifully given by Nature had in Practice failed and misgone, Literature also would never rightly prosper: that striving with his characteristic vehemence to paint this and the other Picture, and ever without success, he at last desperately dashes his brush, full of all colours, against the canvass, to try whether it will paint Foam? With all his stillness, there were perhaps in Teufelsdröckh desperation enough for this.

This answer stresses the expressive rather than the communicative nature of Teufelsdröckh's utterance, which is said to be prompted by internal necessity rather than by conscious artistic choice. Any hesitation one might have in taking the Editor's conjecture about *Die Kleider* as simultaneously an authorial comment on *Sartor Resartus* is dispelled by Carlyle's comments about his book in letters to two of its most sympathetic early readers. Could it be, Emerson asked his Scottish friend, that 'this humour' of Teufelsdröckh's 'proceeds from a despair of finding a contemporary audience'? Carlyle replied that he spoke correctly: 'I have no known public, am *alone* under the Heavens, speaking into friendly or unfriendly Space; add only

[22] Daniel P. Deneau, 'Relationship of Style and Device in *Sartor Resartus*', *Victorian Newsletter*, xvii (1960), 18.

[23] P. A. Dale, '*Sartor Resartus* and the Inverse Sublime: The Art of Humorous Deconstruction', in *Allegory, Myth and Symbol*, ed. M. W. Bloomfield (Cambridge, Mass., 1981), 302.

that I will not defend such attitude, that I call it questionable, tentative, and only the best that I in these mad times could conveniently hit upon.'[24] When John Stuart Mill wrote to Carlyle about *Sartor* he wondered whether his 'mode of writing, between sarcasm or irony and earnest', should have been so unrelievedly employed. Could not things be 'as well or better said in a more direct way? The same doubt has occasionally occurred to me respecting much of your phraseology.' Carlyle's answer was that

You are right about my style . . . I think often of the matter myself; and *see* only that I cannot yet see. Irony is a sharp instrument; but ill to handle without cutting *yourself.* I cannot justify, yet can too well explain what sets me so often on it of late: it is my singularly anomalous position to the world,—and, if you will, my own singularly unreasonable temper. I never know or can even guess what or who my audience is, or whether I have any audience: thus too naturally I adjust myself on the Devil-may-care principle. Besides I have under all my gloom genuine feeling of the ludicrous; and could have been the merriest of men, *had I not* been the sickest & saddest.[25]

Both these answers serve as reminders that the 1820s and 1830s were difficult times for writers who wished to combat the increasing dominance of the rational scientific intellect and of Utilitarian modes of thought and feeling with the great Romantic positives of Fantasy and Intuition. In his essay on Milton of 1825, for example, Thomas Babington Macaulay had observed that in the modern age Romantic prophets were doomed to isolation and probably to derangement. 'As civilisation advances', said Macaulay, 'poetry', that is, the creative and imaginative faculties of the mind, 'almost necessarily declines.' These faculties flourished during the childhood of the race and, like children, visionaries had the ability 'to abandon themselves without reserve to every illusion'. In modern society, however, the truth essential to poetry could only be 'the truth of madness', requiring 'a degree of credulity which almost amounts to a partial and temporary derangement of the intellect':

[24] *The Correspondence of Emerson and Carlyle*, ed. J. Slater (New York, 1964), 98; Appendix III, p. 232 below.

[25] *Collected Letters*, vi. 448–9.

He who, in an enlightened and literary society, aspires to be a great poet, must first become a little child. He must take to pieces the whole web of his mind. He must unlearn much of that knowledge which has perhaps constituted hitherto his chief title to superiority . . . And it is well if, after all his sacrifices and exertions, his works do not resemble a lisping man or a modern ruin. We have seen in our own time great talents, intense labour, and long meditation, employed in this struggle against the spirit of the age, and employed, we will not say absolutely in vain, but with dubious success and feeble applause.[26]

As in the early poems of Tennyson and Browning, which also date from the early 1830s, one finds in *Sartor Resartus* and in Carlyle's comments about the work an intense and brooding self-consciousness, a sense of isolation, and a demoralizing awareness of the lack of any fit audience. One also finds frames and other distancing devices employed to distract attention from the deeply personal and subjective content of the utter- ance. What is being enacted in these texts is part of a complex shift in sensibility that is ultimately the mutation of Romantic into Victorian literature.[27] *Sartor Resartus* itself, as George Levine has argued, 'marks a transition from the Romantics to the Victorians because it adds one quality to the Romantic vision which had not yet become dominant—desperation'. Carlyle 'could not establish himself as a sage in *Sartor* because, though like the Romantics in having won through to a deeply personal affirmation and discovery of his identity, he was not able to see the experience as anything but personal in a world obviously inimical'.[28] No wonder then that after *Sartor*, Car- lyle, like the speaker of Browning's first poem, *Pauline* (also published in 1833), resolved to 'look within no more', but to turn to biography and history for his subjects.

The best recent critical accounts of *Sartor Resartus*, sensitive to the historical moment out of which it comes, make use of methodologies more sophisticated than that of the husk-and- kernel approach. Janice L. Haney, for example, has argued that

[26] *Critical and Historical Essays* (London, 1854), i. 5–9.

[27] See K. McSweeney, *Tennyson and Swinburne as Romantic Naturalists* (Toronto, 1981), 26–37.

[28] '*Sartor Resartus* and the Balance of Fiction', *Victorian Studies*, viii (1964), 153, 154.

the last three chapters of *Sartor* (in which Teufelsdröckh's removal from Weissnichtwo to London is mentioned) show a turning away from an outmoded Romantic vision towards a Victorian social actuality and 'an emerging Victorian mode of making meaning'. Carlyle, says Haney, pits 'an empirical self' against 'a metaphysical and aesthetic self'; together the two 'compose a book about the quest for meaning'.[29] And in her *English Romantic Irony*, Anne Mellor presents *Sartor* as a 'self-consuming artifact' that 'does not preach the truth, but asks that its readers discover the truth for themselves'. *Sartor Resartus* is a fictional work 'designed to consume itself by revealing the limitations both of its own symbolic language and of language as such. It is intended not as a monument of truth but as a goad to action.'[30]

This critical reorientation is a welcome reminder that when he wrote *Sartor Resartus* Carlyle had not yet become Carlylean, and had not yet successfully substituted biography, history, and social prophecy for imaginative fiction. It was perhaps for this reason that John Stuart Mill always regarded *Sartor Resartus* as Carlyle's 'best and greatest work'. Its distinction, however, was not immediately apparent to Mill any more than to most first-time readers, who may take heart from Mill's experience. When first shown the manuscript by Carlyle, he 'made little of it'; but by the time it appeared in *Fraser's Magazine* two years later he had grown sufficiently advanced in 'new modes of thought' to read *Sartor Resartus* 'with enthusiastic admiration and the keenest delight'.[31]

[29] ' "Shadow Hunting": Romantic Irony, *Sartor Resartus*, and Victorian Romanticism', *Studies in Romanticism*, xvii (1978), 329, 319.

[30] *English Romantic Irony* (Cambridge, Mass., 1980), 131, 133.

[31] *Autobiography and Literary Essays*, ed. J. M. Robson and J. Stillinger (Toronto, 1981), 183.

ACKNOWLEDGEMENTS

WE are much indebted to colleagues and friends who have assisted us in various ways: James Critchley, Catherine Harland, Robert Holton, Ross Kilpatrick, Marie Legroulx, George Logan, Susanne McSweeney, Emmi Sabor, M. G. Wiebe, and Gary Wihl. For financial assistance we are grateful to the Advisory Research Committee of the School of Graduate Studies, Queen's University; and to the Humanities Research Grants Committee of the Faculty of Graduate Studies and Research, McGill University.

The letters from Carlyle to James Fraser, Ralph Waldo Emerson, and John Sterling in Appendices I, III, and IV are reprinted from vols. 6, 7, and 8 of the Duke–Edinburgh Edition of *The Collected Letters of Thomas and Jane Welsh Carlyle*, ed. C. R. Saunders *et al.*, by kind permission of Duke University Press. We have incorporated in the Explanatory Notes three corrections made by K. J. Fielding in his review of the edition.

NOTE ON THE TEXT

Sartor Resartus first appeared, anonymously, in the monthly issues of *Fraser's Magazine* from November 1833 to August 1834, with gaps in January and May. These instalments were stitched into book form by Fraser's for an edition of fifty-eight copies, privately issued in August 1834; this was not reset, but the necessary transference of blocks of type occasioned some typographical errors. The first edition of *Sartor* sold to the public was that published in Boston in 1836, with an unsigned preface by Emerson. Here Carlyle's name first appears on the title-page; there are also many changes in paragraphing, spelling, and typography for which Carlyle was not responsible. A second American edition followed in 1837.

For the first English edition of 1838, Carlyle added a subtitle to *Sartor Resartus*: '*the Life and Opinions of Herr Teufelsdröckh*'. He also included the 'Testimonies of Authors' (see Appendix V below) and made some minor revisions to the text, although he claimed in a letter to his brother John of 14 July 1838 that 'there is no change in *Teufk* from the genuine Fraser Copy' (*Collected Letters*, x. 121). Subsequent editions published in Carlyle's lifetime contain further minor revisions; and the 1869 edition contains a new Author's Note, Summary, and Index (see Appendix V below).

The cumulative effect of these revisions is to make *Sartor Resartus* a less exotic, more familiar-seeming work. On numerous occasions, capitals are changed to lower case at the beginning of normally uncapitalized nouns; large numbers of hyphens are inserted to make compound words seem less unusual; and the punctuation, which had followed an individual, highly rhetorical system, is made to conform more closely to conventional usage. There are also about one hundred substantive revisions, the more significant of which are indicated in our notes. Many of the minor revisions follow specific patterns: 'must', for example, is often changed to 'had to', 'has to', etc.; 'whatso' and 'whereso' are changed to 'whatsoever' and 'wheresoever'; and word order is altered for greater elegance.

The present edition is, we believe, the first to reproduce the work as it appeared in *Fraser's Magazine* and thus to present *Sartor Resartus* in its original state, before Carlyle and anonymous compositors began the process of retouching. Many errors in the German passages, which were corrected in later editions, have been silently corrected here, as have other obvious misprints; but in general the text follows closely that of *Fraser's Magazine*. The original divisions into eight monthly instalments are indicated by a row of asterisks after each part. Notes at the foot of the page, indicated by daggers in the text, are Carlyle's.

The manuscript of *Sartor Resartus* is not known to have survived. The fullest account of its publishing history, though now badly outdated, remains that by Isaac Dyer in his *Bibliography of Thomas Carlyle's Writings* (1928). No textual study of *Sartor Resartus* has been published.

SELECT BIBLIOGRAPHY

EDITIONS

THE standard edition of Carlyle's works is the thirty-volume Centenary Edition, ed. H. D. Traill (London, 1896–9). The Duke–Edinburgh edition of *The Collected Letters of Thomas and Jane Welsh Carlyle*, ed. C. R. Sanders *et al.* (Durham, North Carolina, 1970–), will supersede earlier collections. See also *The Correspondence of Emerson and Carlyle*, ed. J. Slater (New York, 1964). The text of *Wotton Reinfred*, Carlyle's unfinished novel, is included in *Last Words of Thomas Carlyle* (London, 1892; reprinted with an introduction by K. J. Fielding, 1971). Several editions of *Sartor Resartus* include extensive introductions and annotation; those by A. MacMechan (Boston, 1896) and C. F. Harrold (New York, 1937) are especially valuable. The complex text of *Sartor* is included in G. B. Tennyson's *A Carlyle Reader: Selections from the Writings of Thomas Carlyle* (New York, 1969: Cambridge, 1984).

BIOGRAPHICAL AND CRITICAL STUDIES

J. A. Froude, *Thomas Carlyle: A History of the First Forty Years of his Life, 1795–1835* (London, 1882) and *Thomas Carlyle: A History of his Life in London, 1834–1881* (London, 1884); Froude's four volumes have been abridged and edited by J. Clubbe (Columbus, Ohio, 1979).

W. Dilthey, 'Sartor Resartus: Philosophical Conflict, Positive and Negative Eras, and Personal Resolution' [1891], *Clio*, i. 3 (1972), 40–60.

L. Cazamian, *Carlyle* (Paris, 1913); trans. E. K. Brown (New York, 1932).

D. A. Wilson and D. W. MacArthur, *Carlyle* (6 vols., London, 1923–34).

E. Neff, *Carlyle and Mill* (New York, 1924).

R. Wellek, 'Carlyle and German Romanticism' [1929] in his *Confrontations* (Princeton, 1965).

E. Neff, *Carlyle* (New York, 1932, 1968).

C. F. Harrold, *Carlyle and German Thought: 1819–1834* (New Haven, 1934).

C. Moore, 'Thomas Carlyle and Fiction: 1822–1834', *Nineteenth-Century Studies*, ed. H. Davis *et al.* (Ithaca, New York, 1940).

J. L. Halliday, *Mr. Carlyle my Patient: A Psychosomatic Biography* (London, 1949).

B. Willey, *Nineteenth-Century Studies: Coleridge to Matthew Arnold* (London, 1949).

H. Shine, *Carlyle's Early Reading to 1834* (Lexington, Kentucky, 1953).

D. DeLaura, 'Arnold and Carlyle', *PMLA*, lxxix (1964), 104–29.

A. J. LaValley, *Carlyle and the Idea of the Modern: Studies in Carlyle's Prophetic Literature and its Relation to Blake, Nietzsche, Marx, and Others* (New Haven, 1968).

H. L. Sussman, *Victorians and the Machine: The Literary Response to Technology* (Cambridge, Mass., 1968).

J. P. Siegel, ed., *Carlyle: The Critical Heritage* (London, 1971).

P. Rosenberg, *The Seventh Hero: Thomas Carlyle and the Theory of Radical Activism* (Cambridge, Mass., 1974).

R. Ashton, *The German Idea: Four English Writers and the Reception of German Thought, 1800–1860* (Cambridge, 1980).

A. L. Le Quesne, *Carlyle* (Oxford, 1982).

F. Kaplan, *Thomas Carlyle: A Biography* (Ithaca, New York, 1983).

J. D. Rosenberg, *Carlyle and the Burden of History* (Cambridge, Mass., 1985).

STUDIES OF '*SARTOR RESARTUS*'

C. Moore, '*Sartor Resartus* and the Problem of Carlyle's Conversion', *PMLA*, lxx (1955), 662–81.

G. Levine, '*Sartor Resartus* and the Balance of Fiction', *Victorian Studies*, viii (1964), 131–60; a revised version appears in Levine's *The Boundaries of Fiction: Carlyle, Macaulay, Newman* (Princeton, 1968).

C. R. Sanders, 'The Byron Closed in *Sartor Resartus*', *Studies in Romanticism*, iii (1964), 77–108.

J. W. Smeed, 'Thomas Carlyle and Jean Paul Richter', *Comparative Literature*, xvi (1964), 226–53.

G. B. Tennyson, *Sartor Called Resartus: The Genesis, Structure and Style of Thomas Carlyle's First Major Work* (Princeton, 1965).

G. H. Brookes, *The Rhetorical Form of Carlyle's 'Sartor Resartus'* (Berkeley, 1972).

P. Brantlinger, ' "Romance", "Biography", and the Making of *Sartor Resartus*', *Philological Quarterly*, lii (1973), 108–18.

J. Clubbe, 'Carlyle on *Sartor Resartus*', in *Carlyle Past and Present: A Collection of New Essays*, ed. K. J. Fielding and R. Tarr (London, 1978).

J. A. Dibble, *The Pythia's Drunken Song: Thomas Carlyle's 'Sartor Resartus' and the Style Problem in German Idealist Philosophy* (The Hague, 1978).

J. L. Haney, ' "Shadow-Hunting": Romantic Irony, *Sartor Resartus*, and Victorian Romanticism', *Studies in Romanticism*, xvii (1978), 307–33.

A. K. Mellor, 'Carlyle's *Sartor Resartus*: A Self-Consuming Artifact', in her *English Romantic Irony* (Cambridge, Mass., 1980).

P. A. Dale, '*Sartor Resartus* and the Inverse Sublime: The Art of Humorous Deconstruction', in *Allegory, Myth and Symbol*, ed. M. W. Bloomfield (Cambridge, Mass., 1981).

B. V. Qualls, *The Secular Pilgrims of Victorian Fiction: The Novel as Book of Life* (Cambridge, 1982).

L. C. R. Baker, 'The Open Secret of *Sartor Resartus*: Carlyle's Method of Converting his Reader', *Studies in Philology*, lxxxiii (1986), 218–35.

L. H. Peterson, 'Carlyle's *Sartor Resartus*: The Necessity of Reconstruction', in her *Victorian Autobiography: The Tradition of Self-Interpretation* (New Haven, 1986).

S. Helming, ' "The Thaumaturgic Art of Thought": Carlyle's *Sartor Resartus*', in his *The Esoteric Comedies of Carlyle, Newman, and Yeats* (Cambridge, 1988).

J. H. Miller, ' "Hieroglyphical Truth" in *Sartor Resartus*: Carlyle and the Language of Parable', in *Victorian Perspectives: Six Essays*, ed. John Clubb and Jerome Meckier (Newark, Delaware, 1989).

D. Riede, 'Transgression, Authority, and the Church of Literature in Carlyle', in *Victorian Connections*, ed. Jerome J. McGann (Charlottesville, 1989).

D. F. Felluga, 'The Critic's New Clothes: *Sartor Resartus* as "Cold Carnival" ', *Criticism*, xxxvii (1995), 583–99.

W. Iser, 'The Emergence of a Cross-Cultural Discourse: Thomas Carlyle's *Sartor Resartus*', in *The Translatability of Cultures: Figurations of the Space Between*, ed. Sanford Budick and Wolfgang Iser (Stanford, 1996).

J. Treadwell, '*Sartor Resartus* and the Work of Writing', *Essays in Criticism*, xlviii (1998), 224–43.

BIBLIOGRAPHY

I. W. Dyer, *A Bibliography of Thomas Carlyle's Writings and Ana* (Portland, Maine, 1928).

G. B. Tennyson, 'Thomas Carlyle', in *Victorian Prose: A Guide to Research*, ed. D. J. DeLaura (New York, 1973), 33–104.

R. L. Tarr, *Thomas Carlyle: A Bibliography of English Language Criticism 1824–1974* (Charlottesville, 1976).

A CHRONOLOGY OF THOMAS CARLYLE

1795   Born 4 December in Ecclefechan, a small market village in Dumfriesshire in south-western Scotland; the first of nine children of James Carlyle, a stonemason, and Margaret Aitken, the daughter of a farmer and like her husband a strict Calvinist in religion.

1806   Sent to Annan Academy, 6 miles from Ecclefechan, to continue his schooling.

1809   Walks to Edinburgh in November to begin his University studies.

1813   Returns for a fifth session at the University of Edinburgh, enrolling in the Divinity Hall of the National Church.

1814   Preaches a sermon in March; in May leaves to teach mathematics at Annan Academy. Makes his first appearance in print with letter on mathematics in the *Dumfries and Galloway Courier*.

1816   Begins teaching at a school in Kirkcaldy, a town on the north shore of the Firth of Forth. Friendship deepens with Edward Irving, who becomes his closest friend.

1817   Breaks off his connection with Divinity Hall and renounces his intention of entering the ministry.

1818   Reads Gibbon's *Decline and Fall*, which weakens his faith in Christianity. Meets Margaret Gordon of Kirkcaldy, with whom he falls in love.

1819   Begins to study German. Moves to Edinburgh, enrols in Scots Law classes, but soon loses interest. Earns money by translating and tutoring.

1820   Romance with Margaret Gordon ends. Writes biographies and articles for Brewster's *Edinburgh Encyclopaedia*.

1821   Meets Jane Baillie Welsh, six years his junior, at her family's home in Haddington, East Lothian; publishes his first original article.

1822   His first article on German literature published, in the *New Edinburgh Review*; completes translation of Legendre's *Elements of Geometry*; writes his first attempt at fiction, 'Cruthers and Johnson'. After a three-year period of intense inner turmoil, undergoes a conversion experience in Leith Walk, Edinburgh.

1824 'Life of Schiller' published in *London Magazine*. Meets Coler-
idge during his first visit to London. Translation of Goethe's
Wilhelm Meister's Apprenticeship published in three volumes;
Goethe writes to thank Carlyle for a presentation copy.

1825 *Life of Friedrich Schiller, Comprehending an Examination of his
Works* published in book form. Begins work on a story, 'Illudo
Chartis', abandoned within a year.

1826 Marries Jane Welsh; they move to Edinburgh.

1827 *German Romance: Specimens of its Chief Authors with Biographical
and Critical Notices* published in four volumes. 'Jean Paul
Friedrich Richter' published, his first contribution to *Edinburgh
Review*. Begins work on an autobiographical novel, *Wotton
Reinfred* (never completed).

1828 Carlyles move to Craigenputtock, a small, remote farming
property in Dumfriesshire. 'Burns' published in *Edinburgh
Review*.

1829 'German Playwrights', 'Voltaire', and 'Novalis' published in
Foreign Review; 'Signs of the Times' in *Edinburgh Review*.
Correspondence with Goethe continues.

1830 'Thoughts on History' published in *Fraser's Magazine*; begins
Sartor Resartus.

1831 Feels he has 'almost done' with German literature. *Sartor
Resartus* finished in July. Arrives in London in August to
arrange for its publication, but negotiations with John Murray
are unsuccessful. First meets John Stuart Mill. 'Characteristics'
published in *Edinburgh Review*.

1832 Death of Carlyle's father; death of Goethe. 'Biography' and
'Boswell's *Life of Johnson*' published in *Fraser's Magazine*,
'Corn-Law Rhymes' in *Edinburgh Review*.

1833 'Diderot' published in the *Foreign Quarterly Review*. Emerson
visits Carlyle at Craigenputtock. Serialization of *Sartor Resartus*
begins in *Fraser's Magazine*.

1834 The Carlyles move to London and settle at 5 Cheyne Row,
Chelsea. Begins work on *French Revolution*. Reception of *Sartor
Resartus* is generally poor; arranges for a small edition of fifty-
eight copies, sewn together from the magazine parts, to
distribute to friends. Death of Edward Irving.

1835 First acquaintance with John Sterling. Manuscript of the first
volume of *French Revolution* inadvertently destroyed by a
servant of John Stuart Mill.

1836   *Sartor Resartus: The Life and Opinions of Herr Teufelsdröckh* published in book form in Boston with preface by Emerson.

1837   'Diamond Necklace' published in *Fraser's Magazine*. Second edition of *Sartor Resartus* published in Boston. *French Revolution: A History* published in three volumes; becomes critical and popular success.

1838   First English edition in book form of *Sartor Resartus*.

1839   *Critical and Miscellaneous Essays* published in four volumes; *Chartism* published.

1841   *On Heroes, Hero-Worship, and the Heroic in History* published.

1843   *Past and Present* published.

1844   Death of Sterling.

1845   *Oliver Cromwell's Letters and Speeches: with Elucidations* published in two volumes.

1850   *Latter-Day Pamphlets* published.

1851   *Life of John Sterling* published.

1852   Begins work on a history of Frederick the Great.

1853   Death of Carlyle's mother.

1856–8   First collected edition of his works published.

1858–65   The six volumes of *History of Friedrich II of Prussia, called Frederick the Great* published.

1866   Inaugural address as Rector of the University of Edinburgh. Death of Jane Welsh Carlyle, who is buried at Haddington. Begins writing *Reminiscences* (posthumously published in 1881).

1867   'Shooting Niagara: and After?' published in *Macmillan's*.

1875   *Early Kings of Norway* and *Essay on the Portraits of John Knox* published.

1881   Dies 5 February at Cheyne Row; burial in Ecclefechan churchyard next to his parents.

Sartor Resartus

IN THREE BOOKS

Mein Vermächtniss, wie herrlich weit und breit!
*Die Zeit ist mein Vermächtniss, mein Acker ist die Zeit.**

BOOK I

CHAPTER I

PRELIMINARY

CONSIDERING our present advanced state of culture, and how the Torch of Science has now been brandished and borne about, with more or less effect, for five thousand years and upwards; how, in these times especially, not only the Torch still burns, and perhaps more fiercely than ever, but innumerable Rush-lights and Sulphur-matches, kindled thereat, are also glancing in every direction, so that not the smallest cranny or doghole in Nature or Art can remain unilluminated,—it might strike the reflective mind with some surprise that hitherto little or nothing of a fundamental character, whether in the way of Philosophy or History, has been written on the subject of Clothes.

Our Theory of Gravitation is as good as perfect: Lagrange, it is well known, has proved that the Planetary System, on this scheme, will endure for ever; Laplace, still more cunningly, even guesses that it could not have been made on any other scheme. Whereby, at least, our nautical Logbooks can be better kept; and water-transport of all kinds has grown more commodious. Of Geology and Geognosy we know enough: what with the labours of our Werners and Huttons, what with the ardent genius of their disciples, it has come about that now, to many a Royal Society, the Creation of a World is little more mysterious than the cooking of a Dumpling; concerning which last, indeed, there have been minds to whom the question, *How the apples were got in,* * presented difficulties. Why mention our disquisitions on the Social Contract, on the Standard of Taste, * on the Migrations of the Herring? Then, have we not a Doctrine of Rent, a Theory of Value; Philosophies of Language, of History, of Pottery, of Apparitions, of Intoxicating Liquors? Man's whole life and environment have been laid open and elucidated; scarcely a fragment or fibre of his Soul,

Body, and Possessions, but has been probed, dissected, distilled, desiccated, and scientifically decomposed: our spiritual Faculties, of which it appears there are not a few, have their Stewarts, Cousins, Royer Collards: every cellular, vascular, muscular Tissue glories in its Lawrences, Majendies, Bichâts.

How, then, comes it, may the reflective mind repeat, that the grand Tissue of all Tissues, the only real *Tissue*, should have been quite overlooked by Science—the vestural Tissue, namely, of woollen or other Cloth; which Man's Soul wears as its outmost wrappage and overall; wherein his whole other Tissues are included and screened, his whole Faculties work, his whole Self lives, moves, and has its being? For if, now and then, some straggling broken-winged thinker has cast an owl's-glance into this obscure region, the most have soared over it altogether heedless; regarding Clothes as a property, not an accident, as quite natural and spontaneous, like the leaves of trees, like the plumage of birds. In all speculations they have tacitly figured man as a *Clothed Animal;* whereas he is by nature a *Naked Animal;* and only in certain circumstances, by purpose and device, masks himself in Clothes. Shakespeare says,* we are creatures that look before and after: the more surprising that we do not look round a little, and see what is passing under our very eyes.

But here, as in so many other cases, Germany, learned, indefatigable, deep-thinking Germany comes to our aid. It is, after all, a blessing that, in these revolutionary times, there should be one country where abstract Thought can still take shelter; that while the din and frenzy of Catholic Emancipations, and Rotten Boroughs, and Revolts of Paris,* deafen every French and every English ear, the German can stand peaceful on his scientific watch-tower; and, to the raging, struggling multitude here and elsewhere, solemnly, from hour to hour, with preparatory blast of cowhorn, emit his *Höret ihr Herren und lasset's Euch sagen;** in other words, tell the Universe, which so often forgets that fact, what o'clock it really is. Not unfrequently the Germans have been blamed for an unprofitable diligence; as if they struck into devious courses, where nothing was to be had but the toil of a rough journey; as if, forsaking the gold-mines of Finance, and that political slaughter of fat oxen whereby a man himself grows fat, they were apt to run goose-hunting into regions of bilberries and crowberries, and be swallowed up at last in remote peat-bogs. Of that unwise science, which, as our Humorist expresses it,

> By geometric scale
> Doth take the size of pots of ale,*

still more, of that altogether misdirected industry, which is seen vigorously enough* thrashing mere straw, there can nothing defensive be said. In so far as the Germans are chargeable with such, let them take the consequence. Nevertheless be it remarked, that even a Russian Steppe has Tumuli and gold ornaments; also many a scene that looks desert and rock-bound from the distance, will unfold itself, when visited, into rare valleys. Nay, in any case, would Criticism erect not only fingerposts and turnpikes, but spiked gates and impassable barriers, for the mind of man? It is written, "Many shall run to and fro, and knowledge shall be increased."* Surely the plain rule is, Let each considerate person have his way, and see what it will lead to. For not this man and that man, but all men make up mankind, and their united tasks the task of mankind. How often have we seen some such adventurous, and perhaps much-censured wanderer light on some outlying, neglected, yet vitally momentous province; the hidden treasures of which he first discovered, and kept proclaiming till the general eye and effort were directed thither, and the conquest was completed;—thereby, in these his seemingly so aimless rambles, planting new standards, founding new habitable colonies, in the immeasurable circumambient realm of Nothingness and Night! Wise man was he who counselled that Speculation should have free course, and look fearlessly towards all the thirty-two points of the compass, whithersoever and howsoever it listed.

Perhaps it is proof of the stinted* condition in which pure Science, especially pure moral Science, languishes among us English; and how our mercantile greatness, and invaluable Constitution, impressing a political or other immediately practical tendency on all English culture and endeavour, cramps the free flight of Thought,—that this, not Philosophy

of Clothes, but recognition even that we have no such Philosophy, stands here for the first time published in our language.
What English intellect could have chosen such a topic, or by
chance stumbled on it? But for that same unshackled, and even
sequestered condition of the German Learned, which permits
and induces them to fish in all manner of waters, with all
manner of nets, it seems probable enough, this abstruse Inquiry
might, in spite of the results it leads to, have continued dormant
for indefinite periods. The Editor of these sheets, though
otherwise boasting himself a man of confirmed speculative
habits, and perhaps discursive enough, is free to confess, that
never, till these last months, did the above very plain considerations, on our total want of a Philosophy of Clothes, occur to
him; and then, by quite foreign suggestion. By the arrival,
namely, of a new Book from Professor Teufelsdröckh of
Weissnichtwo;* treating expressly of this subject; and in a style
which, whether understood or not, could not even by the
blindest be overlooked. In the present Editor's way of thought,
this remarkable Treatise, with its Doctrines, whether as judicially acceded to, or judicially denied, has not remained
without effect.

"*Die Kleider ihr Werden und Wirken* (Clothes, their Origin
and Influence): *von Diog. Teufelsdröckh, J. U. D. etc. Stillschweigen und Co^gnie: Weissnichtwo*, 1833:*

"Here," says the *Weissnichtwo'sche Anzeiger,** "comes a
Volume of that extensive, close-printed, close-meditated sort,
which, be it spoken with pride, is seen only in Germany,
perhaps only in Weissnichtwo: issuing from the hitherto
irreproachable Firm of Stillschweigen and Company, with
every external furtherance, it is of such internal quality as to set
Neglect at defiance." . . . "A work," concludes the well nigh
enthusiastic Reviewer, "interesting alike to the antiquary, the
historian, and the philosophic thinker; a masterpiece of bold-
ness, lynx-eyed acuteness, and rugged independent Germanism
and Philanthropy (*derber Kerndeutschheit und Menschenliebe*);
which will not, assuredly, pass current without opposition in
high places; but must and will exalt the almost new name of
Teufelsdröckh to the first ranks of Philosophy, in our German
Temple-of-Honour."

Mindful of old friendship, the distinguished Professor, in this the first blaze of his fame, which however does not dazzle him, sends hither a Presentation Copy of his Book; with compliments and encomiums which modesty forbids the present Editor to rehearse; yet without indicated wish or hope of any kind, except what may be implied in the concluding phrase: *Möchte es* (this remarkable Treatise) *auch im Brittischen Boden gedeihen!**

CHAPTER 2

EDITORIAL DIFFICULTIES

I<small>F</small> for a speculative man, "whose seedfield," in the sublime words of the Poet, "is Time,"* no conquest is important but that of new Ideas, then might the arrival of Professor Teufels-dröckh's Book be marked with chalk in the Editor's Calendar. It is indeed an "extensive Volume," of boundless, almost formless contents, a very Sea of Thought; neither calm nor clear, if you will; yet wherein the toughest pearl-diver may dive to his utmost depth, and return not only with sea-wreck but with true orients.

Directly on the first perusal, almost on the first deliberate inspection, it became apparent that here a quite new Branch of Philosophy, leading to as yet undescried ulterior results, was disclosed; farther, what seemed scarcely less interesting, a quite new human Individuality, an almost unexampled personal Character, that, namely, of Professor Teufelsdröckh the Dis-closer. Of both which novelties, as far as might be possible, we resolved to master the significance. But as man is emphatically a Proselytising creature, no sooner was such mastery even fairly attempted, than the new question arose: How might this acquired good be imparted to others, perhaps in equal need thereof; how could the Philosophy of Clothes and the Author of such Philosophy be brought home, in any measure, to the business and bosoms of our own English nation? For if new-got gold is said to burn the pockets till it be cast forth into circulation, much more may new Truth.

Here, however, difficulties occurred. The first thought naturally was to publish Article after Article on this remarkable volume, in such widely-circulating Critical Journals as the Editor might stand connected with, or by money or love procure access to. But, on the other hand, was it not clear that such matter as must here be revealed and treated of might endanger the circulation of any Journal extant? If, indeed, the whole Parties of* the State could have been abolished, Whig, Tory, and Radical, embracing in discrepant union; and the whole Journals of the Nation could have been jumbled into one Journal, and the Philosophy of Clothes poured forth in incessant torrents therefrom, the attempt had seemed possible. But, alas, what vehicle of that sort have we, except *Fraser's Magazine?* A vehicle all strewed (figuratively speaking) with the maddest Waterloo-Crackers,* exploding distractively and destructively, wheresoever the mystified passenger stands or sits; nay, in any case, understood to be, of late years, a vehicle full to overflowing, and inexorably shut! Besides, to state the Philosophy of Clothes without the Philosopher, the ideas of Teufelsdröckh without something of his personality, was it not to insure both of entire misapprehension? Now for Biography, had it been otherwise admissible, there were no adequate documents, no hope of obtaining such, but rather, owing to circumstances, a special despair. Thus did the Editor see himself, for the while, shut out from all public utterance of these extraordinary Doctrines, and constrained to revolve them, not without disquietude, in the dark depths of his own mind.

So had it lasted for some months; and now the Volume on Clothes, read and again read, was in several points becoming lucid and lucent; the personality of its Author more and more surprising, but, in spite of all that memory and conjecture could do, more and more enigmatic; whereby the old disquietude seemed fast settling into fixed discontent,—when altogether unexpectedly arrives a Letter from Herr Hofrath Heuschrecke,* our Professor's chief friend and associate in Weissnichtwo, with whom we had not previously corresponded. The Hofrath, after much quite extraneous matter, began dilating largely on the "agitation and attention" which the Philosophy of Clothes was exciting in its own German Republic of Letters; on the deep significance and tendency of his Friend's Volume; and then, at length, with great circumlocution, hinted at the practicability of conveying "some knowledge of it, and of him, to England, and through England to the distant West:" a Work on Professor Teufelsdröckh "were undoubtedly welcome to the *Family,* the *National,** or any other of those patriotic *Libraries,* at present the glory of British Literature;" might work revolutions in Thought; and so forth;—in conclusion, intimating not obscurely, that should the present Editor feel disposed to undertake a Biography of Teufelsdröckh, he, Hofrath Heuschrecke, had it in his power to furnish the requisite Documents.

As in some chemical mixture, that has stood long evaporating, but would not crystallise, instantly when the wire or other fixed substance is introduced, crystallisation commences, and rapidly proceeds till the whole is finished, so was it with the Editor's mind and this offer of Heuschrecke's. Form rose out of void solution and discontinuity; like united itself with like in definite arrangement; and soon either in actual vision and possession, or in fixed reasonable hope, the image of the whole Enterprise had shaped itself, so to speak, into a solid mass. Cautiously yet courageously, through the twopenny post, application to the famed redoubtable OLIVER YORKE* was now made: an interview, interviews with that singular man have taken place; with more of assurance on our side, with less of satire (at least of open satire) on his, than we anticipated;— for the rest, with such issue as is now visible. As to those same "patriotic *Libraries,*" the Hofrath's counsel could only be viewed with silent amazement; but with his offer of Documents we joyfully and almost instantaneously closed. Thus, too, in the sure expectation of these, we already see our task begun; and this our *Sartor Resartus,* which is properly a "Life and Opinions of Herr Teufelsdröckh," hourly advancing.

Of our fitness for the Enterprise, to which we have such title and vocation, it were perhaps uninteresting to say more. Let the British reader study and enjoy, in simplicity of heart, what is here presented him, and with whatever metaphysical acumen, and talent for Meditation he is possessed of. Let him strive to keep a free, open sense; cleared from the mists of Prejudice, above all from the paralysis of Cant; and directed rather to the Book itself than to the Editor of the Book. Who or what such Editor may be, must remain conjectural, and even insignificant:† it is a Voice publishing tidings of the Philosophy of Clothes; undoubtedly a Spirit addressing Spirits: whoso hath ears let him hear.

† With us even he still communicates in some sort of mask, or muffler; and, we have reason to think, under a feigned name!— O. Y.

On one other point the Editor thinks it needful to give warning: namely, that he is animated with a true though perhaps a feeble attachment to the Institutions of our Ancestors; and minded to defend these, according to ability, at all hazards; nay, it was partly with a view to such defence that he engaged in this undertaking. To stem, or if that be impossible, profitably to divert the current of Innovation, such a Volume as Teufelsdröckh's, if cunningly planted down, were no despicable pile, or floodgate, in the Logical wear.*

For the rest, be it nowise apprehended that any personal connexion of ours with Teufelsdröckh, Heuschrecke, or this Philosophy of Clothes, can pervert our judgment, or sway us to extenuate or exaggerate. Powerless, we venture to promise, are those private Compliments themselves. Grateful they may well be; as generous illusions of friendship; as fair mementos of bygone unions, of those nights and suppers of the gods, when lapped in the symphonies and harmonies of Philosophic Eloquence, though with baser accompaniments, the present Editor revelled in that feast of reason, never since vouchsafed him in so full measure! But what then? *Amicus Plato, magis amica veritas;** Teufelsdröckh is our friend, Truth is our divinity. In our historical and critical capacity, we hope, we are strangers to all the world; have feud or favour with no one,—save indeed the Devil, with whom as with the Prince of Lies and Darkness we do at all times wage internecine war. This assurance, at an epoch when Puffery and Quackery have reached a height unexampled in the annals of mankind, and even English Editors, like Chinese Shopkeepers, must write on their door-lintels, *No cheating here,*—we thought it good to premise.

CHAPTER 3
REMINISCENCES

To the Author's private circle the appearance of this singular Work on Clothes must have occasioned little less surprise than it has to the rest of the world. For ourselves, at least, few things have been more unexpected. Professor Teufelsdröckh, at the period of our acquaintance with him, seemed to lead a quite still and self-contained life: a man devoted to the higher Philosophies, indeed; yet more likely, if he published at all, to publish a Refutation of Hegel and Bardili, both of whom, strangely enough, he included under a common ban; than to descend, as he has here done, into the angry noisy Forum, with an Argument that cannot but exasperate and divide. Not, that we can remember, was the Philosophy of Clothes once touched upon between us. If through the high silent, meditative Transcendentalism of our Friend we detected any practical tendency whatever, it was at most Political, and towards a certain prospective, and for the present quite speculative, Radicalism; as indeed some correspondence, on his part, with Herr Oken of Jena was now and then suspected; though his special contributions to the *Isis* could never be more than surmised at. But, at all events, nothing Moral, still less any thing Didactico-Religious, was looked for from him.

Well do we recollect the last words he spoke in our hearing; which indeed, with the Night they were uttered in, are to be forever remembered. Lifting his huge tumbler of *Gukguk*,† and for a moment lowering his tobacco-pipe, he stood up in full coffeehouse (it was *Zum Grünen Ganse,** the largest in Weissnichtwo, where all the Virtuosity, and nearly all the Intellect, of the place assembled of an evening); and there, with low, soul-stirring tone, and the look truly of an angel, though whether of a white or of a black one might be dubious, proposed this toast: *Die Sache der Armen in Gottes und Teufels Namen* (The Cause of the Poor in Heaven's name and ——'s)! One full

† Gukguk is unhappily only an academical—Beer.

shout, breaking the leaden silence; then a gurgle of innumerable emptying bumpers, again followed by universal cheering, returned him loud acclaim. It was the finale of the night: resuming their pipes; in the highest enthusiasm, amid volumes of tobacco-smoke; triumphant, cloudcapt without and within, the assembly broke up, each to his thoughtful pillow. *Bleibt doch ein echter Spass- und Galgen-vogel,** said several; meaning thereby that, one day, he would probably be hanged for his democratic sentiments. *Wo steckt der Schalk?** added they, looking round: but Teufelsdröckh had retired by private alleys, and the Compiler of these pages beheld him no more.

In such scenes has it been our lot to live with this Philosopher, such estimate to form of his purposes and powers. And yet, thou brave Teufelsdröckh, who could tell what lurked in thee? Under those thick locks of thine, so long and lank, overlapping roof-wise the gravest face we ever in this world saw, there dwelt a most busy brain. In thy eyes, too, deep under their shaggy brows, and looking out so still and dreamy, have we not noticed gleams of an ethereal or else a diabolic fire, and half fancied that their stillness was but the rest of infinite motion, the *sleep* of a spinning-top? Thy little figure, there as in loose, ill-brushed, threadbare habiliments, thou sattest, amid litter and lumber, whole days, to "think and smoke tobacco," held in it a mighty heart. The secrets of man's Life were laid open to thee; thou sawest into the mystery of the Universe, farther than another; thou hadst *in petto* thy remarkable Volume on Clothes. Nay, was there not in that clear logically-founded Transcendentalism of thine; still more, in thy meek, silent, deepseated Sansculottism,** combined with a true princely Courtesy of inward nature, the visible rudiments of such speculation? But great men are too often unknown, or what is worse, misknown. Already, when we dreamed not of it, the warp of thy remarkable Volume lay on the loom; and silently, mysterious shuttles were putting in the woof!

How the Hofrath Heuschrecke is to furnish biographical data, in this case, may be a curious question; the answer of which, however, is happily not our concern, but his. To us it appeared, after repeated trial, that in Weissnichtwo, from the archives or memories of the best-informed classes, no Biography of Teufelsdröckh was to be gathered; not so much as a false one. He was a Stranger there, wafted thither by what is called the course of circumstances; concerning whose parentage, birthplace, prospects or pursuits, Curiosity had indeed made inquiries, but satisfied herself with the most indistinct replies. For himself, he was a man so still and altogether unparticipating, that to question him even afar off on such particulars was a thing of more than usual delicacy: besides, in his sly way, he had ever some quaint turn, not without its satirical edge, wherewith to divert such intrusions, and deter you from the like. Wits spoke of him secretly as if he were a kind of Melchizedek, without father or mother of any kind; sometimes, with reference to his great historic and statistic knowledge, and the vivid way he had of expressing himself like an eye-witness of distant transactions and scenes, they called him the *Ewige Jude,* Everlasting, or as we say, Wandering Jew.*

To the most, indeed, he had become not so much a Man as a Thing; which Thing doubtless they were accustomed to see, and with satisfaction; but no more thought of accounting for than for the fabrication of their daily *Allgemeine Zeitung,** or the domestic habits of the Sun. Both were there and welcome; the world enjoyed what good was in them, and thought no more of the matter. The man Teufelsdröckh passed and repassed, in his little circle, as one of those originals and nondescripts, more frequent in German Universities than elsewhere; of whom, though you see them alive, and feel certain enough that they must have a History, no History seems to be discoverable; or only such as men give of mountain rocks and antediluvian ruins: that they have been created by unknown agencies, are in a state of gradual decay, and for the present reflect light and resist pressure; that is, are visible and tangible objects in this phantasm world, where so much other mystery is.

It was to be remarked that though, by title and diploma, *Professor der Allerley-Wissenschaft,* or as we should say in English, "Professor of Things in General," he had never delivered any Course; perhaps never been incited thereto by any public furtherance or requisition. To all appearance, the enlightened Government of Weissnichtwo, in founding their

New University, imagined they had done enough, if "in times like ours," as the half-official Program expressed it, "when all things are, rapidly or slowly, resolving themselves into Chaos, a Professorship of this kind had been established; whereby, as occasion called, the task of bodying somewhat forth again from such Chaos might be, even slightly, facilitated." That actual Lectures should be held, and Public Classes for the "Science of Things in General," they doubtless considered premature; on which ground too they had only established the Professorship, nowise endowed it; so that Teufelsdröckh, "recommended by the highest Names," had been promoted thereby to a Name merely.

Great, among the more enlightened classes, was the admiration of this new Professorship: how an enlightened Government had seen into the Want of the Age (*Zeitbedürfniss*); how at length, instead of Denial and Destruction, we were to have a science of Affirmation and Re-construction; and Germany and Weissnichtwo were, where they should be, in the vanguard of the world. Considerable also was the wonder at the new Professor, dropt opportunely enough into the nascent University; so able to lecture, should occasion call; so ready to hold his peace for indefinite periods, should an enlightened Government consider that occasion did not call. But such admiration and such wonder, being followed by no act to keep them living, could last only nine days; and, long before our visit to that scene, had quite died away. The more cunning heads thought it was all an expiring clutch at popularity, on the part of a Minister, whom domestic embarrassments, court intrigues, old age, and dropsy soon afterwards finally drove from the helm.

As for Teufelsdröckh, except by his nightly appearances at the *Grünen Ganse,* Weissnichtwo saw little of him, felt little of him. Here, over his tumbler of Gukguk, he sat reading Journals; sometimes contemplatively looking into the clouds of his tobacco-pipe, without other visible employment: always, from his mild ways, an agreeable phenomenon there; more especially when he opened his lips for speech; on which occasions the whole Coffeehouse would hush itself into silence, as if sure to hear something noteworthy. Nay, perhaps to hear a whole series and river of the most memorable utterances; such as, when once thawed, he would for hours indulge in, with fit audience: and the more memorable, as issuing from a head apparently not more interested in them, not more conscious of them, than is the sculptured stone head of some public Fountain, which through its brass mouth-tube emits water to the worthy and the unworthy; careless whether it be for cooking victuals or quenching conflagrations; indeed, maintains the same earnest assiduous look, whether any water be flowing or not.

To the Editor of these sheets, as to a young enthusiastic Englishman, however unworthy, Teufelsdröckh opened himself perhaps more than to the most. Pity only that we could not then half guess his importance, and scrutinise him with due power of vision! We enjoyed, what not three men in Weissnichtwo could boast of, a certain degree of access to the Professor's private domicile. It was the attic floor of the highest house in the Wahngasse;* and might truly be called the pinnacle of Weissnichtwo, for it rose sheer up above the contiguous roofs, themselves rising from elevated ground. Moreover, with its windows, it looked towards all the four *Orte,* or as the Scotch say, and we ought to say, *Airts:** the Sitting-room itself commanded three; another came to view in the *Schlafgemach* (Bed-room) at the opposite end; to say nothing of the Kitchen, which offered two, as it were, *duplicates,* and showing nothing new. So that it was in fact the speculum or watch-tower* of Teufelsdröckh; wherefrom, sitting at ease, he might see the whole life-circulation of that considerable City; the streets and lanes of which, with all their doing and driving (*Thun und Treiben*) were for most part visible there.

"I look down into all that wasp-nest or bee-hive," have we heard him say, "and witness their wax-laying and honey-making, and poison-brewing, and choking by sulphur. From the Palace esplanade, where music plays while Serene Highness is pleased to eat his victuals, down to the low lane, where in her door-sill the aged widow, knitting for a thin livelihood, sits to feel the afternoon sun, I see it all; for, except the Schlosskirche* weathercock, no biped stands so high. Couriers arrive bestrapped and bebooted, bearing Joy and Sorrow bagged up in pouches of leather: there, topladen, and with four swift horses, rolls in the country Baron and his household; here, on timber leg, the lamed Soldier hops painfully along, begging alms: a thousand carriages, and wains, and cars, come tumbling in with Food, with young Rusticity, and other Raw Produce, inanimate or animate, and go tumbling out again with Produce manufactured. That living flood, pouring through these streets, of all qualities and ages, knowest thou whence it is coming, whither it is going? *Aus der Ewigkeit, zu der Ewigkeit hin*: From Eternity, onwards to Eternity! These are Apparitions: what else? Are they not Souls rendered visible; in Bodies, that took shape, and will lose it; melting into air? Their solid pavement is a Picture of the Sense; they walk on the bosom of Nothing, blank Time is behind them and before them. Or fanciest thou, the red and yellow Clothes-screen yonder, with spurs on its heels, and feather in its crown, is but of To-day, without a Yesterday or a To-morrow; and had not rather its Ancestor alive when Hengst and Horsa overran thy Island? Friend, thou seest here a living link in that Tissue of History, which inweaves all Being: watch well, or it will be past thee, and seen no more"

"*Ach, mein Lieber!*"* said he once, at midnight, when we had returned from the Coffeehouse in rather earnest talk, "it is a true sublimity to dwell here. These fringes of lamplight, struggling up through smoke and thousandfold exhalation, some fathoms into the ancient reign of Night, what thinks Boötes of them, as he leads his Hunting Dogs* over the Zenith in their leash of sidereal fire? That stifled hum of Midnight, when Traffic has lain down to rest; and the chariot-wheels of Vanity, still rolling here and there through distant streets, are bearing her to Halls roofed in, and lighted to the due pitch for her; and only Vice and Misery, to prowl or to moan like nightbirds, are abroad: that hum, I say, like the stertorous, unquiet slumber of sick Life, is heard in Heaven! Oh, under that hideous coverlid* of vapours, and putrefactions, and unimaginable gases, what a Fermenting-vat lies simmering and hid! The joyful and the sorrowful are there; men are dying there, men are being born; men are praying—on the other side of a brick partition, men are cursing; and around them all is the vast, void Night. The proud Grandee still lingers in his perfumed saloons, or reposes within damask curtains; Wretchedness cowers into truckle-beds, or shivers hunger-stricken into its lair of straw: in obscure cellars, *Rouge-et-Noir** languidly emits its voice-of-destiny to haggard hungry Villains; while Councillors of State sit plotting, and playing their high chess-game, whereof the pawns are Men. The Lover whispers his mistress that the coach is ready; and she, full of hope and fear, glides down, to fly with him over the borders: the Thief, still more silently, sets-to his picklocks and crowbars, or lurks in wait till the watchmen first snore in their boxes. Gay mansions, with supper-rooms and dancing-rooms, are full of light and music and high-swelling hearts; but, in the Condemned Cells, the pulse of life beats tremulous and faint, and bloodshot eyes look out through the darkness, which is around and within, for the light of a stern last morning. Six men are to be hanged on the morrow: comes no hammering from the *Rabenstein?**—their gallows must even now be o' building. Upwards of five hundred thousand two-legged animals without feathers lie round us, in horizontal position; their heads all in nightcaps, and full of the foolishest dreams. Riot cries aloud, and staggers and swaggers in his rank dens of shame; and the Mother, with streaming hair, kneels over her pallid dying infant, whose cracked lips only her tears now moisten.—All these heaped and huddled together, with nothing but a little carpentry and masonry between them;—crammed in, like salted fish, in their barrel;—or weltering, shall I say, like an Egyptian pitcher of tamed Vipers, each struggling to get its *head above* the others: *such* work goes on under that smoke-counterpane!—But I, *mein Werther,** sit above it all; I am alone with the Stars."

We looked in his face to see whether, in the utterance of such extraordinary Night-thoughts, no feeling might be traced there; but with the light we had, which indeed was only a single tallow-light, and far enough from the window, nothing save that old calmness and fixedness was visible.

These were the Professor's talking seasons: most commonly he spoke in mere monosyllables, or sat altogether silent, and smoked; while the visitor had liberty either to say what he listed, receiving for answer an occasional grunt; or to look round for a space, and then take himself away. It was a strange apartment; full of books and tattered papers, and miscellaneous shreds of all conceivable substances, "united in a common element of dust." Books lay on tables, and below tables; here fluttered a sheet of manuscript, there a torn handkerchief, or nightcap hastily thrown aside: ink-bottles alternated with bread-crusts, coffee-pots, tobacco-boxes, Periodical Literature, and Blücher Boots.* Old Lieschen (Lisekin, 'Liza), who was his bed-maker and stove-lighter, his washer and wringer, cook, errand-maid, and general lion's-provider, and for the rest a very orderly creature, had no sovereign authority in this last citadel of Teufelsdröckh; only some once in the month, she half-forcibly made her way thither, with broom and duster, and (Teufelsdröckh hastily saving his manuscripts) effected a partial clearance, a jail-delivery of such lumber as was not Literary. These were her *Erdbebungen** (Earthquakes), which Teufelsdröckh dreaded worse than the pestilence; nevertheless, to such length he had been forced to comply. Glad would he have been to sit here philosophising for ever, or till the litter, by accumulation, drove him out of doors: but Lieschen was his right-arm, and spoon, and necessary of life, and would not be flatly gainsayed. We can still remember the ancient woman; so silent that some thought her dumb; deaf also you would often have supposed her; for Teufelsdröckh and Teufelsdröckh only would she serve or give heed to; and with him she seemed to communicate chiefly by signs; if it were not rather by some secret divination that she guessed all his wants, and supplied them. Assiduous old dame! she scoured, and sorted, and swept, in her kitchen, with the least possible violence to the ear; yet all was tight and right there: hot and black came the coffee ever at the due moment; and the speechless Lieschen herself looked out on you, from under her clean white coif with its lappets, through her clean withered face and wrinkles, with a look of helpful intelligence, almost of benevolence.

Few strangers, as above hinted, had admittance hither: the only one we ever saw there, ourselves excepted, was the Hofrath Heuschrecke, already known, by name and expectation, to the readers of these pages. To us, at that period, Herr Heuschrecke seemed one of those purse-mouthed, crane-necked, clean-brushed, pacific individuals, perhaps sufficiently distinguished in society by this fact, that, in dry weather or in wet, "they never appear without their umbrella." Had we not known with what "little wisdom" the world is governed; and how, in Germany as elsewhere, the ninety and nine Public Men can for most part be but mute train-bearers to the hundredth, perhaps but stalking-horses and willing or unwilling dupes,—it might have seemed wonderful how Herr Heuschrecke should be named a *Rath*, or Councillor, and Counsellor, even in Weissnichtwo. What counsel to any man, or to any woman, could this particular Hofrath give; in whose loose, zigzag figure; in whose thin visage, as it went jerking to and fro, in minute incessant fluctuation,—you traced rather confusion worse confounded; at most, Timidity and physical Cold? Some indeed said withal, he was "the very Spirit of Love embodied:" blue earnest eyes, full of sadness and kindness; purse ever open, and so forth; the whole of which, we shall now hope for many reasons, was not quite groundless. Nevertheless, friend Teufelsdröckh's outline, who indeed handled the burin like few in these cases, was probably the best: *Er hat Gemüth und Geist, hat wenigstens gehabt, doch ohne Organ, ohne Schicksals-Gunst; ist gegenwärtig aber halb-zerrüttet, halb-erstarrt,* "He has heart and talent, at least has had such, yet without fit mode of utterance, or favour of Fortune; and so is now half-cracked, half-congealed."—What the Hofrath shall think of this, when he sees it, readers may wonder: we, safe in the stronghold of Historical Fidelity, are careless.

The main point, doubtless, for us all, is his love of Teufelsdröckh, which indeed was also by far the most decisive feature of Heuschrecke himself. We are enabled to assert that he hung on the Professor with the fondness of a Boswell for his Johnson. And perhaps with the like return; for Teufelsdröckh treated his gaunt admirer with little outward regard, as some half-rational or altogether irrational friend, and at best loved him out of gratitude and by habit. On the other hand, it was curious to observe with what reverent kindness, and a sort of fatherly protection, our Hofrath, being the elder, richer, and as he fondly imagined far more practically influential of the two, looked and tended on his little Sage, whom he seemed to consider as a living oracle. Let but Teufelsdröckh open his mouth, Heuschrecke's also unpuckered itself into a free door-way, besides his being all eye and all ear, so that nothing might be lost: and then, at every pause in the harangue he gurgled out his pursy chuckle of a cough-laugh (for the machinery of laughter took some time to get in motion, and seemed crank and slack), or else his twanging, nasal *Bravo! Das glaub' ich;** in either case, by way of heartiest approval. In short, if Teufels-dröckh was Dalai-Lama, of which except perhaps in his self-seclusion, and god-like Indifference, there was no symptom, then might Heuschrecke pass for his chief Talapoin, to whom no dough-pill he could knead and publish was other than medicinal and sacred.

In such environment, social, domestic, physical, did Teufels-dröckh, at the time of our acquaintance, and most likely does he still, live and meditate. Here, perched up in his high Wahngasse watchtower, and often, in solitude, outwatching the Bear, it was that the indomitable Inquirer fought all his battles with Dulness and Darkness; here, in all probability, that he wrote this surprising Volume on *Clothes*. Additional parti-culars: of his age, which was of that standing middle sort you could only guess at; of his wide surtout; the colour of his trousers, fashion of his broad-brimmed steeple-hat, and so forth, we might report, but do not. The Wisest truly is, in these times, the Greatest; so that an enlightened curiosity leaving Kings and such like to rest very much on their own basis, turns more and more to the Philosophic Class; nevertheless, what reader expects that, with all our writing and reporting, Teufels-dröckh could be brought home to him, till once the Docu-ments arrive? His Life, Fortunes, and Bodily Presence, are as yet hidden from us, or matter only of faint conjecture. But on the other hand, does not his Soul lie enclosed in this remarkable Volume, much more truly than Pedro Garcia's did in the buried Bag of Doubloons?** To the soul of Diogenes Teufels-dröckh, to his opinions namely on the "Origin and Influence of Clothes," we for the present gladly return.

CHAPTER 4
CHARACTERISTICS

It were a piece of vain flattery to pretend that this Work on Clothes entirely contents us; that it is not, like all works of Genius, like the very Sun, which, though the highest published Creation, or work of Genius, has nevertheless black spots and troubled nebulosities amid its effulgence,—a mixture of insight, inspiration, with dulness, double-vision, and even utter blindness.

Without committing ourselves to those enthusiastic praises and prophesyings of the *Weissnichtwo'sche Anzeiger*, we admitted that the Book had in a high degree excited us to self-activity, which is the best effect of any book; that it had even operated changes in our way of thought; nay, that it promised to prove, as it were, the opening of a new mine-shaft, wherein the whole world of Speculation might henceforth dig to unknown depths. More specially it may now be declared that Professor Teufelsdröckh's acquirements, patience of research, philosophic and even poetic vigour, are here made indisputably manifest; and unhappily no less his prolixity and tortuosity and manifold inaptitude; that, on the whole, as in opening new mine-shafts is not unreasonable, there is much rubbish in his Book, though likewise specimens of almost invaluable ore. A paramount popularity in England we cannot promise him. Apart from the choice of such a topic as Clothes, too often the manner of treating it betokens in the Author a rusticity and academic seclusion, unblamable, indeed inevitable in a German, but fatal to his success with our public.

Of good society Teufelsdröckh appears to have seen little, or has mostly forgotten what he saw. He speaks out with a strange plainness; calls many things by their mere dictionary names. To him the Upholsterer is no Pontiff, neither is any Drawing-room a Temple, were it never so begilt and overhung: "a whole immensity of Brussels carpets, and pier-glasses, and ormolu." as he himself expresses it, "cannot hide from me that such Drawing-room is simply a section of Infinite Space, where so many God-created Souls do for the time meet together." To Teufelsdröckh the highest Duchess is respectable, is venerable; but nowise for her pearl-bracelets, and Malines laces: in his eyes, the star of a Lord is little less and little more than the broad button of Birmingham spelter in a Clown's smock; "each is an implement," he says, "in its kind; a tag for *hooking-together;* and, for the rest, was dug from the earth, and hammered on a stithy before smiths' fingers." Thus does the Professor look in men's faces with a strange impartiality, a strange scientific freedom; like a man unversed in the higher circles, like a man dropped thither from the Moon. Rightly considered, it is in this peculiarity, running through his whole system of thought, that all these short-comings, over-shootings, and multiform per-versities, take rise: if indeed they have not a second source, also natural enough, in his Transcendental Philosophies, and humour of looking at all Matter and Material things as Spirit; whereby truly his case were but the more hopeless, the more lamentable.

To the Thinkers of this nation, however, of which class it is firmly believed there are individuals yet extant, we can safely recommend the Work: nay, who knows but among the fashionable ranks too, if it be true, as Teufelsdröckh maintains, that "within the most starched cravat there passes a windpipe and wesand, and under the thickliest embroidered waistcoat beats a heart,"—the force of that rapt earnestness may be felt, and here and there an arrow of the soul pierce through. In our wild Seer, shaggy, unkempt, like a Baptist living on locusts and wild honey,* there is an untutored energy, a silent as it were unconscious strength, which, except in the higher walks of Literature, must be rare. Many a deep glance, and often with unspeakable precision, has he cast into mysterious Nature, and the still more mysterious Life of Man. Wonderful it is with what cutting words, now and then, he severs asunder the confusion; sheers down, were it furlongs deep, into the true centre of the matter; and there not only hits the nail on the head, but with crushing force smites it home, and buries it.— On the other hand, let us be free to admit, he is the most unequal writer breathing. Often after some such feat, he will play truant for long pages, and go dawdling and dreaming, and mumbling and maundering the merest commonplaces, as if he were alseep with eyes open, which indeed he is.

Of his boundless Learning, and how all reading and literature in most known tongues, from *Sanconiathon* to *Dr. Lingard,* from your Oriental *Shasters,* and *Talmuds,* and *Korans,* with Cassini's *Siamese Tables,* and Laplace's *Mécanique Céleste,* down to *Robinson Crusoe* and the *Belfast Town and Country Almanack,* are familiar to him,—we shall say nothing: for unexampled as it is with us, to the Germans such universality of study passes without wonder, as a thing commendable, indeed, but natural, indispensable, and there of course. A man that devotes his life to learning, shall he not be learned?

In respect of style our Author manifests the same genial capability, marred too often by the same rudeness, inequality, and apparent want of intercourse with the higher classes. Occasionally, as above hinted, we find consummate vigour, a true inspiration: his burning Thoughts step forth in fit burning Words, like so many full-formed Minervas, issuing amid flame and splendour from Jove's head; a rich, idiomatic diction, picturesque allusions, fiery poetic emphasis, or quaint tricksy turns; all the graces and terrors of a wild Imagination, wedded to the clearest Intellect, alternate in beautiful vicissitude. Were it not that sheer sleeping and soporific passages; circumlocutions, repetitions, touches even of pure doting jargon, so often intervene! On the whole, Professor Teufelsdröckh is not a cultivated writer. Of his sentences perhaps not more than ninetenths stand straight on their legs; the remainder are in quite angular attitudes, buttressed up by props (of parentheses and dashes), and ever, with this or the other tagrag hanging from them; a few even sprawl out helplessly on all sides quite broken-backed and dismembered. Nevertheless, in almost his very worst moods, there lies in him a singular attraction. A wild tone pervades the whole utterance of the man, like its keynote and regulator; now screwing itself aloft as into the Song of Spirits, or else the shrill mockery of Fiends; now sinking in cadences, not without melodious heartiness, though sometimes abrupt enough, into the common pitch, when we hear it only as a monotonous hum; of which hum the true character is extremely difficult to fix. Up to this hour we have never fully satisfied ourselves whether it is a tone and hum of real Humour, which we reckon among the very highest qualities of genius, or some remote echo* of mere Insanity and Inanity, which doubtless ranks below the very lowest.

Under a like difficulty, in spite even of our personal intercourse, do we still lie with regard to the Professor's moral feeling. Gleams of an ethereal Love burst forth from him, soft wailings of infinite Pity; he could clasp the whole Universe into his bosom, and keep it warm; it seems as if under that rude exterior there dwelt a very seraph. Then again he is so sly and still, so imperturbably saturnine; shews such indifference, malign coolness towards all that men strive after; and ever with some half-visible wrinkle of a bitter sardonic humour, if indeed it be not mere stolid callousness,—that you look on him almost with a shudder, as on some incarnate Mephistopheles, to whom this great terrestrial and celestial Round, after all, were but some huge foolish Whirligig, where kings and beggars, and angels and demons, and stars and street-sweepings, were chaotically whirled; in which only children could take interest. His look, as we mentioned, is probably the gravest ever seen: yet it is not of that cast-iron gravity frequent enough among our own Chancery suitors;* but rather the gravity as of some silent, high-encircled mountain-pool, perhaps the crater of an extinct volcano; into whose black deeps you fear to gaze: those eyes, those lights that sparkle in it, may indeed be reflexes of the heavenly Stars, but perhaps also glances from the region of Nether Fire!

Certainly a most involved, self-secluded, altogether enigmatic nature, this of Teufelsdröckh! Here, however, we gladly recall to mind that once we saw him *laugh;* once only, perhaps it was the first and last time in his life; but then such a peal of laughter, enough to have awakened the Seven Sleepers!* It was of Jean Paul's doing: some single billow in that vast world-Mahlstrom of Humour, with its Heaven-kissing coruscations, which is now, alas, all congealed in the frost of Death! The large-bodied Poet and the small, both large enough in soul, sat talking miscellaneously together, the present Editor being privileged to listen; and now Paul, in his serious way, was giving one of those inimitable "Extra-harangues;" and, as it chanced, On the Proposal for a *Cast-metal King:* gradually a light kindled in our Professor's eyes and face, a beaming, mantling, loveliest light; through those murky features, a radiant ever-young Apollo looked; and he burst forth like the neighing of all Tattersall's,—tears streaming down his cheeks, pipe held aloft, foot clutched into the air,—loud, long-continuing, uncontrollable; a laugh not of the face and diaphragm only, but of the whole man from head to heel. The present Editor, who laughed indeed, yet with measure, began to fear all was not right: however, Teufelsdröckh composed himself, and sank into his old stillness; on his inscrutable countenance there was, if any thing, a slight look of shame; and Richter himself could not rouse him again. Readers who have any tincture of Psychology know how much is to be inferred from this; and that no man who has once heartily and wholly laughed can be altogether irreclaimably bad. How much lies in Laughter: the cipher-key, wherewith we decipher the whole man! Some men wear an everlasting barren simper; in the smile of others lies a cold glitter as of ice: the fewest are able to laugh, what can be called laughing, but only sniff and titter and snigger from the throat outwards; or at best, produce some whiffling husky cachinnation, as if they were laughing through wool: of none such comes good. The man who cannot laugh is not only fit for treasons, stratagems and spoils; but his whole life is already a treason and a stratagem.

Considered as an Author, Herr Teufelsdröckh has one scarcely pardonable fault, doubtless his worst: an almost total want of arrangement. In this remarkable Volume, it is true, his adherence to the mere course of Time produces, through the Narrative portions, a certain shew of outward method; but of true logical method and sequence there is too little. Apart from its multifarious sections and subdivisions, the Work naturally falls into two Parts; a Historical-Descriptive, and a Philosophical-Speculative: but falls, unhappily, by no firm line of demarcation; in that labyrinthic combination, each Part overlaps, and indents, and indeed runs quite through the other. Many sections are of a debatable rubric, or even quite nondescript and unnameable; whereby the Book not only loses in accessibility, but too often distresses us like some mad banquet, wherein all courses had been confounded, and fish and flesh, soup and solid, oyster-sauce, lettuces, Rhine-wine and French mustard, were hurled into one huge tureen or trough, and the hungry Public invited to help itself. To bring what order we can out of this Chaos shall be part of our endeavour.

*   *   *

CHAPTER 5

THE WORLD IN CLOTHES

"As Montesquieu wrote a *Spirit of Laws*," observes our Professor, "so could I write a *Spirit of Clothes;* thus, with an *Esprit des Lois,* properly an *Esprit de Coutumes* we should have an *Esprit de Costumes.** For neither in tailoring nor in legislating does man proceed by mere Accident, but the hand is ever guided on by mysterious operations of the mind. In all his Modes and habilatory endeavours an Architectural Idea will be found lurking; his Body and the Cloth are the site and materials whereon and whereby his beautified edifice, of a Person, is to be built. Whether he flow gracefully out in folded mantles, based on light sandals; tower up in high headgear, from amid peaks, spangles and bell-girdles; swell out in starched ruffs, buckram stuffings and monstrous tuberosities; or girth himself into separate sections, and front the world an Agglomeration of four limbs,—will depend on the nature of such Architectural Idea: whether Grecian, Gothic, Later-Gothic, or altogether Modern, and Parisian or Anglo-Dandiacal. Again, what meaning lies in Colour! From the soberest drab to the high-flaming scarlet, spiritual idiosyncrasies unfold themselves in choice of Colour: if the Cut betoken Intellect and Talent, so does the Colour betoken Temper and Heart. In all which, among nations as among individuals, there is an incessant, indubitable, though infinitely complex working of Cause and Effect: every snip of the Scissors has been regulated and prescribed by ever-active Influences, which doubtless to Intelligences of a superior order are neither invisible nor illegible.

"For such superior Intelligences a Cause-and-effect Philosophy* of Clothes, as of Laws, were probably a comfortable winter-evening entertainment: nevertheless, for inferior Intelligences, like men, such Philosophies have always seemed to me uninstructive enough. Nay, what is your Montesquieu himself but a clever infant spelling Letters from a hieroglyphical prophetic Book, the lexicon of which lies in Eternity, in Heaven?—Let any Cause-and-Effect Philosopher explain, not

why I wear such and such a Garment, obey such and such a
Law; but even why *I* am *here,* to wear and obey any thing!—
Much, therefore, if not the whole, of that same *Spirit of Clothes*
I shall suppress, as hypothetical, ineffectual, and even imperti-
nent: naked Facts, and Deductions drawn therefrom in quite
another than that omniscient style, are my humbler and proper
province."

Acting on which prudent restriction, Teufelsdröckh has
nevertheless contrived to take in a well nigh boundless extent
of field; at least, the boundaries too often lie quite beyond our
horizon. Selection being indispensable, we shall here glance
over his First Part only in the most cursory manner. This First
Part is, no doubt, distinguished by omnivorous learning, and
utmost patience and fairness: at the same time, in its results and
delineations, it is much more likely to interest the Compilers of
some *Library* of General, Entertaining, Useful, or even Useless
Knowledge than the miscellaneous readers of these pages. Was
it this Part of the Book which Heuschrecke had in view, when
he recommended us to that joint-stock vehicle of publication,
"at present the glory of British Literature?" If so, the Library
Editors are welcome to dig in it for their own behoof.

To the First Chapter, which turns on Paradise and Fig-
leaves, and leads us into interminable disquisitions of a mythological, metaphorical, cabalistico-sartorial and quite antediluvian cast, we shall content ourselves with giving an uncon-
cerned approval. Still less have we to do with "Lilis, Adam's
first wife, whom, according to the Talmudists, he had before
Eve, and who bore him, in that wedlock, the whole progeny of
aerial, aquatic, and terrestrial Devils,"—very needlessly, we
think. On this portion of the Work, with its profound glances
into the *Adam-Kadmon,** or Primeval Element, here strangely
brought into relation with the *Nifl* and *Muspel* (Darkness and
Light) of the antique North,* it may be enough to say that its
correctness of deduction, and depth of Talmudic and Rabbini-
cal lore have filled perhaps not the worst Hebraist in Britain
with something like astonishment.

But quitting this twilight region, Teufelsdröckh hastens
from the Tower of Babel, to follow the dispersion of Mankind
over the whole habitable and habilable globe. Walking by the

light of Oriental, Pelasgic, Scandinavian, Egyptian, Otaheitean, Ancient and Modern researches of every conceivable
kind, he strives to give us in compressed shape (as the Nürn-
bergers give an *Orbis Pictus*) an *Orbis Vestitus;** or view of the
costumes of all mankind, in all countries, in all times. It is here
that to the Antiquarian, to the Historian, we can triumphantly
say: Fall to! Here is Learning: an irregular Treasury, if you will;
but inexhaustible as the Hoard of King Nibelung,* which
twelve waggons in twelve days, at the rate of three journeys a
day, could not carry off. Sheepskin cloaks and wampum belts;
phylacteries, stoles, albs; chlamides, togas, Chinese silks,
Afghaun shawls, trunk hose, leather breeches, Celtic philibegs
(though breeches, as the name *Gallia Braccata* indicates, are the
more ancient), Hussar cloaks, Vandyke tippets, ruffs, fardingales,* are brought vividly before us,—even the Kilmarnock
nightcap is not forgotten. For most part too we must admit
that the Learning, heterogeneous as it is, and tumbled down
quite pell-mell, is true concentrated and purified Learning, the
drossy parts smelted out and thrown aside.

Philosophical reflections intervene, and sometimes touching
pictures of human life. Of this sort the following has surprised
us. The first purpose of Clothes, as our Professor imagines, was
not warmth or decency, but ornament. "Miserable indeed,"
says he, "was the condition of the Aboriginal Savage, glaring
fiercely from under his fleece of hair, which with the beard
reached down to his loins, and hung round him like a matted
cloak; the rest of his body sheeted in its thick natural fell. He
loitered in the sunny glades of the forest, living on wild fruits;
or, as the ancient Caledonian, squatted himself in morasses,
lurking for his bestial or human prey; without implements,
without arms, save the ball of heavy Flint, to which, that his
sole possession and defence might not be lost, he had attached a
long cord of plaited thongs; thereby recovering as well as
hurling it with deadly unerring skill. Nevertheless, the pains of
Hunger and Revenge once satisfied, his next care was not
Comfort but Decoration (*Putz*). Warmth he found in the toils
of the chase; or amid dried leaves, in his hollow tree, in his bark
shed, or natural grotto: but for Decoration he must have
Clothes. Nay, among wild people, we find tattooing and

painting even prior to Clothes. The first spiritual want of a barbarous man is Decoration; as indeed we still see among the barbarous classes in civilised countries.

"Reader, the heaven-inspired melodious Singer; loftiest Serene Highness; nay thy own amber-locked, snow-and-rose-bloom Maiden, worthy to glide sylphlike almost on air, whom thou lovest, worshippest as a divine Presence, which indeed, symbolically taken, she is,—has descended, like thyself, from that same hair-mantled, flint-hurling Aboriginal Anthropophagus! Out of the eater cometh forth meat; out of the strong cometh forth sweetness. What changes are wrought not by Time, yet in Time! For not Mankind only, but all that Mankind does or beholds, is in continual growth, re-genesis and self-perfecting vitality. Cast forth thy Act, thy Word, into the ever-living, ever-working Universe: it is a seed-grain that cannot die; unnoticed to-day (says one) it will be found flourishing as a Banyan-grove (perhaps, alas, as a Hemlock-forest!) after a thousand years.

"He who first shortened the labour of Copyists by device of *Movable Types* was disbanding hired Armies, and cashiering most Kings and Senates, and creating a whole new Democratic world; he had invented the Art of Printing. The first ground handful of Nitre, Sulphur, and Charcoal drove Monk Schwartz's pestle through the ceiling: what will the last do? Achieve the final undisputed prostration of Force under Thought, of Animal Courage under Spiritual. A simple invention was it in the old-world Grazier,—sick of lugging his slow Ox about the country till he got it bartered for corn or oil,—to take a piece of Leather, and thereon scratch or stamp the mere Figure of an Ox (or *Pecus*); put it in his pocket, and call it *Pecunia,* Money. Yet hereby did Barter grow Sale, the Leather Money is now Golden and Paper, and all miracles have been out-miracled: for there are Rothschilds and English National Debts; and whoso has sixpence is Sovereign (to the length of sixpence) over all men; commands Cooks to feed him, Philosophers to teach him, Kings to mount guard over him,—to the length of sixpence.—Clothes too, which began in foolishest love of Ornament, what have they not become! Increased Security, and pleasurable Heat soon followed: but what of

these? Shame, divine Shame (*Schaam,* Modesty), as yet a
stranger to the Anthropophagous bosom, arose there mysteriously under Clothes; a mystic grove-encircled shrine for the
Holy in man. Clothes gave us individuality, distinctions, social
polity; Clothes have made Men of us; they are threatening to
make Clothes-screens of us.

"But on the whole," continues our eloquent Professor,
"Man is a Tool-using Animal (*Handthierendes Thier*). Weak in
himself, and of small stature, he stands on a basis, at most for
the flattest-soled, of some half square-foot, insecurely enough;
has to straddle out his legs, lest the very wind supplant him.
Feeblest of bipeds! Three quintals are a crushing load for him;
the Steer of the meadow tosses him aloft, like a waste rag.
Nevertheless he can use Tools, can devise Tools: with these the
granite mountain melts into light dust before him; he kneads
glowing iron, as if it were soft paste; seas are his smooth
highway, winds and fire his unwearying steeds. Nowhere do
you find him without Tools; without Tools he is nothing, with
Tools he is all."

Here may we not, for a moment, interrupt the stream of
Oratory with a remark that this Definition of the Tool-using
Animal, appears to us, of all that Animal-sort, considerably the
precisest and best? Man is called a Laughing Animal: but do not
the apes also laugh, or attempt to do it; and is the manliest man
the greatest and oftenest laugher? Teufelsdröckh himself, as we
said, laughed only once. Still less do we make of that other
French Definition of the Cooking Animal; which, indeed, for
rigorous scientific purposes, is as good as useless. Can a Tartar
be said to Cook, when he only readies his steak by riding on it?
Again, what Cookery does the Greenlander use, beyond
stowing up his whale-blubber, as a marmot, in the like case,
might do? Or how would Monsieur Ude prosper among those
Orinocco Indians who, according to Humboldt, lodge in
crow-nests, on the branches of trees; and, for half the year, have
no victuals but pipe-clay, the whole country being under
water? But on the other hand, show us the human being, of any
period or climate, without his Tools: those very Caledonians,
as we saw, had their Flint-ball, and Thong to it, such as no
brute has or can have.

"Man is a Tool-using animal," concludes Teufelsdröckh in his abrupt way; "of which truth Clothes are but one example: and surely if we consider the interval between the first wooden Dibble fashioned by man, and those Liverpool Steam-carriages,* or the British House of Commons, we shall note what progress he has made. He digs up certain black stones from the bosom of the Earth, and says to them, *Transport me, and this luggage, at the rate of five-and-thirty miles an hour;* and they do it: he collects, apparently by lot, six hundred and fifty-eight miscellaneous individuals, and says to them, *Make this nation toil for us, bleed for us, hunger, and sorrow, and sin for us;* and they do it."

CHAPTER 6

APRONS

ONE of the most unsatisfactory Sections in the whole Volume is that on *Aprons*. What though stout old Gao the Persian Blacksmith, "whose Apron, now indeed hidden under jewels, because raised in revolt which proved successful, is still the royal standard of that country;" what though John Knox's Daughter, "who threatened Sovereign Majesty that she would catch her Husband's head in her Apron, rather than he should lie and be a Bishop;" what though the Landgravine Elizabeth, with many other Apron worthies,—figure here? An idle wire-drawing spirit, sometimes even a tone of levity, approaching to conventional satire, is too clearly discernible. What, for example, are we to make of such sentences as the following?

"Aprons are Defences; against injury to cleanliness, to safety, to modesty, sometimes to roguery. From the thin slip of notched silk (as it were, the Emblem and beatified Ghost of an Apron), which some highest-bred housewife, sitting at Nürnberg Workboxes and Toyboxes, has gracefully fastened on; to the thick-tanned hide, girt round him with thongs, wherein the Builder builds, and at evening sticks his trowel; or to those jingling sheet-iron Aprons, wherein your otherwise half-naked Vulcans hammer and smelt in their Smelt-furnace,—is there not range enough in the fashion and uses of this Vestment? How much has been concealed, how much has been defended in Aprons! Nay, rightly considered, what is your whole Military and Police Establishment, charged at uncalculated millions, but a huge scarlet-coloured, iron-fastened Apron, wherein Society works (uneasily enough); guarding itself from some soil and stithy-sparks, in this Devil's smithy (*Teufelsschmiede*) of a world? But of all Aprons the most puzzling to me hitherto has been the Episcopal, or Cassock. Wherein consists the usefulness of this Apron? The Overseer (*Episcopus*) of Souls, I notice, has tucked in the corner of it, as if his day's work were done: what does he shadow forth thereby?" &c. &c.

Or again, has it often been the lot of our readers to read such stuff as we shall now quote?

"I consider those printed Paper Aprons, worn by the Parisian Cooks, as a new vent, though a slight one, for Typography; therefore as an encouragement to modern Literature, and deserving of approval: nor is it without satisfaction that I hear of a celebrated London Firm having in view to introduce the same fashion, with important extensions, in England."—We who are on the spot hear of no such thing; and indeed have reason to be thankful that hitherto there are other vents for our Literature, exuberant as it is.—Teufelsdröckh continues: "If such supply of printed Paper should rise so far as to choke up the highways and public thoroughfares, new means must of necessity be had recourse to. In a world existing by Industry, we grudge to employ Fire as a destroying element, and not as a creating one. However, Heaven is omnipotent, and will find us an outlet. In the meanwhile, is it not beautiful to see five million quintals of Rags picked annually from the Laystall; and annually, after being macerated, hot-pressed, printed on, and sold,—returned thither; filling so many hungry mouths by the way? Thus is the Laystall, especially with its Rags or Clothes-rubbish, the grand Electric Battery, and Fountain-of-Motion, from which and to which the Social Activities (like vitreous and resinous Electricities) circulate, in larger or smaller circles, through the mighty, billowy, stormtost Chaos of Life, which they keep alive!"—Such passages fill us who love the man, and partly esteem him, with a very mixed feeling.

Farther down we meet with this: "The Journalists are now the true Kings and Clergy: henceforth Historians, unless they are fools, must write not of Bourbon Dynasties, and Tudors and Hapsburgs; but of Stamped Broad-sheet Dynasties, and quite new successive Names, according as this or the other Able Editor, or Combination of Able Editors, gains the world's ear. Of the British Newspaper Press, perhaps the most important of all, and wonderful enough in its secret constitution and procedure, a valuable descriptive History already exists, in that language, under the title of *Satan's Invisible World Displayed;* which, however, by search in all the Weissnichtwo Libraries, I have not yet succeeded in procuring (*vermöchte nicht aufzutreiben*)."

Thus does the good Homer not only nod, but snore. Thus does Teufelsdröckh, wandering in regions where he had little business, confound the old authentic Presbyterian Witchfinder with a new, spurious, imaginary Historian of the *Brittische Journalistik;* and so stumble on perhaps the most egregious blunder in Modern Literature!

CHAPTER 7
MISCELLANEOUS–HISTORICAL

HAPPIER is our Professor, and more purely scientific and historic, when he reaches the Middle Ages in Europe, and down to the end of the Seventeenth Century; the true era of extravagance in Costume. It is here that the Antiquary and Student of Modes comes upon his richest harvest. Fantastic garbs, beggaring all fancy of a Teniers or a Callot, succeed each other, like monster devouring monster in a Dream. The whole too in brief authentic strokes, and touched not seldom with that breath of genius which makes even old raiment live. Indeed, so learned, precise, graphical, and every way interesting have we found these Chapters, that it may be thrown out as a pertinent question for parties concerned, Whether or not a good English Translation thereof might henceforth be profitably incorporated with Mr. Merrick's valuable Work *On Ancient Armour?* Take, by way of example, the following sketch; as authority for which Paullinus's *Zeitkürzende Lust* (11. 678) is, with seeming confidence referred to:

"Did we behold the German fashionable dress of the Fifteenth Century, we might smile; as perhaps those bygone Germans, were they to rise again, and see our haberdashery, would cross themselves, and invoke the Virgin. But happily no bygone German, or man, rises again; thus the Present is not needlessly trammelled with the Past; and only grows out of it, like a Tree, whose roots are not intertangled with its branches, but lie peaceably under ground. Nay it is very mournful, yet not useless, to see and know, how the Greatest and Dearest, in a short while, would find his place quite filled up here, and no room for him; the very Napoleon, the very Byron, in some seven years, has become obsolete, and were now a foreigner to his Europe. Thus is the Law of Progress secured; and in Clothes, as in all other external things whatsoever, no fashion will continue.

"Of the military classes in those old times, whose buff-belts, complicated chains and gorgets, huge churn-boots, and other

riding and fighting gear have been bepainted in modern
Romance, till the whole has acquired somewhat of a signpost
character,—I shall here say nothing: the civil and pacific classes,
less touched upon, are wonderful enough for us.

"Rich men, I find, have *Teusinke*"* (a perhaps untranslate-
able article); "also a silver girdle, whereat hang little bells; so
that when a man walks it is with continual jingling. Some few,
of musical turn, have a whole chime of bells (*Glockenspiel*)
fastened there; which especially, in sudden whirls, and the other
accidents of walking, has a grateful effect. Observe too how
fond they are of peaks, and Gothic-arch intersections. The male
world wears peaked caps, an ell-long, which hang bobbing
over the side (*schief*): their shoes are peaked in front, also to the
length of an ell (and laced on the side with tags); even the
wooden shoes have their ell-long noses: some also clap bells on
the peak. Farther, according to my authority, the men have
breeches without seat (*ohne Gesäss*): these they fasten peakwise
to their shirts; and the long round doublet must overlap them.

"Rich maidens, again, flit abroad in gowns scolloped out
behind and before, so that back and breast are almost bare.
Wives of quality, on the other hand, have train-gowns four or
five ells in length; which trains there are boys to carry. Brave
Cleopatras sailing in their silk-cloth Galley, with a Cupid for
steersman! Consider their welts, a handbreadth thick, which
waver round them by way of hem; the long flood of silver
buttons, or rather silver shells, from throat to shoe, wherewith
these same welt-gowns are buttoned. The maidens have bound
silver snoods about their hair, with gold spangles, and pendent
flames (*Flammen*), that is, sparkling hair-drops: but of their
mothers' headgear who shall speak? Neither in love of grace is
comfort forgotten. In winter weather you behold the whole
fair creation (that can afford it) in long mantles, with skirts
wide below, and, for hem, not one but two sufficient hand-
broad welts: all ending atop in a thick well-starched Ruff, some
twenty inches broad: these are their Ruff-mantles (*Kragenmän-
tel*).

"As yet among the womankind hoop-petticoats are not; but
the men have doublets of fustian, under which lie multiple ruffs
of cloth, pasted together with batter (*mit Teig zusammen-gekleis-*

tert), which create protuberance enough. Thus do the two sexes vie with each other in the art of Decoration; and as usual the stronger carries it."

Our Professor, whether he have Humour himself or not, manifests a certain feeling of the Ludicrous, a sly observance of it, which, could emotion of any kind be confidently predicated of so still a man, we might call a real love. None of those bell-girdles, bushel-breeches, cornuted shoes, or other the like phenomena, of which the History of Dress offers so many, escape him; more especially the mischances, or striking adventures, incident to the wearers of such, are noticed with due fidelity. Sir Walter Raleigh's fine mantle, which he spread in the mud under Queen Elizabeth's feet, appears to provoke little enthusiasm in him; he merely asks, Whether at that period the Maiden Queen "was red-painted on the nose, and white-painted on the cheeks, as her tirewomen, when from spleen and wrinkles she would no longer look in any glass, were wont to serve her?" We can answer that Sir Walter knew well what he was doing, and had the Maiden Queen been stuffed parchment dyed in verdigris, would have done the same.

Thus too, treating of those enormous habiliments, that were not only slashed and galooned, but artificially swollen out on the broader parts of the body, by introduction of Bran,—our Professor fails not to comment on that luckless Courtier, who having seated himself on a chair with some projecting nail on it, and therefrom rising, to pay his *devoir* on the entrance of Majesty, instantaneously emitted several pecks of dry wheat-dust; and stood there diminished to a spindle, his galoons and slashes dangling sorrowful and flabby round him. Whereupon the Professor publishes this reflection:

"By what strange chances do we live in History! Erostratus by a torch; Milo by a bullock; Henry Darnley, an unfledged booby and bustard, by his limbs; most Kings and Queens by being born under such and such a bed-tester; Boileau Des-préaux (according to Helvetius) by the peck of a turkey; and this ill-starred individual by a rent in his breeches,—for no Memoirist of Kaiser Otto's Court omits him. Vain was the prayer of Themistocles for a talent of Forgetting: my Friends, yield cheerfully to Destiny, and read since it is written."—Has

Teufelsdröckh to be put in mind that, nearly related to the impossible talent of Forgetting, stands that talent of Silence, which even travelling Englishmen manifest?

"The simplest costume," observes our Professor, "which I anywhere find alluded to in History, is that used as regimental, by Bolivar's Cavalry, in the late Columbian wars. A square Blanket, twelve feet in diagonal, is provided (some were wont to cut off the corners, and make it circular): in the centre a slit is effected, eighteen inches long; through this the mother-naked Trooper introduces his head and neck; and so rides shielded from all weather, and in battle from many strokes (for he rolls it about his left arm); and not only dressed, but harnessed and draperied."

With which picture of a State of Nature, affecting by its singularity, and Old-Roman contempt of the superfluous, we shall quit this part of our subject.

CHAPTER 8

THE WORLD OUT OF CLOTHES

If in the Descriptive-Historical Portion of his Volume, Teufels-dröckh, discussing merely the *Werden* (Origin and successive Improvement) of Clothes, has astonished many a reader, much more will he in the Speculative-Philosophical Portion, which treats of their *Wirken,* or Influences. It is here that the present Editor first feels the pressure of his task; for here properly the higher and new Philosophy of Clothes commences: an untried, almost inconceivable region, or chaos; in venturing upon which, how difficult, yet how unspeakably important is it to know what course, of survey and conquest, is the true one; where the footing is firm substance and will bear us, where it is hollow, or mere cloud, and may engulf us! Teufelsdröckh undertakes no less than to expound the moral, political, even religious Influences of Clothes; he undertakes to make manifest, in its thousandfold bearings, this grand Proposition, that Man's earthly interests "are all hooked and buttoned together, and held up, by Clothes." He says in so many words, "Society is founded upon Cloth;" and again, "Society sails through the Infinitude on Cloth, as on a Faust's Mantle,* or rather like the Sheet of clean and unclean beasts in the Apostle's Dream;* and without such Sheet or Mantle, would sink to endless depths, or mount to inane limbos, and in either case be no more."

By what chains, or indeed infinitely complected tissues, of Meditation this grand Theorem is here unfolded, and innumerable practical Corollaries are drawn therefrom, it were perhaps a mad ambition to attempt exhibiting. Our Professor's method is not, in any case, that of common school Logic, where the truths all stand in a row, each holding by the skirts of the other; but at best that of practical Reason, proceeding by large Intuition over whole systematic groups and kingdoms; whereby we might say, a noble complexity, almost like that of Nature, reigns in his Philosophy, or spiritual picture of Nature: a mighty maze, yet, as faith whispers, not without a plan. Nay we complained above, that a certain ignoble complexity, what we must call mere confusion, was also discernible. Often, too, must we* exclaim: Would to Heaven those same Biographical Documents were come! For it seems as if the demonstration lay much in the Author's individuality; as if it were not Argument that had taught him, but Experience. At present it is only in local glimpses, and by significant fragments, picked often at wide enough intervals from the original Volume, and carefully collated, that we can hope to impart some outline or foreshadow of this Doctrine. Readers of any intelligence are once more invited to favour us with their most concentrated attention: let these, after intense consideration, and not till then, pronounce, Whether on the utmost verge of our actual horizon there is not a looming as of Land; a promise of new Fortunate Islands,* perhaps whole undiscovered Americas, for such as have canvass to sail thither?—As exordium to the whole, stands here the following long citation:

"With men of a speculative turn," writes Teufelsdröckh, "there come seasons, meditative, sweet, yet awful hours, when in wonder and fear you ask yourself that unanswerable question: Who am I; the thing that can say 'I' (*das Wesen das sich* ICH *nennt*)? The world, with its loud trafficking, retires into the distance; and, through the paper-hangings, and stone-walls, and thick-plied tissues of Commerce and Polity, and all the living and lifeless Integuments (of Society and a Body), wherewith your Existence sits surrounded,—the sight reaches forth into the void Deep, and you are alone with the Universe, and silently commune with it, as one mysterious Presence with another.

"Who am I; what is this ME? A Voice, a Motion, an Appearance;—some embodied, visualised Idea in the Eternal Mind? *Cogito ergo sum.** Alas, poor Cogitator, this takes us but a little way. Sure enough, I am; and lately was not: but Whence? How? Whereto? The answer lies around, written in all colours and motions, uttered in all tones of jubilee and wail, in thousand-figured, thousand-voiced, harmonious Nature: but where is the cunning eye and ear to whom that God-written Apocalypse will yield articulate meaning? We sit as in a boundless Phantasmagoria and Dream-grotto; boundless, for the faintest star, the remotest century, lies not even nearer the verge thereof: sounds and many-coloured visions flit round our sense; but Him, the Unslumbering, whose work both Dream and Dreamer are, we see not; except in rare half-waking moments, suspect not. Creation, says one, lies before us, like a glorious Rainbow; but the Sun that made it lies behind us, hidden from us. Then, in that strange Dream, how we clutch at shadows as if they were substances; and sleep deepest while fancying ourselves most awake! Which of your Philosophical Systems is other than a dream-theorem; a net quotient, confidently given out, where divisor and dividend are both unknown? What are all your national Wars, with their Moscow Retreats,* and sanguinary hate-filled Revolutions, but the Somnambulism of uneasy Sleepers? This Dreaming, this Somnambulism is what we on Earth call Life; wherein the most indeed undoubtingly wander, as if they knew right hand from left; yet they only are wise who know that they know nothing.

"Pity that all Metaphysics had hitherto proved so inexpressibly unproductive! The secret of Man's Being is still like the Sphinx's secret:* a riddle that he cannot rede; and for ignorance of which he suffers death, the worst death, a spiritual. What are your Axioms, and Categories, and Systems, and Aphorisms? Words, words. High Air-castles are cunningly built of Words, the Words well bedded also in good Logic-mortar; wherein, however, no Knowledge will come to lodge. *The whole is greater than the part:* how exceedingly true! *Nature abhors a vacuum:* how exceedingly false and calumnious! Again, *Nothing can act but where it is:* with all my heart; only WHERE is it? Be not the slave of Words: is not the Distant, the Dead, while I love it, and long for it, and mourn for it, Here, in the genuine sense, as truly as the floor I stand on? But that same WHERE, with its brother WHEN, are from the first the master-colours of our Dream-grotto; say rather, the Canvass (the warp and woof thereof) whereon all our Dreams and Life-visions are painted. Nevertheless, has not a deeper meditation taught certain of every climate and age, that the WHERE and WHEN, so mysteriously inseparable from all our thoughts, are but superficial terrestrial adhesions to thought; that the Seer may discern them where they mount up out of the celestial EVERY-WHERE and FOREVER: have not all nations conceived their

God as Omnipresent and Eternal; as existing in a universal HERE, an everlasting NOW? Think well, thou too wilt find that Space is but a mode of our human Sense, so likewise Time; there *is* no Space and no Time: WE are—we know not what;—light-sparkles floating in the æther of Deity!

"So that this so solid-seeming World, after all, were but an air-image, our ME the only reality: and Nature, with its thousandfold production and destruction, but the reflex of our own inward Force, the 'phantasy of our Dream;' or what the Earth-Spirit in *Faust* names it, *the living visible Garment of God:*

> In Being's floods, in Action's storm,
> I walk and work, above, beneath,
> Work and weave in endless motion!
> Birth and Death,
> An infinite ocean;
> A seizing and giving
> The fire of the Living:*
> 'Tis thus at the roaring Loom of Time I ply,
> And weave for God the Garment thou seest Him by.*

Of twenty millions that have read and spouted this thunder-speech of the *Erdgeist*, are there yet twenty units of us that have learned the meaning thereof?"

"It was in some such mood, when wearied and foredone with these high speculations, that I first came upon the question of Clothes. Strange enough, it strikes me, is this same fact of there being Tailors and Tailored. The Horse I ride has his own whole fell: strip him of the girths and flaps and extraneous tags I have fastened round him, and the noble creature is his own sempster and weaver and spinner: nay his own bootmaker, jeweller, and man-milliner; he bounds free through the valleys, with a perennial rainproof court-suit on his body; wherein warmth and easiness of fit have reached perfection; nay, the graces also have been considered, and frills and fringes, with gay variety of colour, featly appended, and ever in the right place, are not wanting. While I—Good Heaven!—have thatched myself over with the dead fleeces of sheep, the bark of vegetables, the entrails of worms, the hides of oxen or seals, the felt of furred beasts; and walk abroad a moving Rag-screen, overheaped with shreds and tatters raked from the Charnel-house of Nature, where they would have rotted, to rot on me more slowly! Day after day, I must thatch myself anew; day after day, this despicable thatch must lose some film of its thickness; some film of it, frayed away by tear and wear, must be brushed off into the Ashpit, into the Laystall; till by degrees the whole has been brushed thither, and I, the dust-making, patent Rag-grinder, get new material to grind down. O subter-brutish! vile! most vile! For have not I too a compact all-enclosing Skin, whiter or dingier? Am I a botched mass of tailors' and cobblers' shreds, then; or a tightly-articulated, homogeneous little Figure, automatic, nay alive?

"Strange enough how creatures of the human-kind shut their eyes to plainest facts; and, by the mere inertia of Oblivion and Stupidity, live at ease in the midst of Wonders and Terrors. But indeed man is, and was always, a blockhead and dullard; much readier to feel and digest, than to think and consider. Prejudice, which he pretends to hate, is his absolute lawgiver; mere use-and-wont everywhere leads him by the nose: thus let but a Rising of the Sun, let but a Creation of the World happen *twice,* and it ceases to be marvellous, to be noteworthy, or noticeable. Perhaps not once in a lifetime does it occur to your ordinary biped, of any country or generation, be he gold-mantled Prince or russet-jerkined Peasant, that his Vestments and his Self are not one and indivisible; that *he* is naked, without vestments, till he buy or steal such, and by forethought sew and button them.

"For my own part, these considerations, of our Clothes-thatch, and how, reaching inwards even to our heart of hearts, it tailorises and demoralises us, fill me with a certain horror at myself and mankind; almost as one feels at those Dutch Cows, which, during the wet season, you see grazing deliberately with jackets and petticoats (of striped sacking), in the meadows of Gouda. Nevertheless there is something great in the moment when a man first strips himself of adventitious wrappages; and sees indeed that he is naked, and, as Swift has it, 'a forked straddling animal with bandy legs;'* yet also a Spirit, and unutterable Mystery of Mysteries."

CHAPTER 9

ADAMITISM

LET no courteous reader take offence at the opinions broached in the conclusion of the last Chapter. The Editor himself, on first glancing over that singular passage, was inclined to exclaim: What, have we got not only a Sansculottist, but an enemy to Clothes in the abstract? A new Adamite, in this century, which flatters itself that it is the Nineteenth, and destructive both to Superstition and Enthusiasm?

Consider, thou foolish Teufelsdröckh, what benefits unspeakable all ages and sexes derive from Clothes. For example, when thou thyself, a watery, pulpy, slobbery freshman and new-comer in this Planet, sattest muling and puking in thy nurse's arms; sucking thy coral, and looking forth into the world in the blankest manner, what hadst thou been, without thy blankets, and bibs, and other nameless hulls? A terror to thyself and mankind! Or hast thou forgotten the day when thou first receivedst breeches, and thy long clothes became short? The village where thou livedst was all apprised of the fact; and neighbour after neighbour kissed thy pudding cheek, and gave thee, as handsel, silver or copper coins, on that the first gala-day of thy existence. Again, wert not thou, at one period of life, a Buck, or Blood, or Macaroni, or Incroyable, or Dandy,* or by whatever name, according to year and place, such phenomenon is distinguished? In that one word lie included mysterious volumes. Nay, now when the reign of folly is over, or altered, and thy clothes are not for triumph but for defence, hast thou always worn them perforce, and as a consequence of Man's Fall; never rejoiced in them as in a warm moveable House, a Body round thy Body, wherein that strange THEE of thine sat snug, defying all variations of Climate? Girt with thick double-milled kerseys; half-buried under shawls and broadbrims, and overalls and mudboots, thy very fingers cased in doeskin and mittens, thou hast bestrode that "Horse I ride;" and, though it were in wild winter, dashed through the world, glorying in it as if thou wert its lord. In vain did the sleet beat round thy temples; it lighted only on thy impenetrable, felted or woven, case of wool. In vain did the winds howl,—forests sounding and creaking, deep calling unto deep,—and the storms heap themselves together into one huge Arctic whirlpool: thou flewest through the middle thereof, striking fire from the highway; wild music hummed in thy ears, thou too wert as a "sailor of the air;" the wreck of matter and the crash of worlds was thy element and propitiously wafting tide. Without Clothes, without bit or saddle, what hadst thou been; what had thy fleet quadruped been?—Nature is good, but she is not the best: here truly was the victory of Art over Nature. A thunderbolt indeed might have pierced thee; all short of this thou couldst defy.

Or, cries the courteous reader, has your Teufelsdröckh forgotten what he said lately about "Aboriginal Savages," and their "condition miserable indeed?" Would he have all this unsaid; and us betake ourselves again to the "matted cloak," and go sheeted in a "thick natural fell?"

Nowise, courteous reader! The Professor knows full well what he is saying; and both thou and we, in our haste, do him wrong. If Clothes, in these times, "so tailorise and demoralise us," have they no redeeming value; can they not be altered to serve better; must they of necessity be thrown to the dogs? The truth is, Teufelsdröckh, though a Sansculottist, is no Adamite: and much perhaps as he might wish to go forth before this degenerate age "as a Sign," would nowise wish to do it, as those old Adamites did, in a state of Nakedness. The utility of Clothes is altogether apparent to him: nay perhaps he has an insight into their more recondite, and almost mystic qualities, what we might call the omnipotent virtue of Clothes, such as was never before vouchsafed to any man. For example:

"You see two individuals," he writes, "one dressed in fine Red, the other in coarse threadbare Blue: Red says to Blue, 'Be hanged and anatomised;' Blue hears with a shudder, and (O wonder of wonders!) marches sorrowfully to the gallows; is there noosed up, vibrates his hour, and the surgeons dissect him, and fit his bones into a skeleton for medical purposes. How is this; or what make ye of your *Nothing can act but where it is?* Red has no physical hold of Blue, no *clutch* of him, is nowise in *contact* with him: neither are those ministering Sheriffs and Lord-Lieutenants and hangmen and Tipstaves so related to commanding Red, that he can tug them hither and thither; but each stands distinct within his own skin. Nevertheless, as it is spoken, so is it done: the articulated Word sets all hands in Action; and Rope and Improved-drop perform their work.

"Thinking reader, the reason seems to me twofold: First, that *Man is a Spirit,* and bound by invisible bonds to *All Men;* Secondly, that *he wears Clothes,* which are the visible emblems of that fact. Has not your Red, hanging individual, a horsehair wig, squirrel skins, and a plush gown; whereby all mortals know that he is a JUDGE?—Society, which the more I think of it astonishes me the more, is founded upon Cloth.

"Often in my atrabiliar moods, when I read of pompous ceremonials, Frankfort Coronations, Royal Drawing-rooms, Levees, Couchees; and how the ushers and macers and pursuivants are all in waiting; how Duke this is presented by Archduke that, and Colonel A by General B, and innumerable Bishops, Admirals, and miscellaneous Functionaries, are advancing gallantly to the Anointed presence; and I strive, in my remote privacy, to form a clear picture of that solemnity,— on a sudden, as by some enchanter's wand, the—shall I speak it?—the Clothes fly off the whole dramatic corps; and Dukes, Grandees, Bishops, Generals, Anointed presence itself, every mother's son of them, stand straddling there, not a shirt on them; and I know not whether to laugh or weep. This physical or psychical infirmity, in which perhaps I am not singular, I have, after hesitation, thought right to publish, for the solace of those afflicted with the like."

Would to Heaven, say we, thou hadst thought right to keep it secret! Who is there now that can read the five columns of Presentations in his Morning Newspaper without a shudder? Hypochondriac men, and all men are to a certain extent hypochondriac, should be more gently treated. With what readiness our fancy, in this shattered state of the nerves, follows out the consequences which Teufelsdröckh, with a devilish coolness, goes on to draw:

"What would Majesty do, could such an accident befall in reality; should the buttons all simultaneously start, and the solid

wool evaporate, in very Deed, as here in Dream? *Ach Gott!*
How each skulks into the nearest hiding-place; their high State
Tragedy (*Haupt- und Staats-Action*) becomes a Pickleherring-
Farce* to weep at, which is the worst kind of Farce; *the tables*
(according to Horace), and with them, the whole fabric of
Government, Legislation, Property, Police, and Civilised
Society, *are dissolved,** in wails and howls."

Lives the man that can figure a naked Duke of Windlestraw
addressing a naked House of Lords? Imagination, choked as in
mephitic air, recoils on itself, and will not forward with the
picture. The Woolsack, the Ministerial, the Opposition
Benches—*infandum! infandum!* * And yet why is the thing
impossible? Was not every soul, or rather every body, of these
Guardians of our Liberties, naked, or nearly so, last night; "a
forked Radish with a head fantastically carved?" And why
might he not, did our stern Fate so order it, walk out to St.
Stephen's, as well as into bed, in that no-fashion; and there,
with other similar Radishes, hold a Bed of Justice?* "Solace of
those afflicted with the like!" Unhappy Teufelsdröckh, had
man ever such a "physical or psychical infirmity" before? And
now how many, perhaps, may thy unparalleled confession
(which we, even to the sounder British world, and goaded on
by Critical and Biographical duty, grudge to re-impart) incur-
ably infect therewith! Art thou the malignest of Sansculottists,
or only the maddest?

"It will remain to be examined," adds the inexorable
Teufelsdröckh, "in how far the SCARECROW, as a Clothed
Person, is not also entitled to benefit of clergy,* and English
trial by jury: nay, perhaps considering his high function (for is
not he too a Defender of Property, and Sovereign armed with
the *terrors* of the Law?), to a certain royal Immunity and
Inviolability; which, however, misers and the meaner class of
persons are not always voluntarily disposed to grant him." ...
"O my Friends, we are (in Yorick Sterne's words)* but as
'turkeys driven, with a stick and red clout, to the market:' or if
some drivers, as they do in Norfolk, take a dried bladder and
put peas in it, the rattle thereof terrifies the boldest!"

CHAPTER 10

PURE REASON

It must now be apparent enough that our Professor, as above hinted, is a speculative Radical, and of the very darkest tinge; acknowledging, for most part, in the solemnities and para-phernalia of civilised Life, which we make so much of, nothing but so many Cloth-rags, turkey-poles, and "Bladders with dried Peas." To linger among such speculations, longer than mere Science requires, a discerning public can have no wish. For our purposes the simple fact that such a *Naked World* is possible, nay actually exists (under the Clothed one), will be sufficient. Much, therefore, we omit about "Kings wrestling naked on the green with Carmen," and the Kings being thrown: "dissect them with scalpels," says Teufelsdröckh; "the same viscera, tissues, livers, lights, and other Life-tackle are there: examine their spiritual mechanism; the same great Need, great Greed, and little Faculty; nay ten to one but the Carman, who understands draught-cattle, the rimming of wheels, some-thing of the laws of unstable and stable equilibrium, with other branches of waggon-science, and has actually put forth his hand and operated on Nature, is the more cunningly gifted of the two. Whence, then, their so unspeakable difference? From Clothes." Much also we shall omit about confusion of Ranks, and Joan and My Lady, and how it would be every where "Hail fellow well met," and Chaos were come again: all which to any one that has once fairly pictured out the grand mother-idea, *Society in a state of Nakedness*, will spontaneously suggest itself. Should some sceptical individual still entertain doubts whether in a World without Clothes, the smallest Politeness, Polity, or even Police, could exist, let him turn to the original Volume, and view there the boundless Serbonian Bogs of Sansculottism, stretching sour and pestilential: over which we have lightly flown; where not only whole armies but whole nations might sink! If indeed the following argument, in its brief rivetting emphasis, be not of itself incontrovertible and final:

"Are we Opossums; have we natural Pouches, like the Kangaroo? Or how, without Clothes, could we possess the master-organ, soul's-seat, and true pineal gland of the Body Social: I mean, a PURSE?"

Nevertheless it is impossible to hate Professor Teufelsdröckh; at worst, one knows not whether to hate or to love him. For though in looking at the fair tapestry of human Life, with its royal and even sacred figures, he dwells not on the obverse alone, but here chiefly on the reverse; and indeed turns out the rough seams, tatters, and manifold thrums of that unsightly wrong-side, with an almost diabolic patience and indifference, which must have sunk him in the estimation of most readers,— there is that within which unspeakably distinguishes him from all other past and present Sansculottists. The grand unparalleled peculiarity of Teufelsdröckh is, that with all this Descendenta-lism,* he combines a Transcendentalism no less superlative; whereby if on the one hand he degrade man below most animals, except those jacketted Gouda Cows, he, on the other, exalts him beyond the visible Heavens, almost to an equality with the gods.

"To the eye of vulgar Logic," says he, "what is man? An omnivorous Biped that wears Breeches. To the eye of Pure Reason what is he? A Soul, a Spirit, and divine Apparition. Round his mysterious ME, there lies, under all those wool-rags, a Garment of Flesh (or of Senses), contextured in the Loom of Heaven; whereby he is revealed to his like, and dwells with them in UNION and DIVISION; and sees and fashions for himself a universe, with azure Starry Spaces, and long Thou-sands of Years. Deep-hidden is he under that strange Garment; amid Sounds and Colours and Forms, as it were, swathed in, and inextricably overshrouded: yet is it sky-woven, and worthy of a God. Stands he not thereby in the centre of Immensities, in the conflux of Eternities? He feels; power has been given him to Know, to Believe; nay does not the spirit of Love, free in its celestial primeval brightness, even here, though but for moments, look through? Well said Saint Chrysostom, with his lips of gold, 'the true SHEKINAH* is Man:' where else is the GOD'S-PRESENCE manifested not to our eyes only, but to our hearts, as in our fellow man?"

In such passages, unhappily too rare, the high Platonic Mysticism of our Author, which is perhaps the fundamental element of his nature, bursts forth, as it were, in full flood: and, through all the vapour and tarnish of what is often so perverse, so mean in his exterior and environment, we seem to look into a whole inward Sea of Light and Love;—though, alas, the grim coppery clouds soon roll together again, and hide it from view.

Such tendency to Mysticism is every where traceable in this man; and indeed, to attentive readers, must have been long ago apparent. Nothing that he sees but has more than a common meaning, but has two meanings: thus, if in the highest Imperial Sceptre and Charlemagne-Mantle,* as well as in the poorest Ox-goad and Gipsy-Blanket, he finds Prose, Decay, Contemptibility; there is in each sort Poetry also, and a reverend Worth. For Matter, were it never so despicable, is Spirit, the manifestation of Spirit: were it never so honourable, can it be more? The thing Visible, nay the thing Imagined, the thing in any way conceived as Visible, what is it but a Garment, a Clothing of the higher, celestial Invisible, "unimaginable, formless, dark with excess of bright?" Under which point of view the following passage, so strange in purport, so strange in phrase, seems characteristic enough:

"The beginning of all Wisdom is to look fixedly on Clothes, or even with armed eyesight, till they become *transparent*. 'The Philosopher,' says the wisest of this age,* 'must station himself in the middle:' how true! The Philosopher is he to whom the Highest has descended, and the Lowest has mounted up; who is the equal and kindly brother of all.

"Shall we tremble before clothwebs and cobwebs, whether woven in Arkwright looms, or by the silent Arachnes that weave unrestingly in our Imagination? Or, on the other hand, what is there that we cannot love; since all was created by God?

"Happy he who can look through the Clothes of a Man (the woollen, and fleshly, and official Bank-paper and State-paper Clothes), into the Man himself; and discern, it may be, in this or the other Dread Potentate, a more or less incompetent Digestive-apparatus; yet also an inscrutable venerable Mystery, in the meanest Tinker that sees with eyes!"

For the rest, as is natural to a man of this kind, he deals much in the feeling of Wonder; insists on the necessity and high worth of universal Wonder, which he holds to be the only reasonable temper for the denizen of so singular a Planet as ours. "Wonder," says he, "is the basis of Worship: the reign of Wonder is perennial, indestructible in Man; only at certain stages (as the present), it is, for some short season, a reign *in partibus infidelium.*"* That progress of Science, which is to destroy Wonder, and in its stead substitute Mensuration and Numeration, finds small favour with Teufelsdröckh, much as he otherwise venerates these two latter processes.

"Shall your Science," exclaims he, "proceed in the small chink-lighted, or even oil-lighted, underground workshop of Logic alone; and man's mind become an Arithmetical Mill, whereof Memory is the Hopper, and mere Tables of Sines and Tangents, Codification, and Treatises of what you call Political Economy, are the Meal? And what is that Science, which the scientific Head alone, were it screwed off, and (like the Doctor's in the Arabian Tale)* set in a basin, to keep it alive, could prosecute without shadow of a heart,—but one other of the mechanical and menial handicrafts, for which the Scientific Head (having a Soul in it) is too noble an organ? I mean that Thought without Reverence is barren, perhaps poisonous; at best, dies like Cookery with the day that called it forth; does not live, like sowing, in successive tilths and wider-spreading harvests, bringing food and plenteous increase to all Time."

In such wise does Teufelsdröckh deal hits, harder or softer, according to ability; yet ever, as we would fain persuade ourselves, with charitable intent. Above all, that class of "Logic-choppers, and treble-pipe Scoffers, and professed Enemies to Wonder; who, in these days, so numerously patrol as night-constables about the Mechanics' Institute* of Science, and cackle, like true Old-Roman geese* and goslings round their Capitol, on any alarm, or on none; nay who often, as illuminated Sceptics, walk abroad into peaceable society, in full daylight, with rattle and lantern, and insist on guiding you and guarding you therewith, though the Sun is shining, and the street populous with mere justice-loving men:" that whole class is inexpressibly wearisome to him. Hear with what uncommon animation he perorates:

"The man who cannot wonder, who does not habitually wonder (and worship), were he President of innumerable Royal Societies, and carried the whole *Mécanique Céleste* and *Hegel's Philosophy,* and the epitome of all Laboratories and Observatories with their results, in his single head,—is but a Pair of Spectacles behind which there is no Eye. Let those who have Eyes look through him, then he may be useful.

"Thou wilt have no Mystery and Mysticism; wilt walk through thy world by the sunshine of what thou callest Truth, or even by the Hand-lamp of what I call Attorney Logic; and 'explain' all, 'account' for all, or believe nothing of it? Nay, thou wilt attempt laughter; whoso recognises the unfathomable, all-pervading domain of Mystery, which is everywhere under our feet and among our hands; to whom the Universe is an Oracle and Temple, as well as a Kitchen and Cattle-stall,— he shall be a (delirious) Mystic; to him thou, with sniffing charity, wilt protrusively proffer thy Handlamp, and shriek, as one injured, when he kicks his foot through it?—*Armer Teufel!* * Doth not thy Cow calve, doth not thy Bull gender? Thou thyself, wert thou not Born, wilt thou not Die? 'Explain' me all this, or do one of two things: Retire into private places with thy foolish cackle; or, what were better, give it up, and weep, not that the reign of wonder is done, and God's world all disembellished and prosaic, but that thou hitherto art a Dilettante and sandblind Pedant."

CHAPTER II

PROSPECTIVE

THE Philosophy of Clothes is now to all readers, as we predicted it would do, unfolding itself into new boundless expansions, of a cloudcapt, almost chimerical aspect, yet not without azure loomings in the far distance, and streaks as of an Elysian brightness; the highly questionable purport and promise of which it is becoming more and more important for us to ascertain. Is that a real Elysian brightness, cries many a timid wayfarer, or the reflex of Pandemonian lava? Is it of a truth leading us into beatific Asphodel meadows, or the yellow-burning marl of a Hell-on-Earth?

Our Professor, like other Mystics, whether delirious or inspired, gives an Editor enough to do. Ever higher and dizzier are the heights he leads us to; more piercing, all-comprehending, all-confounding are his views and glances. For example, this of Nature being not an Aggregate but a Whole:

"Well sang the Hebrew Psalmist: 'If I take the wings of the morning and dwell in the uttermost parts of the universe, God is there.'* Thou too, O cultivated reader, who too* probably art no Psalmist, but a Prosaist, knowing GOD only by tradition, knowest thou any corner of the world where at least FORCE is not? The drop which thou shakest from thy wet hand, rests not where it falls, but to-morrow thou findest it swept away; already, on the wings of the Northwind, it is nearing the Tropic of Cancer. How came it to evaporate, and not lie motionless? Thinkest thou there is aught motionless; without Force, and utterly dead?

"As I rode through the Schwarzwald, I said to myself; That little fire which glows star-like across the dark-growing (*nachtende*) moor, where the sooty smith bends over his anvil, and thou hopest to replace thy lost horse-shoe,—is it a detached, separated speck, cut off from the whole universe; or indissolubly joined to the whole? Thou fool, that smithy-fire was (primarily) kindled at the Sun; is fed by air that circulates from before Noah's Deluge, from beyond the Dogstar; therein, with

Iron Force, and Coal Force, and the far stronger Force of Man, are cunning affinities and battles and victories of Force brought about: it is a little ganglion, or nervous centre, in the great vital system of Immensity. Call it, if thou wilt, an unconscious Altar, kindled on the bosom of the All; whose iron sacrifice, whose iron smoke and influence reach quite through the All; whose Dingy Priest, not by word, yet by brain and sinew, preaches forth the mystery of Force; nay preaches forth (exoterically enough) one little textlet from the Gospel of Freedom, the Gospel of Man's Force, commanding, and one day to be all-commanding.

"Detached, separated! I say there is no such separation: nothing hitherto was ever stranded, cast aside; but all, were it only a withered leaf, works together with all; is borne forward on the bottomless, shoreless flood of Action, and lives through perpetual metamorphoses. The withered leaf is not dead and lost, there are Forces in it and around it, though working in inverse order; else how could it *rot?* Despise not the rag from which man makes Paper, or the litter from which the Earth makes Corn. Rightly viewed no meanest object is insignificant; all objects are as windows, through which the philosophic eye looks into Infinitude itself."

Again, leaving that wondrous Schwarzwald Smithy-Altar, what vacant, high-sailing air-ships are these, and whither will they sail with us?

"All visible things are Emblems; what thou seest is not there on its own account; strictly taken, is not there at all: Matter exists only spiritually, and to represent some Idea, and *body* it forth. Hence Clothes, as despicable as we think them, are so unspeakably significant. Clothes, from the King's-mantle downwards, are Emblematic, not of want only, but of a manifold cunning Victory over Want. On the other hand, all Emblematic things are properly Clothes, thought-woven or hand-woven: must not the Imagination weave Garments, visible Bodies, wherein the else invisible creations and inspirations of our Reason are, like Spirits, revealed, and first become all-powerful;—the rather if, as we often see, the Hand too aid her, and (by wool Clothes or otherwise) reveal such even to the outward eye?

"Men are properly said to be clothed with Authority, clothed with Beauty, with Curses, and the like. Nay, if you consider it, what is Man himself, and his whole terrestrial Life, but an Emblem; a Clothing or visible Garment for that divine ME of his, cast hither, like a light-particle, down from Heaven? Thus is he said also to be clothed with a Body.

"Language is called the Garment of Thought: however, it should rather be, Language is the Flesh-Garment, the Body, of Thought. I said that Imagination wove this Flesh-Garment; and does she not? Metaphors are her stuff: examine Language; what, if you except some few primitive elements (of natural sound), what is it all but Metaphors, recognised as such, or no longer recognised; still fluid and florid, or now solid-grown and colourless? If those same primitive elements are the osseous fixtures in the Flesh-garment, Language,—then are Metaphors its muscles and tissues and living integuments. An unmetaphorical style you shall in vain seek for: is not your very *Attention* a *Stretching-to?* * The difference lies here: some styles are lean, adust, wiry, the muscle itself seems osseous; some are even quite pallid, hunger-bitten, and dead-looking; while others again glow in the flush of health and vigorous self-growth, sometimes (as in my own case) not without an apoplectic tendency. Moreover, there are sham Metaphors, which overhanging that same Thought's-Body (best naked), and deceptively bedizening, or bolstering it out, may be called its false stuffings, superfluous show-cloaks (*Putz-Mäntel*), and tawdry woollen rags: whereof he that runs and reads may gather whole hampers,—and burn them."

Than which paragraph on Metaphors did the reader ever chance to see a more surprisingly metaphorical? However, that is not our chief grievance; the Professor continues:

"Why multiply instances? It is written the Heavens and the Earth shall fade away like a Vesture; which indeed they are: the Time-vesture of the Eternal. Whatsoever sensibly exists, whatsoever represents Spirit to Spirit, is properly a Clothing, a suit of Raiment, put on for a season, and to be laid off. Thus in this one pregnant subject of CLOTHES, rightly understood, is included all that men have thought, dreamed, done, and been: the whole external Universe and what it holds is but Clothing;

and the essence of all Science lies in the PHILOSOPHY OF
CLOTHES."

Towards these dim infinitely-expanded regions, close-bor-
dering on the impalpable Inane, it is not without apprehension,
and perpetual difficulties, that the Editor sees himself journey-
ing and struggling. Till lately a cheerful daystar of hope hung
before him, in the expected Aid of Hofrath Heuschrecke;
which daystar, however, melts now, not into the red of
morning, but into a vague, gray, half-light, uncertain whether
dawn of day or dusk of utter darkness. For the last week, these
so-called Biographical Documents are in his hand. By the
kindness of a Scottish Hamburgh Merchant, whose name,
known to the whole mercantile world, he must not mention;
but whose honourable courtesy, now and often before spontaneously manifested to him, a mere literary stranger, he cannot
soon forget,—the bulky Weissnichtwo Packet, with all its
Customhouse seals, foreign hieroglyphs, and miscellaneous
tokens of Travel, arrived here in perfect safety, and free of cost.
The reader shall now fancy with what hot haste it was broken
up, with what breathless expectation glanced over; and, alas,
with what unquiet disappointment it has, since then, been often
thrown down, and again taken up.

Hofrath Heuschrecke, in a too long-winded Letter, full of
compliments, Weissnichtwo politics, dinners, dining repartees,
and other ephemeral trivialities, proceeds to remind us of what
we knew well already: that however it may be with Metaphysics, and other abstract Science originating in the Head (Verstand) alone, no Life-Philosophy (Lebensphilosophie), such as
this of Clothes pretends to be, which originates equally in the
Character (Gemüth), and equally speaks thereto, can attain its
significance till the Character itself is known and seen; "till the
Author's View of the World (Weltansicht), and how he
actively and passively came by such view, are clear: in short, till
a Biography of him has been philosophico-poetically written,
and philosophico-poetically read." "Nay," adds he, "were the
speculative scientific Truth even known, you still, in this
inquiring age, ask yourself, Whence came it, and Why, and
How?—and rest not, till, if no better may be, Fancy have
shaped out an answer; and, either in the authentic lineaments of

Fact, or the forged ones of Fiction, a complete picture and Genetical History of the Man and his spiritual Endeavour lies before you. But why," says the Hofrath, and indeed say we, "do I dilate on the uses of our Teufelsdröckh's Biography? The great Herr Minister von Goethe has penetratingly remarked* that 'Man is properly the *only* object that interests man:' thus I too have noted, that in Weissnichtwo our whole conversation is little or nothing else but Biography or Autobiography; ever humano-anecdotical (*menschlich-anekdotisch*). Biography is by nature the most universally profitable, universally pleasant of all things: especially Biography of distinguished individuals.

"By this time, *mein Verehrtester* (my Most Esteemed)," continues he, with an eloquence which, unless the words be purloined from Teufelsdröckh, or some trick of his, as we suspect, is well-nigh unaccountable, "by this time, you are fairly plunged (*vertieft*) in that mighty forest of Clothes-Philosophy; and looking round, as all readers do, with astonishment enough. Such portions and passages as you have already mastered, and brought to paper, could not but awaken a strange curiosity touching the mind they issued from; the perhaps unparalleled psychical mechanism, which manufactured such matter, and emitted it to the light of day. Had Teufelsdröckh also a father and mother; did he, at one time, wear drivel-bibs, and live on spoon-meat? Did he ever, in rapture and tears, clasp a friend's bosom to his; looks he also wistfully into the long burial-aisle of the Past, where only winds, and their low harsh moan, give inarticulate answer? Has he fought duels;—good Heaven! how did he comport himself when in Love? By what singular stair-steps, in short, and subterranean passages, and sloughs of Despair, and steep Pisgah hills, has he reached this wonderful prophetic Hebron (a true Old-Clothes Jewry)* where he now dwells?

"To all these natural questions the voice of public History is as yet silent. Certain only that he has been, and is, a Pilgrim, and Traveller from a far Country; more or less footsore and travel-soiled; has parted with road-companions; fallen among thieves, been poisoned by bad cookery, blistered with bugbites; nevertheless, at every stage (for they have let him pass), has had the Bill to discharge. But the whole particulars of his Route, his

Weather-observations, the picturesque Sketches he took, though all regularly jotted down (in indelible sympathetic-ink* by an invisible interior Penman), are these nowhere forthcoming? Perhaps quite lost: one other leaf of that mighty Volume (of human Memory) left to fly abroad, unprinted, unpublished, unbound up, as waste paper; and rot, the sport of rainy winds?

"No, *verehrtester Herr Herausgeber,** in no wise! I here, by the unexampled favour you stand in with our Sage, send not a Biography only, but an Autobiography: at least the materials for such; wherefrom, if I misreckon not, your perspicacity will draw fullest insight; and so the whole Philosophy and Philosopher of Clothes stand* clear to the wondering eyes of England; nay thence, through America, through Hindostan, and the antipodal New Holland, finally conquer (*einnehmen*) great part of this terrestrial Planet!"

And now let the sympathising reader judge of our feeling when, in place of this same Autobiography with "fullest insight," we find—Six considerable PAPER-BAGS, carefully sealed, and marked successively, in gilt China-ink, with the symbols of the Six southern Zodiacal Signs, beginning at Libra; in the inside of·which sealed Bags, lie miscellaneous masses of Sheets, and oftener Shreds and Snips, written in Professor Teufelsdröckh's scarce-legible *cursiv-schrift;** and treating of all imaginable things under the Zodiac and above it, but of his own personal history only at rare intervals, and then in the most enigmatic manner!

Whole fascicles there are, wherein the Professor, or, as he here speaking in the third person calls himself, "the Wanderer," is not once named. Then again, amidst what seems to be a Metaphysico-theological Disquisition, "Detached Thoughts on the Steam-engine," or "The continued Possibility of Prophecy," we shall meet with some quite private, not unimportant Biographical fact. On certain sheets stand Dreams, authentic or not, while the circumjacent waking Actions are omitted. Anecdotes, oftenest without date of place or time, fly loosely on separate slips, like Sibylline leaves.* Interspersed also are long purely Autobiographical delineations, yet without connexion, without recognisable coherence;

so unimportant, so superfluously minute, they almost remind us of "P. P. Clerk of this Parish."* Thus does famine of intelligence alternate with waste. Selection, order appears to be unknown to the Professor. In all Bags the same imbroglio; only perhaps in the Bag *Capricorn,* and those near it, the confusion a little worse confounded. Close by a rather eloquent Oration "On receiving the Doctor's-Hat," lie washbills marked *bezahlt* (settled). His Travels are indicated by the Street-Advertisements of the various cities he has visited; of which Street-Advertisements, in most living tongues, here is perhaps the completest collection extant.

So that if the Clothes Volume itself was too like a Chaos, we have now instead of the solar Luminary that should still it, the airy Limbo which by intermixture will farther volatilise and discompose it! As we shall perhaps see it our duty ultimately to deposit these Six Paper Bags in the British Museum, farther description, and all vituperation of them, may be spared. Biography or Autobiography of Teufelsdröckh there is, clearly enough, none to be gleaned here: at most some sketchy, shadowy, fugitive likeness of him may, by unheard-of efforts, partly of intellect partly of imagination, on the side of Editor and of Reader, rise up between them. Only as a gaseous-chaotic Appendix to that aqueous-chaotic Volume can the contents of the Six Bags hover round us, and portions thereof be incorporated with our delineation of it.

Daily and nightly does the Editor sit (with green spectacles) deciphering these unimaginable Documents from their perplexed *cursiv-schrift;* collating them with the almost equally unimaginable Volume, which stands in legible print. Over such a universal medley of high and low, of hot, cold, moist and dry, is he here struggling (by union of like with like, which is Method) to build a firm Bridge for British travellers. Never perhaps since our first Bridge-builders, Sin and Death, built that stupendous Arch from Hell-gate to the Earth, did any Pontifex, or Pontiff, undertake such a task as the present Editor. For in this Arch too, leading as we humbly presume, far otherwards than that grand primeval one, the materials are to be fished up from the weltering deep, and down from the simmering air, here one mass, there another, and cunningly cemented, while the elements boil beneath: nor is there any supernatural force to do it with; but simply the Diligence and feeble thinking Faculty of an English Editor, endeavouring to evolve printed Creation out of a German printed and written Chaos, wherein, as he shoots to and fro in it, gathering clutching, piecing the Why to the far-distant Wherefore, his whole Faculty and Self are like to be swallowed up.

Patiently, under these incessant toils and agitations, does the Editor, dismissing all anger, see his otherwise robust health declining; some fraction of his allotted natural sleep nightly leaving him, and little but an inflamed nervous-system to be looked for. What is the use of Health, or of Life, if not to do some work therewith? And what work nobler than transplanting foreign Thought into the barren domestic soil; except indeed planting Thought of your own, which the fewest are privileged to do? Wild as it looks, this Philosophy of Clothes, can we ever reach its real meaning, promises to reveal new-coming Eras, the first dim rudiments and already-budding germs of a nobler Era, in Universal History. Is not such a prize worth some striving? Forward with us, courageous reader; be it towards failure, or towards success! The latter thou sharest with us, the former also is not all our own.

*　　　*　　　*

BOOK II

GENESIS

In a psychological point of view, it is perhaps questionable whether from birth and genealogy, how closely scrutinised soever, much insight is to be gained. Nevertheless, as in every phenomenon the Beginning remains always the most notable moment; so, with regard to any great man, we rest not till, for our scientific profit or not, the whole circumstances of his first appearance in this Planet, and what manner of Public Entry he made, are with utmost completeness rendered manifest. To the Genesis of our Clothes-Philosopher, then, be this First Chapter consecrated. Unhappily, indeed, he seems to be of quite obscure extraction; uncertain, we might almost say, whether of any: so that this Genesis of his can properly be nothing but an Exodus (or transit out of Invisibility into Visibility); whereof the preliminary portion is nowhere forthcoming.

"In the village of Entepfuhl,"* thus writes he, in the Bag *Libra,* on various Papers, which we arrange with difficulty, "dwelt Andreas Futteral and his wife; childless, in still seclusion, and cheerful though now verging towards old age. Andreas had been grenadier Sergeant, and even regimental Schoolmaster under Frederick the Great; but now, quitting the halbert and ferule for the spade and pruning-hook, cultivated a little Orchard, on the produce of which he, Cincinnatus-like, lived not without dignity. Fruits, the peach, the apple, the grape, with other varieties came in their season; all which Andreas knew how to sell: on evenings he smoked largely, or read (as beseemed a regimental Schoolmaster), and talked to neighbours that would listen about the Victory of Rossbach; and how Fritz the Only (*der Einzige*) had once with his own royal lips spoken to him, had been pleased to say, when Andreas as camp-sentinel demanded the pass-word, *Schweig Du Hund* (Peace, hound!) before any of his staff-adjutants could answer. *'Das nenn' ich mir einen König,* there is what I call a King,' would Andreas exclaim: 'but the smoke of Kunersdorf was still smarting his eyes.'

"Gretchen, the housewife, won like Desdemona by the deeds rather than the looks of her now veteran Othello,* lived not in altogether military subordination; for, as Andreas said, 'the womankind will not drill (*wer kann die Weiberchen dres-siren*):' nevertheless she at least* loved him both for valour and wisdom; to her a Prussian grenadier Sergeant and Regiment's-Schoolmaster was little other than a Cicero and Cid: what you see, yet cannot see over, is as good as infinite. Nay, was not Andreas in very deed a man of order, courage, downrightness (*Geradheit*); that understood Büsching's Geography, had been in the victory of Rossbach, and left for dead in the camisade* of Hochkirch? The good Gretchen, for all her fretting, watched over him and hovered round him, as only a true housemother can: assiduously she cooked and sewed and scoured for him; so that not only his old regimental sword and grenadier-cap, but the whole habitation and environment where, on pegs of honour, they hung, looked ever trim and gay: a roomy painted Cottage, embowered in fruit-trees and forest-trees, evergreens and honeysuckles; rising many-coloured from amid shaven grass-plots, flowers struggling in through the very windows; under its long projecting eaves nothing but garden-tools in methodic piles (to screen them from rain), and seats, where, especially on summer nights, a King might have wished to sit and smoke and call it his. Such a *Bauergut* (Copyhold) had Gretchen given her veteran; whose sinewy arms, and long-disused gardening talent, had made it what you saw.

"Into this umbrageous Man's-nest, one meek yellow evening or dusk, when the Sun, hidden indeed from terrestrial Entepfuhl, did nevertheless journey visible and radiant along the celestial Balance (*Libra*), it was that a Stranger of reverend aspect entered; and, with grave salutation, stood before the two rather astonished housemates. He was close-muffled in a wide mantle; which without farther parley unfolding, he deposited therefrom what seemed some Basket, overhung with green Persian silk; saying only: *Ihr lieben Leute, hier bringe ein unschätz-bares Verleihen; nehmt es in aller Acht, sorgfältigst benützt es: mit hohem Lohn, oder wohl mit schweren Zinsen, wird's einst zurückge-fordert,* 'Good Christian people, here lies for you an invaluable Loan; take all heed thereof, in all carefulness employ it: with high recompense, or else with heavy penalty, will it one day be required back.' Uttering which singular words, in a clear, bell-like, forever memorable tone, the Stranger gracefully with-drew; and before Andreas or his wife gazing in expectant wonder, had time to fashion either question or answer, was clean gone. Neither out of doors could aught of him be seen or heard; he had vanished in the thickets, in the dusk; the Orchard-gate stood quietly closed: the Stranger was gone once and always. So sudden had the whole transaction been, in the autumn stillness and twilight, so gentle, noiseless, that the Futterals could have fancied it all a trick of Imagination, or some visit from an authentic Spirit. Only that the green-silk Basket, such as neither Imagination nor authentic Spirits are wont to carry, still stood visible and tangible on their little parlour-table. Towards this the astonished couple, now with lit candle, hastily turned their attention. Lifting the green veil, to see what invaluable it hid, they descried there, amid down and rich white wrappages, no Pitt Diamond* or Hapsburg Regalia, but in the softest sleep, a little red-coloured Infant! Beside it, lay a roll of gold Friedrichs,* the exact amount of which was never publicly known; also a *Taufschein* (baptismal certificate), wherein unfortunately nothing but the Name was decipher-able; other document or indication none whatever.

"To wonder and conjecture was unavailing, then and always thenceforth. Nowhere in Entepfuhl, on the morrow or next day, did tidings transpire of any such figure as the Stranger; nor could the Traveller, who had passed through the neighbouring Town in coach-and-four, be connected with this Apparition, except in the way of gratuitous surmise. Meanwhile, for Andreas and his wife, the grand practical problem was: What to do with this little sleeping red-coloured Infant? Amid amazements and curiosities, which had to die away without external satisfying, they resolved, as in such circumstances charitable prudent people needs must, on nursing it, though with spoon-meat, into whiteness, and if possible into manhood. The Heavens smiled on their endeavour: thus has that same mysterious Individual ever since had a status for himself, in this visible Universe, some modicum of victual and lodging and parade-ground; and now expanded in bulk, faculty, and knowledge of good and evil, he, as HERR DIOGENES TEUFELSDRÖCKH, professes or is ready to profess, perhaps not altogether without effect, in the new University of Weissnichtwo, the new Science of Things in General."

Our Philosopher declares here, as indeed we should think he well might, that these facts, first communicated, by the good Gretchen Futteral, in his twelfth year, "produced on the boyish heart and fancy a quite indelible impression. Who this reverend Personage," he says, "that glided into the Orchard Cottage when the Sun was in Libra, and then, as on spirit's wings, glided out again, might be? An inexpressible desire, full of love and of sadness, has often since struggled within me to shape an answer. Ever, in my distresses and my loneliness, has Fantasy turned, full of longing (*sehnsuchtsvoll*), to that unknown Father, who perhaps far from me, perhaps near, either way invisible, might have taken me to his paternal bosom, there to lie screened from many a woe. Thou beloved Father, dost thou still, shut out from me only by thin penetrable curtains of earthly Space, wend to and fro among the crowd of the living? Or art thou hidden by those far thicker curtains of the Everlasting Night, or rather of the Everlasting Day, through which my mortal eye and outstretched arms need not strive to reach? Alas! I know not, and in vain vex myself to know. More than once, heart-deluded, have I taken for thee this and the other noble-looking Stranger; and approached him wistfully, with infinite regard: but he too must repel me, he too was not thou.

"And yet, O Man born of Woman," cries the Autobiographer, with one of his sudden whirls, "wherein is my case peculiar? Hadst thou, any more than I, a Father whom thou knowest? The Andreas and Gretchen, or the Adam and Eve, who led thee into Life, and for a time suckled and pap-fed thee there, whom thou namest Father and Mother; these were, like mine, but thy nursing-father and nursing-mother: thy true Beginning and Father is in Heaven, whom with the bodily eye thou shalt never behold, but only with the spiritual."

"The little green veil," adds he, among much similar moralising, and embroiled discoursing, "I yet keep; still more inseparably the Name, Diogenes Teufelsdröckh. From the veil can nothing be inferred: a piece of now quite faded Persian silk, like thousands of others. On the Name I have many times meditated and conjectured; but neither in this lay there any clue. That it was my unknown Father's name I must hesitate to believe. To no purpose have I searched through all the Herald's Books, in and without the German Empire, and through all manner of Subscriber-Lists (*Pränumeranten*), Militia-Rolls, and other Name-catalogues; extraordinary names as we have in Germany, the name Teufelsdröckh, except as appended to my own person, nowhere occurs. Again, what may the unchristian rather than Christian 'Diogenes' mean? Did that reverend Basket-bearer intend, by such designation, to shadow forth my future destiny, or his own present malign humour? Perhaps the latter, perhaps both. Thou ill-starred Parent, who like an Ostrich must leave thy ill-starred offspring to be hatched into self-support by the mere sky-influences of Chance, can thy pilgrimage have been a smooth one? Beset by Misfortune thou doubtless hast been; or indeed by the worst figure of Misfortune, by Misconduct. Often have I fancied how, in thy hard life-battle, thou wert shot at and slung at, wounded, handfettered, hamstrung, browbeaten and bedevilled, by the Time-Spirit (*Zeitgeist*) in thyself and others, till the good soul first given thee was seared into grim rage; and thou hadst nothing for it but to leave in me an indignant appeal to the Future, and living speaking Protest against the Devil, as that same Spirit not of the Time only, but of Time itself, is well named! Which Appeal and Protest, may I now modestly add, was not perhaps quite lost in air.

"For indeed as Walter Shandy often insisted, there is much, nay almost all, in Names.* The Name is the earliest Garment you wrap round the Earth-visiting ME; to which it thenceforth cleaves, more tenaciously (for there are Names that have lasted nigh thirty centuries) than the very skin. And now from without, what mystic influences does it not send inwards, even to the centre; especially in those plastic first-times, when the whole soul is yet infantine, soft, and the invisible seed-grain

will grow to be an all overshadowing tree! Names? Could I
unfold the influence of Names, which are the most important
of all Clothings, I were a second greater Trismegistus. Not only
all common Speech, but Science, Poetry itself is no other, if
thou consider it, than a right *Naming*. Adam's first task was
giving names to natural Appearances: what is ours still but a
combination of the same; be the Appearances exotic-vegetable,
organic, mechanic, stars, or starry movements (as in Science);
or (as in Poetry) passions, virtues, calamities, God-attributes,
Gods?—In a very plain sense the Proverb says, *Call one a thief
and he will steal;* in an almost similar sense, may we not perhaps
say, *Call one Diogenes Teufelsdröckh and he will open the Philosophy of Clothes.*"

"Meanwhile the incipient Diogenes, like others, all ignorant
of his Why, his How or Whereabout, was opening his eyes to
the kind Light; sprawling out his ten fingers and toes; listening,
tasting, feeling; in a word, by all his Five Senses, still more by
his Sixth Sense of Hunger, and a whole infinitude of inward,
spiritual, half awakened Senses, endeavouring daily to acquire
for himself some knowledge of this strange Universe where he
had arrived, be his task therein what it might. Infinite was his
progress; thus in some fifteen months, he could perform the
miracle of—Speech! To breed a fresh Soul, is it not like
brooding a fresh (celestial) Egg; wherein as yet all is formless,
powerless; yet by degrees organic elements and fibres shoot
through the watery albumen; and out of vague Sensation,
grows Thought, grows Fantasy and Force, and we have
Philosophies, Dynasties, nay Poetries and Religions!

"Young Diogenes, or rather young Gneschen,* for by such
diminutive had they in their fondness named him, travelled
forward to those high consummations, by quick yet easy
stages. The Futterals, to avoid vain talk, and moreover keep the
roll of gold Friedrichs safe, gave out that he was a grand-
nephew; the orphan of some sister's daughter, suddenly deceased, in Andreas's distant Prussian birth-land; of whom, as of
her indigent sorrowing widower, little enough was known at
Entepfuhl. Heedless of all which, the Nurseling took to his
spoon-meat, and throve. I have heard him noted as a still infant,
that kept his mind much to himself; above all, that seldom or

never cried. He already felt that Time was precious; that he had other work cut out for him than whimpering."

Such, after utmost painful search and collation among these miscellaneous Paper-masses, is all the notice we can gather of Herr Teufelsdröckh's genealogy. More imperfect, more enigmatic it can seem to few readers than to us. The Professor, in whom truly we more and more discern a certain satirical turn, and deep undercurrents of roguish whim, for the present stands pledged in honour, so we will not doubt him: but seems it not conceivable that, by the "good Gretchen Futteral," or some other perhaps interested party, he has himself been deceived? Should these Sheets, translated or not, ever reach the Entepfuhl Circulating-Library, some cultivated native of that district might feel called to afford explanation. Nay, since Books, like invisible scouts, permeate the whole habitable globe, and Tombuctoo itself is not safe from British Literature, may not some Copy find out even the mysterious Basket-bearing Stranger, who in a state of extreme senility perhaps still exists; and gently force even him to disclose himself; to claim openly a son, in whom any father may feel pride?

CHAPTER 2
IDYLLIC

"Happy season of Childhood!" exclaims Teufelsdröckh: "Kind Nature, that art to all a bountiful mother; that visitest the poor man's hut with auroral radiance; and for thy Nurseling hast provided a soft swathing of Love and infinite Hope, wherein he waxes and slumbers, danced-round (*umgaukelt*) by sweetest Dreams! If the paternal Cottage still shuts us in, its roof still screens us; with a Father we have as yet a prophet, priest and king, and an Obedience that makes us Free. The young spirit has awakened out of Eternity, and knows not what we mean by Time; as yet Time is no fast-hurrying stream, but a sportful sunlit ocean; years to the child are as ages: ah! the secret of Vicissitude, of that slower or quicker decay and ceaseless downrushing of the universal World-fabric, from the granite mountain to the man or day-moth, is yet unknown; and in a motionless Universe we taste, what afterwards in this quick-whirling Universe is forever denied us, the balm of Rest. Sleep on, thou fair Child, for thy long rough journey is at hand! A little while, and thou too shalt sleep no more, but thy very dreams shall be mimic battles; thou too, with old Arnauld, must say in stern patience: 'Rest? Rest? Shall I not have all Eternity to rest in?'* Celestial Nepenthe! though a Pyrrhus conquer empires, and an Alexander sack the world, he finds thee not; and thou hast once fallen gently, of thy own accord, on the eyelids, on the heart of every mother's child. For as yet, sleep and waking are one: the fair Life-garden rustles infinite around, and everywhere is dewy fragrance, and the budding of Hope; which budding, if in youth, too frost-nipt, it grow to flowers, will in manhood yield no fruit, but a prickly, bitter-rinded stone-fruit, of which the fewest can find the kernel."

In such rose-coloured light does our Professor, as Poets are wont, look back on his childhood; the historical details of which (to say nothing of much other vague oratorical matter) he accordingly dwells on, with an almost wearisome minuteness. We hear of Entepfuhl standing "in trustful derangement"

among the woody slopes; the paternal Orchard flanking it as
extreme outpost from below; the little Kuhbach* gushing
kindly by, among beech-rows, through river after river, into
the Donau, into the Black Sea, into the Atmosphere and
Universe; and how "the brave old Linden, stretching like a
parasol of twenty ells in radius, overtopping all other rows and
clumps, towered up from the central *Agora* and *Campus Martius*
of the Village, like its Sacred Tree; and how the old men sat
talking under its shadow (Gneschen often greedily listening),
and the wearied labourers reclined, and the unwearied children
sported, and the young men and maidens often danced to flute-
music. "Glorious summer twilights," cries Teufelsdröckh,
"when the Sun like a proud Conqueror and Imperial Taskmas-
ter turned his back, with his gold-purple emblazonry, and all
his fire-clad bodyguard (of Prismatic Colours); and the tired
brickmakers of this clay Earth might steal a little frolic, and
those few meek Stars would not tell of them!"

Then we have long details of the *Weinlesen* (Vintage), the
Harvest-Home, Christmas, and so forth; with a whole cycle of
the Entepfuhl Children's-games, differing apparently by mere
superficial shades from those of other countries. Concerning all
which, we shall here, for obvious reasons, say nothing. What
cares the world for our as yet miniature Philosopher's achieve-
ments under that "brave old Linden?" Or even where is the use
of such practical reflections as the following? "In all the sports
of Children, were it only in their wanton breakages and
defacements, you shall discern a creative instinct (*schaffenden
Trieb*): the Mankin feels that he is a born Man, that his
vocation is to Work. The choicest present you can make him is
a Tool; be it knife or pengun,* for construction or for
destruction; either way it is for Work, for Change. In gregarious sports of skill or strength, the Boy trains himself to Co-
operation, for war or peace, as governor or governed: the little
Maid again, provident of her domestic destiny, takes with
preference to Dolls."

Perhaps, however, we may give this anecdote, considering
who it is that relates it: "My first short-clothes were of yellow
serge; or rather, I should say, my first short-cloth, for the
vesture was one and indivisible, reaching from neck to ankle, a

mere body with four limbs: of which fashion how little could I then divine the architectural, how much less the moral significance!"

More graceful is the following little picture: "On fine evenings I was wont to carry forth my supper (bread-crumb boiled in milk), and eat it out of doors. On the coping of the Orchard-wall, which I could reach by climbing, or still more easily if Father Andreas would set up the pruning-ladder, my porringer was placed: there, many a sunset, have I, looking at the distant western Mountains, consumed, not without relish, my evening meal. Those hues of gold and azure, that hush of World's expectation as Day died, were still a Hebrew Speech for me; nevertheless I was looking at the fair illuminated Letters, and had an eye for their gilding."

With "the little one's friendship for the cattle and poultry" we shall not much intermeddle. It may be that hereby he acquired "a certain deeper sympathy with animated Nature:" but when, we would ask, saw any man, in a collection of Biographical Documents, such a piece as this: "Impressive enough (*bedeutungsvoll*) was it to hear, in early morning, the Swineherd's horn; and know that so many hungry, happy quadrupeds, were on all sides starting in hot haste to join him, for breakfast on the Heath. Or to see them, at eventide, all marching in again, with short squeak, almost in military order; and each, topographically correct, trotting off in succession to the right or left, through its own lane, to its own dwelling; till old Kunz, at the Village-head, now left alone, blew his last blast, and retired for the night. We are wont to love the Hog chiefly in the form of Ham: yet did not these bristly thick-skinned beings here manifest intelligence, perhaps humour of character; at any rate, a touching, trustful submissiveness to Man,—who were he but a Swineherd, in darned gabardine, and leather breeches more resembling slate or discoloured tin breeches, is still the Hierarch of this lower world?"

It is maintained, by Helvetius and his set, that an infant of genius is quite the same as any other infant, only that certain surprisingly favourable influences accompany him through life, especially through childhood, and expand him, while others lie close-folded and continue dunces. Herein, say they, consists the whole difference between an inspired Prophet and a double-barrelled Game-preserver:* the inner man of the one has been fostered into generous development; that of the other, crushed down perhaps by vigour of animal digestion, and the like, has exuded and evaporated, or at best sleeps now irresuscitably stagnant at the bottom of his stomach. "With which opinion," cries Teufelsdröckh, "I should as soon agree as with this other, that an acorn might, by favourable or unfavourable influences of soil and climate, be nursed into a cabbage, or the cabbage-seed into an oak.

"Nevertheless," continues he, "I too acknowledge the all but omnipotence of early culture and nurture: hereby we have either a doddered dwarf bush, or a high-towering, wide-shadowing tree; either a sick yellow cabbage, or an edible, luxuriant, green one. Of a truth, it is the duty of all men, especially of all philosophers, to note down with accuracy the characteristic circumstances of their Education, what furth-ered, what hindered, what in any way modified it: to which duty, now-a-days so pressing for many a German Autobiogra-pher, I also zealously address myself."—Thou rogue! Is it by short-clothes of yellow serge, and swineherd horns, that an infant of genius is educated? And yet, as usual, it ever remains doubtful whether he is laughing in his sleeve at these Autobio-graphical times of ours, or writing from the abundance of his own fond ineptitude. For he continues: "If among the ever-streaming currents of Sights, Hearings, Feelings for Pain or Pleasure, whereby, as in a Magic Hall, young Gneschen went about environed, I might venture to select and specify, perhaps these following were also of the number:

"Doubtless, as childish sports call forth Intellect, Activity, so the young creature's Imagination was stirred up, and a Histori-cal tendency given him by the narrative habits of Father Andreas; who, with his battle-reminiscences, and gray, austere, yet hearty patriarchal aspect, could not but appear another Ulysses and 'Much-enduring Man.' Eagerly I hung upon his tales, when listening neighbours enlivened the hearth: from these perils and these travels, wild and far almost as Hades itself, a dim world of Adventure expanded itself within me. Incred-ible* also was the knowledge I acquired in standing by the Old Men under the Linden-tree: the whole of Immensity was yet new to me; and had not these reverend seniors, talkative enough, been employed in partial surveys thereof for nigh fourscore years? With amazement I began to discover that Entepfuhl stood in the middle of a Country, of a World; that there was such a thing as History, as Biography; to which I also, one day, by hand and tongue, might contribute.

"In a like sense worked the *Postwagen* (Stage-Coach), which, slow-rolling under its mountains of men and luggage, wended through our Village: northwards, truly, in the dead of night; yet southwards visibly at eventide. Not till my eighth year, did I reflect that this Postwagen could be other than some terrestrial Moon, rising and setting by mere Law of Nature, like the heavenly one; that it came on made highways, from far cities towards far cities; weaving them like a monstrous shuttle into closer and closer union. It was then that, independently of Schiller's *Wilhelm Tell,* I made this not quite insignificant reflection (so true also in spiritual things): *Any road, this simple Entepfuhl road, will lead you to the end of the World!* *

"Why mention our Swallows, which, out of far Africa as I learned, threading their way over seas and mountains, corporate cities and belligerent nations, yearly found themselves, with the month of May, snug-lodged in our Cottage Lobby? The hospitable Father (for cleanliness' sake) had fixed a little bracket, plumb under their nest: there they built, and caught flies, and twittered, and bred; and all, I chiefly, from the heart loved them. Bright, nimble creatures, who taught *you* the mason-craft; nay, stranger still, gave you a masonic incorporation, almost social police? For if, by ill chance, and when time pressed, your House fell, have I not seen five neighbourly Helpers appear next day; and swashing to and fro, with animated, loud, long-drawn chirpings, and activity almost super-hirundine, complete it again before nightfall?

"But undoubtedly the grand summary of Entepfuhl child's-culture, where as in a funnel its manifold influences were concentrated and simultaneously poured down on us, was the annual Cattle-fair. Here, assembling from all the four winds, came the elements of an unspeakable hurly-burly. Nutbrown maids and nutbrown men, all clear-washed, loud-laughing, bedizened and be-ribanded; who came for dancing, for treating, and if possible, for happiness. Topbooted Graziers from the North; Swiss Brokers, Italian Drovers, also topbooted, from the South; these with their subalterns in leather jerkins, leather skullcaps, and long oxgoads; shouting in half-articulate speech, amid the inarticulate barking and bellowing. Apart stood Potters from far Saxony, with their crockery in fair rows; Nürnberg Pedlars, in booths that to me seemed richer than Ormuz bazaars; Showmen from the Lago Maggiore; detachments of the *Wiener Schub* (Offscourings of Vienna) vociferously superintending games of chance. Ballad-singers brayed, Auctioneers grew hoarse; cheap New Wine (*heuriger*) flowed like water, still worse confounding the confusion; and high over all, vaulted, in ground-and-lofty tumbling, a parti-coloured Merry Andrew, like the genius of the place and of Life itself.

"Thus encircled by the mystery of Existence; under the deep heavenly Firmament; waited on by the four golden Seasons, with their vicissitudes of contribution, for even grim Winter brought its skating-matches and shooting-matches, its snow-storms and Christmas carols,—did the Child sit and learn. These things were the Alphabet, whereby in after-time he was to syllable and partly read the grand Volume of the World: what matters it whether such Alphabet be in large gilt letters or in small ungilt ones, so you have an eye to read it? For Gneschen, eager to learn, the very act of looking thereon was a blessedness that gilded all: his existence was a bright, soft element of Joy; out of which, as in Prospero's Island,* wonder after wonder bodied itself forth, to teach by charming.

"Nevertheless I were but a vain dreamer to say, that even then my felicity was perfect. I had, once for all, come down from Heaven into the Earth. Among the rainbow colours that glowed on my horizon, lay even in childhood a dark ring of Care, as yet no thicker than a thread, and often quite over-shone; yet always it reappeared, nay, ever waxing broader and broader; till in after-years it almost overshadowed my whole canopy, and threatened to engulf me in final night. It was the ring of Necessity, whereby we are all begirt: happy he for whom a kind heavenly Sun brightens it into a ring of Duty, and plays round it with beautiful prismatic diffractions; yet ever, as basis and as bourne for our whole being, it is there.

"For the first few years of our terrestrial Apprenticeship, we have not much work to do; but, boarded and lodged gratis, are set down mostly to look about us over the workshop, and see others work, till we have understood the tools a little, and can handle this and that. If good Passivity alone, and not good Passivity and good Activity together, were the thing wanted, then was my early position favourable beyond the most. In all that respects openness of Sense, affectionate Temper, ingenuous Curiosity, and the fostering of these, what more could I have wished? On the other side, however, things went not so well. My Active Power (*Thatkraft*) was unfavourably hemmed in; of which misfortune how many traces yet abide with me! In an orderly house, where the litter of children's sports is hateful enough, your training is too stoical; rather to bear and forbear than to make and do. I was forbid much: wishes in any measure bold I had to renounce; every where a strait bond of Obedience inflexibly held me down. Thus already Freewill often came in painful collision with Necessity; so that my tears flowed, and at seasons the Child itself might taste that root of bitterness, wherewith the whole fruitage of our life is mingled and tempered.

"In which habituation to Obedience, truly, it was beyond measure safer to err by excess than by defect. Obedience is our universal duty and destiny; wherein whoso will not bend must break: too early and too thoroughly we cannot be trained to know that Would, in this world of ours, is as mere zero to Should, and for most part as the smallest of fractions even to Shall. Hereby was laid for me the basis of worldly Discretion, nay, of Morality itself. Let me not quarrel with my upbringing! It was rigorous, too frugal, compressively secluded, every way unscientific: yet in that very strictness and domestic solitude might there not lie the root of deeper Earnestness, of the stem from which all noble fruit must grow? Above all, how unskilful soever, it was loving, it was well-meant, honest; whereby every deficiency was helped. My kind Mother, for as such I must ever love the good Gretchen, did me one altogether invaluable service: she taught me, less indeed by word than by act and daily reverent look and habitude, her own simple version of the Christian Faith. Andreas, too, attended Church; yet more like a parade-duty, for which he in the other world expected pay with arrears,—as, I trust, he has received: but my Mother, with a true woman's heart, and fine though uncultivated sense, was in the strictest acceptation Religious. How indestructibly the Good grows, and propagates itself, even among the weedy entanglements of Evil! The highest whom I knew on Earth I here saw bowed down, with awe unspeakable, before a Higher in Heaven: such things, especially in infancy, reach inwards to the very core of your being; mysteriously does a Holy of Holies build itself into visibility in the mysterious deeps; and Reverence, the divinest in man, springs forth undying from its mean envelopment of Fear. Wouldst thou rather be a peasant's son that knew, were it never so rudely, there was a God in Heaven and in Man; or a duke's son that only knew there were two and thirty quarters on the family-coach?"

To which last question we must answer: Beware, O Teufelsdröckh, of spiritual pride!

CHAPTER 3

PEDAGOGY

HITHERTO we see young Gneschen, in his indivisible case of yellow serge, borne forward mostly on the arms of kind Nature alone; seated, indeed, and much to his mind, in the terrestrial workshop; but (except his soft hazel eyes, which we doubt not already gleamed with a still intelligence) called upon for little voluntary movement there. Hitherto accordingly his aspect is rather generic, that of an incipient Philosopher and Poet in the abstract: perhaps it would puzzle Herr Heuschrecke himself to say wherein the special Doctrine of Clothes is as yet foreshadowed or betokened. For with Gneschen, as with others, the Man may indeed stand pictured in the Boy (at least, all the pigments are there); yet only some half of the Man stands in the Child, or young Boy, namely his Passive endowment, not his Active. The more impatient are we to discover what figure he cuts in this latter capacity; how when, to use his own words, "he understands the tools a little, and can handle this or that," he will proceed to handle it.

Here, however, may be the place to state that, in much of our Philosopher's history, there is something of an almost Hindoo character:* nay, perhaps in that so well-fostered and every-way excellent "Passivity" of his, which, with no free development of the antagonist Activity, distinguished his childhood, we may detect the rudiments of much that, in after-days, and still in these present days, astonishes the world. For the shallow-sighted, Teufelsdröckh is oftenest a man without Activity of any kind, a No-man; for the deep-sighted, again, a man with Activity almost superabundant, yet so spiritual, close-hidden, enigmatic, that no mortal can foresee its explosions, or even when it has exploded, so much as ascertain its significance. A dangerous, difficult temper for the modern European; above all, disadvantageous in the hero of a Biography! Now as heretofore it will behove the Editor of these pages, were it never so unsuccessfully, to do his endeavour.

Among the earliest tools of any complicacy which a man, especially a man of letters, gets to handle, are his Class-books. On this portion of his History, Teufelsdröckh looks down professedly as indifferent. Reading he "cannot remember ever to have learned;" so perhaps had it by nature. He says generally: "Of the insignificant portion of my Education, which depended on Schools, there need almost no notice be taken. I learned what others learn; and kept it stored by in a corner of my head, seeing as yet no manner of use in it. My Schoolmaster, a downbent, brokenhearted, underfoot martyr, as others of that guild are, did little for me, except discover that he could do little: he, good soul, pronounced me a genius, fit for the learned professions; and that I must be sent to the Gymnasium,* and one day to the University. Meanwhile, what printed thing soever I could meet with I read. My very copper pocket-money I laid out on stall-literature; which, as it accumulated, I with my own hands sewed into volumes. By this means was the young head furnished with a considerable miscellany of things and shadows of things: History in authentic fragments lay mingled with Fabulous chimeras, wherein also was reality; and the whole not as dead stuff, but as living pabulum, tolerably nutritive for a mind as yet so peptic."

That the Entepfuhl Schoolmaster judged well we now know. Indeed, already in the youthful Gneschen, with all his outward stillness, there may have been manifest an inward vivacity that promised much; symptoms of a spirit singularly open, thoughtful, almost poetical. Thus, to say nothing of his Suppers on the Orchard-wall, and other phenomena of that earlier period, have many readers of these pages stumbled, in their twelfth year, on such reflections as the following? "It struck me much, as I sat by the Kuhbach, one silent noontide, and watched it flowing, gurgling, to think how this same streamlet had flowed and gurgled, through all changes of weather and of fortune, from beyond the earliest date of History. Yes, probably on the morning when Joshua forded Jordan; even as at the mid-day when Cæsar, doubtless with difficulty, swam the Nile, yet kept his *Commentaries* dry,—this little Kuhbach, assiduous as Tiber, Eurotas, or Siloa, was murmuring on across the wilderness, as yet unnamed, unseen:

here, too, as in the Euphrates and the Ganges, is a Vein or
Veinlet of the grand World-circulation of Waters, which, with
its atmospheric Arteries, has lasted and lasts simply with the
World. Thou fool! Nature alone is antique, and the oldest Art a
mushroom; that idle crag thou sittest on is six thousand years of
age." In which little thought, as in a little fountain, may there
not lie the beginning of those well-nigh unutterable meditations on the grandeur and the mystery of TIME, and its
relation to ETERNITY, which play such a part in this Philosophy of Clothes?

Over his Gymnasic and Academic years the Professor by no
means lingers so lyrical and joyful as over his childhood. Green
sunny tracts there are still; but intersected by bitter rivulets of
tears, here and there stagnating into sour marshes of discontent.
"With my first view of the Hinterschlag* Gymnasium," writes
he, "my evil days began. Well do I still remember the red
sunny Whitsuntide morning, when trotting full of hope, by the
side of Father Andreas, I entered the main street of the place,
and saw its steeple-clock (then striking Eight), and *Schuldthurm*
(Jail), and the aproned or disaproned Burghers moving in to
breakfast: a little dog, in mad terror, was rushing past; for some
human imps had tied a tin kettle to its tail; thus did the agonised
creature loud-jingling career through the whole length of the
Borough, and become notable enough. Fit emblem of many a
Conquering Hero, to whom Fate (wedding Fantasy to Sense, as
it often elsewhere does) has malignantly appended a tin kettle
of Ambition, to chase him on; which, the faster he runs, urges
him the faster, the more loudly and more foolishly! Fit emblem
also of much that awaited myself, in that mischievous Den; as
in the World, whereof it was a portion and epitome!

"Alas, the kind beech-rows of Entepfuhl were hidden in the
distance: I was among strangers, harshly, at best indifferently,
disposed towards me; the young heart felt, for the first time,
quite orphaned and alone." His schoolfellows, as is usual,
persecuted him: "They were Boys," he says, "mostly rude
Boys, and obeyed the impulse of rude Nature, which bids the
deerherd fall upon any stricken hart, the duck-flock put to
death any broken-winged brother or sister, and on all hands the
strong tyrannise over the weak." He admits that though

"perhaps in an unusual degree morally courageous," he succeeded ill in battle, and would fain have avoided it; a result, as
would appear, owing less to his small personal stature (for, in
passionate seasons, he was "incredibly nimble"), than to his
"virtuous principles:" "if it was disgraceful to be beaten," says
he, "it was only a shade less disgraceful to have so much as
fought; thus was I drawn two ways at once, and in this
important element of school history, the war-element, had
little but sorrow." On the whole, that same excellent "Passivity," so notable in Teufelsdröckh's childhood, is here visibly
enough again getting nourishment. "He wept often; indeed to
such a degree, that he was nicknamed *Der Weinende* (the
Tearful), which epithet, till towards his thirteenth year, was
indeed not quite unmerited. Only at rare intervals did the
young soul burst forth into fire-eyed rage, and, with a Storm-
fulness (*Ungestüm*) under which the boldest quailed, assert that
he too had Rights of Man, or at least of Mankin." In all which,
who does not discern a fine flower-tree and cinnamon-tree (of
genius) nigh choked among pumpkins, reedgrass, and ignoble
shrubs; and forced, if it would live, to struggle upwards only,
and not outwards; into a *height* quite sickly and dispropor-
tioned to its *breadth?*

We find, moreover, that his Greek and Latin were "mechanically" taught; Hebrew scarce even mechanically; much else
which they called History, Cosmography, Philosophy, and so
forth, no better than not at all. So that, except inasmuch as
Nature was still busy; and he himself "went about, as was of
old his wont, among the Craftsmen's workshops, there learning many things;" and farther lighted on some small store of
curious reading, in Hans Wachtel the Cooper's house, where he
lodged,—his time, it would appear, was utterly wasted. Which
facts the Professor has not yet learned to look upon with any
contentment. Indeed, throughout the whole of this Bag *Scorpio,* where we now are, and often in the following Bag, he
shews himself unusually animated on the matter of Education,
and not without some touch of what we might presume to be
anger.

"My Teachers," says he, "were hide-bound Pedants, without knowledge of man's nature or of boy's; or of aught save

their lexicons and quarterly account-books. Innumerable dead Vocables (no dead Language, for they themselves knew no Language) they crammed into us, and called it fostering the growth of mind. How can an inanimate, mechanical Gerund-grinder, the like of whom will, in a subsequent century, be manufactured, at Nürnberg, out of wood and leather, foster the growth of any thing; much more of Mind, which grows, not like a vegetable (by having its roots littered with etymo-logical compost), but like a Spirit, by mysterious contact of Spirit; Thought kindling itself at the fire of living Thought? How shall *he* give kindling, in whose own inward man there is no live coal, but all is burnt out to a dead grammatical cinder? The Hinterschlag Professors knew Syntax enough; and of the human soul thus much: that it had a faculty called Memory, and could be acted on through the muscular integument by appliance of birch rods.

"Alas, so is it every where, so will it ever be; till the Hodman is discharged, or reduced to Hodbearing; and an Architect is hired, and on all hands fitly encouraged: till communities and individuals discover, not without surprise, that fashioning the souls of a generation by Knowledge can rank on a level with blowing their bodies to pieces by Gunpowder; that with Generals and Field-marshals for killing, there should be world-honoured Dignitaries, and were it possible, true God-ordained Priests, for teaching. But as yet, though the Soldier wears openly, and even parades, his butchering-tool, nowhere, far as I have travelled, did the Schoolmaster make show of his instruct-ing-tool: nay, were he to walk abroad with birch girt on thigh, as if he therefrom expected honour, would not, among the idler class, a certain levity be excited?"

In the third year of this Gymnasic period, Father Andreas seems to have died: the young Scholar, otherwise so mal-treated, saw himself for the first time clad outwardly in sables, and inwardly in quite inexpressible melancholy. "The dark boundless* Abyss, that lies under our feet, had yawned open; the pale kingdoms of Death, with all their innumerable silent nations and generations stood before him; the inexorable word, NEVER! now first showed its meaning. My mother wept, and her sorrow got vent; but in my heart there lay a whole lake of tears, pent up in silent desolation. Nevertheless, the unworn Spirit is strong, Life is so healthful that it even finds nourishment in Death: these stern experiences, planted down by Memory in my Imagination, rose there to a whole cypress forest, sad but beautiful; waving, with not unmelodious sighs, in dark luxuriance, in the hottest sunshine, through long years of youth:—as in manhood also it does, and will do; for I have now pitched my tent under a Cypress tree; the Tomb is now my inexpugnable Fortress, ever close by the gate of which I look upon the hostile armaments, and pains and penalties, of tyrannous Life placidly enough, and listen to its loudest threatenings with a still smile. O ye loved ones, that already sleep in the noiseless Bed of Rest, whom in life I could only weep for and never help; and ye, who wide-scattered still toil lonely in the monster-bearing Desert, dyeing the flinty ground with your blood,—yet a little while, and we shall all meet THERE, and our Mother's bosom will screen us all; and Oppression's harness, and Sorrow's fire-whip, and all the Gehenna Bailiffs that patrol and inhabit ever-vexed Time, cannot thenceforth harm us any more!"

Close by which rather beautiful apostrophe, lies a laboured Character of the deceased Andreas Futteral; of his natural ability, his deserts in life (as Prussian Sergeant); with long historical inquiries into the genealogy of the Futteral family, here traced back as far as Henry the Fowler: the whole of which we pass over, not without astonishment. It only concerns us to add that now was the time when Mother Gretchen revealed to her foster-son that he was not at all of this kindred; or indeed of any kindred, having come into historical existence in the way already known to us. "Thus was I doubly orphaned," says he; "bereft not only of Possession, but even of Remembrance. Sorrow and Wonder, here suddenly united, could not but produce abundant fruit. Such a disclosure, in such a season, struck its roots through my whole nature: ever till the years of mature manhood, it mingled with my whole thoughts, was as the stem whereon all my day-dreams and night-dreams grew. A certain poetic elevation, yet also a corresponding civic depression, it naturally imparted: *I was like no other;* in which fixed-idea, leading sometimes to highest, and oftener to frightfullest results, may there not lie the first spring of Tendencies, that in my Life have become remarkable enough? As in birth, so in action, speculation, and social position, my fellows are perhaps not numerous."

In the Bag *Sagittarius*, as we at length discover, Teufelsdröckh has become a University man; though how, when, or of what quality, will nowhere disclose itself with the smallest certainty. Few things, in the way of confusion and capricious indistinctness, can now surprise our readers; not even the total want of dates, almost without parallel in a Biographical work. So enigmatic, so chaotic we have always found, and must always look to find, these scattered Leaves. In *Sagittarius*, however, Teufelsdröckh begins to shew himself even more than usually Sibylline: fragments of all sorts; scraps of regular Memoir, College Exercises, Programs, Professional Testimoniums, Milkscores, torn Billets, sometimes to appearance of an amatory cast; all blown together as if by merest chance, henceforth bewilder the sane Historian. To combine any picture of these University, and the subsequent, years; much more, to decipher therein any illustrative primordial elements of the Clothes-Philosophy, becomes such a problem as the reader may imagine.

So much we can see; darkly, as through the foliage of some wavering thicket: a youth of no common endowment, that has passed happily through Childhood, less happily yet still vigorously through Boyhood, now at length perfect in "dead vocables," and set down, as he hopes, by the living Fountain, there to superadd Ideas and Capabilities. From such Fountain he draws, diligently, thirstily, yet nowise* with his whole heart, for the water nowise suits his palate; discouragements, entanglements, aberrations are discoverable or supposable. Nor perhaps are even pecuniary distresses wanting; for "the good Gretchen, who in spite of advices from not disinterested relatives has sent him hither, must after a time withdraw her willing but too feeble hand." Nevertheless in an atmosphere of Poverty and manifold Chagrin, the Humour of that young Soul, what character is in him, first decisively reveals itself; and, like strong sunshine in weeping skies, gives out variety of colours, some of which are prismatic. Thus with the aid of

Time, and of what Time brings, has the stripling Diogenes
Teufelsdröckh waxed into manly stature; and into so questionable an aspect, that we ask with new eagerness How he
specially came by it, and regret anew that there is no more
explicit answer. Certain of the intelligible and partially significant fragments, which are few in number, shall be extracted
from that Limbo of a Paperbag, and presented with the usual
preparation.

As if, in the Bag *Scorpio*, Teufelsdröckh had not already
expectorated his antipedagogic spleen; as if, from the name
Sagittarius, he had thought himself called upon to shoot arrows,
we here again fall in with such matter as this: "The University
where I was educated still stands vivid enough in my remembrance, and I know its name well; which name, however, I
from tenderness to existing interests and persons, shall in no
wise divulge. It is my painful duty to say that, out of England
and Spain, ours was the worst of all hitherto discovered
Universities. This is indeed a time when right Education is, as
nearly as may be, impossible: however, in degrees of wrong-
ness there is no limit; nay, I can conceive a worse system than
that of the Nameless itself; as poisoned victual may be worse
than absolute hunger.

"It is written, When the blind lead the blind, both shall fall
into the ditch: wherefore, in such circumstances, may it not
sometimes be safer, if both leader and led simply—sit still? Had
you, any where in Crim Tartary, walled in a square enclosure;
furnished it with a small, ill-chosen Library; and then turned
loose into it eleven hundred Christian striplings, to tumble
about as they listed, from three to seven years; certain persons,
under the title of Professors, being stationed at the gates, to
declare aloud that it was a University, and exact considerable
admission-fees,—you had, not indeed in mechanical structure,
yet in spirit and result, some imperfect resemblance of our
High Seminary. I say, imperfect; for if our mechanical structure was quite other, so neither was our result altogether the
same: unhappily, we were not in Crim Tartary, but in a
corrupt European city, full of smoke and sin; moreover, in the
middle of a Public, which, without far costlier apparatus, than
that of the Square Enclosure, and Declaration aloud, you could
not be sure of gulling.

"Gullible, however, by fit apparatus, all Publics are; and gulled, with the most surprising profit. Towards any thing like a *Statistics of Imposture*, indeed, little as yet has been done: with a strange indifference, our Economists, nigh buried under Tables for minor Branches of Industry, have altogether overlooked the grand all-overtopping Hypocrisy Branch; as if our whole arts of Puffery, of Quackery, Priestcraft, Kingcraft, and the innumerable other crafts and mysteries of that genus, had not ranked in Productive Industry at all! Can any one, for example, so much as say, What monies, in Literature and Shoeblacking, are realised by actual Instruction and actual jet Polish; what by fictitious-persuasive Proclamation of such; specifying, in distinct items, the distributions, circulations, disbursements, incomings of said monies, with the smallest approach to accuracy? But to ask, How far, in all the several infinitely complected departments of social business, in government, education, in manual, commercial, intellectual fabrication of every sort, man's Want is supplied by true Ware; how far by the mere Appearance of true Ware:—in other words, To what extent, by what methods, with what effects, in various times and countries, Deception takes the place and wages of Performance: here truly is an Inquiry big with results for the future time, but to which hitherto only the vaguest answer can be given. If for the present, in our Europe, we estimate the ratio of Ware to Appearance of Ware so high even as at One to a Hundred (which, considering the Wages of a Pope, Russian Autocrat, or English Game-Preserver, is probably not far from the mark),—what almost prodigious saving may there not be anticipated, as the *Statistics of Imposture* advances, and so the manufacturing of Shams (that of Realities rising into clearer and clearer distinction therefrom) gradually declines, and at length becomes all but wholly unnecessary!

"This for the coming golden ages. What I had to remark, for the present brazen one, is, that in several provinces, as in Education, Polity, Religion, where so much is wanted and indispensable, and so little can as yet be furnished, probably Imposture is of sanative, anodyne nature, and man's Gullibility not his worst blessing. Suppose your sinews of war quite broken; I mean your military chest insolvent, forage all but exhausted; and that the whole army is about to mutiny, disband, and cut your and each other's throat,—then were it not well could you, as if by miracle, pay them in any sort of fairy-money, feed them on coagulated water, or mere imagination of meat; whereby, till the real supply came up, they might be kept together, and quiet? Such perhaps was the aim of Nature, who does nothing without aim, in furnishing her favourite, Man, with this his so omni-potent or rather omni-patient Talent of being Gulled.

"How beautifully it works, with a little mechanism; nay, almost makes mechanism for itself! These Professors in the Nameless lived with ease, with safety, by a mere Reputation, constructed in past times, and then too with no great effort, by quite another class of persons. Which Reputation, like a strong, brisk-going, undershot-wheel, sunk into the general current, bade fair, with only a little annual repainting on their part, to hold long together, and of its own accord, assiduously grind for them. Happy that it was so for the Millers! They themselves needed not to work; their attempts at working, at what they called Educating, now when I look back on it, fill me with a certain mute admiration.

"Besides all this, we boasted ourselves a Rational University; in the highest degree, hostile to Mysticism: thus was the young vacant mind furnished with much talk about Progress of the Species, Dark Ages, Prejudice, and the like; so that all were quickly enough blown out into a state of windy argumentativeness; whereby the better sort must soon end in sick, impotent Scepticism; the worser sort explode (*crepiren*) in finished Self-conceit, and to all spiritual intents become dead.—But this too is portion of mankind's lot. If our era is the Era of Unbelief, why murmur under it; is there not a better coming, nay come? As in longdrawn Systole and longdrawn Diastole, must the period of Faith alternate with the period of Denial; must the vernal growth, the summer luxuriance of all Opinions, Spiritual Representations and Creations, be followed by, and again follow, the autumnal decay, the winter dissolution. For man lives in Time, has his whole earthly being, endeavour, and destiny shaped for him by Time: only in the transitory Time-Symbol is the ever-motionless Eternity we stand on made manifest. And yet, in such winter-seasons of Denial, it is for the nobler-minded perhaps a comparative misery to have been born, and to be awake, and work; and for the duller a felicity, if like hibernating animals, safe-lodged in some Salamanca University, or Sybaris City, or other superstitious or voluptuous Castle of Indolence, they can slumber through, in stupid dreams, and only awaken when the loud-roaring hailstorms have all done their work, and to our prayers and martyrdoms the new Spring has been vouchsafed."

That in the environment, here mysteriously enough shadowed forth, Teufelsdröckh must have felt ill at ease, cannot be doubtful. "The hungry young," he says, "looked up to their spiritual Nurses; and, for food, were bidden eat the east wind. What vain jargon of controversial Metaphysic, Etymology, and mechanical Manipulation, falsely named Science, was current there, I indeed learned, better perhaps than the most. Among eleven hundred Christian youths, there will not be wanting some eleven eager to learn. By collision with such, a certain warmth, a certain polish was communicated; by instinct and happy accident, I took less to rioting (*renommiren*), than to thinking and reading, which latter also I was free to do. Nay from the chaos of that Library, I succeeded in fishing up more books perhaps than had been known to the very keepers thereof. The foundation of a Literary Life was hereby laid: I learned, on my own strength, to read fluently in almost all cultivated languages, on almost all subjects, and sciences; farther, as man is ever the prime object to man, already it was my favourite employment to read character in speculation, and from the Writing to construe the Writer. A certain groundplan of Human Nature and Life began to fashion itself in me; wondrous enough, now when I look back on it; for my whole Universe, physical and spiritual, was as yet a Machine! However, such a conscious, recognised groundplan, the truest I had, *was* beginning to be there, and by additional experiments, might be corrected and indefinitely extended."

Thus from poverty does the strong educe nobler wealth; thus in the destitution of the wild desert, does our young Ishmael acquire for himself the highest of all possessions, that of Self-help. Nevertheless a desert this was, waste, and howling with savage monsters. Teufelsdröckh gives us long details of his "fever-paroxysms of Doubt;" his Inquiries concerning Miracles, and the Evidences of religious Faith; and how "in the silent night-watches, still darker in his heart than over sky and earth, he has cast himself before the All-seeing, and with audible prayers, cried vehemently for Light, for deliverance from Death and the Grave. Not till after long years, and unspeakable agonies, did the believing heart surrender; sink into spell-bound sleep, under the nightmare, Unbelief; and, in this hag-ridden dream, mistake God's fair living world for a pallid, vacant Hades and extinct Pandemonium. But through such Purgatory pain," continues he, "it is appointed us to pass: first must the dead Letter of Religion own itself dead, and drop piecemeal into dust, if the living Spirit of Religion, freed from this its charnel-house, is to arise on us, newborn of Heaven, and with new healing under its wings."

To which Purgatory pains, seemingly severe enough, if we add a liberal measure of Earthly distresses, want of practical guidance, want of sympathy, want of money, want of hope; and all this in the fervid season of youth, so exaggerated in imagining, so boundless in desires, yet here so poor in means,—do we not see a strong incipient spirit oppressed and overloaded from without and from within; the fire of genius struggling up among fuel-wood of the greenest, and as yet with more of bitter vapour than of clear flame?

From various fragments of Letters and other documentary scraps, it is to be inferred that Teufelsdröckh, isolated, shy, retiring as he was, had not altogether escaped notice: certain established men are aware of his existence; and, if stretching out no helpful hand, have at least their eyes on him. He appears, though in dreary enough humour, to be addressing himself to the Profession of Law;—whereof, indeed, the world has since seen him a public graduate. But omitting these broken, unsatisfactory thrums of Economical relation, let us present rather the following small thread of Moral relation; and therewith, the reader for himself weaving it in at the right place, conclude our dim arras-picture of these University years.

"Here also it was that I formed acquaintance with Herr Towgood, or, as it is perhaps better written, Herr Toughgut; a young person of quality (*von Adel*), from the interior parts of England. He stood connected, by blood and hospitality, with the Counts von Zähdarm,* in this quarter of Germany; to which noble Family I likewise was, by his means, with all friendliness, brought near. Towgood had a fair talent, unspeakably ill-cultivated; with considerable humour of character: and, bating his total ignorance, for he knew nothing except Boxing and a little Grammar, shewed less of that aristocratic impassivity and silent fury than for most part belongs to Travellers of his nation. To him I owe my first practical knowledge of the English and their ways; perhaps also something of the partiality with which I have ever since regarded that singular people. Towgood was not without an eye, could he have come at any light. Invited doubtless by the presence of the Zähdarm Family, he had travelled hither, in the almost frantic hope of perfecting his studies; he, whose studies had been as yet those of infancy, hither to a University where so much as the notion of perfection, not to say the effort after it, no longer existed! Often we would condole over the hard destiny of the Young in this era: how, after all our toil, we were to be turned out into the world, with beards on our chins, indeed, but with few other attributes of manhood; no existing thing that we were trained to Act on, nothing that we could so much as Believe. 'How has our Head on the outside a polished Hat,' would Towgood exclaim, 'and in the inside Vacancy, or a froth of Vocables and Attorney Logic! At a small cost men are educated to make leather into shoes; but, at a great cost, what am I educated to make? By Heaven, Brother! what I have already eaten and worn, as I came thus far, would endow a considerable Hospital of Incurables.'—'Man, indeed,' I would answer, 'has a Digestive faculty, which must be kept working, were it even partly by stealth. But as for our Miseducation, make not bad worse; waste not the time yet ours, in trampling on thistles because they have yielded us no figs. *Frisch zu, Bruder!* * Here are Books, and we have brains to read them; here is a whole Earth and a whole Heaven and we have eyes to look on them: *Frisch zu!*'

"Often also our talk was gay; not without brilliancy, and even fire. We looked out on Life, with its strange scaffolding, where all at once harlequins dance, and men are beheaded and quartered: motley, not unterrific was the aspect; but we looked on it like brave youths. For myself, these were perhaps my most genial hours. Towards this young warmhearted, strong-headed and wrongheaded Herr Towgood, I was even near experiencing the now obsolete sentiment of Friendship. Yes, foolish Heathen that I was, I felt that, under certain conditions, I could have loved this man, and taken him to my bosom, and been his brother once and always. By degrees, however, I understood the new time, and its wants. If man's *Soul* is indeed, as in the Finnish Language, and Utilitarian Philosophy, a kind of *Stomach* ,* what else is the true meaning of Spiritual Union but an Eating together? Thus we, instead of Friends, are Dinner-guests; and here as elsewhere have cast away chimeras."

So ends, abruptly as is usual, and enigmatically, this little incipient romance. What henceforth becomes of the brave Herr Towgood, or Toughgut? He has dived under, in the Autobiographical Chaos, and swims we see not where. Does any reader "in the interior parts of England" know of such a man?

CHAPTER 4
GETTING UNDER WAY

"THUS nevertheless," writes our Autobiographer, apparently as quitting College, "was there realised Somewhat; namely, I, Diogenes Teufelsdröckh: a visible Temporary Figure (*Zeit-bild*), occupying some cubic feet of Space, and containing within it Forces both physical and spiritual; hopes, passions, thoughts; the whole wondrous furniture, in more or less perfection, belonging to that mystery, a Man. Capabilities there were in me to give battle, in some small degree, against the great Empire of Darkness: Does not the very Ditcher and Delver, with his spade, extinguish many a thistle and puddle; and so leave a little Order, where he found the opposite? Nay your very Daymoth has capabilities in this kind; and ever organises something (into its own Body, if no otherwise), which was before Inorganic; and of r ate dead air makes living music, though only of the faintest, by humming.

"How much more, one whose capabilities are spiritual; who has learned or begun learning the grand thaumaturgic art of Thought! Thaumaturgic I name it; for hitherto all Miracles have been wrought thereby, and henceforth innumerable will be wrought; whereof we, even in these days, witness some. Of the Poet's and Prophet's inspired Message, and how it makes and unmakes whole worlds, I shall forbear mention: but cannot the dullest hear Steam-engines clanking around him? Has he not seen the Scottish Brassmith's IDEA* (and this but a mechanical one) travelling on fire-wings round the Cape, and across two Oceans; and stronger than any other Enchanter's Familiar, on all hands unweariedly fetching and carrying: at home, not only weaving Cloth; but rapidly enough overturn-ing the whole old system of Society; and, for Feudalism and Preservation of the Game, preparing us, by indirect but sure methods, Industrialism and the Government of the Wisest. Truly a Thinking Man is the worst enemy the Prince of Darkness can have; every time such a one announces himself, I doubt not, there runs a shudder through the Nether Empire;

and new Emissaries are trained, with new tactics, to, if possible, entrap him, and hoodwink and handcuff him.

"With such high vocation had I too, as denizen of the Universe, been called. Unhappy it is, however, that though born to the amplest Sovereignty, in this way, with no less than sovereign right of Peace and War against the Time-Prince (*Zeitfürst*), or Devil, and all his Dominions, your coronation ceremony costs such trouble, your sceptre is so difficult to get at, or even to get eye on!"

By which last wiredrawn similitude, does Teufelsdröckh mean no more than that young men find obstacles in what we call "getting under way?" "Not what I Have," continues he, "but what I Do is my Kingdom. To each is given a certain inward Talent, a certain outward Environment of Fortune; to each, by wisest combination of these two, a certain maximum of Capability. But the hardest problem were ever this first: To find by study of yourself, and of the ground you stand on, what your combined inward and outward Capability specially is. For, alas, our young soul is all budding with Capabilities, and we see not yet which is the main and true one. Always too the new man is in a new time, under new conditions; his course can be the *facsimile* of no prior one, but is by its nature original. And then how seldom will the outward Capability fit the inward: though talented wonderfully enough, we are poor, unfriended, dyspeptical, bashful; nay what is worse than all, we are foolish. Thus, in a whole imbroglio of Capabilities, we go stupidly groping about, to grope which is ours, and often clutch the wrong one: in this mad work, must several years of our small term be spent, till the purblind Youth, by practice, acquire notions of distance, and become a seeing Man. Nay, many so spend their whole term, and in ever new expectation, ever new disappointment, shift from enterprise to enterprise, and from side to side; till at length, as exasperated striplings of threescore and ten, they shift into their last enterprise, that of getting buried.

"Such, since the most of us are too ophthalmic, would be the general fate; were it not that one thing saves us: our Hunger. For on this ground, as the prompt nature of Hunger is well known, must a prompt choice be made: hence have we, with

wise foresight, Indentures and Apprenticeships for our irrational young; whereby, in due season, the vague universality
of a Man shall find himself ready-moulded into a specific
Craftsman; and so thenceforth work, with much or with little
waste of Capability, as it may be; yet not with the worst waste,
that of time. Nay even in matters spiritual, since the spiritual
artist too is born blind, and does not, like certain other
creatures, receive sight in nine days, but far later, sometimes
never,—is it not well that there should be what we call
Professions, or Bread-studies (*Brod-zwecke*), preappointed us?
Here, circling like the gin-horse,* for whom partial or total
blindness is no evil, the Bread-artist can travel contentedly
round and round, still fancying that it is forward and forward,
and realise much: for himself victual; for the world an additional horse's power in the grand corn-mill or hemp-mill of
Economic Society. For me too had such a leading-string been
provided; only that it proved a neck-halter, and had nigh
throttled me, till I broke it off. Then, in the words of Ancient
Pistol,* did the World generally become mine oyster, which I,
by strength or cunning, was to open, as I would and could.
Almost had I deceased (*fast wär ich umgekommen*), so obstinately
did it continue shut."

We see here, significantly foreshadowed, the spirit of much
that was to befall our Autobiographer; the historical embodyment of which, as it painfully takes shape in his Life, lies
scattered, in dim disastrous details, through this Bag *Pisces,* and
those that follow. A young man of high talent, and high
though still temper, like a young mettled colt, "breaks off his
neck-halter," and bounds forth, from his peculiar manger, into
the wide world; which, alas, he finds all rigourously fenced in.
Richest clover-fields tempt his eye; but to him they are
forbidden pasture: either pining in progressive starvation, he
must stand; or, in mad exasperation, must rush to and fro,
leaping against sheer stone-walls, which he cannot leap over,
which only lacerate and lame him; till at last, after thousand
attempts and endurances, he, as if by miracle, clears his way;
not indeed into luxuriant and luxurious clover, yet into a
certain bosky wilderness where existence is still possible, and
Freedom though waited on by Scarcity is not without sweet-

ness. In a word, Teufelsdröckh having thrown up his legal Profession, finds himself without landmark of outward guidance; whereby his previous want of decided Belief, or inward guidance, is frightfully aggravated. Necessity urges him on; Time will not stop, neither can he, a Son of Time; wild passions without solacement, wild faculties without employment, ever vex and agitate him. He too must enact that stern Monodrama, *No Object and no Rest;* must front its successive destinies, work through to its catastrophe, and deduce therefrom what moral he can.

Yet let us be just to him, let us admit that his "neck-halter" sat nowise easy on him; that he was in some degree forced to break it off. If we look at the young man's civic position, in this Nameless Capital, as he emerges from its Nameless University, we can discern well that it was far from enviable. His first Law Examination he has come through triumphantly; and can even boast that the *Examen Rigorosum* need not have frightened him: but though he is hereby "an *Auscultator* * of respectability," what avails it? There is next to no employment to be had. Neither, for a youth without connexions is the process of Expectation very hopeful in itself; nor for one of his disposition much cheered from without. "My fellow Auscultators," he says, "were Auscultators: they dressed, and digested, and talked articulate words; other vitality shewed they almost none. Small speculation in those eyes, that they did glare withal! Sense neither for the high nor for the deep, nor for aught human or divine, save only for the faintest scent of coming Preferment." In which words, indicating a total estrangement on the part of Teufelsdröckh, may there not also lurk traces of a bitterness as from wounded vanity? Doubtless these prosaic Auscultators may have sniffed at him, with his strange ways; and tried to hate, and, what was much more impossible, to despise him. Friendly communion, in any case, there could not be: already has the young Teufelsdröckh left the other young geese; and swims apart, though as yet uncertain whether he himself is cygnet or gosling.

Perhaps too what little employment he had was performed ill, at best unpleasantly. "Great practical method and expertness" he may brag of; but is there not also great practical pride, though deep-hidden, only the deeper-seated? So shy a man can never have been popular. We figure to ourselves, how in those days he may have played strange freaks with his Independence, and so forth: do not his own words betoken as much? "Like a very young person, I imagined it was with Work alone, and not also with Folly and Sin, in myself and others, that I had been appointed to struggle." Be this as it may, his progress from the passive Auscultatorship, towards any active Assessorship, is evidently of the slowest. By degrees, those same established men, once partially inclined to patronise him, seem to withdraw their countenance, and give him up as "a man of genius;" against which procedure he, in these Papers loudly protests. "As if," says he, "the higher did not presuppose the lower; as if he who can fly into heaven, could not also walk post if he resolved on it! But the world is an old woman, and mistakes any gilt farthing for a gold coin; whereby being often cheated she will thenceforth trust nothing but the common copper."

How our winged sky-messenger, unaccepted as a terrestrial runner, contrived, in the meanwhile, to keep himself from flying skyward without return, is not too clear from these Documents. Good old Gretchen seems to have vanished from the scene, perhaps from the Earth; other Horn of Plenty, or even of Parsimony, no where flows for him; so that "the prompt nature of Hunger being well known," we are not without our anxiety. From private Tuition, in never so many languages and sciences, the aid derivable is small; neither, to use his own words, "does the young Adventurer hitherto suspect in himself any literary gift; but at best earns bread-and-water wages, by his wide faculty of Translation. Nevertheless," continues he, "that I subsisted is clear, for you find me even now alive." Which fact, however, except upon the principle of our true-hearted, kind old Proverb, that "there is ever Life for the Living,"* we must profess ourselves unable to explain.

Certain Landlords' Bills, and other economic Documents, bearing the mark of Settlement, indicate that he was not without money; but, like an independent Hearth-holder, if not House-holder, paid his way. Here also occur, among many others, two little mutilated Notes, which perhaps throw light on his condition. The first has now no date, or writer's name, but a huge Blot; and runs to this effect: "The (*Inkblot*), tied down by previous promise, cannot, except by best wishes, forward the Herr Teufelsdröckh's views on the Assessorship in question; and sees himself under the cruel necessity of forbearing for the present, what were otherwise his duty and joy, to assist in opening the career for a man of genius, on whom far higher triumphs are yet waiting." The other is on gilt paper; and interests us like a sort of epistolary mummy now dead, yet which once lived and beneficently worked. We give it in the original: "*Herr Teufelsdröckh wird von der Frau Gräfinn, auf Donnerstag, zum* ÆSTHETISCHEN THEE, *schönstens eingeladen.*" *

Thus, in answer to a cry for solid pudding, whereof there is the most urgent need, comes, epigrammatically enough, the invitation to a wash of quite fluid *Æsthetic Tea!* How Teufelsdröckh, now at actual handgrips with Destiny herself, may have comported himself among these Musical and Literary Dilettanti of both sexes, like a hungry lion invited to a feast of chickenweed, we can only conjecture. Perhaps in expressive silence, and abstinence: otherwise if the lion, in such case, is to feast at all, it cannot be on the chickenweed, but only on the chickens. For the rest, as this Frau Gräfinn dates from the *Zähdarm House,* she can be no other than the Countess and mistress of the same; whose intellectual tendencies, and good will to Teufelsdröckh, whether on the footing of Herr Towgood, or on his own footing, are hereby manifest. That some sort of relation, indeed, continued, for a time, to connect our Autobiographer, though perhaps feebly enough, with this noble House, we have elsewhere express evidence. Doubtless, if he expected patronage, it was in vain; enough for him if he here obtained occasional glimpses of the great world, from which we at one time fancied him to have been always excluded. "The Zähdarms," says he, "lived in the soft, sumptuous garniture of Aristocracy; whereto Literature and Art, attracted and attached from without, must serve as the handsomest fringing. It was to the *Gnädigen Frau* (her Ladyship) that this latter improvement was due: assiduously she gathered, dexterously she fitted on, what fringing was to be had; lace or cobweb, as the place yielded." Was Teufelsdröckh also a fringe, of lace or cobweb; or promising to be such? "With His *Excellenz* (the Count)," continues he, "I have more than once had the honour to converse; chiefly on general affairs, and the aspect of the world, which he, though now past middle life, viewed in no unfavourable light; finding indeed, except the Outrooting of Journalism (*die auszurottende Journalistik*), little to desiderate therein. On some points, as his *Excellenz* was not uncholeric, I found it more pleasant to keep silence. Besides, his occupation being that of Owning Land, there might be faculties enough, which, as superfluous for such use, were little developed in him."

That to Teufelsdröckh the aspect of the world was nowise so faultless, and many things, besides "the Outrooting of Journalism," might have seemed improvements, we can readily conjecture. With nothing but a barren Auscultatorship from without, and so many mutinous thoughts and wishes from within, his position was no easy one. "The Universe," he says, "was as a mighty Sphinx-riddle, which I knew so little of, yet must rede, or be devoured. In red streaks of unspeakable grandeur, yet also in the blackness of darkness, was Life, to my too-unfurnished Thought, unfolding itself. A strange contradiction lay in me; and I as yet knew not the solution of it; knew not that spiritual music can spring only from discords set in unison;* that but for Evil there were no Good, as Victory is only possible by Battle."

"I have heard affirmed (surely in jest)," observes he else-where, "by not unphilanthropic persons, that it were a real increase of human happiness, could all young men from the age of nineteen be covered under barrels, or rendered otherwise invisible; and there left to follow their lawful studies and callings, till they emerged, sadder and wiser, at the age of twenty-five. With which suggestion, at least as considered in the light of a practical scheme, I need scarcely say that I nowise coincide. Nevertheless it is plausibly urged that, as young ladies (*Mädchen*) are, to mankind, precisely the most delightful in those years; so young gentlemen (*Bübchen*)* do then attain their maximum of detestability. Such gawks (*Gecken*) are they, and foolish peacocks, and yet with such a vulturous hunger for self-indulgence; so obstinate, obstreperous, vainglorious; in all senses, so froward and so forward. No mortal's endeavour or attainment will in the smallest content the as yet unendeavouring, unattaining young gentleman; but he could make it all infinitely better, were it worthy of him. Life every where is the most manageable matter, simple as a question in the Rule of Three: multiply your second and third term together, divide the product by the first, and your quotient will be the answer,—which you are but an ass if you cannot come at. The booby has not yet found out, by any trial, that, do what one will, there is ever a cursed fraction, oftenest a decimal repeater, and no net integer quotient so much as to be thought of."

In which passage, does there not lie an implied confession that Teufelsdröckh himself, besides his outward obstructions, had an inward, still greater, to contend with; namely, a certain temporary, youthful, yet still afflictive derangement of head? Alas! on the former side alone, his case was hard enough. "It continues ever true," says he, "that Saturn, or Chronos, or what we call TIME, devours all his Children: only by incessant Running, by incessant Working, may you (for some threescore and ten years) escape him; and you too he devours at last. Can any Sovereign, or Holy Alliance of Sovereigns,* bid Time stand still; even in thought, shake themselves free of Time? Our whole terrestrial being is based on Time, and built of Time; it is wholly a Movement, a Time-impulse; Time is the author of it, the material of it. Hence also our Whole Duty, which is to Move, to Work,—in the right direction. Are not our Bodies and our Souls in continual movement, whether we will or not; in a continual Waste, requiring a continual Repair? Utmost satisfaction of our whole outward and inward Wants were but satisfaction for a space of Time; thus whatso we have done, is done, and for us annihilated, and ever must we go and do anew. O Time-Spirit, how hast thou environed and imprisoned us, and sunk us so deep in thy troublous dim Time-Element; that, only in lucid moments, can so much as glimpses of our upper Azure Home be revealed to us! Me, however, as a Son of Time, unhappier than some others, was Time threatening to eat quite prematurely; for strive as I might, there was no good Running, so obstructed was the path, so gyved were the feet." That is to say, we presume, speaking in the dialect of this lower world, that Teufelsdröckh's whole duty and necessity was, like other men's, "to work,—in the right direction," and that no work was to be had; whereby he became wretched enough. As was natural: with haggard Scarcity threatening him in the distance; and so vehement a soul languishing in restless inaction, and forced thereby, like Sir Hudibras's sword by rust,

> To eat into itself, for lack
> Of something else to hew and hack!*

But on the whole, that same "excellent Passivity," as it has all along done, is here again vigorously flourishing; in which circumstance, may we not trace the beginnings of much that now characterises our Professor; and perhaps, in faint rudiments, the origin of the Clothes-Philosophy itself? Already the attitude he has assumed towards the World is too defensive; not, as would have been desirable, a bold attitude of attack. "So far hitherto," he says, "as I had mingled with mankind, I was notable, if for any thing, for a certain stillness of manner, which, as my friends often rebukingly declared, did but ill express the keen ardour of my feelings. I, in truth, regarded men with an excess both of love and of fear. The mystery of a Person, indeed, is ever divine, to him that has a sense for the Godlike. Often, notwithstanding, was I blamed, and by half-strangers hated, for my so-called Hardness (Härte), my Indifferentism towards men; and the seemingly ironic tone I had adopted, as my favourite dialect in conversation. Alas, the panoply of Sarcasm was but as a buckram-case, wherein I had striven to envelope myself; that so my own poor Person might live safe there; and in all friendliness, being no longer exasperated by wounds. Sarcasm I now see to be, in general, the language of the Devil; for which reason I have, long since, as good as renounced it. But how many individuals did I, in those days, provoke into some degree of hostility thereby! An ironic man, with his sly stillness, and ambuscading ways, more especially an ironic young man, from whom it is least expected, may be viewed as a pest to society. Have we not seen persons of weight and name, coming forward, with gentlest indifference, to tread such a one out of sight, as an insignificancy and worm, start ceiling-high (*balkenhoch*), and thence fall shattered and supine, to be borne home on shutters, not without indignation, when he proved electric and a torpedo!"

Alas, how can a man with this devilishness of temper make way for himself in Life; where the first problem, as Teufelsdröckh too admits, is "to unite yourself with some one and with somewhat (*sich anzuschliessen*)?" Division, not union, is written on most part of his procedure. Let us add too that, in no great length of time, the only important connexion he had ever succeeded in forming, his connexion with the Zähdarm Family, seems to have been paralysed, for all practical uses, by the death of the "not uncholeric" old Count. This fact stands recorded, quite incidentally, in a certain *Discourse on Epitaphs,* huddled into the present Bag, among so much else; of which Essay the learning and curious penetration are more to be approved of than the spirit. His grand principle is, that lapidary inscriptions, of what sort soever, should be Historical rather than Lyrical. "By request of that worthy Nobleman's survivors," says he, "I undertook to compose his Epitaph; and not unmindful of my own rules, produced the following; which, however, for an alleged defect of Latinity, a defect never yet fully visible to myself, still remains unengraven;"—wherein, we may predict, there is more than the Latinity that will surprise an English reader:

HIC JACET

PHILIPPUS ZAEHDARM, COGNOMINE MAGNUS,

ZAEHDARMI COMES,

EX IMPERII CONCILIO,

VELLERIS AUREI, PERISCELIDIS, NECNON VULTURIS NIGRI EQUES.

QUI DUM SUB LUNA AGEBAT,

QUINQUIES MILLE PERDICES

PLUMBO CONFECIT:

VARII CIBI

CENTUMPONDIA MILLIES CENTENA MILLIA,
PER SE, PERQUE SERVOS QUADRUPEDES BIPEDESVE,
HAUD SINE TUMULTU DEVOLVENS,

IN STERCUS

PALAM CONVERTIT.

NUNC A LABORE REQUIESCENTEM
OPERA SEQUUNTUR.

SI MONUMENTUM QUÆRIS
FIMETUM ADSPICE.

PRIMUM IN ORBE DEJECIT [*sub dato*]; POSTREMUM
[*sub dato*].*

*   *   *

CHAPTER 5

ROMANCE

"FOR long years," writes Teufelsdröckh, "had the poor Hebrew, in this Egypt of an Auscultatorship, painfully toiled, baking bricks without stubble, before ever the question once struck him with entire force: For what?—*Beym Himmel!* For Food and Warmth! And are Food and Warmth nowhere else, in the whole wide Universe, discoverable?—Come of it what might, I resolved to try."

Thus then are we to see him in a new independent capacity, though perhaps far from an improved one. Teufelsdröckh is now a man without Profession. Quitting the common Fleet of herring-busses* and whalers, where indeed his leeward, laggard condition was painful enough, he desperately steers off, on a course of his own, by sextant and compass of his own. Unhappy Teufelsdröckh! Though neither Fleet, nor Traffic, nor Commodores pleased thee, still was it not *a Fleet,* sailing in prescribed track, for fixed objects; above all, in combination, wherein, by mutual guidance, by all manner of loans and borrowings, each could manifoldly aid the other? How wilt thou sail in unknown seas; and for thyself find that shorter, Northwest Passage to thy fair Spice-country of a Nowhere?— A solitary rover, on such a voyage, with such nautical tactics, will meet with adventures. Nay, as we forthwith discover, a certain Calypso-Island* detains him at the very outset; and as it were falsifies and oversets his whole reckoning.

"If in youth," writes he once, "the Universe is majestically unveiling, and everywhere Heaven revealing itself on Earth, nowhere to the Young Man does this Heaven on Earth so immediately reveal itself as in the Young Maiden. Strangely enough, in this strange life of ours, it has been so appointed. On the whole, as I have often said, a Person (*Persönlichkeit*) is ever holy to us; a certain orthodox Anthropomorphism connects my *Me* with all *Thees* in bonds of Love: but it is in this approximation of the Like and Unlike, that such heavenly attraction, as between Negative and Positive, first burns out into a flame. Is the pitifullest mortal Person, think you, indifferent to us? Is it not rather our heartfelt wish to be made one with him; to unite him to us, by gratitude, by admiration, even by fear; or failing all these, unite ourselves to him? But how much more, in this case of the Like-Unlike! Here is conceded us the higher mystic possibility of such a union, the highest in our Earth; thus, in the conducting medium of Fantasy, flames forth that *fire*-development of the universal Spiritual Electricity, which, as unfolded between man and woman, we first emphatically denominate LOVE.

"In every well-conditioned stripling, as I conjecture, there already blooms a certain prospective Paradise, cheered by some fairest Eve; nor in the stately vistas, and flowerage and foliage, of that Garden is a Tree of Knowledge, beautiful and awful in the midst thereof, wanting. Perhaps too the whole is but the lovelier if Cherubim and a flaming sword divide it from all footsteps of men; and grant him, the imaginative stripling, only the view, not the entrance. Happy season of virtuous youth, when Shame is still an impassable celestial barrier; and the sacred air-cities of Hope have not shrunk into the mean clay-hamlets of Reality; and man, by his nature, is yet infinite and free!

"As for our young Forlorn," continues Teufelsdröckh, evidently meaning himself, "in his secluded way of life, and with his glowing Fantasy, the more fiery that it burnt under cover, as in a reverberating furnace, his feeling towards the Queens of this Earth was, and indeed is, altogether unspeakable. A visible Divinity dwelt in them; to our young Friend all women were holy, were heavenly. As yet he but saw them flitting past, in their many-coloured angel-plumage; or hovering mute and inaccessible on the outskirts of Æsthetic Tea: all of air they were, all Soul and Form; so lovely, like mysterious priestesses, in whose hand was the invisible Jacob's-ladder, whereby man might mount into very Heaven. That he, our poor Friend, should ever win for himself one of these Gracefuls (*Holden*)—*Ach Gott!* how could he hope it; should he not have died under it? There was a certain delirious vertigo in the thought.

"Thus was the young man, if all sceptical of Demons and

Angels, such as the vulgar had once believed in, nevertheless not unvisited by hosts of true Skyborn, who visibly and audibly hovered round him whereso he went; and they had that religious worship in his thought, though as yet it was by their mere earthly and trivial name that he named them. But now, if on a soul so circumstanced, some actual Air-maiden, incorporated into tangibility and reality, should cast any electric glance of kind eyes, saying thereby, 'Thou too mayest love and be loved;' and so kindle him,—good Heaven, what a volcanic, earthquake-bringing, all-consuming fire were probably kindled!"

Such a fire, it afterwards appears, did actually burst forth, with explosions more or less Vesuvian, in the inner man of Herr Diogenes; as indeed how could it fail? A nature, which, in his own figurative style, we might say, had now not a little carbonised tinder, of Irritability; with so much nitre of latent Passion, and sulphurous Humour enough; the whole lying in such hot neighbourhood, close by "a reverberating furnace of Fantasy:" have we not here the components of driest Gunpowder, ready, on occasion of the smallest spark, to blaze up? Neither, in this our Life-element, are sparks anywhere wanting. Without doubt, some Angel, whereof so many hovered round, must one day, leaving "the outskirts of Æsthetic Tea," flit nigher; and, by electric Promethean glance, kindle no despicable firework. Happy, if it indeed proved a Firework, and flamed off rocket-wise, in successive beautiful bursts of splendour, each growing naturally from the other, through the several stages of a happy Youthful Love; till the whole were safely burnt out; and the young soul relieved, with little damage! Happy, if it did not rather prove a Conflagration and mad Explosion; painfully lacerating the heart itself; nay perhaps bursting the heart in pieces (which were Death); or at best, bursting the thin walls of your "reverberating furnace," so that it rage thenceforth all unchecked among the contiguous combustibles (which were Madness): till of the so fair and manifold internal world of our Diogenes, there remained Nothing, or only the "Crater of an extinct volcano!"

From multifarious Documents in this Bag *Capricornus,* and in the adjacent ones on both sides thereof, it becomes manifest that our Philosopher, as stoical and cynical as he now looks, was heartily and even franticly in Love: here therefore may our old doubts whether his heart were of stone or of flesh, give way. He loved once; not wisely but too well. And once only: for as your Congreve needs a new case or wrappage for every new rocket, so each human heart can properly exhibit but one Love, if even one; the "First Love which is infinite" can be followed by no second like unto it. In more recent years, accordingly, the Editor of these Sheets was led to regard Teufelsdröckh as a man not only who would never wed, but who would never even flirt; whom the grand-climacteric itself, and *St. Martin's Summer** of incipient Dotage, would crown with no new myrtle garland. To the Professor, women are henceforth Pieces of Art; of Celestial Art, indeed; which celestial pieces he glories to survey in galleries, but has lost thought of purchasing.

Psychological readers are not without curiosity to see how Teufelsdröckh, in this for him unexampled predicament, de-means himself; with what specialties of successive configu-ration, splendour and colour, his Firework blazes off. Small, as usual, is the satisfaction that such can meet with here. From amid these confused masses of Eulogy and Elegy, with their mad Petrarchan and Werterean* ware lying madly scattered among all sorts of quite extraneous matter, not so much as the fair one's name can be deciphered. For, without doubt, the title *Blumine,* whereby she is here designated, and which means simply Goddess of Flowers, must be fictitious. Was her real name Flora, then? But what was her surname, or had she none? Of what station in Life was she; of what parentage, fortune, aspect? Specially, by what Pre-established Harmony of occur-rences did the Lover and the Loved meet one another in so wide a world; how did they behave in such meeting? To all which questions, not unessential in a Biographic work, mere Con-jecture must for most part return answer. "It was appointed," says your Philosopher, "that the high celestial orbit of Blumine should intersect the low sublunary one of our Forlorn; that he, looking in her empyrean eyes, should fancy the upper Sphere of Light was come down into this nether sphere of Shadows; and finding himself mistaken, make noise enough."

We seem to gather that she was young, hazel-eyed, beautiful, and some one's Cousin; highborn, and of high spirit; but unhappily dependent and insolvent; living, perhaps, on the not too gracious bounty of monied relatives. But how came "the Wanderer" into her circle? Was it by the humid vehicle of *Æsthetic Tea,* or by the arid one of mere Business? Was it on the hand of Herr Towgood; or of the Gnädige Frau, who, as an ornamental Artist, might sometimes like to promote flirtation, especially for young cynical Nondescripts? To all appearance, it was chiefly by Accident, and the grace of Nature.

"Thou fair Waldschloss," writes our Autobiographer, "what stranger ever saw thee, were it even an absolved Auscultator, officially bearing in his pocket the last *Relatio ex Actis** he would ever write; but must have paused to wonder! Noble Mansion! There stoodest thou, in deep Mountain Amphitheatre, on umbrageous lawns, in thy serene solitude; stately, massive, all of granite; glittering in the western Sunbeams, like a palace of El Dorado, overlaid with precious metal. Beautiful rose up, in wavy curvature, the slope of thy guardian Hills: of the greenest was their sward, embossed with its dark-brown frets of crag, or spotted by some spreading solitary Tree and its shadow. To the unconscious Wayfarer thou wert also as an Ammon's Temple, in the Libyan Waste; where, for joy and woe, the tablet of his Destiny lay written. Well might he pause and gaze; in that glance of his were prophecy and nameless forebodings."

But now let us conjecture that the so presentient Auscultator has handed in his *Relatio ex Actis;* been invited to a glass of Rhine-wine; and so, instead of returning dispirited and athirst to his dusty Town-home, is ushered into the Gardenhouse, where sit the choicest party of dames and cavaliers; if not engaged in Æsthetic Tea, yet in trustful evening conversation, and perhaps Musical Coffee, for we hear of "harps and pure voices making the stillness live." Scarcely, it would seem, is the Gardenhouse inferior in respectability to the noble Mansion itself. "Embowered amid rich foliage, rose-clusters, and the hues and odours of thousand flowers, here sat that brave company; in front, from the wide-opened doors, fair outlook over blossom and bush, over grove and velvet green, stretching, undulating onwards to the remote Mountain peaks: so bright, so mild, and everywhere the melody of birds and happy creatures: it was all as if man had stolen a shelter from the Sun in the bosom-vesture of Summer herself. How came it that the Wanderer advanced thither with such forecasting heart (*ahnungsvoll*),* by the side of his gay host? Did he feel that to these soft influences his hard bosom ought to be shut; that here, once more, Fate had it in view to try him; to mock him, and see whether there were Humour in him?

"Next moment he finds himself presented to the party; and specially by name to—Blumine! Peculiar among all dames and damosels, glanced Blumine, there in her modesty, like a star among earthly lights. Noblest maiden! whom he bent to, in body and in soul; yet scarcely dared look at, for the presence filled him with painful yet sweetest embarrassment.

"Blumine's was a name well known to him; far and wide, was the fair one heard of, for her gifts, her graces, her caprices: from all which vague colourings of Rumour, from the censures no less than from the praises, had our Friend painted for himself a certain imperious Queen of Hearts, and blooming, warm Earth-angel, much more enchanting than your mere white Heaven-angels of women, in whose placid veins circulates too little naphtha-fire. Herself also he had seen in public places; that light yet so stately form; those dark tresses, shading a face where smiles and sunlight played over earnest deeps: but all this he had seen only as a magic vision, for him inaccessible, almost without reality. Her sphere was too far from his; how should she ever think of him; O Heaven! How should they so much as once meet together? And now that Rose-goddess sits in the same circle with him; the light of *her* eyes has smiled on him, if he speak she will hear it! Nay, who knows, since the heavenly Sun looks into lowest valleys, but Blumine herself might have aforetime noted the so unnotable; perhaps, from his very gainsayers, as he had from hers, gathered wonder, gathered favour for him? Was the attraction, the agitation mutual, then; pole and pole trembling towards contact, when once brought into neighbourhood? Say rather, heart swelling in presence of the Queen of Hearts; like the Sea swelling when once near its Moon! With the Wanderer it was even so: as in heavenward gravitation, suddenly as at the touch of a Seraph's wand, his whole soul is roused from its deepest recesses; and all that was painful, and that was blissful there, dim images, vague feelings of a whole Past and a whole Future are heaving in unquiet eddies within him.

"Often, in far less agitating scenes, had our still Friend shrunk forcibly together; and shrouded up his tremours and flutterings, of what sort soever, in a safe cover of Silence, and perhaps of seeming Stolidity. How was it, then, that here, when trembling to the core of his heart, he did not sink into swoons, but rose into strength, into fearlessness and clearness? It was his guiding Genius (*Dämon*) that inspired him; he must go forth and meet his Destiny. Shew thyself now, whispered it, or be forever hid. Thus sometimes it is even when your anxiety becomes transcendental, that the soul first feels herself able to transcend it; that she rises above it, in fiery victory; and, borne on new-found wings of victory, moves so calmly, even because so rapidly, so irresistibly. Always must the Wanderer remember, with a certain satisfaction and surprise, how in this case he sat not silent, but struck adroitly into the stream of conversation; which thenceforth, to speak with an apparent not a real vanity, he may say that he continued to lead. Surely, in those hours, a certain inspiration was imparted him, such inspiration as is still possible in our late era. The self-secluded unfolds himself in noble thoughts, in free, glowing words; his soul is as one sea of light, the peculiar home of Truth and Intellect; wherein also Fantasy bodies forth form after form, radiant with all prismatic hues."

It appears, in this otherwise so happy meeting, there talked one "Philistine;" who even now, to the general weariness, was dominantly pouring forth Philistinism (*Philistriositäten*); little witting what hero was here entering to demolish him! We omit the series of Socratic, or rather Diogenic utterances, not unhappy in their way, whereby the monster, "persuaded into silence," seems soon after to have withdrawn for the night. "Of which dialectic marauder," writes our hero, "the discomfiture was visibly felt as a benefit by most: but what were all applauses to the glad smile, threatening every moment to become a laugh, wherewith Blumine herself repaid the victor? He ventured to address her, she answered with attention: nay, what if there were a slight tremour in that silver voice; what if the red glow of evening were hiding a transient blush!

"The conversation took a higher tone, one fine thought called forth another: it was one of those rare seasons, when the soul expands with full freedom, and man feels himself brought near to man. Gaily in light, graceful abandonment, the friendly talk played round that circle: for the burden was rolled from every heart; the barriers of Ceremony, which are indeed the laws of polite living, had melted as into vapour; and the poor claims of Me and Thee, no longer parted by rigid fences, now flowed softly into one another; and Life lay all harmonious, many-tinted, like some fair royal champaign, the sovereign and owner of which were Love only. Such music springs from kind hearts, in a kind environment of place and time. And yet as the light grew more aërial on the mountain tops, and the shadows fell longer over the valley, some faint tone of sadness may have breathed through the heart; and, in whispers more or less audible, reminded every one that as this bright day was drawing towards its close, so likewise must the Day of man's Existence decline into dusk and darkness; and with all its sick toilings, and joyful and mournful noises, sink in the still Eternity.

"To our Friend the hours seemed moments; holy was he and happy: the words from those sweetest lips came over him like dew on thirsty grass; all better feelings in his soul seemed to whisper: It is good for us to be here. At parting, the Blumine's hand was in his: in the balmy twilight, with the kind stars above them, he spoke something of meeting again, which was not contradicted; he pressed gently those small soft fingers, and it seemed as if they were not hastily, not angrily withdrawn."

Poor Teufelsdröckh! it is clear to demonstration thou art smit: the Queen of Hearts would see a "man of genius" also sigh for her; and there, by art magic, in that preternatural hour, has she bound and spell-bound thee. "Love is not altogether a Delirium," says he elsewhere; "yet has it many points in common therewith. I call it rather a discerning of the Infinite in the Finite, of the Idea made Real; which discerning again may be either true or false, either seraphic or demoniac, Inspiration or Insanity. But in the former case, too, as in common

Madness, it is Fantasy that superadds itself to Sight; on the so petty domain of the Actual, plants its Archimedes-lever,* whereby to move at will the infinite Spiritual. Fantasy I might call the true Heaven-gate and Hell-gate of man: his sensuous life is but the small temporary stage (*Zeitbühne*), whereon thick-streaming influences from both these far yet near regions meet visibly, and act tragedy and melodrama. Sense can support herself handsomely, in most countries, for some eighteenpence a-day; but for Fantasy planets and solar-systems will not suffice. Witness your Pyrrhus conquering the world, yet drinking no better red wine than he had before." Alas, witness also your Diogenes, flame-clad, scaling the upper Heaven, and verging towards Insanity, for prize of a "highsouled Brunette," as if the Earth held but one, and not several of these!

He says that, in Town, they met again: "day after day, like his heart's sun, the blooming Blumine shone on him. Ah! a little while ago, and he was yet all in darkness: him what Graceful (*Holde*) would ever love? Disbelieving all things, the poor youth had never learned to believe in himself. Withdrawn, in proud timidity, within his own fastnesses; solitary from men, yet baited by night-spectres enough, he saw himself, with a sad indignation, constrained to renounce the fairest hopes of existence. And now, O now! 'She looks on thee,' cried he: 'she the fairest, noblest; do not her dark eyes tell thee, thou are not despised? The Heaven's-Messenger! All Heaven's blessings be hers!' Thus did soft melodies flow through his heart; tones of an infinite gratitude; sweetest intimations that he also was a man, that for him also unutterable joys had been provided.

"In free speech, earnest or gay, amid lambent glances, laughter, tears, and often with the inarticulate mystic speech of Music: such was the element they now lived in; in such a many-tinted, radiant Aurora, and by this fairest of Orient Light-bringers must our Friend be blandished, and the new Apocalypse of Nature unrolled to him. Fairest Blumine! And, even as a Star, all Fire and humid Softness, a very Light-ray incarnate! Was there so much as a fault, a 'caprice,' he could have dispensed with? Was she not to him in very deed a Morning-Star; did not her presence bring with it airs from Heaven? As from Æolean Harps in the breath of dawn, as from the Memnon's Statue struck by the rosy-finger of Aurora, unearthly music was around him, and lapped him into untried balmy Rest. Pale Doubt fled away to the distance; Life bloomed up with happiness and hope. The Past, then, was all a haggard dream; he had been in the Garden of Eden, then, and could not discern it! But lo now! the black walls of his prison melt away; the captive is alive, is free. If he loved his Disenchantress? *Ach Gott!* His whole heart and soul and life were hers, but never had he named it Love: existence was all a Feeling, not yet shaped into a Thought."

Nevertheless, into a Thought, nay into an Action, it must be shaped; for neither Disenchanter nor Disenchantress, mere "Children of Time," can abide by Feeling alone. The Professor knows not, to this day, "how in her soft, fervid bosom, the Lovely found determination, even on hest of Necessity, to cut asunder these so blissful bonds." He even appears surprised at the "Duenna Cousin," whoever she may have been, "in whose meagre, hunger-bitten philosophy, the religion of young hearts was, from the first, faintly approved of." We, even at such distance, can explain it without necromancy. Let the Philosopher answer this one question: What figure, at that period, was a Mrs. Teufelsdröckh likely to make in polished society? Could she have driven so much as a brass-bound Gig, or even a simple iron-spring one? Thou foolish "absolved Auscultator," before whom lies no prospect of capital, will any yet known "religion of young hearts" keep the human Kitchen warm? Pshaw! thy divine Blumine, when she "resigned herself to wed some richer," shews more philosophy, though but "a woman of genius," than thou, a pretended man.

Our readers have witnessed the origin of this Love-mania, and with what royal splendour it waxes, and rises. Let no one ask us to unfold the glories of its dominant state; much less the horrors of its almost instantaneous dissolution. How from such inorganic masses, henceforth madder than ever, as lie in these Bags, can even fragments of a living delineation be organised? Besides, of what profit were it? We view, with a lively pleasure, the gay silk Montgolfier start from the ground, and shoot upwards, cleaving the liquid deeps, till it dwindle to a luminous star: but what is there to look longer on, when once, by natural elasticity, or accident of fire, it has exploded? A hapless air-navigator, plunging, amid torn parachutes, sand-bags, and confused wreck, fast enough, into the jaws of the Devil! Suffice it to know that Teufelsdröckh rose into the highest regions of the Empyrean, by a natural parabolic track, and returned thence in a quick perpendicular one. For the rest, let any feeling reader who has been unhappy enough to do the like, paint it out for himself; considering only that if he, for his perhaps comparatively insignificant mistress, underwent such agonies and frenzies, what must Teufelsdröckh's have been, with a fire-heart, and for a nonpareil Blumine! We glance merely at the final scene:

"One morning, he found his Morning-star all dimmed and dusky-red; the fair creature was silent, absent, she seemed to have been weeping. Alas, no longer a Morning-star, but a troublous skyey Portent, announcing that the Doomsday had dawned! She said, in a tremulous voice, they were to meet no more." The thunderstruck Air-sailor is not wanting to himself in this dread hour: but what avails it? We omit the passionate expostulations, entreaties, indignations, since all was vain, and not even an explanation was conceded him; and hasten to the catastrophe. "Farewell, then, Madam! said he, not without sternness, for his stung pride helped him. She put her hand in his, she looked in his face, tears started to her eyes: in wild audacity he clasped her to his bosom; their lips were joined, their two souls, like two dew-drops, rushed into one,—for the first time, and for the last!" Thus was Teufelsdröckh made immortal by a kiss. And then? Why, then—"thick curtains of Night rushed over his soul, as rose the immeasurable Crash of Doom; and through the ruins as of a shivered Universe, was he falling, falling, towards the Abyss."

CHAPTER 6

SORROWS OF TEUFELSDRÖCKH

WE have long felt that, with a man like our Professor, matters must often be expected to take a course of their own; that, in so multiplex, intricate a nature, there might be channels, both for admitting and emitting, such as the Psychologist had seldom noted; in short, that on no grand occasion and convulsion, neither in the joy-storm nor in the woe-storm, could you predict his demeanour.

To our less philosophical readers, for example, it is now clear that the so passionate Teufelsdröckh, precipitated through "a shivered Universe" in this extraordinary way, has only one of three things which he can next do: Establish himself in Bedlam; begin writing Satanic Poetry;* or blow out his brains. In the progress towards any of which consummations, do not such readers anticipate extravagance enough: breast-beating, brow-beating (against walls), lion-bellowings of blasphemy and the like, stampings, smitings, breakages of furniture, if not arson itself?

Nowise so does Teufelsdröckh deport him. He quietly lifts his *Pilgerstab* (Pilgrim-staff), "old business being soon wound up;" and begins a perambulation and circumambulation of the terraqueous Globe! Curious it is, indeed, how with such vivacity of conception, such intensity of feeling; above all, with these unconscionable habits of Exaggeration in speech, he combines that wonderful stillness of his, that stoicism in external procedure. Thus if his sudden bereavement, in this matter of the Flower-goddess, is talked of as a real Doomsday and Dissolution of Nature, in which light doubtless it partly appeared to himself, his own nature is nowise dissolved there-by; but rather is compressed closer. For once, as we might say, a Blumine by magic appliances has unlocked that shut heart of his, and its hidden things rush out tumultuous, boundless, like genii enfranchised from their glass phial: but no sooner are your magic appliances withdrawn, than the strange casket of a heart springs-to again; and perhaps there is now no key extant that will open it; for a Teufelsdröckh, as we remarked, will not love a second time. Singular Diogenes! No sooner has that heart-rending occurrence fairly taken place, than he affects to regard it as a thing natural, of which there is nothing more to be said. "One highest Hope, seemingly legible in the eyes of an Angel, had recalled him as out of Death-shadows into celestial Life: but a gleam of Tophet passed over the face of his Angel; he was rapt away in whirlwinds, and heard the laughter of Demons. It was a Calenture," adds he, "whereby the Youth saw green Paradise-groves in the waste Ocean-waters: a lying vision, yet not wholly a lie, for *he* saw it." But what things soever passed in him, when he ceased to see it; what ragings and despairings soever Teufelsdröckh's soul was the scene of, he has the goodness to conceal under a quite opaque cover of Silence. We know it well; the first mad paroxysm past, our brave Gneschen collected his dismembered philosophies, and buttoned himself together; he was meek, silent, or spoke of the weather, and the Journals: only by a transient knitting of those shaggy brows, by some deep flash of those eyes, glancing one knew not whether with tear-dew or with fierce fire,—might you have guessed what a Gehenna was within; that a whole Satanic School were spouting, though inaudibly, there. To consume your own choler, as some chimneys consume their own smoke; to keep a whole Satanic School spouting, if it must spout, inaudibly, is a negative yet no slight virtue, nor one of the commonest in these times.

Nevertheless, we will not take upon us to say, that in the strange measure he fell upon, there was not a touch of latent Insanity; whereof indeed the actual condition of these Documents in *Capricornus* and *Aquarius* is no bad emblem. His so unlimited Wanderings, toilsome enough, are without assigned or perhaps assignable aim; internal Unrest seems his sole guidance; he wanders, wanders, as if that curse of the Prophet had fallen on him, and he were "made like unto a wheel." Doubtless, too, the chaotic nature of these Paperbags aggravates our obscurity. Quite without note of preparation, for example, we come upon the following slip: "A peculiar feeling is it that will rise in the Traveller, when turning some hill-range in his desert road, he descries lying far below, embosomed among its groves and green natural bulwarks, and all diminished to a toybox, the fair Town, where so many souls, as it were seen and yet unseen, are driving their multifarious traffic. Its white steeple is then truly a starward-pointing finger; the canopy of blue smoke seems like a sort of Life-breath: for always, of its own unity, the soul gives unity to whatso it looks on with love: thus does the little Dwellingplace of men, in itself a congeries of houses and huts, become for us an individual, almost a person. But what thousand other thoughts unite thereto, if the place has to ourselves been the arena of joyous or mournful experiences; if perhaps the cradle we were rocked in still stands there, if our Loving ones still dwell there, if our Buried ones there slumber!" Does Teufelsdröckh, as the wounded eagle is said to make for its own eyrie, and indeed military deserters, and all hunted outcast creatures, turn as if by instinct in the direction of their birthland,—fly first, in this extremity, towards his native Entepfuhl; but reflecting that there no help awaits him, take but one wistful look from the distance, and then wend elsewhither?

Little happier seems to be his next flight: into the wilds of Nature; as if in her mother-bosom he would seek healing. So at least we incline to interpret the following Notice, separated from the former by some considerable space, wherein, however, is nothing noteworthy:

"Mountains were not new to him; but rarely are Mountains seen in such combined majesty and grace as here. The rocks are of that sort called Primitive by the mineralogists, which always arrange themselves in masses of a rugged, gigantic character; which ruggedness, however, is here tempered by a singular airiness of form, and softness of environment: in a climate favourable to vegetation, the gray cliff, itself covered with lichens, shoots up through a garment of foliage or verdure; and white, bright cottages, tree-shaded, cluster round the everlasting granite. In fine vicissitude, Beauty alternates with Grandeur: you ride through stony hollows, along strait passes, traversed by torrents, overhung by high walls of rock; now winding amid broken shaggy chasms, and huge fragments; now suddenly emerging into some emerald valley, where the streamlet collects itself into a Lake, and man has again found a fair dwelling, and it seems as if Peace had established herself in the bosom of Strength.

"To Peace, however, in this vortex of existence, can the son of Time not pretend: still less if some Spectre haunt him from the Past; and the Future is wholly a Stygian Darkness, spectre-bearing. Reasonably might the Wanderer exclaim to himself: Are not the gates of this world's Happiness inexorably shut against thee; hast thou a hope that is not mad? Nevertheless, one may still murmur audibly, or in the original Greek if that suit* better: 'Whoso can look on Death will start at no shadows?'

"From such meditations is the Wanderer's attention called outwards: for now the Valley closes in abruptly, intersected by a huge mountain mass, the stony water-worn ascent of which is not to be accomplished on horseback. Arrived aloft, he finds himself again lifted into the evening sunset light; and cannot but pause, and gaze round him, some moments there. An upland irregular expanse of wold, where valleys in complex branchings are suddenly or slowly arranging their descent towards every quarter of the sky. The mountain-ranges are beneath your feet, and folded together; only the loftier summits look down here and there as on a second plain; lakes also lie clear and earnest in their solitude. No trace of man now visible; unless indeed it were he who fashioned that little visible link of Highway, here, as would seem, scaling the inaccessible to unite Province with Province. But sun-wards, lo you! how it towers sheer up, a world of Mountains, the diadem and centre of the mountain region! A hundred and a hundred savage peaks, in the last light of Day; all glowing, of gold and amethyst, like giant spirits of the wilderness; there in their silence, in their solitude, even as on the night when Noah's deluge first dried! Beautiful, nay solemn, was the sudden aspect to our Wanderer. He gazed over those stupendous masses with wonder, almost with longing desire; never till this hour had he known Nature, that she was One, that she was his Mother and divine. And as the ruddy glow was fading into clearness in the sky, and the Sun had now departed, a murmur of Eternity and Immensity, of Death and of Life, stole through his soul; and he felt as if Death and Life were one, as if the Earth were not dead, as if the Spirit of the Earth had its throne in that splendour, and his own spirit were therewith holding communion.

"The spell was broken by a sound of carriage-wheels. Emerging from the hidden Northward, to sink soon into the hidden Southward, came a gay barouche-and-four: it was open; servants and postilions wore wedding-favours: that happy pair, then, had found each other, it was their marriage-evening! Few moments brought them near: *Du Himmel!* * It was Herr Towgood and ——Blumine! With slight, unrecognising salutation they passed me; plunged down amid the neighbouring thickets, onwards, to Heaven, and to England; and I, in my friend Richter's words, *I remained alone, behind them, with the Night*."*

Were it not cruel in these circumstances, here might be the place to insert an observation, gleaned long ago from the great *Clothes-Volume,* where it stands with quite other intent: "Some time before Small-pox was extirpated," says the Professor, "there came a new malady of the spiritual sort on Europe: I mean the epidemic, now endemical, of view-hunting. Poets of old date, being privileged with Senses, had also enjoyed external Nature; but chiefly as we enjoy the crystal cup which holds good or bad liquor for us; that is to say, in silence, or with slight incidental commentary: never, as I compute, till after the *Sorrows of Werter,* was there man found who would say: Come let us make a Description! Having drunk the liquor, come let us eat the glass! Of which endemic the Jenner is unhappily still to seek." Too true!

We reckon it more important to remark that the Professor's Wanderings, so far as his stoical and cynical envelopement admits us to clear insight, here first take their permanent character, fatuous or not. That basilisk-glance of the Barouche-and-four seems to have withered up what little remnant of a purpose may have still lurked in him: Life has become wholly a dark labyrinth; wherein, through long years, our Friend, flying from spectres, must stumble about at random, and naturally with more haste than progress.

Foolish were it in us to attempt following him, even from afar, in this extraordinary world-pilgrimage of his; the simplest record of which, were clear record possible, would fill volumes. Hopeless is the obscurity, unspeakable the confusion. He glides from country to country, from condition to condition; vanishing and reappearing, no man can calculate how or where. Through all quarters of the world he wanders, and apparently through all circles of society. If in any scene, perhaps difficult to fix geographically, he settles for a time, and forms connexions, be sure he will snap them abruptly asunder. Let him sink out of sight as Private Scholar (*Privatisirender*), living by the grace of God, in some European capital, you may next find him as Hadjee in the neighbourhood of Mecca. It is an inexplicable Phantasmagoria, capricious, quick-changing; as if our Traveller, instead of limbs and highways, had transported himself by some wishing-carpet, or Fortunatus' Hat.* The whole too imparted emblematically, in dim multifarious tokens (as that collection of Street-Advertisements); with only some touch of direct historical notice sparingly interspersed: little light-islets in the world of haze! So that from this point, the Professor is more of an enigma than ever. In figurative language, we might say he becomes, not indeed a spirit, yet spiritualised, vaporised. Fact unparalleled in Biography! The river of his History, which we have traced from its tiniest fountains, and hoped to see flow onward, with increasing current, into the ocean, here dashes itself over that terrific Lover's Leap;* and, as a mad-foaming cataract, flies wholly into tumultuous clouds of spray! Low down it indeed collects again into pools and plashes; yet only at a great distance, and with difficulty, if at all, into a general stream. To cast a glance into certain of those pools and plashes, and trace whither they run, must, for a chapter or two, form the limit of our endeavour.

For which end doubtless those direct historical Notices, where they can be met with, are the best. Nevertheless, of this sort too there occurs much, which, with our present light, it were questionable to emit. Teufelsdröckh, vibrating everywhere between the highest and the lowest levels, comes into contact with Public History itself. For example, those conversations and relations with illustrious Persons, as Sultan Mahmoud, the Emperor Napoleon, and others, are they not as yet rather of a diplomatic character, than of a biographic? The

Editor, appreciating the sacredness of crowned heads, nay perhaps suspecting the possible trickeries of a Clothes-Philosopher, will eschew this province for the present: a new time may bring new insight and a different duty.

If we ask now, not indeed with what ulterior Purpose, for there was none, yet with what immediate outlooks; at all events, in what mood of mind, the Professor undertook and prosecuted this world-pilgrimage,—the answer is more distinct than favourable. "A nameless Unrest," says he, "urged me forward; to which the outward motion was some momentary lying solace. Whither should I go? My Loadstars were blotted out; in that canopy of grim fire shone no star. Yet forward must I; the ground burnt under me; there was no rest for the sole of my foot. I was alone! alone! Ever too the strong inward longing shaped Fantasms for itself: towards these, one after the other, must I fruitlessly wander. A feeling I had that, for my fever-thirst, there was and must be somewhere a healing Fountain. To many fondly imagined Fountains, the Saints' Wells of these days, did I pilgrim; to great Men, to great Cities, to great Events: but found there no healing. In strange countries, as in the well-known; in savage deserts as in the press of corrupt civilisation, it was ever the same: how could your Wanderer escape from—*his own Shadow?* Nevertheless still Forward! I felt as if in great haste; to do I saw not what. From the depths of my own heart, it called to me, Forwards! The winds and the streams, and all Nature sounded to me, Forwards! *Ach Gott!* I was even, once for all, a Son of Time."

From which is it not clear that the internal Satanic School was still active enough? He says elsewhere: "The *Enchiridion* of Epictetus I had ever with me, often as my sole rational companion; and regret to mention that the nourishment it yielded was trifling." Thou foolish Teufelsdröckh! How could it else? Hadst thou not Greek enough to understand thus much: *The end of Man is an Action, and not a Thought,* * though it were the noblest?

"How I lived?" writes he once: "Friend, hast thou considered the 'rugged all-nourishing Earth,' as Sophocles well names her;* how she feeds the sparrow on the housetop, much more her darling, man? While thou stirrest and livest, thou hast a probability of victual. My breakfast of tea has been cooked by a Tartar woman, with water of the Amur, who wiped her earthen-kettle with a horse-tail. I have roasted wild eggs in the sand of Sahara; I have awakened in Paris *Estrapades* and Vienna *Malzleins,* with no prospect of breakfast beyond elemental liquid. That I had my Living to seek saved me from Dying,— by suicide. In our busy Europe, is there not an everlasting demand for Intellect, in the chemical, mechanical, political, religious, educational, commercial departments? In Pagan countries, cannot one write Fetishes? Living! Little knowest thou what alchemy is in an inventive Soul; how, as with its little finger, it can create provision enough for the body (of a Philosopher); and then, as with both hands, create quite other than provision; namely, spectres to torment itself withal."

Poor Teufelsdröckh! Flying with Hunger always parallel to him; and a whole Infernal Chace in his rear; so that the countenance of Hunger is comparatively a friend's! Thus must he, in the temper of ancient Cain, or of the modern Wandering Jew, save only that he feels himself not guilty and but suffering the pains of guilt,—wend to and fro with aimless speed. Thus must he, over the whole surface of the Earth (by foot-prints), write his *Sorrows of Teufelsdröckh;* even as the great Goethe, in passionate words, must write his *Sorrows of Werter,* before the spirit freed herself, and he could become a Man. Vain truly is the hope of your swiftest Runner "to escape from his own Shadow!" Nevertheless, in these sick days, when the Born of Heaven first descries himself (about the age of twenty) in a world such as ours, richer than usual in two things: in Truths grown obsolete, and Trades grown obsolete,—what can the fool think but that it is all a Den of Lies, wherein whoso will not speak Lies and act Lies, must stand Idle, and despair? Whereby it happens that, for your nobler minds, the publishing of some such Work of Art, in one or the other dialect, becomes almost a necessity. For what is it properly but an Altercation with the Devil, before you begin honestly Fighting him? Your Byron publishes his *Sorrows of Lord George,* in verse and in prose, and copiously otherwise: your Bonaparte represents his *Sorrows of Napoleon* Opera, in an all-too stupendous style; with music of cannon-vollies, and murder-shrieks of a

world; his stage-lights are the fires of Conflagration; his rhyme
and recitative are the tramp of embattled Hosts and the sound
of falling Cities.—Happier is he who, like our Clothes-Philosopher, can write such matter, since it must be written, on the
insensible Earth, with his shoe-soles only; and also survive the
writing thereof!

CHAPTER 7
THE EVERLASTING NO

UNDER the strange nebulous envelopment, wherein our Professor has now shrouded himself, no doubt but his spiritual nature is nevertheless progressive, and growing: for how can the "Son of Time," in any case, stand still? We behold him, through those dim years, in a state of crisis, of transition: his new* Pilgrimings, and general solution into aimless Discontinuity, what is all this but a mad Fermentation; wherefrom, the fiercer it is, the clearer product will one day evolve itself?

Such transitions are ever full of pain: thus the Eagle, when he moults, is sickly; and, to attain his new beak, must harshly dash off the old one upon rocks. What Stoicism soever our Wanderer, in his individual acts and motions may affect, it is clear that there is a hot fever of anarchy and misery raging within; coruscations of which flash out: as, indeed, how could there be other? Have we not seen him disappointed, bemocked of Destiny, through long years? All that the young heart might desire and pray for has been denied; nay, as in the last worst instance, offered and then snatched away. Ever an "excellent Passivity;" but of useful, reasonable Activity, essential to the former as Food to Hunger, nothing granted: till at length, in this wild Pilgrimage, he must forcibly seize for himself an Activity, though useless, unreasonable. Alas! his cup of bitterness, which had been filling drop by drop, ever since that first "ruddy morning" in the Hinterschlag Gymnasium, was at the very lip; and then with that poison-drop, of the Towgood-and-Blumine business, it runs over, and even hisses over in a deluge of foam.

He himself says once, with more justness than originality: "Man is, properly speaking, based upon Hope, he has no other possession but Hope; this world of his is emphatically the Place of Hope." What then was our Professor's possession? We see him, for the present, quite shut out from Hope; looking not into the golden orient, but vaguely all round into a dim copper firmament, pregnant with earthquake and tornado.

Alas, shut out from Hope, in a deeper sense than we yet
dream of! For as he wanders wearisomely through this world,
he has now lost all tidings of another and higher. Full of
religion, or at least of religiosity, as our Friend has since
exhibited himself, he hides not that, in those days, he was
wholly irreligious: "Doubt had darkened into Unbelief," says
he; "shade after shade goes grimly over your soul, till you have
the fixed, starless, Tartarean black." To such readers as have
reflected, what can be called reflecting, on man's life, and
happily discovered, in contradiction to much Profit-and-Loss
Philosophy,* speculative and practical, that Soul is *not* synonymous with Stomach; who understand, therefore, in our
Friend's words, "that, for man's well-being, Faith is properly
the one thing needful; how, with it, Martyrs, otherwise weak,
can cheerfully endure the shame and the cross; and, without it,
Wordlings puke up their sick existence, by suicide, in the midst
of luxury:" to such it will be clear that, for a pure moral nature,
the loss of his religious Belief was the loss of every thing.
Unhappy young man! All wounds, the crush of long-conti-
nued Destitution, the stab of false Friendship, and of false Love,
all wounds in thy so genial heart would have healed again, had
not its life-warmth been withdrawn. Well might he exclaim, in
his wild way: "Is there no God, then; but at best an absentee
God, sitting idle, ever since the first Sabbath, at the outside of
his Universe, and *seeing* it go? Has the word Duty no meaning:
is what we call Duty no divine Messenger and Guide, but a
false earthly Fantasm, made up of Desire and Fear, of emana-
tions from the Gallows and from Doctor Graham's Celestial-
Bed? Happiness of an approving Conscience! Did not Paul of
Tarsus, whom admiring men have since named Saint, feel that
he was 'the chief of sinners;' and Nero of Rome, jocund in spirit
(*wohlgemuth*), spend much of his time in fiddling? Foolish
Word-monger, and Motive-grinder, that in thy Logic-mill
hast an earthly mechanism for the Godlike itself, and wouldst
fain grind me out Virtue from the husks of Pleasure,—I tell
thee, Nay! To the unregenerate Prometheus Vinctus* of a man,
it is even* the bitterest aggravation of his wretchedness that he
is conscious of Virtue, that he feels himself the victim not of
suffering only, but of injustice. What then? Is the heroic

inspiration we name Virtue but some Passion; some bubble of the blood, bubbling in the direction others *profit* by? I know not: only this I know, If what thou namest Happiness be our true aim, then are we all astray. With Stupidity and sound Digestion man may front much. But what, in these dull unimaginative days, are the terrors of Conscience to the diseases of the Liver! Not on Morality, but on Cookery let us build our stronghold: there brandishing our fryingpan, as censer, let us offer sweet incense to the Devil, and live at ease on the fat things which *he* has provided for his Elect!"

Thus must the bewildered Wanderer stand, as so many have done, shouting question after question into the Sibyl-cave of Destiny, and receive no Answer but an Echo. It is all a grim Desert, this once fair world of his; wherein is heard only the howling of wild beasts, or the shrieks of despairing, hate-filled men; and no Pillar of Cloud by day, and no Pillar of Fire by night, any longer guides the Pilgrim. To such length has the spirit of Inquiry carried him. "But what recks* it (*was thut's*)?" cries he: "it is but the common lot in this era. Not having come to spiritual majority prior to the *Siècle de Louis Quinze,** and not being born purely a Loghead (*Dummkopf*), thou hadst no other outlook. The whole world is, like thee, sold to Unbelief: their old Temples of the Godhead, which for long have not been rainproof, crumble down; and men ask now: Where is the Godhead; our eyes never saw him!"

Pitiful enough were it, for all these wild utterances, to call our Diogenes wicked. Unprofitable Servants as we all are, perhaps at no era of his life was he more decisively the Servant of Goodness, the Servant of God, than even now when doubting God's existence. "One circumstance I note," says he: "after all the nameless woe that Inquiry, which for me, what it is not always, was genuine Love of Truth, had wrought me, I nevertheless still loved Truth, and would bate no jot of my allegiance to her. 'Truth!' I cried, 'though the Heavens crush me for following her: no Falsehood! though a whole celestial Lubberland* were the price of Apostasy.' In conduct it was the same. Had a divine Messenger from the clouds, or miraculous Handwriting on the wall, convincingly proclaimed to me, *This shalt thou do*, with what passionate readiness, as I often thought, would I have done it, had it been leaping into the infernal Fire! Thus, in spite of all Motive-grinders, and Mechanical Profit-and-Loss Philosophies, with the sick ophthalmia and hallucination they had brought on, was the Infinite nature of Duty still dimly present to me: living without God in the world, of God's light I was not utterly bereft; if my as yet sealed eyes, with their unspeakable longing, could nowhere see Him, nevertheless in my heart He was present, and His Heaven-written Law still stood legible and sacred there."

Meanwhile, under all these tribulations, and temporal and spiritual destitutions, what must the Wanderer, in his silent soul, have endured! "The painfullest feeling," writes he, "is that of your own Feebleness (*Unkraft*); ever, as the English Milton says, to be weak is the true misery.* And yet of your Strength there is and can be no clear feeling, save by what you have prospered in, by what you have done. Between vague wavering Capability and fixed indubitable Performance, what a difference! A certain inarticulate Self-consciousness dwells dimly in us; which only our Works can render articulate and decisively discernible. Our Works are the mirror wherein the spirit first sees its natural lineaments. Hence, too, the folly of that impossible Precept, *Know thyself;* till it be translated into this partially possible one, *Know what thou canst work at.*

"But for me, so strangely unprosperous had I been, the net result of my Workings amounted as yet simply to—Nothing. How then could I believe in my Strength, when there was as yet no mirror to see it in? Ever did this agitating, yet as I now perceive, quite frivolous question, remain to me insoluble: Hast thou a certain Faculty, a certain Worth, such even as the most have not; or art thou the completest Dullard of these modern times? Alas! the fearful Unbelief is unbelief in yourself; and how could I believe? Had not my first, last Faith in myself, when even to me the Heavens seemed laid open, and I dared to love, been all too-cruelly belied? The speculative Mystery of Life grew ever more mysterious to me: neither in the practical Mystery had I made the slightest progress, but been every-where buffeted, foiled, and contemptuously cast out. A feeble unit in the middle of a threatening Infinitude, I seemed to have nothing given me but eyes, whereby to discern my own wretchedness. Invisible yet impenetrable walls, as of Enchantment, divided me from all living: was there, in the wide world, any true bosom I could press trustfully to mine? O Heaven, No, there was none! I kept a lock upon my lips; why should I speak much with that shifting variety of so-called Friends, in whose withered, vain, and too-hungry souls, Friendship was but an incredible tradition? In such cases, your resource is to talk little, and that little mostly from the Newspapers. Now when I look back, it was a strange isolation I then lived in. The men and women round me, even speaking with me, were but Figures; I had, practically, forgotten that they were alive, that they were not merely automatic. In midst of their crowded streets, and assemblages, I walked solitary; and (except as it was my own heart, not another's, that I kept devouring) savage also, as the tiger in his jungle. Some comfort it would have been, could I, like a Faust, have fancied myself tempted and tormented of the Devil; for a Hell, as I imagine, without Life, though only Diabolic Life, were more frightful: but in our age of Downpulling and Disbelief, the very Devil has been pulled down, you cannot so much as believe in a Devil. To me the Universe was all void of Life, of Purpose, of Volition, even of Hostility: it was one huge, dead, immeasurable Steam-engine, rolling on, in its dead indifference, to grind me limb from limb. O the vast, gloomy, solitary Golgotha, and Mill of Death! Why was the Living banished thither companionless, conscious? Why if there is no Devil; nay, unless the Devil is your God?"

A prey incessantly to such corrosions, might not, moreover, as the worst aggravation to them, the iron constitution even of a Teufelsdröckh threaten to fail? We conjecture that he has known sickness; and, in spite of his locomotive habits, perhaps sickness of the chronic sort. Hear this, for example: "How beautiful to die of broken-heart, on Paper! Quite another thing in Practice; every window of your Feeling, even of your Intellect, as it were, begrimed and mud-bespattered, so that no pure ray can enter; a whole Drugshop in your inwards; the foredone soul drowning slowly in quagmires of Disgust!"

Putting all which external and internal miseries together, may we not find in the following sentences, quite in our

Professor's still vein, significance enough: "From Suicide a certain after-shine (*Nachschein*) of Christianity withheld me; perhaps also a certain indolence of character; for, was not that a remedy I had at any time within reach? Often, however, was there a question present to me: Should some one now, at the turning of that corner, blow thee suddenly out of Space, into the other World, or other No-world, by pistol-shot,—how were it? On which ground, too, I have often,* in sea-storms and sieged cities and other death-scenes, exhibited an imperturbability, which passed, falsely enough, for courage."

"So had it lasted," concludes the Wanderer, "so had it lasted, as in bitter protracted Death-agony, through long years. The heart within me, unvisited by any heavenly dew-drop, was smouldering in sulphurous, slow-consuming fire. Almost since earliest memory I had shed no tear; or once only when I, murmuring half-audibly, recited Faust's Deathsong,* that wild *Selig der den er im Siegesglanze findet* (Happy whom He finds in Battle's splendour), and thought that of this last Friend even I was not forsaken, that Destiny itself could not doom me not to die. Having no Hope, neither had I any definite Fear, were it of Man or of Devil: nay, I often felt as if it might be solacing, could the Arch-Devil himself, though in Tartarean terrors, but rise to me, that I might tell him a little of my mind. And yet, strangely enough, I lived in a continual, indefinite, pining Fear; tremulous, pusillanimous, apprehensive of I knew not what: it seemed as if all things in the Heavens above and the Earth beneath would hurt me; as if the heavens and the Earth were but boundless Jaws of a devouring Monster, wherein I, palpitating, waited to be devoured.

"Full of such humour, and perhaps the miserablest man in the whole French Capital or Suburbs, was I, one sultry Dogday, after much perambulation, toiling along the dirty little *Rue Saint Thomas de l'Enfer,** among civic rubbish enough, in a close atmosphere, and over pavements hot as Nebuchadnezzar's Furnace; whereby doubtless my spirits were little cheered; when, all at once, there rose a Thought in me, and I asked myself: 'What *art* thou afraid of? Wherefore, like a coward, dost thou for ever pip and whimper, and go cowering and trembling? Despicable biped! what is the sum-total of the worst that lies before thee? Death? Well, Death; and say the pangs of Tophet too, and all that the Devil and Man may, will, or can do against thee! Hast thou not a heart; canst thou not suffer whatso it be; and, as a Child of Freedom, though outcast, trample Tophet itself under thy feet, while it consumes thee? Let it come, then; I will meet it and defy it!' And as I so thought, there rushed like a stream of fire over my whole soul; and I shook base Fear away from me for ever. I was strong, of unknown strength; a spirit, almost a god. Ever from that time, the temper of my misery was changed: not Fear or whining Sorrow was it, but Indignation and grim fire-eyed Defiance.

"Thus had the EVERLASTING NO (*das Ewige Nein*) pealed authoritatively through all the recesses of my Being, of my ME; and then was it that my whole ME stood up, in native God-created majesty, and with emphasis recorded its Protest. Such a Protest, the most important transaction in Life, may that same Indignation and Defiance, in a psychological point of view, be fitly called. The Everlasting No had said: 'Behold, thou art fatherless, outcast, and the Universe is mine (the Devil's);' to which my whole Me now made answer: '*I* am not thine, but Free, and for ever hate thee!'

"It is from this hour that I incline to date my Spiritual New-birth, or Baphometic Fire-baptism;* perhaps I directly thereupon began to be a Man."

*   *   *

CHAPTER 8

CENTRE OF INDIFFERENCE*

THOUGH, after this "Baphometic Fire-baptism" of his, our Wanderer signifies that his Unrest was but increased; as, indeed, "Indignation and Defiance," especially against things in general, are not the most peaceable inmates; yet can the Psychologist surmise that it was no longer a quite hopeless Unrest; that henceforth it had at least a fixed centre to revolve round. For the fire-baptised soul, long so scathed and thunder-riven, here feels its own Freedom, which feeling is its Baphometic Baptism: the citadel of its whole kingdom it has thus gained by assault, and will keep inexpugnable; outwards from which the remaining dominions, not indeed without hard battling, will doubtless by degrees be conquered and pacificated. Under another figure, we might say, if in that great moment, in the *Rue Saint Thomas de l'Enfer,* the old inward Satanic School was not yet thrown out of doors, it received peremptory judicial notice to quit;—whereby, for the rest, its howl-chauntings, Ernulphus-cursings, and rebellious gnashings of teeth, might, in the meanwhile, become only the more tumultuous, and difficult to keep secret.

Accordingly, if we scrutinize these Pilgrimings well, there is perhaps discernible henceforth a certain incipient method in their madness. Not wholly as a Spectre does Teufelsdröckh now storm through the world; at worst as a spectre-fighting Man, nay that will one day be a Spectre-queller. If pilgriming restlessly to so many "Saints' Wells," and ever without quenching of his thirst, he nevertheless finds little secular wells, whereby from time to time some alleviation is ministered. In a word, he is now, if not ceasing, yet intermitting to "eat his own heart;" and clutches round him outwardly, on the NOT-ME for wholesomer food. Does not the following glimpse exhibit him in a much more natural state?

"Towns also and Cities, especially the ancient, I failed not to look upon with interest. How beautiful to see thereby, as through a long vista, into the remote Time; to have, as it were, an actual section of almost the earliest Past brought safe into the Present, and set before your eyes! There, in that old City, was a live ember of Culinary Fire put down, say only two thousand years ago; and there, burning more or less triumphantly, with such fuel as the region yielded, it has burnt, and still burns, and thou thyself seest the very smoke thereof. Ah! and the far more mysterious live ember of Vital Fire was then also put down there; and still miraculously burns and spreads; and the smoke and ashes thereof (in these Judgment-Halls and Churchyards), and its bellows-engines (in these Churches), thou still seest; and its flame, looking out from every kind countenance, and every hateful one, still warms thee or scorches thee.

"Of Man's Activity and Attainment the chief results are aeriform, mystic, and preserved in Tradition only: such are his Forms of Government, with the Authority they rest on; his Customs, or Fashions both of Cloth-habits and of Soul-habits; much more his collective stock of Handicrafts, the whole Faculty he has required* of manipulating Nature: all these things, as indispensable and priceless as they are, cannot in any way be fixed under lock and key, but must flit, spirit-like, on impalpable vehicles, from Father to Son; if you demand sight of them, they are nowhere to be met with. Visible Ploughmen and Hammermen there have been, ever from Cain and Tubal-cain downwards: but where does your accumulated Agricul-tural, Metallurgic, and other Manufacturing SKILL lie ware-housed? It transmits itself on the atmospheric air, on the sun's rays (by Hearing and by Vision); it is a thing aeriform, impalpable, of quite spiritual sort. In like manner, ask me not, Where are the LAWS; where is the GOVERNMENT? In vain wilt thou go to Schönbrunn, to Downing Street, to the Palais Bourbon: thou findest nothing there, but brick or stone houses, and some bundles of Papers tied with tape. Where then is that same cunningly-devised almighty GOVERNMENT of theirs to be laid hands on? Everywhere, yet nowhere: seen only in its works, this too is a thing aeriform, invisible; or if you will, mystic and miraculous. So spiritual (*geistig*) is our whole daily Life: all that we do springs out of Mystery, Spirit, invisible Force; only like a little Cloud-image, or Armida's Palace,* air-built, does the Actual body itself forth from the great mystic Deep.

"Visible and tangible products of the Past, again, I reckon up to the extent of three: Cities, with their Cabinets and Arsenals; then tilled Fields, to either or to both of which divisions Roads with their Bridges may belong; and thirdly——Books. In which third truly, the last-invented, lies a worth far surpassing that of the two others. Wondrous indeed is the virtue of a true Book. Not like a dead City of stones, yearly crumbling, yearly needing repair; more like a tilled Field, but then a spiritual Field: like a spiritual Tree, let me rather say, it stands from year to year, and from age to age (we have Books that already number some hundred-and-fifty human ages); and yearly comes its new produce of Leaves (Commentaries, Deductions, Philosophical, Political Systems; or were it only Sermons, Pamphlets, Journalistic Essays), every one of which is talismanic and thaumaturgic, for it can persuade men. O thou who art able to write a Book, which once in the two centuries or oftener there is a man gifted to do, envy not him whom they name City-builder, and inexpressibly pity him whom they name Conqueror or City-burner! Thou too art a Conqueror and Victor; but of the true sort, namely over the Devil: thou too hast built what will outlast all marble and metal, and be a wonder-bringing City of the Mind, a Temple and Seminary and Prophetic Mount, whereto all kindreds of the Earth will pilgrim.—Fool! why journeyest thou wearisomely, in thy antiquarian fervour, to gaze on the stone Pyramids of Geeza, or the clay ones of Sacchara? These stand there, as I can tell thee, idle and inert, looking over the Desart, foolishly enough, for the last three thousand years: but canst thou not open thy Hebrew BIBLE, then, or even Luther's Version thereof?"

No less satisfactory is his sudden appearance not in Battle, yet on some Battle-field; which, we soon gather, must be that of Wagram; so that here, for once, is a certain approximation to distinctness of date. Omitting much, let us impart what follows:

"Horrible enough! A whole Marchfeld strewed with shell-splinters, cannon-shot, ruined tumbrils, and dead men and horses; stragglers still remaining not so much as buried. And those red mould heaps: aye, there lie the Shells of Men, out of which all the Life and Virtue has been blown; and now are they swept together, and crammed down out of sight, like blown Egg-shells!—Did Nature, when she bade the Donau bring down his mould-cargos from the Carinthian and Carpathian Heights, and spread them out here into the softest, richest level,—intend thee, O Marchfeld, for a corn-bearing Nursery, whereon her children might be nursed; or for a Cockpit, wherein they might the more commodiously be throttled and tattered? Were thy three broad Highways, meeting here from the ends of Europe, made for Ammunition-waggons, then? Were thy Wagrams and Stillfrieds but so many ready-built Casemates, wherein the house of Hapsburg might batter with artillery, and with artillery be battered? König Ottokar, amid yonder hillocks, dies under Rodolf's truncheon; here Kaiser Franz falls a-swoon under Napoleon's: within which five centuries, to omit the others, how has thy breast, fair Plain, been defaced and defiled! The greensward is torn up and trampled down; man's fond care of it, his fruit-trees, hedge-rows, and pleasant dwellings, blown away with gunpowder; and the kind seedfield lies as a desolate, hideous Place-of-Sculls.—Nevertheless, Nature is at work; neither shall these Powder-Devilkins with their utmost devilry gainsay her: but all that gore and carnage will be shrouded in, absorbed into manure; and next year the Marchfeld will be green, nay greener. Thrifty unwearied Nature, ever out of our great waste educing some little profit of thy own,—how dost thou, from the very carcass of the Killer, bring Life for the Living!

"What, speaking in quite unofficial language, is the net purport and upshot of War? To my own knowledge, for example, there dwell and toil, in the British village of Dum-drudge,* usually some five hundred souls. From these, by certain 'Natural Enemies' of the French, there are successively selected, during the French war, say thirty able-bodied men: Dumdrudge, at her own expense, has suckled and nursed them; she has, not without difficulty and sorrow, fed them up to manhood, and even trained them to crafts, so that one can weave, another build, another hammer, and the weakest can stand under thirty stone avoirdupois. Nevertheless, amid much weeping and swearing, they are selected; all dressed in red; and shipped away, at the public charges, some two thousand miles, or say only to the south of Spain; and fed there till wanted. And now, to that same spot in the south of Spain, are thirty similar French artisans, from a French Dumdrudge, in like manner wending: till at length, after infinite effort, the two parties come into actual juxta-position; and Thirty stands fronting Thirty, each with a gun in his hand. Straightway the word 'Fire!' is given; and they blow the souls out of one another; and in place of sixty brisk useful craftsmen, the world has sixty dead carcasses, which it must bury, and anew shed tears for. Had these men any quarrel? Busy as the Devil is, not the smallest! They lived far enough apart; were the entirest strangers; nay, in so wide a Universe, there was even, unconsciously, by Commerce, some mutual helpfulness between them. How then? Simpleton! Their Governors had fallen out; and, instead of shooting one another, had the cunning to make these poor blockheads shoot.—Alas so is it in Deutschland, and hitherto in all other lands; still as of old, 'what devilry soever Kings do, the Greeks must pay the piper!'—In that fiction of the English Smollett,* it is true, the final Cessation of War is perhaps prophetically shadowed forth; where the two Natural Enemies, in person, take each a Tobacco-pipe, filled with Brimstone; light the same, and smoke in one another's faces, till the weaker gives in: but from such predicted Peace-Era, what blood-filled trenches, and contentious centuries, may still divide us!' "

Thus can the Professor, at least in lucid intervals, look away from his own sorrows, over the many-coloured world, and pertinently enough note what is passing there. We may remark, indeed, that for the matter of spiritual culture, if for nothing else, perhaps few periods of his life were richer than this. Internally, there is the most momentous instructive Course of Practical Philosophy, with Experiments, going on; towards the right comprehension of which his Peripatetic habits, favourable to Meditation, might help him rather than hinder. Externally, again, as he wanders to and fro, there are, if for the longing heart little substance, yet for the seeing eye Sights enough: in these so boundless Travels of his, granting that the Satanic School was even partially kept down, what an incredible Knowledge of our Planet, and its Inhabitants and their Works, that is to say, of all knowable things, might not Teufelsdröckh acquire!

"I have read in most Public Libraries," says he, "including those of Constantinople and Samarcand: in most Colleges, except the Chinese Mandarin ones, I have studied, or seen that there was no studying. Unknown Languages have I oftenest gathered from their natural repertory, the Air, by my organ of Hearing; Statistics, Geographics, Topographics came, through the Eye, almost of their own accord. The ways of Man, how he seeks food, and warmth, and protection for himself, in most regions, are ocularly known to me. Like the great Hadrian, I meted out much of the terraqueous Globe with a pair of Compasses that belonged to myself only.

"Of great Scenes, why speak? Three summer days, I lingered reflecting, and even composing (*dichtete*), by the Pine-chasms of Vaucluse; and in that clear Lakelet moistened my bread. I have sat under the palm-trees of Tadmor; smoked a pipe among the ruins of Babylon. The great Wall of China I have seen; and can testify that it is of grey brick, coped and covered with granite, and shows only second-rate masonry.—Great Events, also, have I not witnessed? Kings sweated down (*ausgemergelt*) into Berlin-and-Milan Customhouse-officers;* the World well won, and the World well lost; oftener than once a hundred thousand individuals shot (by each other) in one day. All kindreds and peoples and nations dashed together, and shifted and shovelled into heaps, that they might ferment there, and in time unite. The birth-pangs of Democracy, wherewith con-vulsed Europe was groaning in cries that reached Heaven, could not escape me.

"For great Men I have ever had the warmest predilection; and can perhaps boast that few such in this era have wholly escaped me. Great Men are the inspired (speaking and acting) Texts of that divine BOOK OF REVELATIONS, whereof a Chapter is completed from epoch to epoch, and by some named HISTORY; to which inspired Texts your numerous talented men, and your innumerable untalented men, are the better or worse exegetic Commentaries, and waggon-load of too-stupid, heretical or orthodox, weekly Sermons. For my study, the inspired Texts themselves! Thus, did I not, in very early days, having disguised me as tavern-waiter, stand behind the field-chairs, under that shady Tree at Treisnitz by the Jena Highway; waiting upon the great Schiller and greater Goethe; and hearing what I have not forgotten. For——"

——But at this point the Editor recalls his principle of caution, some time ago laid down, and must suppress much. Let not the sacredness of Laurelled, still more, of Crowned Heads, be tampered with. Should we, at a future day, find circumstances altered, and the time come for Publication, then may these glimpses into the privacy of the Illustrious be conceded; which for the present were little better than treacherous, perhaps traitorous Eavesdroppings. Of Lord Byron, therefore, of Pope Pius, Emperor Tarakwang, and the "White Water-roses" (Chinese Carbonari) with their mysteries, no notice here! Of Napoleon himself we shall only, glancing from afar, remark that Teufelsdröckh's relation to him seems to have been of very varied character. At first we find our poor Professor on the point of being shot as a spy; then taken into private conversation, even pinched on the ear, yet presented with no money; at last indignantly dismissed, almost thrown out of doors, as an "Ideologist." "He himself," says the Professor, "was among the completest Ideologists, at least Ideopraxists: in the Idea (*in der Idee*) he lived, moved, and fought. The man was a divine Missionary, though unconscious of it; and preached, through the cannon's throat, that great doctrine, *La carrière ouverte aux talens** (The Tools to him that can handle them), which is our ultimate Political Evangile, wherein alone can Liberty lie. Madly enough he preached, it is true, as Enthusiasts and first Missionaries are wont, with imperfect utterance, amid much frothy rant; yet as articulately perhaps as the case admitted. Or call him, if you will, an American Backwoods-man, who had to fell unpenetrated forests, and battle with innumerable wolves, and did not entirely forbear strong liquor, rioting, and even theft; whom, notwithstanding, the peaceful Sower will follow, and, as he cuts the boundless harvest, bless."

More legitimate and decisively authentic is Teufelsdröckh's appearance and emergence (we know not well whence) in the solitude of the North Cape, on that June Midnight. He has a "light-blue Spanish cloak" hanging round him, as his "most commodious, principal, indeed sole upper-garment;" and stands there, on the World-promontory, looking over the infinite Brine, like a little blue Belfry (as we figure), now motionless indeed, yet ready, if stirred, to ring quaintest changes.

"Silence as of Death," writes he; "for Midnight, even in the Arctic latitudes, has its character: nothing but the granite cliffs ruddy-tinged, the peaceable gurgle of that slow-heaving Polar Ocean, over which in the utmost North the great Sun hangs low and lazy, as if he too were slumbering. Yet is his cloud-couch wrought of crimson and cloth of gold; yet does his light stream over the mirror of waters, like a tremulous fire-pillar, shooting downwards to the abyss, and hide itself under my feet. In such moments, Solitude also is invaluable; for who would speak, or be looked on, when behind him lies all Europe and Africa, fast asleep, except the watchmen; and before him the silent Immensity, and Palace of the Eternal, whereof our Sun is but a porch-lamp.

"Nevertheless, in this solemn moment, comes a man, or monster, scrambling from among the rock-hollows; and, shaggy, huge as the Hyperborean Bear, hails me in Russian speech: most probably, therefore, a Russian Smuggler. With courteous brevity, I signify my indifference to contraband trade, my humane intentions, yet strong wish to be private. In vain: the monster, counting doubtless on his superior stature, and minded to make sport for himself, or perhaps profit, were it with murder, continues to advance; ever assailing me with his importunate train-oil breath; and now has advanced till we stand both on the verge of the rock, the deep Sea rippling greedily down below. What argument will avail? On the thick Hyperborean, cherubic reasoning, seraphic eloquence were lost. Prepared for such extremity, I, deftly enough, whisk aside one step; draw out, from my interior reservoirs, a sufficient Birmingham Horse-pistol, and say: 'Be so obliging as retire, Friend (*Er ziehe sich zurück, Freund*), and with promptitude!' This logic even the Hyperborean understands: fast enough, with apologetic, petitionary growl, he sidles off; and, except for suicidal, as well as homicidal purposes, need not return.

"Such I hold to be the genuine use of Gunpowder: that it makes all men alike tall. Nay, if thou be cooler, cleverer than I, if thou have more *Mind,* though all but no *Body* whatever, then canst thou kill me first, and art the taller. Hereby, at least, is the Goliath powerless, and the David resistless; savage Animalism is nothing, inventive Spiritualism is all.

"With respect to Duels, indeed, I have my own ideas. Few things, in this so surprising world, strike me with more surprise. Two little visual Spectra of men, hovering with insecure enough cohesion in the midst of the UNFATHOM-ABLE, and to dissolve therein, at any rate, very soon,—make pause at the distance of twelve paces asunder; whirl round; and, simultaneously by the cunningest mechanism, explode one another into Dissolution; and off-hand become Air, and Non-extant! Deuce on it (*verdammt*)! The little spitfires!—Nay, I think with old Hugo von Trimberg; 'God must needs laugh outright, could such a thing be, to see his wondrous Mannikins here below.' "

But amid these specialities, let us not forget the great genera-lity, which is our chief quest here: How prospered the inner man of Teufelsdröckh under so much outward shifting? Does Legion still lurk in him, though repressed; or has he exorcised that Devil's Brood? We can answer that the symptoms con-tinue promising. Experience is the grand spiritual Doctor; and with him Teufelsdröckh has now been long a patient, swallow-ing many a bitter bolus. Unless our poor Friend belong to the numerous class of Incurables, which seems not likely, some cure will doubtless be effected. We should rather say that Legion, or the Satanic School, was now pretty well extirpated and cast out, but next to nothing introduced in its room; whereby the heart remains, for the while, in a quiet but no comfortable state.

"At length, after so much roasting," thus writes our Auto-biographer, "I was what you might name calcined. Pray only that it be not rather, as is the more frequent issue, reduced to a *caput-mortuum!* * But in any case, by mere dint of practice, I had grown familiar with many things. Wretchedness was still wretched; but I could now partly see through it, and despise it.

Which highest mortal, in this inane Existence, had I not found a Shadow-hunter, or Shadow-hunted; and, when I looked through his brave garnitures, miserable enough? Thy wishes have all been sniffed aside, thought I: but what, had they even been all granted! Did not the Boy Alexander weep because he had not two Planets to conquer; or a whole Solar System; or after that, a whole Universe? *Ach Gott!* when I gazed into these Stars, have they not looked down on me as if with pity from their serene spaces; like Eyes glistening with heavenly tears over the little lot of man! Thousands of human generations, all as noisy as our own, have been swallowed up of Time, and there remains no wreck of them any more; and Arcturus and Orion and Sirius and the Pleiades are still shining in their courses, clear and young, as when the Shepherd first noted them in the plain of Shinar. Pshaw! what is this paltry little Dog-cage of an Earth; what art thou that sittest whining there? Thou art still Nothing, Nobody: true; but who then is Something, Somebody? For thee the Family of Man has no use; it rejects thee; thou art wholly as a dissevered limb: so be it; perhaps it is better so!"

Too heavy-laden Teufelsdröckh! Yet surely his bands are loosening; one day he will hurl the burden far from him, and bound forth free, and with a second youth.

"This," says our Professor, "was the CENTRE OF INDIFFERENCE I had now reached; through which whoso travels from the Negative Pole to the Positive must necessarily pass."

CHAPTER 9
THE EVERLASTING YEA

"TEMPTATIONS in the Wilderness!" exclaims Teufelsdröckh: "Have we not all to be tried with such? Not so easily can the old Adam, lodged in us by birth, be dispossessed. Our Life is compassed round with Necessity; yet is the meaning of Life itself no other than Freedom, than Voluntary Force: thus have we a warfare; in the beginning, especially, a hard-fought Battle. For the God-given mandate, *Work thou in Welldoing,* lies mysteriously written, in Promethean, Prophetic Characters, in our hearts; and leaves us no rest, night or day, till it be deciphered and obeyed; till it burn forth, in our conduct, a visible, acted Gospel of Freedom. And as the clay-given mandate, *Eat thou and be filled,* at the same time, persuasively proclaims itself through every nerve,—must there not be a confusion, a contest, before the better Influence can become the upper?

"To me nothing seems more natural than that the Son of Man, when such God-given mandate first prophetically stirs within him, and the Clay must now be vanquished or vanquish,—should be carried of the spirit into grim Solitudes, and there fronting the Tempter do grimmest battle with him; defiantly setting him at nought, till he yield and fly. Name it as we choose; with or without visible Devil, whether in the natural Desert of rocks and sands, or in the populous, moral Desert of selfishness and baseness,—to such Temptation are we all called. Unhappy if we are not! Unhappy if we are but Half-men, in whom that divine handwriting has never blazed forth, all-subduing, in true sun-splendour; but quivers dubiously amid meaner lights; or smoulders, in dull pain, in darkness, under earthly vapours!—Our Wilderness is the wide World in an Atheistic Century; our Forty Days are long years of suffering and fasting: nevertheless, to these also comes an end. Yes, to me also was given, if not Victory, yet the consciousness of Battle, and the resolve to persevere therein while life or faculty is left. To me also, entangled in the enchanted forests, demon-peopled, doleful of sight and of sound, it was given, after weariest wanderings, to work out my way into the higher sunlit slopes—of that Mountain which has no summit, or whose summit is in Heaven only!"

He says elsewhere, under a less ambitious figure; as figures are, once for all, natural to him: "Has not thy Life been that of most sufficient men (*tüchtigen Männer*) thou hast known in this generation? An outflush of foolish young Enthusiasm, like the first fallow-crop, wherein are as many weeds as valuable herbs: this all parched away, under the Droughts of practical and spiritual Unbelief; as Disappointment, in thought and act, often-repeated gave rise to Doubt, and Doubt gradually settled into Denial! If I have had a second-crop, and now see the perennial greensward, and sit under umbrageous cedars, which defy all Drought (and Doubt): herein too, be the Heavens praised I am not without examples, and even exemplars."

So that for Teufelsdröckh also there has been a "glorious revolution:" these mad shadow-hunting and shadow-hunted Pilgrimings of his, were but some purifying "Temptation in the Wilderness," before his apostolic work (such as it was) could begin; which Temptation is now happily over, and the Devil once more worsted! Was "that high moment in the *Rue de l'Enfer*," then, properly the turning point of the battle; when the Fiend said, *Worship me or be torn in shreds,* and was answered valiantly with an *Apage Satanas?**—Singular Teufelsdröckh, would thou hadst told thy singular story in plain words! But it is fruitless to look there, in those Paper-bags, for such. Nothing but innuendoes, figurative crotchets: a typical Shadow, fitfully wavering, prophetico-satiric; no clear logical Picture. "How paint to the sensual eye," asks he once, "what passes in the Holy-of-Holies of Man's Soul; in what words, known to these profane times, speak even afar off of the Unspeakable?" We ask in turn: Why perplex these times, profane as they are, with needless obscurity, by omission and by commission? Not mystical only is our Professor, but whimsical; and involves himself, now more than ever, in eye-bewildering *chiaroscuro*. Successive glimpses, here faithfully imparted, our more gifted readers must endeavour to combine for their own behoof.

He says: "The hot Harmattan-wind had raged itself out; its

howl went silent within me; and the long-deafened soul could now hear. I paused in my wild wanderings; and sat me down to wait, and consider; for it was as if the hour of change drew nigh. I seemed to surrender, to renounce utterly, and say: Fly, then, false shadows of Hope; I will chase you no more, I will believe you no more. And ye too, haggard spectres of Fear, I care not for you; ye too are all shadows and a lie. Let me rest here; for I am way-weary and life-weary; I will rest here, were it but to die: to die or to live is alike to me; alike insignificant."—And again: "Here, then, as I lay in that CENTRE OF INDIFFERENCE; cast, doubtless, by benignant upper Influence, into a healing sleep, the heavy dreams rolled gradually away, and I awoke to a new Heaven and a new Earth. The first preliminary moral Act, Annihilation of Self (*Selbst-tödtung*), had been happily accomplished; and my mind's eyes were now unsealed, and its hands ungyved."

Might we not also conjecture that the following passage refers to his Locality, during this same "healing sleep;" that his Pilgrim-staff lies cast aside here, on "the high table-land;" and indeed that the repose is already taking wholesome effect on him? Were it not that the tone, in some parts, has more of riancy, even of levity, than we could have expected. However, in Teufelsdröckh, there is always the strangest Dualism: light dancing, with guitar-music, will be going on in the forecourt, while by fits from within comes the faint whimpering of woe and wail. We transcribe the piece entire:

"Beautiful it was to sit there, as in my skyey Tent, musing and meditating; on the high table-land, in front of the Mountains; over me, as roof, the azure Dome; and around me, for walls, four azure flowing curtains,—namely, of the Four azure Winds, on whose bottom-fringes also I have seen gilding. And then to fancy the fair Castles that stood sheltered in these Mountain hollows; with their green flower-lawns, and white dames and damosels, lovely enough: or better still, the straw-roofed Cottages, wherein stood many a Mother baking bread, with her children round her:—all hidden and protectingly folded up in the valley-folds; yet there and alive, as sure as if I beheld them. Or to see, as well as fancy, the nine Towns and Villages, that lay round my mountain-seat, which, in still weather, were wont to speak to me (by their steeple-bells) with metal tongue; and, in almost all weather, proclaimed their vitality by repeated Smoke-clouds; whereon, as on a culinary horologe, I might read the hour of the day. For it was the smoke of cookery, as kind housewives, at morning, midday, eventide, were boiling their husbands' kettles; and ever a blue pillar rose up into the air, successively or simultaneously, from each of the nine, saying, as plainly as smoke could say: Such and such a meal is getting ready here. Not uninteresting! For you have the whole Borough, with all its love-makings and scandal-mongeries, contentions and contentments, as in minia-ture, and could cover it all with your hat.—If, in my wide Wayfarings, I had learned to look into the business of the World in its details, here perhaps was the place for combining it into general propositions, and deducing inferences therefrom.

"Often also could I see the black Tempest marching in anger through the Distance: round some Schreckhorn, as yet grim-blue, would the eddying vapour gather, and there tumul-tuously eddy, and flow down like a mad witch's hair; till, after a space, it vanished, and, in the clear sunbeam, your Schreck-horn stood smiling grim-white, for the vapour had held snow. How thou fermentest and elaboratest, in thy great fermenting-vat and laboratory of an Atmosphere, of a World, O Nature!— Or what is Nature? Ha! why do I not name thee GOD? Art thou not the 'Living Garment of God?' O Heavens, is it, in very deed, HE, then, that ever speaks through thee; that lives and loves in thee, that lives and loves in me?

"Foreshadows, call them rather fore-splendours, of that Truth, and Beginning of Truths, fell mysteriously over my soul. Sweeter than Dayspring to the Shipwrecked in Nova Zembla; ah! like the mother's voice to her little child that strays bewildered, weeping, in unknown tumults; like soft streamings of celestial music to my too exasperated heart, came that Evangile. The Universe is not dead and demoniacal, a charnel-house with spectres; but god-like, and my Father's!

"With other eyes too could I now look upon my fellow man; with an infinite Love, an infinite Pity. Poor, wandering, wayward man! Art thou not tried, and beaten with stripes, even as I am? Ever, whether thou bear the Royal mantle or the

Beggar's gabardine, art thou not so weary, so heavy-laden; and thy Bed of Rest is but a Grave. O my Brother, my Brother! why cannot I shelter thee in my bosom, and wipe away all tears from thy eyes.—Truly, the din of many-voiced Life, which, in this solitude, with the mind's organ, I could hear, was no longer a maddening discord, but a melting one: like inarticulate cries, and sobbings of a dumb creature, which in the ear of Heaven are prayers. The poor Earth, with her poor joys, was now my needy Mother, not my cruel Stepdame; Man, with his so mad Wants and so mean Endeavours, had become the dearer to me; and even for his sufferings and his sins, I now first named him Brother. Thus was I standing in the porch of that 'Sanctuary of Sorrow;' by strange, steep ways, had I too been guided thither; and ere long its sacred gates would open, and the 'Divine Depth of Sorrow' lie disclosed to me."

The Professor says, he here first got eye on the Knot that had been strangling him, and straightway could unfasten it, and was free. "A vain interminable controversy," writes he, "touching what is at present called Origin of Evil, or some such thing, arises in every soul, since the beginning of the world; and in every soul, that would pass from idle Suffering into actual Endeavouring, must first be put an end to. The most, in our time, have to go content with a simple, incomplete enough Suppression of this controversy; to a few some Solution of it is indispensable. In every new era, too, such Solution comes out in different terms; and ever the Solution of the last era has become obsolete, and is found unserviceable. For it is man's nature to change his Dialect from century to century; he cannot help it though he would. The authentic Church-Catechism of our present century has not yet fallen into my hands: meanwhile, for my own private behoof, I attempt to elucidate the matter so. Man's Unhappiness, as I construe, comes of his Greatness; it is because there is an Infinite in him, which with all his cunning he cannot quite bury under the Finite. Will the whole Finance Ministers and Upholsterers and Confectioners of modern Europe undertake, in joint-stock company, to make one Shoeblack HAPPY? They cannot accomplish it, above an hour or two; for the Shoeblack also has a Soul quite other than his Stomach; and would require, if you consider it, for his permanent satisfaction and saturation, simply this allotment, no more, and no less: *God's infinite Universe altogether to himself,* therein to enjoy infinitely, and fill every wish as fast as it rose. Oceans of Hochheimer, a Throat like that Ophiuchus!* Speak not of them; to the infinite Shoeblack they are as nothing. No sooner is your ocean filled, than he grumbles that it might have been of better vintage. Try him with half of a Universe, of an Omnipotence, he sets to quarrelling with the proprietor of the other half, and declares himself the most maltreated of men.— Always there is a black spot in our sunshine: it is even, as I said, the *Shadow of Ourselves.*

"But the whim we have of Happiness is somewhat thus. By certain valuations, and averages, of our own striking, we come upon some sort of average terrestrial lot; this we fancy belongs to us by nature, and of indefeasible right. It is simple payment of our wages, of our deserts; requires neither thanks nor complaint: only such *overplus* as there may be do we account Happiness; any *deficit* again is Misery. Now consider that we have the valuation of our own deserts ourselves, and what a fund of Self-conceit there is in each of us,—do you wonder that the balance should so often dip the wrong way, and many a Blockhead cry: See there, what a payment; was ever worthy gentleman so used!—I tell thee, Blockhead, it all comes of thy Vanity; of what thou *fanciest* those same deserts of thine to be. Fancy that thou deservest to be hanged (as is most likely), thou wilt feel it happiness to be only shot: fancy that thou deservest to be hanged in a hair-halter, it will be a luxury to die in hemp.

"So true is it, what I then said, that *the Fraction of Life can be increased in value not so much by increasing your Numerator, as by lessening your Denominator.* Nay, unless my Algebra deceive me, *Unity* itself divided by *Zero* will give *Infinity.* Make thy claim of wages a zero, then; thou hast the world under thy feet. Well did the Wisest of our time write: 'It is only with Renunciation *(Entsagen)* that Life, properly speaking, can be said to begin.'*

"I asked myself: What is this that, ever since earliest years, thou hast been fretting and fuming, and lamenting and self-tormenting, on account of? Say it in a word: is it not because thou art not HAPPY? Because the THOU (sweet gentleman) is not sufficiently honoured, nourished, soft-bedded, and lovingly cared for? Foolish soul! What Act of Legislature was there that *thou* shouldst be Happy? A little while ago thou hadst no right to *be* at all. What if thou wert born and predestined not to be Happy, but to be Unhappy! Art thou nothing other than a Vulture, then, that fliest through the Universe seeking after somewhat to *eat;* and shrieking dolefully because carrion enough is not given thee? Close thy *Byron;* open thy *Goethe.*"

"*Es leuchtet mir ein,* I see a glimpse of it!" cries he elsewhere: "there is in man a HIGHER than Love of Happiness: he can do without Happiness, and instead thereof find Blessedness! Was it not to preach forth this same HIGHER that sages and martyrs, the Poet and the Priest, in all times, have spoken and suffered; bearing testimony, through life and through death, of the Godlike that is in Man, and how in the Godlike only has he Strength and Freedom? Which God-inspired Doctrine art thou too honoured to be taught; O Heavens! and broken with manifold merciful Afflictions, even till thou become contrite, and learn it! O thank thy Destiny for these; thankfully bear what yet remain: thou hadst need of them; the Self in thee needed to be annihilated. By benignant fever-paroxysms is Life rooting out the deep-seated chronic Disease, and triumphs over Death. On the roaring billows of Time, thou art not engulphed, but borne aloft into the azure of Eternity. Love not Pleasure; love God. This is the EVERLASTING YEA, wherein all contradiction is solved; wherein whoso walks and works, it is well with him."

And again: "Small is it that thou canst trample the Earth with its injuries under thy feet, as old Greek Zeno trained thee: thou canst love the Earth while it injures thee, and even because it injures thee; for this a Greater than Zeno was needed, and he too was sent. Knowest thou that '*Worship of Sorrow?*' The Temple thereof, opened* some eighteen centuries ago, now lies in ruins, overgrown with jungle, the habitation of doleful creatures: nevertheless, venture forward; in a low crypt, arched out of falling fragments, thou findest the Altar still there, and its sacred Lamp perennially burning."

Without pretending to comment on which strange utterances, the Editor will only remark that there lies beside them, much of a still more questionable character; unsuited to the general apprehension; nay wherein he himself does not see his way. Nebulous disquisitions on Religion, yet not without bursts of splendour; on the "perennial continuance of Inspiration;" on Prophecy; that there are "true Priests, as well as Baal-Priests, in our own day:" with more of the like sort. We select some fractions, by way of finish to this farrago.

"Cease, my much-respected Herr von Voltaire," thus apostrophises the Professor: "shut thy sweet voice; for the task appointed thee seems finished. Sufficiently hast thou demonstrated this proposition, considerable or otherwise: That the Mythus of the Christian Religion looks not in the eighteenth century as it did in the eighth. Alas, were thy six-and-thirty quartos, and the six-and-thirty thousand other quartos and folios, and flying sheets or reams, printed before and since on the same subject, all needed to convince us of so little! But what next? Wilt thou help us to embody the divine Spirit of that Religion in a new Mythus, in a new vehicle and vesture, that our Souls, otherwise too like perishing, may live? What! thou hast no faculty in that kind? Only a torch for burning, no hammer for building? Take our thanks, then, and——thyself away.

'Meanwhile what are antiquated Mythuses to me? Or is the God present, felt in my own Heart a thing which Herr von Voltaire will dispute out of me; or dispute into me? To the 'Worship of Sorrow' ascribe what origin and genesis thou pleasest, *has* not that Worship originated, and been generated; is it not *here?* Feel it in thy heart, and then say whether it is of God! This is Belief; all else is Opinion,—for which latter whoso will let him worry and be worried."

"Neither," observes he elsewhere, "shall ye tear out one another's eyes, struggling over 'Plenary Inspiration,' and such like: try rather to get a little even Partial Inspiration, each of you for himself. One BIBLE I know, of whose Plenary Inspiration doubt is not so much as possible; nay with my own eyes I saw the God's-Hand writing it: thereof all other Bibles are but Leaves,—say, in Picture-Writing to assist the weaker faculty."

Or to give the wearied reader relief, and bring it to an end, let him take the following perhaps more intelligible passage:

"To me, in this our Life," says the Professor, "which is an internecine warfare with the Time-spirit, other warfare seems questionable. Hast thou in any way a Contention with thy brother, I advise thee, think well what the meaning thereof is. If thou gauge it to the bottom, it is simply this: 'Fellow, see! thou art taking more than thy share of Happiness in the world, something from *my* share: which, by the Heavens, thou shalt not; nay I will fight thee rather.'—Alas! and the whole lot to be divided is such a beggarly matter, truly a 'feast of shells,' for the substance has been spilled out: not enough to quench one Appetite; and the collective human species clutching at them!—Can we not, in all such cases, rather say: 'Take it, thou too-ravenous individual; take that pitiful additional fraction of a share, which I reckoned mine, but which thou so wantest; take it with a blessing: would to Heaven I had enough for thee!'—If Fichte's *Wissenschaftslehre** be 'to a certain extent, Applied Christianity,' surely to a still greater extent, so is this. We have here not a Whole Duty of Man,* yet a Half Duty, namely the Passive half: could we but do it, as we can demonstrate it!

"But indeed Conviction, were it never so excellent, is worthless till it convert itself into Conduct. Nay properly Conviction is not possible till then; inasmuch as all Speculation is by nature endless, formless, a vortex amid vortices: only, by a felt indubitable certainty of Experience, does it find any centre to revolve round, and so fashion itself into a system. Most true is it, as a wise man teaches us, that 'Doubt of any sort cannot be removed except by Action.'* On which ground too let him who gropes painfully in darkness or uncertain light, and prays vehemently that the dawn may ripen into day, lay this other precept well to heart, which to me was of invaluable service: '*Do the Duty which lies nearest thee,*'* which thou knowest to be a Duty! Thy second Duty will already have become clearer.

"May we not say, however, that the hour of Spiritual Enfranchisement is even this: When your Ideal World, wherein the whole man has been dimly struggling and inexpressibly languishing to work, becomes revealed, and thrown open; and you discover, with amazement enough, like the Lothario in *Wilhelm Meister,* that your 'America is here or nowhere?'* The

Situation that has not its Duty, its Ideal, was never yet occupied by man. Yes here, in this poor, miserable, hampered, despicable Actual, wherein thou even now standest, here or nowhere is thy Ideal: work it out therefrom; and working, believe, live, be free. Fool! The Ideal is in thyself, the Impediment too is in thyself: thy Condition is but the stuff thou art to shape that same Ideal out of: what matters whether such stuff be of this sort or of that, so the Form thou give it be heroic, be poetic? O thou that pinest in the imprisonment of the Actual, and criest bitterly to the gods for a kingdom wherein to rule and create, know this of a truth: the thing thou seekest is already with thee, 'here or nowhere,' couldst thou only see!

"But it is with man's Soul as it was with Nature: the beginning of Creation is—Light. Till the eye have vision, the whole members are in bonds. Divine moment, when over the tempest-tost Soul, as once over the wild-weltering Chaos, it is spoken: Let there be Light! Ever to the greatest that has felt such moment, is it not miraculous and God-announcing; even, as under simpler figures, to the simplest and least? The mad primeval Discord is hushed; the rudely-jumbled conflicting elements bind themselves into separate Firmaments: deep silent rock-foundations are built beneath; and the skyey vault with its everlasting Luminaries above: instead of a dark wasteful Chaos, we have a blooming, fertile, Heaven-encompassed World.

"I too could now say to myself: Be no longer a Chaos, but a World, or even Worldkin. Produce! Produce! Were it but the pitifullest infinitesimal fraction of a Product, produce it in God's name! 'Tis the utmost thou hast in thee; out with it then. Up, up! Whatsoever thy hand findeth to do, do it with thy whole might. Work while it is called To-day, for the Night cometh wherein no man can work."

CHAPTER 10

PAUSE

THUS have we, as closely and perhaps satisfactorily as, in such circumstances, might be, followed Teufelsdröckh through the various successive states and stages of Growth, Entanglement, Unbelief, and almost Reprobation, into a certain clearer state of what he himself seems to consider as Conversion. "Blame not the word," says he; "rejoice rather that such a word, signifying such a thing, has come to light in our Modern Era, though hidden from the wisest Ancients. The Old World knew nothing of Conversion: instead of an *Ecce Homo*, they had only some *Choice of Hercules*.* It was a new-attained progress in the Moral Development of man: hereby has the Highest come home to the bosoms of the most Limited; what to Plato was but a hallucination, and to Socrates a chimera, is now clear and certain to your Zinzendorfs, your Wesleys, and the poorest of their Pietists and Methodists."

It is here then that the spiritual majority of Teufelsdröckh commences: we are henceforth to see him "Work in Welldoing," with the spirit and clear aims of a Man. He has discovered that the Ideal Workshop he so panted for, is even this same Actual ill-furnished Workshop he has so long been stumbling in. He can say to himself: "Tools? Thou hast no Tools? Why, there is not a Man, or a Thing, now alive but has tools. The basest of created animalcules, the Spider itself, has a spinning-jenny, and warping-mill, and power-loom, within its head; the stupidest of Oysters has a Papin's-Digester, with stone-and-lime house to hold it in: every being that can live can do something; this let him *do.*—Tools? Hast thou not a Brain, furnished, furnishable with some glimmerings of Light; and three fingers to hold a Pen withal? Never since Aaron's Rod went out of practice, or even before it, was there such a wonder-working Tool: greater than all recorded miracles have been performed by Pens. For strangely in this so solid-seeming World, which nevertheless is in continual restless flux, it is appointed that *Sound,* to appearance the most fleeting, should be the most continuing of all things. The WORD is well said to be omnipotent in this world; man, thereby divine, can create as by a *Fiat*. Awake, arise! Speak forth what is in thee; what God has given thee, what the Devil shall not take away. Higher task than that of Priesthood was allotted to no man: wert thou but the meanest in that sacred Hierarchy, is it not honour enough therein to spend and be spent?

"By this Art, which whoso will may sacrilegiously degrade into a handicraft," adds Teufelsdröckh, "have I thenceforth abidden. Writings of mine, not indeed known as mine (for what am *I*?), have fallen, perhaps not altogether void, into the mighty seedfield of Opinion; fruits of my unseen sowing gratifyingly meet me here and there. I thank the Heavens that I have now found my Calling; wherein, with or without perceptible result, I am minded diligently to persevere.

"Nay how knowest thou," cries he, "but this and the other pregnant Device, now grown to be a world-renowned far-working Institution; like a grain of right mustard-seed once cast into the right soil, and now stretching out strong boughs to the four winds, for the birds of the air to lodge in,—may have been properly my doing? Some one's doing it without doubt was; from some Idea in some single Head it did first of all take beginning: why not from some Idea in mine?" Does Teufelsdröckh here glance at that "SOCIETY FOR THE CONSERVATION OF PROPERTY (*Eigenthums-conservirende Gesellschaft*)," of which so many ambiguous notices glide spectre-like through these inexpressible Paperbags? "An Institution," hints he, "not unsuitable to the wants of the time; as indeed such sudden extension proves: for already can the Society number, among its office-bearers or corresponding members, the highest Names, if not the highest Persons, in Germany, England, France; and contributions, both of money and of meditation, pour in from all quarters; to, if possible, enlist the remaining Integrity of the world, and, defensively and with forethought, marshal it round this Palladium." Does Teufelsdröckh mean, then, to give himself out as the originator of that so notable *Eigenthums-conservirende* ("Owndom-conserving") *Gesellschaft;* and, if so, what, in the Devil's name, is it? He again hints: "At a time when the divine Commandment, *Thou shalt not steal,*

wherein truly, if well understood, is comprised the whole
Hebrew Decalogue, with Solon's and Lycurgus's Constitu-
tions, Justinian's Pandects, the Code Napoléon,* and all Codes,
Catechisms, Divinities, Moralities whatsoever, that man has
hitherto devised (and enforced with Altar-fire and Gallows-
ropes) for his social guidance: at a time, I say, when this divine
Commandment has all but faded away from the general
remembrance; and, with little disguise, a new opposite Commandment, *Thou shalt steal,* is every where promulgated,—it
perhaps behoved, in this universal dotage and deliration,* the
sound portion of mankind to bestir themselves and rally. When
the widest and wildest violations of that divine right of
Property, the only divine right now extant or conceivable, are
sanctioned and recommended by a vicious Press, and the world
has lived to hear it asserted that *we have no Property in our very
Bodies, but only an accidental Possession, and Liferent,* what is the
issue to be looked for? Hangmen and Catchpoles may, by their
noose-gins and baited fall-traps, keep down the smaller sort of
vermin: but what, except perhaps some such Universal Asso-
ciation, can protect us against whole meat-devouring and man-
devouring hosts of Boa Constrictors? If, therefore, the more
sequestered Thinker have wondered, in his privacy, from what
hand that perhaps not ill-written *Program* in the Public Journals,
with its high *Prize-Questions* and so liberal *Prizes,* could have
proceeded,—let him now cease such wonder; and, with undi-
vided faculty, betake himself to the *Concurrenz* (Competition)."

We ask: Has this same "perhaps not ill-written *Program,*" or
any other authentic Transaction of that Property-conserving
Society, fallen under the eye of the British Reader, in any
Journal, foreign or domestic? If so, what are those *Prize-
Questions;* what are the terms of Competition, and when, and
where? No printed Newspaper leaf, no farther light of any sort,
to be met with in these Paperbags! Or is the whole business one
other of those whimsicalities, and perverse inexplicabilities,
whereby Herr Teufelsdröckh, meaning much or nothing, is
pleased so often to play fast and loose with us?

Here, indeed, at length, must the Editor give utterance to a painful suspicion which, through late Chapters, has begun to haunt him; paralysing any little enthusiasm, that might still have rendered his thorny Biographical task a labour of love. It is a suspicion grounded perhaps on trifles, yet confirmed almost into certainty by the more and more discernible humouristico-satirical tendency of Teufelsdröckh, in whom underground humours, and intricate sardonic rogueries, wheel within wheel, defy all reckoning: a suspicion, in one word, that these Autobiographical Documents are partly a Mystification! What if many a so-called Fact were little better than a Fiction; if here we had no direct Camera-obscura Picture of the Professor's History; but only some more or less fantastic Adumbration, symbolically, perhaps significantly enough, shadowing forth the same! Our theory begins to be that, in receiving as literally authentic what was but hieroglyphically so, Hofrath Heusch-recke, whom in that case we scruple not to name Hofrath Nose-of-Wax, was made a fool of, and set adrift to make fools of others. Could it be expected, indeed, that a man so known for impenetrable reticence as Teufelsdröckh, would all at once frankly unlock his private citadel to an English Editor and a German Hofrath; and not rather deceptively *in*lock both Editor and Hofrath, in the labyrinthic tortuosities and covered ways of said citadel (having enticed them thither), to see, in his half-devilish way, how the fools would look?

Of one fool, however, the Herr Professor will perhaps find himself short. On a small slip, formerly thrown aside as blank, the ink being all but invisible, we lately notice, and with effort decipher, the following: "What are your historical Facts; still more your biographical? Wilt thou know a Man, above all, a Mankind, by stringing together beadrolls of what thou namest Facts? The Man is the spirit he worked in; not what he did, but what he became. Facts are engraved Hierograms, for which the fewest have the key. And then how your Blockhead (*Dumm-kopf*) studies not their Meaning; but simply whether they are well or ill cut, what he calls Moral or Immoral! Still worse is it with your Bungler (*Pfuscher*): such I have seen reading some Rousseau, with pretences of interpretation; and mistaking the ill-cut Serpent-of-Eternity for a common poisonous Reptile." Was the Professor apprehensive lest an Editor, selected as the present boasts himself, might mistake the Teufelsdröckh Serpent-of-Eternity in like manner? For which reason it was to be altered, not without underhand satire, into a plainer Symbol? Or is this merely one of his half-sophisms, half-truisms, which if he can but set on the back of a Figure, he cares not whither it gallop? We say not with certainty; and indeed, so strange is the Professor, can never say. If our Suspicion be wholly unfounded, let his own questionable ways, not our necessary circumspectness, bear the blame.

But be this as it will, the somewhat exasperated and indeed exhausted Editor determines here to shut these Paper-bags, for the present. Let it suffice that we know of Teufelsdröckh, so far, if "not what he did, yet what he became:" the rather, as his character has now taken its ultimate bent, and no new revolution, of importance, is to be looked for. The imprisoned Chrysalis is now a winged Psyche; and such, wheresoever be its flight, it will continue. To trace by what complex gyrations (flights or involuntary waftings) through the mere external Life-element, Teufelsdröckh reaches his University Professorship, and the Psyche clothes herself in civic Titles, without altering her now fixed nature,—would be comparatively an unproductive task; were we even unsuspicious of its being, for us at least, a false and impossible one. His outward Biography, therefore, which, at the Blumine Lover's-Leap, we saw churned utterly into spray-vapour, may hover in that condition, for aught that concerns us here. Enough that by survey of certain "pools and plashes," we have ascertained its general direction: do we not already know that, by one way and other, it *has* long since rained down again into a stream; and even now, at Weissnichtwo, flows deep and still, fraught with the *Philosophy of Clothes,* and visible to whoso will cast eye thereon? Over much invaluable matter that lies scattered, like jewels among quarry-rubbish, in those Paper-catacombs, we may have occasion to glance back, and somewhat will demand insertion at the right place: meanwhile be our toilsome diggings therein suspended.

If now, before reopening the great *Clothes-Volume,* we ask what our degree of progress, during these Ten Chapters, has been, towards right understanding of the *Clothes-Philosophy,* let not our discouragement become total. To speak in that old figure of the Hell-gate Bridge over Chaos, a few flying pontoons have perhaps been added, though as yet they drift straggling on the Flood; how far they will reach, when once the chains are straightened and fastened, can, at present, only be matter of conjecture.

So much we already calculate. Through many a little loophole, we have had glimpses into the internal world of Teufelsdröckh: his strange mystic, almost magic Diagram of the Universe, and how it was gradually drawn, is not henceforth altogether dark to us. Those mysterious ideas on TIME, which merit consideration, and are not wholly unintelligible with such, may by and by prove significant. Still more may his somewhat peculiar view of Nature; the decisive Oneness he ascribes to Nature. How all Nature and Life are but one *Garment,* a "Living Garment," woven and ever a-weaving in the "Loom of Time:" is not here, indeed, the outline of a whole *Clothes-Philosophy;* at least the arena it is to work in? Remark too that the Character of the man, nowise without meaning in such a matter, becomes less enigmatic: amid so much tumultuous obscurity, almost like diluted madness, do not a certain indomitable Defiance and yet a boundless Reverence seem to loom forth, as the two mountain summits, on whose rock-strata all the rest were based and built?

Nay farther, may we not say that Teufelsdröckh's Biography, allowing it even, as suspected, only a hieroglyphical truth, exhibits a man, as it were preappointed for Clothes-Philosophy? To look through the Shows of things into Things themselves he is led and compelled. The "Passivity" given him by birth is fostered by all turns of his fortune. Everywhere cast out, like oil out of water, from mingling in any Employment, in any public Communion, he has no portion but Solitude, and a life of Meditation. The whole energy of his existence is directed, through long years, on one task: that of enduring pain, if he cannot cure it. Thus everywhere do the Shows of things oppress him, withstand him, threaten him with fearfullest destruction: only by victoriously penetrating into Things themselves can he find peace and a stronghold. But is not this same looking through the Shows or Vestures into the Things even the first preliminary to a *Philosophy of Clothes?* Do we not, in all this, discern some beckonings towards the true higher purport of such a Philosophy; and what shape it must assume with such a man, in such an era?

Perhaps in entering on Book Third, the courteous Reader is not utterly without guess whither he is bound: nor, let us hope, for all the fantastic Dream-Grottoes through which, as is our lot with Teufelsdröckh, he must wander, will there be wanting between whiles some twinkling of a steady Polar Star.

* * *

BOOK III

CHAPTER I
INCIDENT IN MODERN HISTORY

As a wonder-loving and wonder-seeking man, Teufelsdröckh, from an early part of this Clothes-Volume, has more and more exhibited himself. Striking it was, amid all his perverse cloudiness, with what force of vision and of heart he pierced into the mystery of the World; recognising in the highest sensible phenomena, so far as Sense went, only fresh or faded Raiment; yet ever, under this, a celestial Essence thereby rendered visible: and while, on the one hand, he trod the old rags of Matter, with their tinsels, into the mire, he on the other every where exalted Spirit above all earthly principalities and powers, and worshipped it, though under the meanest shapes, with a true Platonic Mysticism. What the man ultimately purposed by this casting his Greek-fire into the general Wardrobe of the Universe; what such more or less complete rending and burning of Garments throughout the whole compass of Civilised Life and Speculation, should lead to; the rather as he was no Adamite, in any sense, and could not, like Rousseau, recommend either bodily or intellectual Nudity, and a return to the savage state: all this our readers are now bent to discover; this is, in fact, properly the gist and purport of Professor Teufelsdröckh's Philosophy of Clothes.

Be it remembered, however, that such purport is here not so much evolved as detected to lie ready for evolving. We are to guide our British Friends into the new Gold-country, and shew them the mines; nowise to dig out and exhaust its wealth, which indeed remains for all time inexhaustible. Once there, let each dig for his own behoof, and enrich himself.

Neither, in so capricious inexpressible a Work as this of the Professor's, can our course now more than formerly be straightforward, step by step, but at best leap by leap. Significant Indications stand out here and there; which for the critical eye, that looks both widely and narrowly, shape themselves into some ground-scheme of a Whole: to select these with judgement, so that a leap from one to the other be possible, and (in our old figure) by chaining them together, a passable Bridge be effected: this as heretofore continues our only method. Among such light-spots, the following, floating in much wild matter about *Perfectibility,* has seemed worth clutching at:

"Perhaps the most remarkable incident in Modern History," says Teufelsdröckh, "is not the Diet of Worms, still less the Battle of Austerlitz, Waterloo, Peterloo,* or any other Battle; but an incident passed carelessly over by most Historians, and treated with some degree of ridicule by others; namely, George Fox's making to himself a Suit of Leather. This man, the first of the Quakers, and by trade a Shoemaker, was one of those, to whom, under ruder or purer form, the Divine Idea of the Universe is pleased to manifest itself; and, across all the hulls of Ignorance and earthly Degradation, shine through, in unspeakable Awfulness, unspeakable Beauty, on their souls: who therefore are rightly accounted Prophets, God-possessed; or even Gods, as in some periods it has chanced. Sitting in his stall; working on tanned hides, amid pincers, paste-horns, rosin, swine-bristles, and a nameless flood of rubbish, this youth had nevertheless a Living Spirit belonging to him; also an antique Inspired Volume, through which, as through a window, it could look upwards, and discern its celestial Home. The task of a daily pair of shoes, coupled even with some prospect of victuals, and an honourable Mastership in Cordwainery, and perhaps the post of Thirdborough in his Hundred,* as the crown of long faithful sewing,—was nowise satisfaction enough to such a mind: but ever amid the boring and hammering, came tones from that far country, came Splendours and Terrors; for this poor Cordwainer, as we said, was a Man; and the Temple of Immensity, wherein as Man he had been sent to minister, was full of holy mystery to him.

"The Clergy of the neighbourhood, the ordained Watchers and Interpreters of that same holy mystery, listened with unaffected tedium to his consultations, and advised him, as the solution of such doubts, to 'drink beer, and dance with the girls.' Blind leaders of the blind! For what end were their tithes levied and eaten; for what were their shovel-hats scooped out, and their surplices and cassock-aprons girt on; and such a church-repairing, and chaffering, and organing, and other racketting, held over that spot of God's Earth,—if Man were but a Patent Digester, and the Belly with its adjuncts the grand Reality? Fox turned from them, with tears and a sacred scorn, back to his Leather-parings and his Bible. Mountains of encumbrance, higher than Ætna, had been heaped over that Spirit: but it was a Spirit, and would not lie buried there. Through long days and nights of silent agony, it struggled and wrestled, with a man's force, to be free: how its prison-mountains heaved and swayed tumultuously, as the giant spirit shook them to this hand and that, and emerged into the light of Heaven! That Leicester shoe-shop, had men known it, was a holier place than any Vatican or Loretto-shrine.—'So bandaged, and hampered, and hemmed in,' groaned he, 'with thousand requisitions, obligations, straps, tatters, and tagrags, I can neither see nor move: not my own am I, but the World's; and Time flies fast, and Heaven is high, and Hell is deep: Man! bethink thee, if thou hast power of Thought! Why not; what binds me here? Want! Want!—Ha, of what? Will all the shoe-wages under the Moon ferry me across into that far Land of Light? Only Meditation can, and devout Prayer to God. I will to the woods: the hollow of a tree will lodge me, wild berries feed me; and for Clothes, cannot I stitch myself one perennial Suit of Leather!'

"Historical Oil-painting," continues Teufelsdröckh, "is one of the Arts I never practised; therefore shall I not decide whether this subject were easy of execution on the canvass. Yet often has it seemed to me as if such first outflashing of man's Freewill, to lighten, more and more into Day, the Chaotic Night that threatened to engulph him in its hindrances and its horrors, were properly the only grandeur there is in history. Let some living Angelo or Rosa, with seeing eye and understanding heart, picture George Fox on that morning, when he spreads out his cutting-board for the last time, and cuts cow-hides by unwonted patterns, and stitches them together into one continuous all-including Case, the farewell service of his awl! Stitch away, thou noble Fox: every prick of that little instrument is pricking into the heart of Slavery, and World-worship, and the Mammon-god. Thy elbows jerk, as in strong swimmer-strokes, and every stroke is bearing thee across the Prison-ditch, within which Vanity holds her Workhouse and Rag-fair, into lands of true Liberty; were the work done, there is in broad Europe one Free Man, and thou art he!

"Thus from the lowest depth there is a path to the loftiest height: and for the Poor also a Gospel has been published. Surely, if, as D'Alembert asserts, my illustrious namesake, Diogenes, was the greatest man of Antiquity, only that he wanted Decency, then by stronger reason is George Fox the greatest of the Moderns; and greater than Diogenes himself: for he too stands on the adamantine basis of his Manhood, casting aside all props and shoars; yet not, in half-savage Pride, undervaluing the Earth; valuing it rather, as a place to yield him warmth and food, he looks Heavenward from his Earth, and dwells in an element of Mercy and Worship, with a still Strength, such as the Cynic's Tub did nowise witness. Great, truly, was that Tub; a temple from which man's dignity and divinity was scornfully preached abroad: but greater is the Leather Hull, for the same sermon was preached there, and not in Scorn but in Love."

George Fox's "perennial suit," with all that it held, has been worn quite into ashes for nigh two centuries; why, in a discussion on the *Perfectibility of Society*, reproduce it now? Not out of blind sectarian partisanship: Teufelsdröckh himself is no Quaker; with all his pacific tendencies, did we not see him, in that scene at the North Cape, with the Archangel Smuggler, exhibit fire-arms?

For us, aware of his deep Sansculottism, there is more meant in this passage than meets the ear. At the same time, who can avoid smiling at the earnestness and Bœotian simplicity (if indeed there be not an underhand satire in it), with which that "Incident" is here brought forward; and, in the Professor's ambiguous way, as clearly perhaps as he durst in Weissnichtwo, recommended to imitation! Does Teufelsdröckh anticipate that, in this age of refinement, any considerable class of the community, by way of testifying against the "Mammon-god," and escaping from what he calls "Vanity's Workhouse and Ragfair," where doubtless some of them are toiled and whipped and hoodwinked sufficiently,—will sheathe themselves in close-fitting cases of Leather? The idea is ridiculous in the extreme. Will Majesty lay aside its robes of state, and Beauty its frills, and train-gowns, for a second-skin of tanned hide? By which change Huddersfield and Manchester, and Coventry and Paisley, and the Fancy-Bazaar, were reduced to hungry solitudes; and only Day and Martin* could profit. For neither would Teufelsdröckh's mad daydream, here as we presume covertly intended, of levelling Society (*levelling* it indeed with a vengeance, into one huge drowned marsh!), and so attaining the political effects of Nudity without its frigorific or other consequences,—be thereby realized. Would not the rich man purchase a waterproof suit of Russia Leather; and the highborn Belle step forth in red or azure morocco, lined with shamoy: the black cowhide being left to the Drudges and Gibeonites of the world; and so all the old Distinctions re-established?

Or has the Professor his own deeper intention; and laughs in his sleeve at our strictures and glosses, which indeed are but a part thereof?

CHAPTER 2

CHURCH CLOTHES

NOT less questionable is his Chapter on *Church Clothes,* which has the farther distinction of being the shortest in the Volume. We here translate it entire:

"By Church Clothes, it need not be premised, that I mean infinitely more than Cassocks and Surplices; and do not at all mean the mere haberdasher Sunday Clothes that men go to Church in. Far from it! Church Clothes are, in our vocabulary, the Forms, the *Vestures,* under which men have at various periods embodied and represented for themselves the Religious Principle; that is to say, invested the Divine Idea of the World with a sensible and practically active Body, so that it might dwell among them as a living and life-giving WORD.

"These are unspeakably the most important of all the vestures and garnitures of Human Existence. They are first spun and woven, I may say, by that wonder of wonders, SOCIETY; for it is still only when 'two or three are gathered together' that Religion, spiritually existent, and indeed indestructible however latent, in each, first outwardly manifests itself (as with 'cloven tongues of fire'), and seeks to be embodied in a visible Communion and Church Militant. Mystical, more than magical, is that Communing of Soul with Soul, both looking heavenward: here properly Soul first speaks with Soul; for only in looking heavenward, take it in what sense you may, not in looking earthward, does what we can call Union, mutual Love, Society, begin to be possible. How true is that of Novalis: 'It is certain, my Belief gains quite *infinitely* the moment I can convince another mind thereof!' Gaze thou in the face of thy Brother, in those eyes where plays the lambent fire of Kindness, or in those where rages the lurid conflagration of Anger; feel how thy own so quiet Soul is straightway involuntarily kindled with the like, and ye blaze and reverberate on each other, till it is all one limitless confluent flame (of embracing Love, or of deadly-grappling Hate); and then say what miraculous virtue goes out of man into man. But if so, through all the thick-plied hulls of our Earthly Life; how much more when it is of the Divine Life we speak, and inmost ME is, as it were, brought into contact with inmost ME!

"Thus was it that I said, the Church Clothes are first spun and woven by Society; outward Religion originates by Society, Society becomes possible by Religion. Nay, perhaps every conceivable Society, past and present, may well be figured as properly and wholly a Church, in one or other of these three predicaments: an audibly preaching and prophesying Church, which is the best; second, a Church that struggles to preach and prophesy, but cannot as yet, till its Pentecost come; and third and worst, a Church gone dumb with old age, or which only mumbles delirium prior to dissolution. Whoso fancies that by Church is here meant Chapterhouses and Cathedrals, or by preaching and prophesying, mere speech and chaunting, let him," says the oracular Professor, "read on light of heart (*getrosten Muthes*).

"But with regard to your Church proper, and the Church Clothes specially recognised as Church Clothes, I remark, fearlessly enough, that without such Vestures and sacred Tissues Society has not existed, and will not exist. For if Government is, so to speak, the outward SKIN of the Body Politic, holding the whole together and protecting it; and all your Craft-Guilds, and Associations for Industry, of hand or of head, are the Fleshly Clothes, the muscular and osseous Tissues (lying *under* such SKIN), whereby Society stands and works;—then is Religion the inmost Pericardial and Nervous Tissue, which ministers Life and warm Circulation to the whole. Without which Pericardial Tissue the Bones and Muscles (of Industry) were inert, or animated only by a Galvanic vitality; the SKIN would become a shrivelled pelt, or fast-rotting raw-hide; and Society itself a dead carcass,—deserving to be buried. Men were no longer Social, but Gregarious; which latter state also could not continue, but must gradually issue in universal selfish discord, hatred, savage isolation, and dispersion;—whereby, as we might continue to say, the very dust and dead body of Society would have evaporated and become abolished. Such, and so all-important, all-sustaining, are the Church Clothes, to civilised or even to rational man.*

"Meanwhile, in our era of the World, those same Church Clothes have gone sorrowfully out at elbows: nay, far worse, many of them have become mere hollow Shapes, or Masks, under which no living Figure or Spirit any longer dwells; but only spiders and unclean beetles, in horrid accumulation, drive their trade; and the Mask still glares on you with its glass-eyes, in ghastly affectation of Life,—some generation and half after Religion has quite withdrawn from it, and in unnoticed nooks is weaving for herself new Vestures, wherewith to reappear, and bless us, or our sons or grandsons. As a Priest, or Interpreter of the Holy, is the noblest and highest of all men, so is a Sham-priest (*Scheinpriester*) the falsest and basest: neither is it doubtful that his Canonicals, were they Popes' Tiaras, will one day be torn from him, to make bandages for the wounds of mankind; or even to burn into tinder, for general scientific or culinary purposes.

"All which, as out of place here, falls to be handled in my Second Volume, *On the Palingenesia, or Newbirth of Society;* which volume, as treating practically of the Wear, Destruction, and Re-texture of Spiritual Tissues, or Garments, forms, properly speaking, the Transcendental or ultimate Portion of this my Work *on Clothes,* and is already in a state of forwardness."

And herewith, no farther exposition, note, or commentary being added, does Teufelsdröckh, and must his Editor now, terminate the Singular Chapter on Church Clothes!

CHAPTER 3
SYMBOLS

PROBABLY it will elucidate the drift of these foregoing obscure utterances, if we here insert somewhat of our Professor's speculations on *Symbols*. To state his whole doctrine, indeed, were beyond our compass: nowhere is he more mysterious, impalpable, than in this of "Fantasy being the organ of the Godlike;" and how "Man thereby, though based, to all seeming, on the small Visible, does nevertheless extend down into the infinite deeps of the Invisible, of which Invisible, indeed, his Life is properly the bodying forth." Let us, omitting these high transcendental aspects of the matter, study to glean (whether from the Paperbags or the Printed Volume) what little seems logical and practical, and cunningly arrange it into such degree of coherence as it will assume. By way of proem, take the following not injudicious remarks:

"The benignant efficacies of Concealment," cries our Professor, "who shall speak or sing? SILENCE and SECRECY! Altars might still be raised to them (were this an altar-building time) for universal worship. Silence is the element in which great things fashion themselves together; that at length they may emerge, full-formed and majestic, into the daylight of Life, which they are thenceforth to rule. Not William the Silent only, but all the considerable men I have known, and the most undiplomatic and unstrategic of these, forbore to babble of what they were creating and projecting. Nay, in thy own mean perplexities, do thou thyself but *hold thy tongue for one day*: on the morrow, how much clearer are thy purposes, and duties; what wreck and rubbish have those mute workmen within thee swept away, when intrusive noises were shut out! Speech is too often not, as the Frenchman defined it, the art of concealing Thought;* but of quite stifling and suspending Thought, so that there is none to conceal. Speech too is great, but not the greatest. As the Swiss Inscription says: *Sprechen ist silbern, Schweigen ist golden* (Speech is silvern, Silence is golden);

or as I might rather express it: Speech is of Time, Silence is of Eternity.

"Bees will not work except in darkness; Thought will not work except in Silence: neither will Virtue work except in Secrecy. Let not thy right hand know what thy left hand* doeth! Neither shalt thou prate even to thy own heart of 'those secrets known to all.' Is not Shame* the soil of all Virtue, of all good manners, and good morals? Like other plants, Virtue will not grow unless its root be hidden, buried from the eye of the sun. Let the Sun shine on it, nay, do but look at it privily thyself, the root withers, and no flower will glad thee. O my Friends, when we view the fair clustering flowers that over-wreathe, for example, the Marriage-bower, and encircle man's life with the fragrance and hues of Heaven, what hand will not smite the foul plunderer that grubs them up by the roots, and, with grinning, grunting satisfaction, shews us the dung they flourish in! Men speak much of the Printing Press with its Newspapers: *du Himmel!* what are these to Clothes and the Tailor's Goose?"

"Of kin to the so incalculable influences of Concealment, and connected with still greater things, is the wondrous agency of *Symbols*. In a Symbol there is concealment and yet revelation: here, therefore, by Silence and by Speech acting together, comes a doubled significance. And if both the Speech be itself high, and the Silence fit and noble, how expressive will their union be! Thus in many a painted Device, or simple Seal-emblem, the commonest Truth stands out to us proclaimed with quite new emphasis.

"For it is here that Fantasy with her mystic wonderland plays into the small prose domain of Sense, and becomes incorporated therewith. In the Symbol proper, what we can call a Symbol, there is ever, more or less distinctly and directly, some embodyment and revelation of the Infinite; the Infinite is made to blend itself with the Finite, to stand visible, and as it were attainable, there. By Symbols, accordingly, is man guided and commanded, made happy, made wretched. He every where finds himself encompassed with Symbols, recognised as such or not recognised: the Universe is but one vast Symbol of God; nay, if thou wilt have it, what is man himself but a Symbol of

God, is not all that he does symbolical; a revelation to Sense of the mystic god-given Force that is in him; a 'Gospel of Freedom,' which he, the 'Messias of Nature,' preaches, as he can, by act and word? Not a Hut he builds but is the visible embodyment of a Thought; but bears visible record of invisible things; but is, in the transcendental sense, symbolical as well as real."

"Man," says the Professor elsewhere, in quite antipodal contrast with these high-soaring delineations, which we have here cut short on the verge of the inane, "man is by birth somewhat of an owl. Perhaps too of all the owleries that ever possessed him, the most owlish, if we consider it, is that of your actually existing Motive-Millwrights.* Fantastic tricks enough has man played in his time; has fancied himself to be most things, down even to an animated heap of Glass: but to fancy himself a dead Iron-Balance for weighing Pains and Pleasures on, was reserved for this his latter era. There stands he, his Universe one huge Manger, filled with hay and thistles to be weighed against each other; and looks long-eared enough.* Alas, poor devil! spectres are appointed to haunt him: one age, he is hagridden, bewitched; the next, priestridden, befooled; in all ages, bedevilled. And now the Genius of Mechanism smothers him worse than any Nightmare did; till the Soul is nigh choked out of him, and only a kind of Digestive, Mechanic life remains. In Earth and in Heaven he can see nothing but Mechanism; has fear for nothing else, hope in nothing else: the world would indeed grind him to pieces; but cannot he fathom the Doctrine of Motives, and cunningly compute them to grind the other way?

"Were he not, as has been said, purblinded by enchantment, you had but to bid him open his eyes and look. In which country, in which time, was it hitherto that man's history, or the history of any man, went on by calculated or calculable 'Motives?' What make ye of your Christianities, and Chivalries, and Reformations, and Marseillese Hymns, and Reigns of Terror?* Nay, has not perhaps the Motive-grinder himself been *in Love?* Did he never stand so much as a contested Election? Leave him to Time, and the medicating virtue of Nature."

"Yes, Friends," elsewhere observes the Professor, "not our Logical, Mensurative faculty, but our Imaginative one is King over us; I might say, Priest and Prophet to lead us heavenward; or Magician and Wizard to lead us hellward. Nay, even for the basest Sensualist, what is Sense but the implement of Fantasy; the vessel it drinks out of? Ever in the dullest existence, there is a sheen either of Inspiration or of Madness (thou partly hast it in thy choice, which of the two) that gleams in from the circumambient Eternity, and colours with its own hues our little islet of Time. The Understanding is indeed thy window, too clear thou canst not make it; but Fantasy is thy eye, with its colour-giving retina, healthy or diseased. Have not I myself known five hundred living soldiers sabred into crows' meat, for a piece of glazed cotton, which they called their Flag; which, had you sold it at any market-cross, would not have brought above three groschen?* Did not the whole Hungarian Nation rise, like some tumultuous moon-stirred Atlantic, when Kaiser Joseph pocketed their Iron Crown; an implement, as was sagaciously observed, in size and commercial value, little differing from a horse-shoe? It is in and through *Symbols* that man, consciously or unconsciously, lives, works, and has his being: those ages, moreover, are accounted the noblest which can the best recognise symbolical worth, and prize it the highest. For is not a Symbol ever, to him who has eyes for it, some dimmer or clearer revelation of the Godlike?

"Of Symbols, however, I remark farther, that they have both an extrinsic and intrinsic value; oftenest the former only. What, for instance, was in that clouted Shoe which the Peasants bore aloft with them as ensign in their *Bauernkrieg* (Peasants' War)?* Or in the Wallet-and-staff round which the Netherland *Gueux,* glorying in that nickname of Beggars, heroically rallied and prevailed, though against King Philip himself? Intrinsic significance these had none: only extrinsic; as the accidental Standards of multitudes more or less sacredly uniting together; in which union itself, as above noted, there is ever something mystical and borrowing of the Godlike. Under a like category too, stand, or stood, the stupidest heraldic coats-of-arms; military Banners every where; and generally all national or other sectarian Costumes and Customs: they have no intrinsic, necessary divineness, or even worth; but have acquired an extrinsic one. Nevertheless through all these there glimmers something of a Divine Idea; as through military Banners themselves, the Divine Idea of Duty, of heroic Daring; in some instances of Freedom, of Right. Nay, the highest ensign that men ever met and embraced under, the Cross itself, had no meaning save an accidental extrinsic one.

"Another matter it is, however, when your Symbol has intrinsic meaning, and is of itself *fit* that men should unite round it. Let but the Godlike manifest itself to Sense; let but Eternity look, more or less visibly, through the Time-Figure (*Zeitbild*)! Then is it fit that men unite there; and worship together before such Symbol; and so from day to day, and from age to age, superadd to it new divineness.

"Of this latter sort are all true Works of Art: in them (if thou know a Work of Art from a Daub of Artifice) wilt thou discern Eternity looking through Time; the Godlike rendered visible. Here too may an extrinsic value gradually superadd itself: thus certain *Iliads,* and the like, have, in three thousand years, attained quite new significance. But nobler than all in this kind are the Lives of heroic, god-inspired Men; for what other Work of Art is so divine? In Death too, in the Death of the Just, as the last perfection of a Work of Art, may we not discern symbolic meaning? In that divinely transfigured Sleep, as of Victory, resting over the beloved face which now knows thee no more, read (if thou canst for tears) the confluence of Time with Eternity, and some gleam of the latter peering through.

"Highest of all Symbols are those wherein the Artist or Poet has risen into Prophet, and all men can recognise a present God, and worship the same: I mean religious Symbols. Various enough have been such religious Symbols, what we call *Religions;* as men stood in this stage of culture or the other, and could worse or better body forth the Godlike: some Symbols with a transient intrinsic worth; many with only an extrinsic. If thou ask to what height man has carried it in this matter, look on our divinest Symbol: on Jesus of Nazareth, and his Life, and his Biography, and what followed therefrom. Higher has the human Thought not yet reached: this is Christianity and Christendom; a Symbol of quite perennial, infinite character; whose significance will ever demand to be anew inquired into, and anew made manifest.

"But, on the whole, as Time adds much to the sacredness of Symbols, so likewise in his progress he at length defaces, or even desecrates them; and Symbols, like all terrestrial Garments, wax old. Homer's Epos has not ceased to be true; yet it is no longer *our* Epos, but shines in the distance, if clearer and clearer, yet also smaller and smaller, like a receding Star. It needs a scientific telescope, it needs to be reinterpreted and artificially brought near us, before we can so much as know that it *was* a Sun. So likewise a day comes when the Runic Thor, with his Eddas, must withdraw into dimness; and many an African Mumbo-Jumbo, and Indian Wau-Wau* be utterly abolished. For all things, even Celestial Luminaries, much more atmospheric meteors, have their rise, their culmination, their decline.

"Small is this which thou tellest me that the Royal Sceptre is but a piece of gilt wood; that the Pyx has become a most foolish box, and truly, as Ancient Pistol thought, 'of little price.'* A right Conjuror might I name thee, couldst thou conjure back into these wooden tools the divine virtue they once held.

"Of this thing however be certain: woulds thou plant for Eternity, then plant into the deep infinite faculties of man, his Fantasy and Heart; wouldst thou plant for Year and Day, then plant into his shallow superficial faculties, his Self-love and Arithmetical Understanding, what will grow there. A Hierarch, therefore, and Pontiff of the World will we call him, the Poet and inspired Maker; who, Prometheus-like, can shape new Symbols, and bring new Fire from Heaven to fix it there. Such too will not always be wanting; neither perhaps now are. Meanwhile, as the average of matters goes, we account him Legislator and wise who can so much as tell when a Symbol has grown old, and gently remove it.

"When, as the last English† Coronation was preparing," concludes this wonderful Professor, "I read in their Newspapers that the 'Champion of England,'* he who must offer battle to the Universe for his new King, had brought it so far that he could now 'mount his horse with little assistance,' I said

† *Now* last but one—ED.*

to myself: Here also have we a Symbol well nigh superannuated. Alas, move whithersoever you may, are not the tatters and rags of superannuated worn-out Symbols (in this Ragfair of a World) dropping off every where, to hoodwink, to halter, to tether you; nay, if you shake them not aside, threatening to accumulate, and perhaps produce suffocation!"

CHAPTER 4

HELOTAGE*

AT this point we determine on adverting shortly, or rather reverting, to a certain Tract of Hofrath Heuschrecke's, entitled *Institute for the Repression of Population;* which lies, dishonourably enough (with torn leaves, and a perceptible smell of aloetic drugs), stuffed into the Bag *Pisces*. Not indeed for sake of the Tract itself, which we admire little; but of the marginal Notes, evidently in Teufelsdröckh's hand, which rather copiously fringe it. A few of these may be in their right place here.

Into the Hofrath's *Institute,* with its extraordinary schemes, and machinery of Corresponding Boards and the like, we shall not so much as glance. Enough for us to understand that Heuschrecke is a disciple of Malthus; and so zealous for the doctrine, that his zeal almost literally eats him up. A deadly fear of Population possesses the Hofrath; something like a fixed-idea; undoubtedly akin to the more diluted forms of Madness. Nowhere, in that quarter of his intellectual world, is there light; nothing but a grim shadow of Hunger; open mouths opening wider and wider; a world to terminate by the frightfullest consummation: by its too dense inhabitants, famished into delirium, universally eating one another. To make air for himself in which strangulation, choking enough to a benevolent heart, the Hofrath founds, or proposes to found, this *Institute* of his, as the best he can do. It is only with our Professor's comments thereon that we concern ourselves.

First, then, remark that Teufelsdröckh, as a speculative Radical, has his own notions about human dignity; that the Zähdarm palaces and courtesies have not made him forgetful of the Futteral cottages. On the blank cover of Heuschrecke's Tract, we find the following, indistinctly engrossed:

"Two men I honour, and no third. First, the toilworn Craftsman that with earth-made Implement laboriously conquers the Earth, and makes her man's. Venerable to me is the hard Hand; crooked, coarse; wherein notwithstanding lies a cunning virtue, indefeasibly royal, as of the Sceptre of this

Planet. Venerable too is the rugged face, all weather-tanned, besoiled, with its rude intelligence; for it is the face of a Man living manlike. Oh, but the more venerable for thy rudeness, and even because we must pity as well as love thee! Hardly-entreated Brother! For us was thy back so bent, for us were thy straight limbs and fingers so deformed: thou wert our Conscript, on whom the lot fell, and fighting our battles wert so marred. For in thee too lay a god-created Form, but it was not to be unfolded; encrusted must it stand with the thick adhesions and defacements of Labour; and thy body like thy soul was not to know freedom. Yet toil on, toil on: *thou* art in thy duty, be out of it who may; thou toilest for the altogether indispensable, for daily bread.

"A second man I honour, and still more highly: Him who is seen toiling for the spiritually indispensable; not daily bread, but the Bread of Life. Is not he too in his duty; endeavouring towards inward Harmony; revealing this, by act or by word, through all his outward endeavours, be they high or low? Highest of all, when his outward and his inward endeavour are one: when we can name him Artist; not earthly Craftsman only, but inspired Thinker, that with heaven-made Implement conquers Heaven for us! If the poor and humble toil that we have Food, must not the high and glorious toil for him in return that he have Light and Guidance; Freedom, Immortality?—These two, in all their degrees, I honour: all else is chaff and dust, which let the wind blow whither it listeth.

"Unspeakably touching is it, however, when I find both dignities united; and he that must toil outwardly for the lowest of man's wants, is also toiling inwardly for the highest. Sublimer in this world know I nothing than a Peasant Saint, could such now any where be met with. Such a one will take thee back to Nazareth itself; thou wilt see the splendour of Heaven spring forth from the humblest depths of Earth, like a light shining in great darkness."

And again: "It is not because of his toils that I lament for the poor: we must all toil, or steal (howsoever we name our stealing) which is worse; no faithful workman finds his task a pastime. The poor is hungry and athirst, but for him also there is food and drink: he is heavy-laden and weary; but for him also the Heavens send Sleep, and of the deepest; in his smoky cribs, a clear dewy heaven of Rest envelopes him, and fitful glitterings of cloud-skirted Dreams. But what I do mourn over is that the lamp of his soul should go out; that no ray of heavenly, or even of earthly knowledge, should visit him; but, only in the haggard darkness, like two spectres, Fear and Indignation.* Alas, while the Body stands so broad and brawny, must the Soul lie blinded, dwarfed, stupified, almost annihilated! Alas, was this too a Breath of God: bestowed in Heaven, but on Earth never to be unfolded!—That there should one Man die ignorant who had capacity for Knowledge, this I call a tragedy, were it to happen more than twenty times in the minute, as by some computations it does. The miserable fraction of Science which united* mankind, in a wide Universe of Nescience, has acquired, why is not this, with all diligence, imparted to all?"

Quite in an opposite strain is the following: "The old Spartans had a wiser method; and went out and hunted down their Helots, and speared and spitted them, when they grew too numerous. With our improved fashions of hunting, Herr Hofrath, now after the invention of fire-arms, and standing armies, how much easier were such a hunt! Perhaps in the most thickly-peopled country, some three days annually might suffice to shoot all the able-bodied Paupers that had accumulated within the year. Let Governments think of this. The expense were trifling: nay, the very carcasses would pay it. Have them salted and barrelled; could not you victual therewith, if not Army and Navy, yet richly such infirm Paupers, in workhouses and elsewhere, as enlightened Charity, dreading no evil of them, might see good to keep alive?"

"And yet," writes he farther on, "there must be something wrong. A full-formed Horse will, in any market, bring from twenty to as high as two hundred Friedrichs d'or: such is his worth to the world. A full-formed Man is not only worth nothing to the world, but the world could afford him a round sum would he simply engage to go and hang himself. Nevertheless, which of the two was the more cunningly-devised article, even as an Engine? Good Heavens! A white European Man, standing on his two Legs, with his two five-fingered Hands at his shackle-bones, and miraculous Head on his shoulders, is worth, I should say, from fifty to a hundred Horses!"

"True, thou Gold-Hofrath!" cries the Professor elsewhere: "Too crowded indeed. Meanwhile, what portion of this inconsiderable terraqueous Globe have ye actually tilled and delved, till it will grow no more? How thick stands your Population in the Pampas and Savannas of America; round ancient Carthage, and in the interior of Africa; on both slopes of the Altaic chain, in the central Platform of Asia; in Spain, Greece, Turkey, Crim Tartary, the Curragh of Kildare? One man, in one year, as I have understood it, if you lend him Earth, will feed himself and nine others. Alas, where now are the Hengsts and Alarics of our still glowing, still expanding Europe; who, when their home is grown too narrow, will enlist and, like Fire-pillars, guide onwards those superfluous masses of indomitable living Valour; equipped, not now with the battle-axe and war-chariot, but with the steam-engine and ploughshare? Where are they?—Preserving their Game!"

THE PHŒNIX

PUTTING which four singular Chapters together, and alongside of them numerous hints, and even direct utterances, scattered over these Writings of his, we come upon the startling yet not quite unlooked-for conclusion, that Teufelsdröckh is one of those who consider Society, properly so called, to be as good as extinct; and that only the Gregarious feelings, and old inherited habitudes, at this juncture, hold us from Dispersion, and universal national, civil, domestic and personal war! He says expressly: "For the last three centuries, above all, for the last three quarters of a century, that same Pericardial Nervous Tissue (as we named it) of Religion, where lies the Life-essence of Society, has been smote at and perforated, needfully and needlessly; till now it is quite rent into shreds; and Society, long pining, diabetic, consumptive, can be regarded as defunct; for those spasmodic, galvanic sprawlings are not life, neither indeed will they endure, galvanise as you may, beyond two days."

"Call ye that a Society," cries he again, "where there is no longer any Social Idea extant; not so much as the Idea of a common Home, but only of a common, over-crowded Lodging-house? Where each, isolated, regardless of his neighbour, turned against his neighbour, clutches what he can get, and cries 'Mine!' and calls it Peace, because, in the cut-purse and cut-throat Scramble, no steel knives, but only a far cunninger sort, can be employed? Where Friendship, Communion, has become an incredible tradition; and your holiest Sacramental Supper is a smoking Tavern Dinner, with Cook for Evangelist? Where your Priest has no tongue but for plate-licking: and your high Guides and Governers cannot guide; but on all hands hear it passionately proclaimed: *Laissez faire*: Leave us alone of your guidance, such light is darker than darkness; eat your wages, and sleep!

"Thus, too," continues he, "must an observant eye discern every where that saddest spectacle: The Poor perishing, like neglected, foundered Draught-Cattle, of Hunger and Overwork; the Rich, still more wretchedly, of Idleness, Satiety, and Overgrowth. The Highest in rank, at length, without honour from the Lowest; scarcely, with a little mouth-honour, as from tavern-waiters who expect to put it in the bill. Once sacred Symbols fluttering as empty Pageants, whereof men grudge even the expense; a World becoming dismantled: in one word, the CHURCH fallen speechless, from obesity and apoplexy; the STATE shrunken into a Police-Office, straitened to get its pay!"

We might ask, are there many "observant eyes," belonging to Practical men, in England or elsewhere, which have descried these phenomena; or is it only from the mystic elevation of a German *Wahngasse* that such wonders are visible? Teufels-dröckh contends that the aspect of a "deceased or expiring Society" fronts us everywhere, so that whoso runs may read. "What, for example," says he, "is the universally-arrogated Virtue, almost the sole remaining Catholic Virtue, of these days? For some half century, it has been the thing you name 'Independence.' Suspicion of 'Servility,' of reverence for Superiors, the very dogleech* is anxious to disavow. Fools! Were your Superiors worthy to govern, and you worthy to obey, reverence for them were even your only possible freedom. Independence, in all kinds, is rebellion; if unjust rebellion, why parade it, and every where prescribe it?"

But what then? Are we returning, as Rousseau prayed, to the state of Nature? "The Soul Politic having departed," says Teufelsdröckh, "what can follow but that the Body Politic be decently interred, to avoid putrescence? Liberals, Economists, Utilitarians enough I see marching with its bier, and chaunting loud pæans, towards the funeral-pile, where, amid wailings from some, and saturnalian revelries from the most, the venerable Corpse is to be burnt. Or, in plain words, that these men, Liberals, Utilitarians, or whatsoever they are called, will ultimately carry their point, and dissever and destroy most existing Institutions of Society, seems a thing which has some time ago ceased to be doubtful.

"Do we not see a little subdivision of the grand Utilitarian Armament come to light even in insulated England? A living nucleus, that will attract and grow, does at length appear there also; and under curious phasis; properly as the inconsiderable fag-end, and so far in rear of the others as to fancy itself the van. Our European Mechanisers are a Sect of boundless diffusion, activity, and co-operative spirit: has not Utilitarianism flourished in high places of Thought, here among ourselves, and in every European country, at some time or other, within the last fifty years? If now in all countries, except perhaps England, it has ceased to flourish, or indeed to exist, among Thinkers, and sunk to Journalists and the popular mass,—who sees not that, as hereby it no longer preaches, so the reason is, it now needs no Preaching, but is in full universal Action, the doctrine every where known and enthusiastically laid to heart? The fit pabulum, in these times, for a certain rugged workshop-intellect and heart, nowise without their corresponding workshop-strength and ferocity, it requires but to be stated in such scenes to make proselytes enough.—Admirably calculated for destroying, only not for rebuilding! It spreads like a sort of Dog-madness; till the whole World-kennel will be rabid: then woe to the Huntsmen, with or without their whips! They should have given the quadrupeds water," adds he, "the water, namely, of Knowledge and of Life, while it was yet time."

Thus, if Professor Teufelsdröckh can be relied on, we are at this hour in a most critical condition; beleaguered by that boundless "Armament of Mechanisers" and Unbelievers, threatening to strip us bare! "The World," says he, "as it needs must, is under a process of devastation and waste, which, whether by silent assiduous corrosion, or open quicker combustion, as the case chances, will effectually enough annihilate the past Forms of Society; replace them with what it may. For the present, it is contemplated that when man's whole Spiritual Interests are once *divested,* these innumerable stript-off Garments shall mostly be burnt; but the sounder Rags among them be quilted together into one huge Irish watch-coat for the defence of the Body only!"—This, we think, is but Job's news* to the humane reader.

"Nevertheless," cries Teufelsdröckh, "who can hinder it; who is there that can clutch into the wheel-spokes of Destiny, and say to the Spirit of the Time: Turn back, I command thee?—Wiser were it that we yielded to the Inevitable and Inexorable, and accounted even this the best."

Nay, might not an attentive Editor, drawing his own inferences from what stands written, conjecture that Teufelsdröckh individually had yielded to this same "Inevitable and Inexorable" heartily enough; and now sat waiting the issue, with his natural diabolico-angelical Indifference, if not even Placidity? Did we not hear him complain that the World was a "huge Ragfair," and the "rags and tatters of old Symbols" were raining down every where, like to drift him in, and suffocate him? What with those "unhunted Helots" of his; and the uneven *sic-vos-non-vobis** pressure, and hard crashing collision he is pleased to discern in existing things; what with the so hateful "empty Masks," full of beetles and spiders, yet glaring out on him, from their glass-eyes, "with a ghastly affectation of life,"—we feel entitled to conclude him even willing that much should be thrown to the Devil, so it were but done gently! Safe himself in that "Pinnacle of Weissnichtwo," he would consent, with a tragic solemnity, that the monster UTILITARIA, held back, indeed, and moderated by nose-rings, halters, footshackles, and every conceivable modification of rope, should go forth to do her work;—to tread down old ruinous Palaces and Temples, with her broad hoof, till the whole were trodden down, that new and better might be built! Remarkable in this point of view are the following sentences.

"Society," says he, "is not dead: that Carcass, which you call dead Society, is but her mortal coil which she has shuffled off, to assume a nobler; she herself, through perpetual metamorphoses, in fairer and fairer developement, has to live till Time also merge in Eternity. Wheresoever two or three Living Men are gathered together, there is Society; or there it will be, with its cunning mechanisms and stupendous structures, overspreading this little Globe, and reaching upwards to Heaven and downwards to Gehenna: for always, under one or the other figure, has it two authentic Revelations, of a God and of a Devil; the Pulpit, namely, and the Gallows."

Indeed, we already heard him speak of "Religion, in unnoticed nooks, weaving for herself new Vestures;"—Teufelsdröckh himself being one of the loom-treaddles? Elsewhere he quotes without censure that strange aphorism of Saint-Simon's, concerning which and whom so much were to be said: *L'age d'or qu'une aveugle tradition a placé jusqu'ici dans le passé est devant nous;* The golden age which a blind tradition has hitherto placed in the Past is Before us.—But listen again:

"When the Phœnix is fanning her funeral pyre, will there not be sparks flying? Alas, some millions of men, and among them such as a Napoleon, have already been licked into that high-eddying Flame, and like moths, consumed there. Still also have we to fear that incautious beards will get singed.

"For the rest, in what year of grace such Phœnix-cremation will be completed, you need not ask. The law of Perseverance is among the deepest in man: by nature he hates change; seldom will he quit his old house till it has actually fallen about his ears. Thus have I seen Solemnities linger as Ceremonies, sacred Symbols as idle Pageants, to the extent of three hundred years and more after all life and sacredness had evaporated out of them. And then, finally, what time the Phœnix Death-Birth itself will require depends on unseen contingencies.—Meanwhile, would Destiny offer Mankind that after, say two centuries of convulsion and conflagration, more or less vivid, the fire-creation should be accomplished, and we find* ourselves again in a Living Society, and no longer fighting but working,—were it not perhaps prudent in Mankind to strike the bargain?"

Thus is Teufelsdröckh content that old sick Society should be deliberately burnt (alas! with quite other fuel than spicewood); in the faith that she is a Phœnix; and that a new heavenborn young one will rise out of her ashes! We ourselves, restricted to the duty of Indicator, shall forbear commentary. Meanwhile, will not the judicious reader shake his head, and reproachfully, yet more in sorrow than in anger, say or think: From a *Doctor Utriusque Juris,** titular Professor in a University, and man to whom hitherto, for his services, Society, bad as she is, has given not only food and raiment (of a kind), but books, tobacco and gukguk, we expected more gratitude to his benefactress; and less of a blind Trust in the future, which resembles that rather of a philosophical Fatalist and Enthusiast, than of a solid householder paying scot and lot in a Christian country.

*   *   *

CHAPTER 6

OLD CLOTHES

As mentioned above, Teufelsdröckh, though a Sansculottist, is in practice probably the politest man extant: his whole heart and life are penetrated and informed with the spirit of Politeness; a noble natural Courtesy shines through him, beautifying his vagaries; like sun-light, making a rosy-fingered, rainbow-dyed Aurora out of mere aqueous clouds; nay, brightening London smoke itself into gold vapour, as from the crucible of an alchemist. Hear in what earnest though fantastic wise he expresses himself on this head:

"Shall Courtesy be done only to the rich, and only by the rich? In Good-breeding, which differs, if at all, from High-breeding, only as it gracefully remembers the rights of others, rather than gracefully insists on its own rights, I discern no special connexion with wealth or birth: but rather that it lies in human nature itself, and is due from all men towards all men. Of a truth, were your Schoolmaster at his post, and worth any thing when there, this, with so much else, would be reformed. Nay, each man were then also his neighbour's schoolmaster; till at length a rude-visaged, unmannered Peasant, could no more be met with than a Peasant unacquainted with botanical Physiology, or who felt not that the clod he broke was created in Heaven.

"For whether thou bear a sceptre or a sledge-hammer, art thou not ALIVE; is not this thy brother ALIVE? 'There is but one Temple in the world,' says Novalis, 'and that Temple is the Body of Man. Nothing is holier than this high Form. Bending before men is a reverence done to this Revelation in the Flesh. We touch Heaven, when we lay our hands on a human Body.'

"On which ground, I would fain carry it farther than most do; and whereas the English Johnson only bowed to every Clergyman, or man with a shovel-hat, I would bow to every Man with any sort of hat, or with no hat whatever. Is he not a Temple, then; the visible Manifestation and Impersonation of the Divinity? And yet, alas, such indiscriminate bowing serves not. For there is a Devil dwells in man, as well as a Divinity; and too often the bow is but pocketed by the *former*. It would go to the pocket of Vanity (which is your clearest phasis of the Devil, in these times); therefore must we withhold it.

"The gladder am I, on the other hand, to do reverence to those Shells and outer Husks of the Body, wherein no devilish passion any longer lodges, but only the pure emblem and effigies of Man: I mean, to Empty, or even to Cast Clothes. Nay, is it not to Clothes that most men do reverence; to the fine frogged broad-cloth, nowise to the 'straddling animal with bandy legs' which it holds, and makes a Dignitary of? Who ever saw any Lord my-lorded in tattered blanket, fastened with wooden skewer? Nevertheless, I say, there is in such worship a shade of hypocrisy, a practical deception: for how often does the Body appropriate what was meant for the Cloth only! Whoso would avoid Falsehood, which is the essence of all Sin, will perhaps see good to take a different course. That reverence which cannot act without obstruction and perversion when the Clothes are full, may have free course when they are empty. Even as, for Hindoo Worshippers, the Pagoda is not less sacred than the God; so do I too worship the hollow cloth Garment with equal fervour, as when it contained the Man: nay, with more, for I now fear no deception, of myself or of others.

"Did not King *Toomtabard,* or, in other words, John Balliol, reign long over Scotland; the man John Balliol being quite gone, and only the 'Toom Tabard' (Empty Gown) remaining? What still dignity dwells in a suit of Cast Clothes! How meekly it bears its honours! No haughty looks, no scornful gesture; silent and serene, it fronts the world; neither demanding worship, nor afraid to miss it. The Hat still carries the physiognomy of its Head: but the vanity and the stupidity, and goose-speech which was the sign of these two, are gone. The Coat-arm is stretched out, but not to strike; the Breeches, in modest simplicity, depend at ease, and now at last have a graceful flow; the Waistcoat hides no evil passion, no riotous desire; hunger or thirst now dwells not in it. Thus all is purged from the grossness of Sense, from the carking Cares and foul Vices of the World; and rides there, on its Clothes-horse; as, on a Pegasus, might some skyey Messenger, or purified Apparition, visiting our low Earth.

"Often, while I sojourned in that monstrous Tuberosity of Civilised Life, the Capital of England; and meditated, and questioned Destiny, under that ink-sea of vapour, black, thick, and multifarious as Spartan broth;* and was one lone Soul amid those grinding millions;—often have I turned into their Old-Clothes Market to worship. With awe-struck heart I walk through that Monmouth Street, with its empty Suits, as through a Sanhedrim of stainless Ghosts. Silent are they, but expressive in their silence: the past witnesses and instruments of Woe and Joy, of Passions, Virtues, Crimes, and all the fathomless tumult of Good and Evil in 'the Prison called* Life.' Friends! trust not the heart of that man for whom Old Clothes are not venerable. Watch too, with reverence, that bearded Jewish Highpriest, who with hoarse voice, like some Angel of Doom, summons them from the four winds! On his head, like the Pope, he has three Hats,—a real triple tiara; on either hand, are the similitude of Wings, whereon the summoned Garments come to alight; and ever, as he slowly cleaves the air, sounds forth his deep fateful note, as if through a trumpet he were proclaiming: 'Ghosts of Life, come to Judgment!' Reck not, ye fluttering Ghosts: he will purify you in his Purgatory, with fire and with water; and, one day, new-created ye shall reappear. Oh! let him in whom the flame of Devotion is ready to go out, who has never worshipped, and knows not what to worship, pace and repace, with austerest thought, the pavement of Monmouth Street, and say whether his heart and his eyes still continue dry. If Field Lane, with its long fluttering rows of yellow handkerchiefs, be a Dionysius' Ear, where, in stifled jarring hubbub, we hear the Indictment which Poverty and Vice bring against lazy Wealth, that it has left them there cast out and trodden under foot of Want, Darkness, and the Devil,—then is Monmouth Street a Mirza's Hill,* where, in motley vision, the whole Pageant of Existence passes awfully before us; with its wail and jubilee, mad loves and mad hatreds, church-bells and gallows-ropes, farce-tragedy, beast-godhood,—the Bedlam of Creation!"

To most men, as it does to ourselves, all this will seem overcharged. We too have walked through Monmouth Street; but with little feeling of "Devotion:" probably in part because the contemplative process is so fatally broken in upon by the brood of money-changers, who nestle in that Church, and importune the worshipper with merely secular proposals. Whereas Teufelsdröckh might be in that happy middle-state, which leaves to the Clothes-broker no hope either of sale or of purchase, and so be allowed to linger there without molestation.—Something we would have given to see the little philosophical Figure, with its steeple-hat and loose-flowing skirts, and eyes in a fine frenzy, "pacing and repacing in austerest thought" that foolish Street; which to him was a true Delphic avenue, and supernatural Whispering-gallery,* where the "Ghosts of Life" rounded strange secrets in his ear. O thou philosophic Teufelsdröckh, that listenest while others only gabble, and with thy quick tympanum hearest the grass grow!

At the same time, is it not strange that, in Paperbag Documents, destined for an English Work, there exists nothing like an authentic diary of this his sojourn in London; and of his Meditations among the Clothes-shops only the obscurest emblematic shadows? Neither, in conversation (for, indeed, he was not a man to pester you with his Travels), have we heard him more than allude to the subject.

For the rest, however, it cannot be uninteresting that we here find how early the significance of Clothes had dawned on the now so distinguished Clothes-Professor. Might we but fancy it to have been even in Monmouth Street, at the bottom of our own English "ink-sea," that this remarkable Volume first took being, and shot forth its salient point in his soul,—as in Chaos did the Egg of Eros, one day to be hatched into a Universe!

CHAPTER 7

ORGANIC FILAMENTS

FOR us, who happen to live while the World-Phœnix is burning herself, and burning so slowly that, as Teufelsdröckh calculates, it were a handsome bargain would she engage to have done "within two centuries," there seems to lie but an ashy prospect. Not altogether so, however, does the Professor figure it. "In the living subject," says he, "change is wont to be gradual: thus, while the serpent sheds its old skin, the new is already formed beneath. Little knowest thou of the burning of a World-Phœnix, who fanciest that she must first burn out, and lie as a dead cinereous heap; and therefrom the young one start up by miracle, and fly heavenward. Far otherwise! In that Fire-whirlwind, Creation and Destruction proceed together; ever as the ashes of the Old are blown about, do organic filaments of the New mysteriously spin themselves; and amid the rushing and the waving of the Whirlwind-Element, come tones of a melodious Deathsong, which end not but in tones of a more melodious Birthsong. Nay, look into the Fire-whirlwind with thy own eyes, and thou wilt see." Let us actually look, then: to poor individuals, who cannot expect to live two centuries, those same organic filaments, mysteriously spinning themselves, will be the best part of the spectacle. First, therefore, this of Mankind in general:

"In vain thou deniest it," says the Professor; "thou *art* my Brother. Thy very Hatred, thy very Envy, those foolish Lies thou tellest of me in thy splenetic humour: what is all this but an inverted Sympathy? Were I a Steam-engine, wouldst thou take the trouble to tell Lies of me? Not thou! I should grind all unheeded, whether badly or well.

"Wondrous truly are the bonds that unite us one and all; whether by the soft binding of Love, or the iron chaining of Necessity, as we like to choose it. More than once, have I said to myself, of some perhaps whimsically strutting Figure, such as provokes whimsical thoughts: 'Wert thou, my little Brother-kin, suddenly covered up with even* the largest imaginable

Glass-bell,—what a thing it were, not for thyself only, but for the world! Post Letters, more or fewer, from all the four winds, impinge against thy Glass walls, but must drop unread: neither from within comes there question or response into any Post-bag; thy Thoughts fall into no friendly ear or heart, thy Manufacture into no purchasing hand; thou art no longer a circulating venous-arterial Heart, that, taking and giving, circulatest through all Space and all Time: there has a Hole fallen out in the immeasurable, universal World-tissue, which must be darned up again!'

"Such venous-arterial circulation, of Letters, verbal Messages, paper and other Packages, going out from him and coming in, are a blood-circulation, visible to the eye: but the finer nervous circulation, by which all things, the minutest that he does, minutely influence all men, and the very look of his face blesses or curses whomso it lights on, and so generates ever new blessing or new cursing: all this you cannot see, but only imagine. I say, there is not a red Indian, hunting by Lake Winnipic, can quarrel with his squaw, but the whole world must smart for it: will not the price of beaver rise? It is a mathematical fact that the casting of this pebble from my hand alters the centre of gravity of the Universe.

"If now an existing generation of men stand so woven together, not less indissolubly does generation with generation. Hast thou ever meditated on that word, Tradition: how we inherit not Life only, but all the garniture and form of Life; and work, and speak, and even think and feel, as our Fathers, and primeval grandfathers, from the beginning, have given it us?— Who printed thee, for example, this unpretending Volume on the Philosophy of Clothes? Not the Herren Stillschweigen and Company: but Cadmus of Thebes, Faust of Mentz, and innumerable others whom thou knowest not. Had there been no Mæsogothic Ulfila, there had been no English Shakespeare, or a different one. Simpleton! It was Tubalcain that made thy very Tailor's needle, and sewed that court suit of thine.

"Yes, truly, if Nature is one, and a living indivisible whole, much more is Mankind, the Image that reflects and creates Nature, without which Nature were not. As palpable life-

streams in that wondrous Individual, Mankind, among so
many life-streams that are not palpable, flow on those main-
currents of what we call Opinion; as preserved in Institutions,
Polities, Churches, above all in Books. Beautiful it is to
understand and know that a Thought did never yet die; that as
thou, the originator thereof, has gathered it and created it from
the whole Past, so thou wilt transmit it to the whole Future. It
is thus that the heroic Heart, the seeing Eye of the first times,
still feels and sees in us of the latest; that the Wise Man stands
ever encompassed, and spiritually embraced, by a cloud of
witnesses and brothers; and there is a living, literal *Communion
of Saints,* wide as the World itself, and as the History of the
World.

"Noteworthy also, and serviceable for the progress of this
same Individual, wilt thou find his subdivision into Generations. Generations are as the Days of toilsome Mankind; Death
and Birth are the vesper and the matin bells, that summon
Mankind to sleep, and to rise refreshed for new advancement.
What the Father has made the Son can make and enjoy; but has
also work of his own appointed him. Thus all things wax, and
roll onwards; Arts, Establishments, Opinions, nothing is completed, but ever completing. Newton has learned to see what
Kepler saw; but there is also a fresh heaven-derived force in
Newton; he must mount to still higher points of vision. So too
the Hebrew Lawgiver is, in due time, followed by an Apostle
of the Gentiles.* In the business of Destruction, as this also is
from time to time a necessary work, thou findest a like
sequence and perseverance: for Luther it was as yet hot enough
to stand by that burning of the Pope's Bull; Voltaire could not
warm himself at the glimmering ashes, but required quite other
fuel. Thus likewise, I note, the English Whig has, in the second
generation, become an English Radical; who, in the third again,
it is to be hoped, will become an English Rebuilder. Find
Mankind where thou wilt, thou findest it in living movement,
in progress faster or slower: the Phœnix soars aloft, hovers with
outstretched wings, filling Earth with her music; or, as now,
she sinks, and with spheral swan-song immolates herself in
flame, that she may soar the higher and sing the clearer."

Let the friends of social order, in such a disastrous period, lay this to heart, and derive from it any little comfort they can. We subjoin another passage, concerning Titles:

"Remark, not without surprise," says Teufelsdröckh, "how all high Titles of Honour come hitherto from Fighting. Your *Herzog* (Duke, *Dux*) is Leader of Armies; your Earl (*Jarl*) is Strong Man; your Marshall* cavalry Horse-shoer. A Millennium, or reign of Peace and Wisdom, having from of old been prophesied, and becoming now daily more and more indubitable, may it not be apprehended that such Fighting-titles will cease to be palatable, and new and higher need to be devised?

"The only Title wherein I, with confidence, trace eternity, is that of King. *König* (King), anciently *Könning*, means Ken-ning (Cunning), or which is the same thing, Can-ning. Ever must the Sovereign of Mankind be fitly entitled King."

"Well, also," says he elsewhere, "was it written by Theologians: a King rules by divine right. He carries in him an authority from God, or man will never give it him. Can I choose my own King? I can choose my own King Popinjay,* and play what farce or tragedy I may with him: but he who is to be my Ruler, whose will is to be higher than my will, was chosen for me in Heaven. Neither except in such Obedience to the Heaven-chosen is Freedom so much as conceivable."

The Editor will here admit that, among all the wondrous provinces of Teufelsdröckh's spiritual world, there is none he walks in with such astonishment, hesitation, and even pain, as in the Political. How, with our English love of Ministry and Opposition, and that generous conflict of Parties, mind warming itself against mind in their mutual wrestle for the Public Good, by which wrestle, indeed, is our invaluable Constitution kept warm and alive; how shall we domesticate ourselves in this spectral Necropolis, or rather City both of the Dead and of the Unborn, where the Present seems little other than an inconsiderable Film dividing the Past and the Future? In those dim longdrawn expanses, all is so immeasurable; much so disastrous, ghastly; your very radiances, and straggling light-beams, have a supernatural character. And then with such an Indifference, such a prophetic peacefulness (accounting the inevitably-coming as already here, to him all one whether it be distant by centuries or only by days), does he sit;—and live, you would say, rather in any other age than in his own! It is our painful duty to announce, or repeat, that, looking into this man, we discern a deep, silent, slow-burning, inextinguishable Radicalism, such as fills us with shuddering admiration.

Thus, for example, he appears to make little even of the Elective Franchise; at least so we interpret the following: "Satisfy yourselves," he says, "by universal, indubitable experiment, even as ye are now doing or will do, whether FREEDOM heavenborn and leading heavenward, and so vitally essential for us all, cannot peradventure be mechanically hatched and brought to light in that same Ballot-Box* of yours; or at worst, in some other discoverable or devisable Box, Edifice, or Steam-mechanism. It were a mighty convenience; and beyond all feats of manufacture witnessed hitherto." Is Teufelsdröckh acquainted with the British Constitution, even slightly?—He says, under another figure: "But after all, were the problem, as indeed it now everywhere is, To rebuild your old House from the top downwards (since you must live in it the while), what better, what other, than the Representative Machine will serve your turn? Meanwhile, however, mock me not with the name of Free, 'when you have but knit up my chains into ornamental festoons.'"—Or what will any member of the Peace Society* make of such an assertion as this: "The lower people every-where desire War. Not so unwisely; there is then a demand for lower people—to be shot!"

Gladly, therefore, do we emerge from those soul-confusing labyrinths of speculative Radicalism, into somewhat clearer regions. Here, looking round, as was our hest, for "organic filaments," we ask, may not this, touching "Hero-worship," be of the number? It seems of a cheerful character; yet so quaint, so mystical, one knows not what, or how little, may lie under it. Our readers shall look with their own eyes:

"True is it that, in these days, man can do almost all things, only not obey. True likewise that whoso cannot obey cannot be free, still less bear rule; he that is the inferior of nothing, can be the superior of nothing, the equal of nothing. Nevertheless, believe not that man has lost his faculty of Reverence; that if it slumber in him, it has gone dead. Painful for man is that same rebellious Independence, when it has become inevitable; only in loving companionship with his fellows does he feel safe; only in reverently bowing down before the Higher does he feel himself exalted.

"Or what if the character of our so troublous Era lay even in this: that man had for ever cast away Fear, which is the lower; but not yet risen into perennial Reverence, which is the higher and highest?

"Meanwhile, observe with joy, so cunningly has Nature ordered it, that whatsoever man ought to obey he cannot but obey. Before no faintest revelation of the Godlike did he ever stand irreverent; least of all, when the Godlike shewed itself revealed in his fellow-man. Thus is there a true religious Loyalty for ever rooted in his heart; nay, in all ages, even in ours, it manifests itself as a more or less orthodox *Hero-worship*. In which fact, that Hero-worship exists, has existed, and will for ever exist, universally among Mankind, mayst thou discern the corner-stone of living rock, whereon all Polities for the remotest time may stand secure."

Do our readers discern any such corner-stone, or even so much as what Teufelsdröckh is looking at? He exclaims: "Or hast thou forgotten Paris and Voltaire?* How the aged, withered man, though but a Sceptic, Mocker, and millinery Court-poet, yet because even he seemed the Wisest, Best, could drag mankind at his chariot-wheels, so that princes coveted a smile from him, and the loveliest of France would have laid their hair beneath his feet! All Paris was one vast Temple of Hero-Worship; though their Divinity, moreover, was of feature too apish.

"But if such things," continues he, "were done in the dry tree, what will be done in the green? If, in the most parched season of man's History, in the most parched spot of Europe, when Parisian life was at best but a scientific *Hortus Siccus,* bedizened with some Italian Gumflowers,* such virtue could come out of it: what is it to be looked for when Life again waves leafy and bloomy, and your Hero-Divinity shall have nothing apelike, but be wholly human? Know that there is in man a quite indestructible Reverence for whatsoever holds of Heaven, or even plausibly counterfeits such holding. Shew the dullest clodpole, shew the haughtiest featherhead, that a soul Higher than himself is actually here; were his knees stiffened into brass, he must down and worship."

Organic filaments, of a more authentic sort, mysteriously spinning themselves, some will perhaps discover in the following passage:

"There is no Church, sayest thou? The voice of Prophecy has gone dumb? This is even what I dispute: but, in any case, hast thou not still Preaching enough? A Preaching Friar settles himself in every village; and builds a pulpit, which he calls Newspaper. Therefrom he preaches what most momentous doctrine is in him, for man's salvation; and dost not thou listen, and believe? Look well, thou seest every where a new Clergy of the Mendicant Orders, some bare-footed, some almost bare-backed, fashion itself into shape, and teach and preach, zealously enough, for copper alms and the love of God. These break in pieces the ancient idols; and, though themselves too often reprobate, as idol-breakers are wont to be, mark out the sites of new Churches, where the true God-ordained, that are to follow, may find audience, and minister. Said I not, Before the old skin was shed, the new had formed itself beneath it?"

Perhaps, also, in the following; wherewith we now hasten to knit up this ravelled sleeve:

"But there is no Religion?" reiterates the Professor. "Fool! I tell thee, there is. Hast thou well considered all that lies in this immeasurable froth-ocean we name LITERATURE? Fragments of a genuine Church-*Homiletic* lie scattered there, which Time will assort: nay, fractions even of a *Liturgy* could I point out. And knowest thou no Prophet, even in the vesture, environment, and dialect of this age? None to whom the Godlike had revealed itself, through all meanest and highest forms of the Common; and by him been again prophetically revealed: in whose inspired melody, even in these rag-gathering and rag-burning days, Man's Life again begins, were it but afar off, to be divine? Knowest thou none such? I know him, and name him—Goethe.

"But thou as yet standest in no Temple; joinest in no Psalm-worship; feelest well that, where there is no ministering Priest, the people perish? Be of comfort! Thou art not alone, if thou have Faith. Spake we not of a Communion of Saints, unseen, yet not unreal, accompanying and brother-like embracing thee, so thou be worthy? Their heroic Sufferings rise up melodiously together to Heaven, out of all lands, and out of all times, as a sacred *Miserere;** their heroic Actions also, as a boundless, everlasting Psalm of Triumph. Neither say that thou hast now no Symbol of the Godlike. Is not God's Universe a Symbol of the Godlike; is not Immensity a Temple; is not Man's History, and Men's History, a perpetual Evangile? Listen, and for organ-music thou wilt ever, as of old, hear the Morning Stars sing together.''

CHAPTER 8

NATURAL SUPERNATURALISM

IT is in his stupendous Section, headed *Natural Supernaturalism,* that the Professor first becomes a Seer; and, after long effort, such as we have witnessed, finally subdues under his feet this refractory Clothes-Philosophy, and takes victorious possession thereof. Phantasms enough he has had to struggle with; "Cloth-webs and Cob-webs," of Imperial Mantles, Superannuated Symbols, and what not: yet still did he courageously pierce through. Nay, worst of all, two quite mysterious, world-embracing Phantasms, TIME and SPACE, have ever hovered round him, perplexing and bewildering: but with these also he now resolutely grapples, these also he victoriously rends asunder. In a word, he has looked fixedly on Existence, till one after the other, its earthly hulls and garnitures, have all melted away; and now to his rapt vision the interior, celestial Holy of Holies, lies disclosed.

Here therefore properly it is that the Philosophy of Clothes attains to Transcendentalism; this last leap, can we but clear it, takes us safe into the promised land, where *Palingenesia,* in all senses, may be considered as beginning. "Courage, then!" may our Diogenes exclaim, with better right than Diogenes the First* once did. This stupendous Section we, after long, painful meditation, have found not to be unintelligible; but on the contrary to grow clear, nay radiant, and all-illuminating. Let the reader, turning on it what utmost force of speculative intellect is in him, do his part; as we, by judicious selection and adjustment, shall study to do ours:

"Deep has been, and is, the significance of Miracles," thus quietly begins the Professor; "far deeper perhaps than we imagine. Meanwhile, the question of questions were: What specially is a Miracle? To that Dutch King of Siam,* an icicle had been a miracle; whoso had carried with him an air-pump, and phial of vitriolic ether, might have worked a miracle. To my Horse again, who unhappily is still more unscientific, do not I work a miracle, and magical *'open sesame!'* every time I please to pay twopence, and open for him an impassable *Schlagbaum,* or shut Turnpike?

" 'But is not a real Miracle simply a violation of the Laws of Nature?' ask several. Whom I answer by this new question: What are the Laws of Nature? To me perhaps the rising of one from the dead were no violation of these Laws, but a confirmation; were some far deeper Law, now first penetrated into, and by Spiritual Force, even as the rest have all been, brought to bear on us with its Material Force.

"Here too may some inquire, not without astonishment: On what ground shall one, that can make Iron swim, come and declare that therefore he can teach Religion? To us, truly, of the Nineteenth Century, such declaration were inept enough; which nevertheless to our fathers, of the First Century, was full of meaning.

" 'But is it not the deepest Law of Nature that she be constant?' cries an illuminated class: 'Is not the Machine of the Universe fixed to move by unalterable rules?' Probable enough, good friends: nay, I too must believe that the God, whom ancient, inspired men assert to be 'without variableness or shadow of turning,' does indeed never change; that Nature, that the Universe, which no one whom it so pleases can be prevented from calling a Machine, does move by the most unalterable rules. And now of you too I make the old inquiry: What those same unalterable rules, forming the complete Statute-Book of Nature, may possibly be?

"They stand written in our Works of Science, say you; in the accumulated records of man's Experience?—Was man with his Experience present at the Creation, then, to see how it all went on? Have any deepest scientific individuals yet dived down to the foundations of the Universe, and gauged every thing there? Did the Maker take them into His counsel; that they read His ground-plan of the incomprehensible All; and can say, This stands marked therein, and no more than this? Alas, not in anywise! These scientific individuals have been nowhere but where we also are; have seen some handbreadths deeper than we see into the Deep that is infinite, without bottom as without shore.

"Laplace's Book on the Stars, wherein he exhibits that certain Planets, with their Satellites, gyrate round our worthy

Sun, at a rate and in a course, which, by greatest good fortune, he and the like of him have succeeded in detecting,—is to me as precious as to another. But is this what thou namest 'Mechanism of the Heavens,' and 'System of the World;' this, wherein Sirius and the Pleiades, and all Herschel's Fifteen thousand Suns per minute, being left out, some paltry handful of Moons, and inert Balls, had been—looked at, nicknamed, and marked in the Zodiacal Waybill; so that we can now prate of their Whereabout; their How, their Why, their What, being hid from us as in the signless Inane?

"System of Nature! To the wisest man, wide as is his vision, Nature remains of quite *infinite* depth, of quite infinite expansion; and all Experience thereof limits itself to some few computed centuries, and measured square-miles. The course of Nature's phases, on this our little fraction of a Planet, is partially known to us; but who knows what deeper courses these depend on; what infinitely larger Cycle (of causes) our little Epicycle revolves on? To the Minnow every cranny and pebble, and quality and accident, of its little native Creek may have become familiar: but does the Minnow understand the Ocean Tides and periodic Currents, the Trade-winds, and Monsoons, and Moon's Eclipses; by all which the condition of its little Creek is regulated, and may, from time to time (*un*miraculously enough), be quite overset and reversed? Such a minnow is man; his Creek this Planet Earth; his Ocean the immeasurable All; his Monsoons and periodic Currents the mysterious Course of Providence through Æons of Æons.

"We speak of the Volume of Nature: and truly a Volume it is,—whose Author and Writer is God. To read it! Dost thou, does man, so much as well know the Alphabet thereof? With its Words, Sentences, and grand descriptive Pages, poetical and philosophical, spread out through Solar Systems, and Thousands of Years, we shall not try thee. It is a Volume written in celestial hieroglyphs, in the true Sacred-writing; of which even Prophets are happy that they can read here a line and there a line. As for your Institutes, and Academies of Science, they strive bravely; and, from amid the thick-crowded, inextricably intertwisted hieroglyphic writing, pick out, by dextrous combination, some Letters in the vulgar Character, and therefrom put together this and the other economic Recipe, of high avail in Practice. That Nature is more than some boundless Volume of such Recipes, or huge, well-nigh inexhaustible Domestic-Cookery Book, of which the whole secret will, in this wise,* one day, evolve itself, the fewest dream.

"Custom," continues the Professor, "doth make dotards of us all. Consider well, thou wilt find that Custom is the greatest of Weavers; and weaves air-raiment for all the Spirits of the Universe; whereby indeed these dwell with us visibly, as ministering servants, in our houses and workshops; but their spiritual nature becomes, to the most, for ever hidden. Philosophy complains that Custom has hoodwinked us, from the first; that we do every thing by Custom, even Believe by it; that our very Axioms, let us boast of Free-thinking as we may, are oftenest simply such Beliefs as we have never heard questioned. Nay, what is Philosophy throughout but a continual battle against Custom; an ever-renewed effort to *transcend* the sphere of blind Custom, and so become Transcendental?

"Innumerable are the illusions and legerdemain tricks of Custom: but of all these perhaps the cleverest is her knack of persuading us that the Miraculous, by simple repetition, ceases to be Miraculous. True, it is by this means we live; for man must work as well as wonder: and herein is Custom so far a kind nurse, guiding him to his true benefit. But she is a fond foolish nurse, or rather we are false foolish nurselings, when, in our resting and reflecting hours, we prolong the same deception. Am I to view the Stupendous with stupid indifference, because I have seen it twice, or two hundred, or two million times? There is no reason in Nature or in Art why I should: unless, indeed, I am a mere Work-Machine, for whom the divine gift of Thought were no other than the terrestrial gift of Steam is to the Steam-engine; a power whereby Cotton might be spun, and money and money's worth realised.

"Notable enough too, here as elsewhere, wilt thou find the potency of Names; which indeed are but one kind of such Custom-woven, wonder-hiding garments. Witchcraft, and all manner of Spectre-work, and Demonology, we have now named Madness, and Diseases of the Nerves. Seldom reflecting that still the new question comes upon us: What is Madness, what are Nerves? Ever, as before, does Madness remain a mysterious-terrific, altogether *infernal* boiling up of the Nether Chaotic Deep, through this fair-painted Vision of Creation, which swims thereon, which we name the Real. Was Luther's Picture of the Devil* less a Reality, whether it were formed within the bodily eye, or without it? In every the wisest Soul, lies a whole world of internal Madness, an authentic Demon-Empire; out of which, indeed, his world of Wisdom has been creatively built together, and now rests there, as on its dark foundations does a habitable flowery Earth-rind.

"But deepest of all illusory Appearances, for hiding Wonder, as for many other ends, are your two grand fundamental world-enveloping Appearances, SPACE and TIME. These, as spun and woven for us from before Birth itself, to clothe our celestial ME for dwelling here, and yet to blind it,—lie all-embracing, as the universal canvass, or warp and woof, whereby all minor Illusions, in this Phantasm Existence, weave and paint them-selves. In vain, while here on Earth, shall you endeavour to strip them off; you can, at best, but rend them asunder for moments, and look through.

"Fortunatus had a wishing Hat, which when he put it on, and wished himself Anywhere, behold he was There. By this means had Fortunatus triumphed over Space, he had annihi-lated Space; for him there was no Where, but all was Here. Were a Hatter to establish himself, in the Wahngasse of Weissnichtwo, and make felts of this sort for all mankind, what a world we should have of it! Still stranger, should, on the opposite side of the street, another Hatter establish himself; and, as his fellow-craftsman made Space-annihilating Hats, make Time-annihilating! Of both would I purchase, were it with my last groschen; but chiefly of this latter. To clap on your felt, and, simply by wishing that you were Any*where*, straightway to be *There!* Next to clap on your other felt, and, simply by wishing that you were Any*when*, straightway to be *Then!* This were indeed the grander: shooting at will from the Fire-Creation of the World to its Fire-Consummation; here histori-cally present in the First Century, conversing face to face with Paul and Seneca; there prophetically in the Thirty-first, conversing also face to face with other Pauls and Senecas, who as yet stand hidden in the depth of that late Time!

"Or thinkest thou, it were impossible, unimaginable? Is the Past annihilated, then, or only past; is the Future non-extant, or only future? Those mystic faculties of thine, Memory and Hope, already answer: already through those mystic avenues, thou the Earth-blinded summonest both Past and Future, and communest with them, though as yet darkly, and with mute beckonings. The curtains of Yesterday drop down, the curtains of To-morrow roll up; but Yesterday and To-morrow both *are*. Pierce through the Time-Element, glance into the Eternal. Believe what thou findest written in the sanctuaries of Man's Soul, even as all Thinkers, in all ages, have devoutly read it there: that Time and Space are not God, but creations of God; that with God as it is a universal HERE, so is it an Everlasting NOW.

"And seest thou therein any glimpse of IMMORTALITY?—O heaven! Is the white Tomb of our Loved One, who died from our arms, and must be left behind us there, which rises in the distance, like a pale, mournfully receding Milestone, to tell how many toilsome uncheered miles we have journeyed on alone,—but a pale spectral Illusion! Is the lost Friend still mysteriously Here, even as we are Here mysteriously, with God!—Know of a truth that only the Time-shadows have perished, or are perishable; that the real Being of whatever was, and whatever is, and whatever will be, *is* even now and for ever. This, should it unhappily seem new, thou mayst ponder, at thy leisure; for the next twenty years, or the next twenty centuries: believe it thou must; understand it thou canst not.

"That the Thought-forms, Space and Time, wherein, once for all, we are sent into this Earth to live, should condition and determine our whole Practical reasonings, conceptions, and imagings (not imaginings),*—seems altogether fit, just, and unavoidable. But that they should, farthermore, usurp such sway over pure spiritual Meditation, and blind us to the wonder every where lying close on us, seems nowise so. Admit Space and Time to their due rank as Forms of Thought; nay, even, if thou wilt, to their quite undue rank of Realities: and consider, then, with thyself how their thin disguises hide from us the brightest God-effulgences! Thus, were it not miraculous, could I stretch forth my hand, and clutch the Sun? Yet thou seest me daily stretch forth my hand, and therewith clutch many a thing, and swing it hither and thither. Art thou a grown Baby, then, to fancy that the Miracle lies in miles of distance, or in pounds avoirdupois of weight; and not to see that the true inexplicable God-revealing Miracle lies in this, that I can stretch forth my hand at all; that I have free Force to clutch aught therewith? Innumerable other of this sort are the deceptions, and wonder-hiding stupefactions, which Space practises on us.

"Still worse is it with regard to Time. Your grand anti-magician, and universal wonder-hider, is this same lying Time. Had we but the Time-annihilating Hat, to put on for once only, we should see ourselves in a World of Miracles, wherein all fabled or authentic Thaumaturgy, and feats of Magic, were outdone. But unhappily we have not such a Hat; and man, poor fool that he is, can seldom and scantily help himself without one.

"Were it not wonderful, for instance, had Orpheus* built the walls of Thebes by the mere sound of his Lyre? Yet tell me, who built these walls of Weissnichtwo; summoning out all the sandstone rocks, to dance along from the *Steinbruch** (now a huge Troglodyte Chasm, with frightful green-mantled pools); and shape themselves into Doric and Ionic pillars, squared ashlar houses, and noble streets? Was it not the still higher Orpheus, or Orpheuses, who, in past centuries, by the divine Music of Wisdom, succeeded in civilising Man? Our highest Orpheus walked in Judea, eighteen hundred years ago: his sphere-melody, flowing in wild native tones, took captive the ravished souls of men; and, being of a truth* sphere-melody, still flows and sounds, though now with thousandfold Accompaniments, and rich symphonies, through all our hearts; and modulates, and divinely leads them. Is that a wonder, which happens in two hours; and does it cease to be wonderful if happening in two million? Not only was Thebes built by the Music of an Orpheus; but without the music of some inspired Orpheus was no city ever built, no work that man glories in ever done.

"Sweep away the Illusion of Time: glance, if thou have eyes, from the near moving-cause to its far distant Mover: The stroke that came transmitted through a whole galaxy of elastic balls, was it less a stroke than if the last ball only had been struck, and sent flying? Oh, could I (with the Time-annihilating Hat) transport thee direct from the Beginnings to the Endings, how were thy eyesight unsealed, and thy heart set flaming in the Light-sea of celestial wonder! Then sawest thou that this fair Universe, were it in the meanest province thereof, is in very deed the star-domed City of God; that through every star, through every grass-blade, and most through every Living Soul, the glory of a present God still beams. But Nature, which is the Time-vesture of God, and reveals Him to the wise, hides Him from the foolish.

"Again, could any thing be more miraculous than an actual authentic Ghost? The English Johnson longed, all his life, to see one; but could not, though he went to Cock Lane,* and thence to the church-vaults, and tapped on coffins. Foolish Doctor! Did he never, with the mind's eye as well as with the body's, look round him into that full tide of human Life he so loved; did he never so much as look into Himself? The good Doctor was a Ghost, as actual and authentic as heart could wish; well nigh a million of Ghosts were travelling the streets by his side. Once more I say, sweep away the illusion of Time; compress the three-score years into three minutes: what else was he, what else are we? Are we not Spirits, shaped into a body, into an Appearance; and that fade away again into air, and Invisibility? This is no metaphor, it is a simple scientific *fact*: we start out of Nothingness, take figure, and are Apparitions; round us, as round the veriest spectre, is Eternity; and to Eternity minutes are as years and æons. Come there not tones of Love and Faith, as from celestial harp-strings, like the Song of beatified Souls? And again, do we not squeak and gibber (in our discordant, screech-owlish debatings and recriminatings); and glide bodeful, and feeble, and fearful; or uproar (*poltern*), and revel in our mad Dance of the Dead,—till the scent of the morning-air summons us to our still Home; and dreamy Night becomes awake and Day? Where now is Alexander of Macedon: does the steel Host, that yelled in fierce battle-shouts at Issus and

Arbela, remain behind him; or have they all vanished utterly, even as perturbed Goblins must? Napoleon too, and his Moscow Retreats and Austerlitz Campaigns! Was it all other than the veriest Spectre-Hunt; which has now, with its howling tumult that made Night hideous, flitted away?—Ghosts! There are nigh a thousand million walking the earth openly at noontide; some half-hundred have vanished from it, some half-hundred have arisen in it, ere thy watch ticks once.

"O Heaven, it is mysterious, it is awful to consider that we not only carry each a future Ghost within him; but are, in very deed, Ghosts! These Limbs, whence had we them; this stormy Force; this life-blood with its burning Passion? They are dust and shadow; a Shadow-system gathered round our ME; wherein, through some moments or years, the Divine Essence is to be revealed in the Flesh. That warrior on his strong war-horse, fire flashes through his eyes; Force dwells in his arm and heart: but warrior and war-horse are a vision; a revealed Force, nothing more. Stately they tread the Earth, as if it were a firm substance: fool! the Earth is but a film; it cracks in twain, and warrior and war-horse sink beyond plummet's sounding. Plummet's? Fantasy herself will not follow them. A little while ago they were not; a little while and they are not, their very ashes are not.

"So has it been from the beginning, so will it be to the end. Generation after generation takes to itself the Form of a Body; and forth-issuing from Cimmerian Night, on Heaven's mission, APPEARS. What Force and Fire is in each he expends: one grinding in the mill of Industry; one hunter-like climbing the giddy Alpine heights of Science; one madly dashed in pieces on the rocks of Strife, in war with his fellow:—and then the Heaven-sent is recalled; his earthly Vesture falls away, and soon even to Sense becomes a vanished Shadow. Thus, like some wild-flaming, wild-thundering train of Heaven's Artillery, does this mysterious MANKIND thunder and flame, in long-drawn, quick-succeeding grandeur, through the unknown Deep. Thus, like a God-created, fire-breathing Spirit-host, we emerge from the Inane; haste stormfully across the astonished Earth; then plunge again into the Inane. Earth's mountains are levelled, and her seas filled up, in our passage: can the Earth,

which is but dead and a vision, resist Spirits which have reality
and are alive? On the hardest adamant some foot-print of us is
stamped in; the last Rear of the host will read traces of the
earliest Van. But whence?—O Heaven, whither? Sense knows
not; Faith knows not; only that it is through Mystery to
Mystery, from God and to God.

> We *are such stuff*
> As Dreams are made of, and our little Life
> Is rounded with a sleep!*

*   *   *

CHAPTER 9
CIRCUMSPECTIVE

HERE then arises the so momentous question: Have many British Readers actually arrived with us at the new promised country; is the Philosophy of Clothes now at last opening around them? Long and adventurous has the journey been: from those outmost vulgar, palpable Woollen-Hulls of Man; through his wondrous Flesh-Garments, and his wondrous Social Garnitures; inwards to the Garments of his very Soul's Soul, to Time and Space themselves! And now does the spiritual, eternal Essence of Man, and of Mankind, bared of such wrappages, begin in any measure to reveal itself? Can many readers discern, as through a glass darkly, in huge wavering outlines, some primeval rudiments of Man's Being, what is changeable divided from what is unchangeable? Does that Earth-Spirit's speech in *Faust:*

'Tis thus at the roaring Loom of Time I ply,
And weave for God the Garment thou see'st Him by;

or that other thousand-times-repeated speech of the Magician, Shakespeare:

And like the baseless fabric of this vision,
The cloudcapt Towers, the gorgeous Palaces,
The solemn Temples, the great Globe itself,
And all which it inherit, shall dissolve;
And like this unsubstantial pageant faded,
Leave not a wrack behind;*

begin to have some meaning for us? In a word, do we at length stand safe in the far region of Poetic Creation and Palingenesia, where that Phœnix Death-Birth of Human Society, and of all Human things, appears possible, is seen to be inevitable?

Along this most insufficient, unheard-of Bridge, which the Editor, by Heaven's blessing, has now seen himself enabled to conclude, if not complete, it cannot be his sober calculation, but only his fond hope, that many have travelled without accident. No firm arch, overspanning the Impassable with paved highway, could the Editor construct; only, as was said, some zigzag series of rafts floating tumultuously thereon. Alas, and the leaps from raft to raft were too often of a breakneck character; the darkness, the nature of the element, all was against us!

Nevertheless, may not here and there one of a thousand, provided with a discursiveness of intellect rare in our day, have cleared the passage, in spite of all? Happy few, little band of Friends, be welcome, be of courage! By degrees, the eye grows accustomed to its new Whereabout; the hand can stretch itself forth to work there: it is in this grand and indeed highest work of Palingenesia that ye shall labour, each according to ability. New labourers will arrive; new Bridges will be built: nay, may not our own poor rope-and-raft Bridge, in your passings and repassings, be mended in many a point, till it grow quite firm, passable even for the halt?

Meanwhile, of the innumerable multitude that started with us, joyous and full of hope, where now is the innumerable remainder, whom we see no longer by our side? The most have recoiled, and stand gazing afar off, in unsympathetic astonishment, at our career: not a few, pressing forward with more courage, have missed footing, or leaped short; and now swim weltering in the Chaos-flood, some towards this shore, some towards that. To these also a helping hand should be held out; at least some word of encouragement be said.

Or, to speak without metaphor, with which mode of utterance Teufelsdröckh unhappily has somewhat infected us,—can it be hidden from the Editor that many a British Reader sits reading quite bewildered in head, and afflicted rather than instructed by the present Work? Yes, long ago has many a British Reader been, as now, demanding with something like a snarl: Whereto does all this lead; or what use is in it?

In the way of replenishing thy purse, or otherwise aiding thy digestive faculty, O British reader, it leads to nothing, and there is no use in it; but rather the reverse, for it costs thee somewhat. Nevertheless, if through this unpromising Horn-gate,* Teufelsdröckh, and we by means of him, have led thee into the true Land of Dreams; and through the Clothes-Screen, as through a magical Pierre-Pertuis, thou lookest, even for moments, into the region of the Wonderful, and seest and feelest that thy daily life is girt with Wonder, and based on Wonder, and thy very blankets and breeches are Miracles,— then art thou profited beyond money's worth, and hast a thankfulness towards our Professor; nay, perhaps in many a literary Tea-circle, wilt open thy kind lips, and audibly express that same.

Nay, farther art not thou too perhaps by this time made aware that all Symbols are properly Clothes; that all Forms whereby Spirit manifests itself to Sense, whether outwardly or in the imagination, are Clothes; and thus not only the parchment Magna Charta, which a Tailor was nigh cutting into measures,* but the Pomp and Authority of Law, the sacredness of Majesty, and all inferior Worships (Worth-ships) are properly a Vesture and Raiment; and the Thirty-nine Articles* themselves are articles of wearing apparel (for the Religious Idea)? In which case, must it not also be admitted that this Science of Clothes is a high one, and may with infinitely deeper study on thy part yield richer fruit: that it takes scientific rank beside Codification, and Political Economy, and the Theory of the British Constitution; nay, rather, from its prophetic height looks down on all these, as on so many weaving-shops and spinning-mills, where the Vestures which *it* has to fashion, and consecrate, and distribute, are, too often by haggard hungry operatives who see no farther than their nose, mechanically woven and spun?

But omitting all this, much more all that concerns Natural Supernaturalism, and indeed whatever has reference to the Ulterior or Transcendental Portion of the Science, or bears never so remotely on that promised Volume of the *Palingenesie der menschlichen Gesellschaft* (Newbirth of Society),—we humbly suggest that no province of Clothes-Philosophy, even the lowest, is without its direct value, but that innumerable inferences of a practical nature may be drawn therefrom. To say nothing of those pregnant considerations, ethical, political, symbolical, which crowd on the Clothes-Philosopher from the very threshold of his Science: nothing even of those "architectural ideas" which, as we have seen, lurk at the bottom of all Modes, and will one day, better unfolding themselves, lead to

important revolutions,—let us glance, for a moment, and with
the faintest light of Clothes-Philosophy, on what may be called
the Habilatory Class of our fellow-men. Here too overlooking,
whereso much were to be looked on, the million spinners,
weavers, fullers, dyers, washers, and wringers, that puddle and
muddle in their dark recesses, to make us Clothes, and die that
we may live,—let us but turn the reader's attention upon two
small divisions of mankind, who, like moths, may be regarded
as Cloth-animals, creatures that live, move, and have their
being in Cloth: we mean, Dandies and Tailors.

In regard to both which small divisions it may be asserted
without scruple that the public feeling, unenlightened by
Philosophy, is at fault; and even that the dictates of humanity
are violated. As will perhaps abundantly appear to readers of
the two following Chapters.

CHAPTER 10

THE DANDIACAL BODY

First, touching Dandies, let us consider, with some scientific strictness, what a Dandy specially is. A Dandy is a Clothes-wearing Man, a Man whose trade, office, and existence consists in the wearing of Clothes. Every faculty of his soul, spirit, purse, and person is heroically consecrated to this one object, the wearing of Clothes wisely and well: so that as others dress to live, he lives to dress. The all-importance of Clothes, which a German Professor, of unequalled learning and acumen, writes his enormous Volume to demonstrate, has sprung up in the intellect of the Dandy, without effort, like an instinct of genius: he is inspired with Cloth, a Poet of Cloth. What Teufelsdröckh would call a "Divine Idea of Cloth" is born with him; and this, like other such Ideas, will express itself outwardly, or wring his heart asunder with unutterable throes.

But, like a generous, creative enthusiast, he fearlessly makes his Idea an Action; shows himself, in peculiar guise, to mankind; walks forth, a witness and living Martyr to the eternal Worth* of Clothes. We called him a Poet: is not his body the (stuffed) parchment-skin whereon he writes, with cunning Huddersfield dyes, a Sonnet to his mistress' eyebrow? Say, rather, an Epos, and *Clotha Virumque cano,** to the whole world, in Macaronic verses, which he that runs may read. Nay, if you grant, what seems to be admissible, that the Dandy has a Thinking-principle in him, and some notions of Time and Space, is there not in this Life-devotedness to Cloth, in this so willing sacrifice of the Immortal to the Perishable, something (though in reverse order) of that blending and identification of Eternity with Time, which, as we have seen, constitutes the Prophetic character?

And now, for all this perennial Martyrdom, and Poesy, and even Prophecy, what is it that the Dandy asks in return? Solely, we may say, that you would recognise his existence; would admit him to be a living object; or even failing this, a visual object, or thing that will reflect rays of light. Your silver or your gold (beyond what the niggardly Law has already secured him) he solicits not; simply the glance of your eyes. Understand his mystic significance, or altogether miss and misinterpret it; do but look at him, and he is contented. May we not well cry shame on an ungrateful world, that refuses even this poor boon; that will waste its optic faculty on dried Crocodiles, and Siamese Twins; and over the domestic wonderful wonder of wonders, a live Dandy, glance with hasty indifference, and a scarcely concealed contempt! Him no Zoologist classes among the Mammalia, no Anatomist dissects with care: when did we see any injected Preparation of the Dandy, in our Museums; any specimen of him preserved in spirits? Lord Herringbone* may dress himself in a snuff-brown suit, with snuff-brown shirt and shoes: it skills not; the undiscerning public, occupied with grosser wants, passes by regardless on the other side.

The age of Curiosity, like that of Chivalry, is indeed, properly speaking, gone. Yet perhaps only gone to sleep: for here arises the Clothes-Philosophy to resuscitate, strangely enough, both the one and the other! Should sound views of this Science come to prevail, the essential nature of the British Dandy, and the mystic significance that lies in him, cannot always remain hidden under laughable and lamentable hallucination. The following long Extract from Professor Teufelsdröckh may set the matter, if not in its true light, yet in the way towards such. It is to be regretted however that, here as so often elsewhere, the Professor's keen philosophic perspicacity is somewhat marred by a certain mixture of almost owlish purblindness, or else of some perverse, ineffectual, ironic tendency, our readers shall judge which:

"In these distracted times," writes he, "when the Religious Principle, driven out of most Churches, either lies unseen in the hearts of good men, looking and longing and silently working there towards some new Revelation; or else wanders homeless over the world, like a disembodied soul seeking its terrestrial organisation,—into how many strange shapes, of Superstition and Fanaticism, does it not tentatively and errantly cast itself! The higher Enthusiasm of man's nature is for the while without Exponent; yet must it continue indestructible, unweariedly active, and work blindly in the great chaotic deep: thus Sect after Sect, and Church after Church, bodies itself forth, and melts again into new metamorphosis.

"Chiefly is this observable in England, which, as the wealthiest and worst-instructed of European nations, offers precisely the elements (of Heat, namely, and of Darkness), in which such moon-calves and monstrosities are best generated. Among the newer Sects of that country, one of the most notable, and closely connected with our present subject, is that of the *Dandies;* concerning which, what little information I have been able to procure may fitly stand here.

"It is true, certain of the English Journalists, men generally without sense for the Religious Principle, or judgment for its manifestations, speak, in their brief enigmatic notices, as if this were perhaps rather a Secular Sect, and not a Religious one: nevertheless, to the psychologic eye its devotional and even sacrificial character plainly enough reveals itself. Whether it belongs to the class of Fetish-worships, or of Hero-worships or Polytheisms, or to what other class, may in the present state of our intelligence remain undecided (*schweben*). A certain touch of Manicheism, not indeed in the Gnostic shape, is discernible enough: also (for human Error walks in a cycle, and reappears at intervals) a not inconsiderable resemblance to that Superstition of the Athos Monks, who by fasting from all nourishment, and looking intensely for a length of time into their own navels, came to discern therein the true Apocalypse of Nature, and Heaven Unveiled. To my own surmise, it appears as if this Dandiacal Sect were but a new modification, adapted to the new time, of that primeval Superstition, *Self-Worship;* which Zerdusht, Quangfoutchee, Mohamed,* and others, strove rather to subordinate and restrain than to eradicate; and which only in the purer forms of Religion has been altogether rejected. Wherefore, if any one chooses to name it revived Ahrimanism, or a new figure of Demon-Worship, I have, so far as is yet visible, no objection.

"For the rest, these people, animated with the zeal of a new Sect, display courage and perseverance, and what force there is in man's nature though never so enslaved. They affect great purity and separatism; distinguish themselves by a particular

costume (whereof some notices were given in the earlier part of
this Volume); likewise, so far as possible, by a particular speech
(apparently some broken *Lingua-franca,* or English-French);
and, on the whole, strive to maintain a true Nazarene deport-
ment, and keep themselves unspotted from the world.

"They have their Temples, whereof the chief, as the Jewish
Temple did, stands in their metropolis; and is named *Almack's,*
a word of uncertain etymology. They worship principally by
night; and have their Highpriests and Highpriestesses, who,
however, do not continue for life. The rites, by some supposed
to be of the Menadic sort, or perhaps with an Eleusinian or
Cabiric* character, are held strictly secret. Nor are Sacred
Books wanting to the Sect; these they call *Fashionable Novels:*
however, the Canon is not completed, and some are canonical
and others not.

"Of such Sacred Books I, not without expense, procured
myself some samples; and in hope of true insight, and with the
zeal which beseems an Inquirer into Clothes, set to interpret
and study them. But wholly to no purpose: that tough faculty
of reading, for which the world will not refuse me credit, was
here for the first time foiled and set at nought. In vain that I
summoned my whole energies (*mich weidlich anstrengte*), and
did my very utmost: at the end of some short space, I was
uniformly seized with not so much what I can call a drumming
in my ears, as a kind of infinite, unsufferable Jew's-harping and
scrannel-piping there; to which the frightfullest species of
Magnetic Sleep* soon supervened. And if I strove to shake this
away, and absolutely would not yield, came a hitherto unfelt
sensation, as of *Delirium Tremens,* and a melting into total
deliquium:*—till at last, by order of the Doctor, dreading ruin
to my whole intellectual and bodily faculties, and a general
breaking-up of the constitution, I reluctantly but determinedly
forbore. Was there some miracle at work here; like those Fire-
balls, and supernal and infernal prodigies, that, in the case of the
Jewish Mysteries, have also more than once scared back the
Alien?* Be this as it may, such failure on my part, after best
efforts, must excuse the imperfection of this sketch; altogether
incomplete, yet the completest I could give of a Sect too
singular to be omitted.

"Loving my own life and senses as I do, no power shall induce me, as a private individual, to open another *Fashionable Novel*. But luckily, in this dilemma, comes a hand from the clouds; whereby if not victory, deliverance is held out to me. Round one of those Book-packages, which the *Stillschweigen'sche Buchhandlung** is in the habit of importing from England, come, as is usual, various waste printed-sheets (*Maculatur-Blätter*), by way of interior wrappage: into these the Clothes-Philosopher, with a certain Mohamedan reverence even for waste paper,* where curious knowledge will sometimes hover, disdains not to cast his eye. Readers may judge of his astonishment when on such a defaced stray sheet, probably the outcast fraction of some English Periodical, such as they name *Magazine,* appears something like a Dissertation on this very subject of *Fashionable Novels!* It sets out, indeed, chiefly from the Secular point of view; directing itself, not without asperity, against some to me unknown individual, named *Pelham,** who seems to be a mystagogue, and leading Teacher and Preacher of the Sect; so that, what indeed otherwise was not to be expected in such a fugitive fragmentary sheet, the true secret, the Religious physiognomy and physiology of the Dandiacal Body, is nowise laid fully open there. Nevertheless, scattered lights do from time to time sparkle out, whereby I have endeavoured to profit. Nay, in one passage selected from the Prophecies, or Mythic Theogonies, or whatever they are (for the style seems very mixed), of this Mystagogue, I find what appears to be a Confession of Faith, or Whole Duty of Man, according to the tenets of that Sect. Which Confession, or Whole Duty, therefore, as proceeding from a source so authentic, I shall here arrange under Seven distinct Articles, and in very abridged shape, lay before the German world; therewith taking leave of this matter. Observe, also, that to avoid possibility of error, I, as far as may be, quote literally from the Original:

"ARTICLES OF FAITH

1. Coats should have nothing of the triangle about them; at the same time, wrinkles behind should be carefully avoided.
2. The collar is a very important point: it should be low behind, and slightly rolled.

3. No licence of fashion can allow a man of delicate taste to adopt the posterial luxuriance of a Hottentot.

4. There is safety in a swallow-tail.

5. The good sense of a gentleman is nowhere more finely developed than in his rings.

6. It is permitted to mankind, under certain restrictions, to wear white waistcoats.

7. The trowsers must be exceedingly tight across the hips."

All which Propositions, I, for the present, content myself with modestly but peremptorily and irrevocably denying.

"In strange contrast with this Dandiacal Body stands another British Sect, originally, as I understand, of Ireland, where its chief seat still is; but known also in the main Island, and indeed every where rapidly spreading. As this Sect has hitherto emitted no Canonical Books, it remains to me in the same state of obscurity as the Dandiacal, which has published Books that the unassisted human faculties are inadequate to read. The members appear to be designated by a considerable diversity of names, according to their various places of establishment: in England they are generally called the *Drudge* Sect; also, unphilosophically enough, the *White-Negroes;* and, chiefly in scorn by those of other communions, the *Ragged-Beggar* Sect. In Scotland, again, I find them entitled *Hallanshakers,** or the *Stook-of-Duds* Sect; any individual communicant is named *Stook-of-Duds* (that is, Shock of Rags), in allusion, doubtless, to their professional Costume. While in Ireland, which, as mentioned, is their grand parent hive, they go by a perplexing multiplicity of designations, such as *Bogtrotters, Redshanks, Ribbonmen, Cottiers, Peep-of-day Boys, Babes of the Wood, Rockites,** Poor-Slaves;* which last, however, seems to be the primary and generic name; whereto, probably enough, the others are only subsidiary species, or slight varieties; or, at most, propagated offsets from the parent stem, whose minute subdivisions, and shades of difference, it were here loss of time to dwell on. Enough for us to understand, what seems indubitable, that the original Sect is that of the *Poor-Slaves;* whose doctrines, practices, and fundamental characteristics, pervade and animate the whole Body, howsoever denominated or outwardly diversified.

"The precise speculative tenets of this Brotherhood: how the Universe, and Man, and Man's Life, picture themselves to the mind of an Irish Poor-Slave; with what feelings and opinions he looks forward on the Future, round on the Present, back on the Past, it were extremely difficult to specify. Something Monastic there appears to be in their Constitution: we find them bound by the two Monastic Vows, of Poverty and Obedience; which Vows, especially the former, it is said, they observe with great strictness; nay, as I have understood it, they are pledged, and be it by any solemn Nazarene ordination or not, irrevocably enough* consecrated thereto, even *before* birth. That the third Monastic Vow, of Chastity, is rigidly enforced among them, I find no ground to conjecture.

"Furthermore, they appear to imitate the Dandiacal Sect in their grand principle of wearing a peculiar Costume. Of which Irish Poor-Slave Costume no description will indeed be found in the present Volume; for this reason, that by the imperfect organ of Language it seemed indescribable.* Their raiment consists of innumerable skirts, lappets, and irregular wings, of all cloths and of all colours; through the labyrinthic intricacies of which their bodies are introduced by some unknown process. It is fastened together by a multiplex combination of buttons, thrums, and skewers; to which frequently is added a girdle of leather, of hempen or even of straw rope, round the loins. To straw rope, indeed, they seem partial, and often wear it by way of sandals. In head-dress they affect a certain freedom: hats with partial brim, without crown, or with only a loose, hinged, or valved crown; in the former case, they sometimes invert the hat, and wear it brim uppermost, like a University-cap, with what view is unknown.

"The name, Poor-Slaves, seems to indicate a Slavonic, Polish, or Russian origin: not so, however, the interior essence and spirit of their Superstition, which rather displays a Teutonic or Druidical character. One might fancy them worshippers of Hertha, or the Earth: for they dig and affectionately work continually in her bosom; or else, shut up in private Oratories, meditate and manipulate the substances derived from her; seldom looking up towards the Heavenly Luminaries, and then with comparative indifference. Like the Druids, on the other hand, they live in dark dwellings; often even breaking their glass-windows, where they find such, and stuffing them up with pieces of raiment, or other opaque substances, till the fit obscurity is restored. Again, like all followers of Nature-Worship, they are liable to outbreakings of an enthusiasm rising to ferocity; and burn men, if not in wicker idols, yet in sod cottages.

"In respect of diet, they have also their observances. All Poor-Slaves are Rhizophagous (or Root-eaters); a few are Ichthyophagous, and use Salted Herrings: other animal food they abstain from; except indeed, with perhaps some strange inverted fragment of a Brahminical feeling,* such animals as die a natural death. Their universal sustenance is the root named Potato, cooked by fire alone; and generally without condiment or relish of any kind, save an unknown condiment named *Point,* into the meaning of which I have vainly inquired; the victual *Potatoes-and-Point* * not appearing, at least not with specific accuracy of description, in any European Cookery-Book whatever. For drink they use, with an almost epigrammatic counterpoise of taste, Milk, which is the mildest of liquors, and *Potheen,* which is the fiercest. This latter I have tasted, as well as the English *Blue-Ruin,* and the Scotch *Whisky,* analogous fluids used by the Sect in those countries: it evidently contains some form of alcohol, in the highest state of concentration, though disguised with acrid oils; and is, on the whole, the most pungent substance known to me—indeed, a perfect liquid fire. In all their Religious Solemnities, Potheen is said to be an indispensable requisite, and largely consumed.

"An Irish Traveller, of perhaps common veracity, who presents himself under the to me unmeaning title of *The late John Bernard,* * offers the following sketch of a domestic establishment, the inmates whereof, though such is not stated expressly, appear to have been of that Faith. Thereby shall my German readers now behold an Irish Poor-Slave, as it were with their own eyes; and even see him at meat. Moreover, in the so precious waste-paper sheet, above mentioned, I have found some corresponding picture of a Dandiacal Household, painted by that same Dandiacal Mystagogue, or Theogonist:

this also, by way of counterpart and contrast, the world shall look into.

"First, therefore, of the Poor-Slave, who appears likewise to have been a species of Innkeeper. I quote from the original:* *'The furniture of this Caravansera consisted of a large iron Pot, two oaken Tables, two Benches, two Chairs, and a Potheen Noggin. There was a Loft above (attainable by a ladder), upon which the inmates slept; and the space below was divided by a hurdle into two Apartments: the one for their cow and pig, the other for themselves and guests. On entering the house we discovered the family, eleven in number, at dinner: the father sitting at the top, the mother at bottom, the children on each side of a large oaken Board which was scooped out in the middle, like a Trough, to receive the contents of their Pot of Potatoes. Little holes were cut at equal distances to contain Salt; and a bowl of Milk stood on the table: all the luxuries of meat and beer, bread, knives, and dishes were dispensed with.'* The Poor-Slave himself our Traveller found, as he says, broad-backed, black-browed, of great personal strength, and mouth from ear to ear. His Wife was a sun-browned but well-featured woman; and his young ones, bare and chubby, had the appetite of ravens. Of their Philosophical, or Religious tenets or observances, no notice or hint.

"But now, secondly, of the Dandiacal Household; in which, truly, that often-mentioned Mystagogue and inspired Penman himself has his abode:* *'A Dressing-room splendidly furnished: violet-coloured curtains, chairs and ottomans of the same hue. Two full-length Mirrors are placed, one on each side of a table, which supports the luxuries of the Toilet. Several Bottles of Perfumes, arranged in a peculiar fashion, stand upon a smaller table of mother-of-pearl: opposite to these are placed the appurtenances of Lavation richly wrought in frosted silver. A Wardrobe of Buhl is on the left; the doors of which being partly open discover a profusion of Clothes; Shoes of a singularly small size monopolise the lower shelves. Fronting the wardrobe a door ajar gives some slight glimpse of a Bath-room. Folding-doors in the back-ground.—Enter the Author (our Theogonist in person), obsequiously preceded by a French Valet, in white silk Jacket and cambric Apron.'*

"Such are the two Sects which, at this moment, divide the

more unsettled portion of the British People; and agitate that
ever-vexed country. To the eye of the political Seer, their
mutual relation, pregnant with the elements of discord and
hostility, is far from consoling. These two principles of Dandiacal Self-worship or Demon-worship, and Poor-Slavish or
Drudgical Earth-worship, or whatever that same Drudgism
may be, do as yet indeed manifest themselves under distant and
nowise considerable shapes: nevertheless, in their roots and
subterranean ramifications, they extend through the entire
structure of Society, and work unweariedly in the secret depths
of English national Existence; striving to separate and isolate it
into two contradictory, uncommunicating masses.

"In numbers, and even individual strength, the Poor-Slaves
or Drudges, it would seem, are hourly increasing. The Dandiacal, again, is by nature no proselytising Sect; but it boasts of
great hereditary resources, and is strong by union: whereas the
Drudges, split into parties, have as yet no rallying-point; or at
best, only co-operate by means of partial secret affiliations. If,
indeed, there were to arise a *Communion of Drudges,* as there is
already a Communion of Saints, what strangest effects would
follow therefrom! Dandyism as yet affects to look down on
Drudgism: but perhaps the hour of trial, when it will be
practically seen which ought to look down, and which up, is
not so distant.

"To me it seems probable that the two Sects will one day
part England between them; each recruiting itself from the
intermediate ranks, till there be none left to enlist on either side.
Those Dandiacal Manicheans, with the host of Dandyising
Christians, will form one body: the Drudges, gathering round
them whosoever is Drudgical, be he Christian or Infidel pagan;
sweeping up likewise all manner of Utilitarians, Radicals,
refractory Potwalloppers,* and so forth, into their general
mass, will form another. I could liken Dandyism and Drudgism to two bottomless boiling Whirlpools that had broken
out on opposite quarters of the firm land: as yet they appear
only disquieted, foolishly bubbling wells, which man's art
might cover in; yet mark them, their diameter is daily widen-
ing; they are hollow Cones that boil up from the infinite Deep,
over which your firm land is but a thin crust or rind! Thus daily

is the intermediate land crumbling in, daily the empire of the two Buchan-Bullers extending; till now there is but a foot-plank, a mere film of Land between them; this too is washed away; and then—we have the true Hell of Waters, and Noah's Deluge is outdeluged!

"Or better, I might call them two boundless, and indeed unexampled Electric Machines (turned by the "Machinery of Society"), with batteries of opposite quality; Drudgism the Negative, Dandyism the Positive: one attracts hourly towards it and appropriates all the Positive Electricity of the nation (namely, the Money thereof); the other is equally busy with the Negative (that is to say the Hunger), which is equally potent. Hitherto you see only partial transient sparkles and sputters: but wait a little, till the entire nation is in an electric state; till your whole vital Electricity, no longer healthfully Neutral, is cut into two isolated portions of Positive and Negative (of Money and of Hunger); and stands there bottled up in two World-Batteries! The stirring of a child's finger brings the two together; and then—What then? The Earth is but shivered into impalpable smoke by that Doom's-thunder-peal; the Sun misses one of his Planets in Space, and henceforth there are no eclipses of the Moon.—Or better still, I might liken"——

Oh! enough, enough of likenings and similitudes; in excess of which, truly, it is hard to say whether Teufelsdröckh or ourselves sin the more.

We have often blamed him for a habit of wire-drawing and over-refining; from of old we have been familiar with his tendency to Mysticism and Religiosity, whereby in every thing he was still scenting out Religion: but never perhaps did these amaurosis suffusions so cloud and distort his otherwise most piercing vision, as in this of the *Dandiacal Body!* Or was there something of intended satire; is the Professor and Seer not quite the blinkard he affects to be? Of an ordinary mortal we should have decisively answered in the affirmative; but with a Teufels-dröckh there ever hovers some shade of doubt. In the mean-while, if satire were actually intended, the case is little better. There are not wanting men who will answer: Does your Professor take us for simpletons? His irony has overshot itself; we see through it, and perhaps through him.

CHAPTER II

TAILORS

THUS, however, has our first Practical Inference from the Clothes-Philosophy, that which respects Dandies, been sufficiently drawn; and we come now to the second, concerning Tailors. On this latter our opinion happily quite coincides with that of Teufelsdröckh himself, as expressed in the concluding page of his Volume; to whom therefore we willingly give place. Let him speak his own last words, in his own way:

"Upwards of a century," says he, "must elapse, and still the bleeding fight of Freedom be fought, whoso is noblest perishing in the van, and thrones be hurled on altars like Pelion on Ossa,* and the Moloch of Iniquity have his victims, and the Michael of Justice his Martyrs, before Tailors can be admitted to their true prerogatives of manhood, and this last wound of suffering Humanity be closed.

"If aught in the history of the world's blindness could surprise us, here might we indeed pause and wonder. An idea has gone abroad, and fixed itself down into a wide-spreading rooted Error, that Tailors are a distinct species in Physiology, not Men, but fractional Parts of a Man. Call any one a *Schneider* (Cutter, Tailor), is it not, in our dislocated, hoodwinked, and indeed delirious condition of Society, equivalent to defying his perpetual fellest enmity? The epithet *Schneidermässig* (Tailor-like) betokens an otherwise unapproachable degree of pusillanimity: we introduce a *Tailor's-Melancholy*, more opprobrious than any Leprosy, into our Books of Medicine; and fable I know not what of his generating it by living on Cabbage. Why should I speak of Hans Sachs (himself a Shoemaker, or kind of Leather-Tailor), with his *Schneider mit dem Panier?* * Why of Shakespeare, in his *Taming of the Shrew,* * and elsewhere? Does it not stand on record that the English Queen Elizabeth, receiving a deputation of Eighteen Tailors, addressed them with a: Good morning, gentlemen both! Did not the same virago boast that she had a Cavalry Regiment, whereof neither horse nor man could be injured: her Regiment, namely, of Tailors on Mares? Thus everywhere is the falsehood taken for granted, and acted on as an indisputable fact.

"Nevertheless, need I put the question to any Physiologist, Whether it is disputable or not? Seems it not at least presumable, that, under his Clothes, the Tailor has bones, and viscera, and other muscles than the sartorius?* Which function of manhood is the Tailor not conjectured to perform? Can he not arrest for Debt? Is he not in most countries a tax-paying animal?

"To no reader of this Volume can it be doubtful which conviction is mine. Nay, if the fruit of these long vigils, and almost preternatural Inquiries is not to perish utterly, the world will have approximated towards a higher Truth; and the doctrine, which Swift, with the keen forecast of genius, dimly anticipated, will stand revealed in clear light: that the Tailor is not only a Man, but something of a Creator or Divinity.* Of Franklin it was said, that 'he snatched the Thunder from Heaven and the Sceptre from Kings:'* but which is greater, I would ask, he that lends, or he that snatches? For, looking away from individual cases, and how a Man is by the Tailor new-created into a Nobleman, and clothed not only with Wool but with Dignity and a Mystic Dominion,—is not the fair fabric of Society itself, with all its royal mantles and pontifical stoles, whereby, from nakedness and dismemberment, we are organised into Polities, into Nations, and a whole co-operating Mankind, the creation, as has here been often irrefragably evinced, of the Tailor alone?—What too are all poets, and moral Teachers, but a species of Metaphorical Tailors? Touching which high Guild the greatest living Guild-Brother* has triumphantly asked us: 'Nay, if thou wilt have it, who but the Poet first made Gods for men; brought them down to us; and raised us up to them?'

"And this is he, whom sitting downcast, on the hard basis of his Shop-board, the world treats with contumely, as the ninth part of a man! Look up, thou much injured one, look up with the kindling eye of hope, and prophetic bodings of a noble better time. Too long hast thou sat there, on crossed legs, wearing thy ancle-joints to horn; like some sacred Anchorite, or Catholic Fakir, doing penance, drawing down Heaven's richest blessings, for a world that scoffed at thee. Be of hope! Already streaks of blue peer through our clouds; the thick gloom of Ignorance is rolling asunder, and it will be Day. Mankind will repay with interest their long-accumulated debt: the Anchorite that was scoffed at will be worshipped; the Fraction will become not an Integer only, but a Square and Cube. With astonishment the world will recognise that the Tailor is its Hierophant, and Hierarch, or even its God.

"As I stood in the Mosque of St. Sophia, and looked upon these Four-and-Twenty Tailors, sewing and embroidering that rich Cloth, which the Sultan sends yearly for the Caaba of Mecca, I thought within myself: How many other Unholies has your covering Art made holy, besides this Arabian Whin-stone!

"Still more touching was it when, turning the corner of a lane, in the Scottish Town of Edinburgh, I came upon a Signpost, whereon stood written that such and such a one was 'Breeches-Maker to his Majesty;' and stood painted the Effigies of a Pair of Leather Breeches, and between the knees these memorable words, SIC ITUR AD ASTRA.* Was not this the martyr prison-speech of a Tailor sighing indeed in bonds, yet sighing towards deliverance; and prophetically appealing to a better day? A day of justice, when the worth of Breeches would be revealed to man, and the Scissors become for ever venerable.

"Neither, perhaps, may I now say, has his appeal been altogether in vain. It was in this high moment, when the soul, rent, as it were, and shed asunder, is open to inspiring influence, that I first conceived this Work on Clothes; the greatest I can ever hope to do; which has already, after long retardations, occupied, and will yet occupy, so large a section of my Life; and of which the Primary and simpler Portion may here find its conclusion."

CHAPTER 12
FAREWELL

So have we endeavoured, from the enormous, amorphous Plumpudding, more like a Scottish Haggis, which Herr Teufelsdröckh had kneaded for his fellow mortals, to pick out the choicest Plums, and present them separately on a cover of our own. A laborious, perhaps a thankless enterprise; in which, however, something of hope has occasionally cheered us, and of which we can now wash our hands not altogether without satisfaction. If hereby, though in barbaric wise, some morsel of spiritual nourishment have been added to the scanty ration of our beloved British world, what nobler recompense could the Editor desire? If it prove otherwise, why should he murmur? Was not this a Task which Destiny, in any case, had appointed him; which being* now done with, he sees his general Day's-work so much the lighter, so much the shorter?

Of Professor Teufelsdröckh it seems impossible to take leave without a mingled feeling of astonishment, gratitude and disapproval. Who will not regret that talents, which might have profited in the higher walks of Philosophy, or in Art itself, have been so much devoted to a rummaging among lumber-rooms; nay, too often to a scraping in kennels, where lost rings and diamond-necklaces are nowise the sole conquests? Regret is unavoidable; yet Censure were loss of time. To cure him of his mad humours British Criticism would essay in vain: enough for her if she can, by vigilance, prevent the spreading of such among ourselves. What a result, should this piebald, entangled, hyper-metaphorical style of writing, not to say of thinking, become general among our Literary men! As it might so easily do. Thus has not the Editor himself, working over Teufelsdröckh's German, lost much of his own English purity? Even as the smaller whirlpool is sucked into the larger, and made to whirl along with it, so must the lesser mind, in this instance, become portion of the greater, and, like it, see all things figuratively: which habit time, and assiduous effort, will be needed to eradicate.

Nevertheless, wayward as our Professor shows himself, is there any reader that can part with him in declared enmity? Let us confess, there is that in the wild, much-suffering, much-inflicting man, which almost attaches us. His attitude, we will hope and believe, is that of a man who had said to Cant, Begone; and to Dilettantism, Here thou canst not be; and to Truth, Be thou in place of all to me: a man who had manfully defied the "Time-Prince," or Devil, to his face; nay, perhaps, Hannibal-like, was mysteriously consecrated from birth to that warfare, and now stood minded to wage the same, by all weapons, in all places, at all times. In such a cause, any soldier, were he but a Polack Scythe-man, shall be welcome.

Still the question returns on us: How could a man occasionally of keen insight, not without keen sense of propriety, who had real Thoughts to communicate, resolve to emit them in a shape bordering so closely on the absurd? Which question he were wiser than the present Editor who should satisfactorily answer. Our conjecture has sometimes been that perhaps Necessity as well as Choice was concerned in it. Seems it not conceivable that, in a Life like our Professor's, where so much bountifully given by Nature had in Practice failed and mis-gone, Literature also would never rightly prosper: that striving with his characteristic vehemence to paint this and the other Picture, and ever without success, he at last desperately dashes his brush,* full of all colours, against the canvass, to try whether it will paint Foam? With all his stillness, there were perhaps in Teufelsdröckh desperation enough for this.

A second conjecture we hazard with even less warranty. It is that Teufelsdröckh is not without some touch of the universal feeling, a wish to proselytise. How often already have we paused, uncertain whether the basis of this so enigmatic nature were really Stoicism and Despair, or Love and Hope only seared into the figure of these! Remarkable, moreover, is this saying of his: "How were Friendship possible? In mutual devotedness to the Good and True: otherwise impossible; except as Armed Neutrality, or hollow Commercial League. A man, be the Heavens ever praised, is sufficient for himself; yet were ten men, united in Love, capable of being and of doing what ten thousand singly would fail in. Infinite is the help man can yield to man." And now in conjunction therewith consider this other: "It is the Night of the World, and still long till it be Day: we wander amid the glimmer of smoking ruins, and the Sun and the Stars of Heaven are as blotted out for a season; and two immeasurable Fantoms, HYPOCRISY and ATHEISM, with the Gowle,* SENSUALITY, stalk abroad over the Earth, and call it theirs: well at ease are the Sleepers for whom Existence is a shallow Dream."

But what of the awestruck Wakeful who find it a Reality? Should not these unite; since even an authentic Spectre is not visible to Two?—In which case were this enormous Clothes-Volume properly an enormous Pitchpan, which our Teufels-dröckh in his lone watchtower had kindled, that it might flame far and wide through the Night, and many a disconsolately wandering spirit be guided thither to a Brother's bosom!—We say as before, with all his malign Indifference, who knows what mad Hopes this man may harbour?

Meanwhile there is one fact to be stated here, which harmonises ill with such conjecture; and, indeed, were Teufels-dröckh made like other men, might as good as altogether subvert it. Namely, that while the Beaconfire blazed its brightest, the Watchman had quitted it; that no pilgrim could now ask him: Watchman, what of the Night? Professor Teufelsdröckh, be it known, is no longer visibly present at Weissnichtwo, but again to all appearance lost in Space! Some time ago the Hofrath Heuschrecke was pleased to favour us with another copious Epistle; wherein much is said about the "Population-Institute;" much repeated in praise of the Paper-bag Documents, the hieroglyphic nature of which our Hofrath still seems not to have surmised; and, lastly, the strangest occurrence communicated, to us for the first time, in the following paragraph:

"*Ew. Wohlgeboren**" will have seen, from the public Prints, with what affectionate and hitherto fruitless solicitude Weissnichtwo regards the disappearance of her Sage. Might but the united voice of Germany prevail on him to return; nay, could we but so much as elucidate for ourselves by what mystery he went away! But, alas, old Lieschen experiences or affects the pro-

foundest deafness, the profoundest ignorance: in the Wahngasse all lies swept, silent, sealed up; the Privy Council itself can
hitherto elicit no answer.

"It had been remarked that while the agitating news of those
Parisian Three Days flew from mouth to mouth, and dinned
every ear in Weissnichtwo, Herr Teufelsdröckh was not
known, at the *Ganse* or elsewhere, to have spoken, for a whole
week, any syllable except once these three: *Es geht an* (It is
beginning). Shortly after, as *Ew. Wohlgeboren* knows, was the
public tranquillity here, as in Berlin, threatened by a Sedition
of the Tailors. Nor did there want Evil-wishers, or perhaps
mere desperate Alarmists, who asserted that the closing
Chapter of the Clothes-Volume was to blame. In this appalling
crisis, the serenity of our Philosopher was indescribable: nay,
perhaps, through one humble individual, something thereof
might pass into the *Rath* (Council) itself, and so contribute to
the country's deliverance. The Tailors are now entirely pacificated.—To neither of these two incidents can I attribute our
loss: yet still comes there the shadow of a suspicion out of Paris
and its Politics. For example, when the *Saint-Simonian Society*
transmitted its Propositions hither, and the whole *Ganse* was
one vast cackle of laughter, lamentation, and astonishment,
our Sage sat mute; and at the end of the third evening, said
merely: 'Here also are men who have discovered, not without
amazement, that Man is still Man; of which high, long-
forgotten Truth you already see them make a false application.' Since then, as has been ascertained by examination
of the Post Director, there passed at least one Letter
with its Answer between the Messieurs Bazard-Enfantin
and our Professor himself; of what tenor can now only be
conjectured. On the fifth night following, he was seen for the last
time!

"Has this invaluable man, so obnoxious to most of the
hostile Sects that convulse our Era, been spirited away by
certain of their emissaries: or did he go forth voluntarily to
their head-quarters to confer with them, and confront them?
Reason we have, at least of a negative sort, to believe the Lost
still living: our widowed heart also whispers that ere long he
will himself give a sign. Otherwise, indeed, must his archives,

one day, be opened by Authority; where much, perhaps the *Palingenesie* itself, is thought to be reposited."

Thus far the Hofrath; who vanishes, as is his wont, too like an Ignis Fatuus, leaving the dark still darker.—So that Teufelsdröckh's public History were not done, then, or reduced to an even, unromantic tenor; nay, perhaps, the better part thereof were only beginning? We stand in a region of conjectures, where substance has melted into shadow, and one cannot be distinguished from the other. May Time, which solves or suppresses all problems, throw glad light on this also. Our own private conjecture, now amounting almost to certainty, is that, safe-moored in some stillest obscurity, not to lie always still, Teufelsdröckh is actually in London!

Here, however, can the present Editor, with an ambrosial joy as of over-weariness falling into sleep, lay down his pen. Well does he know, if human testimony be worth aught, that to innumerable British readers likewise, it* is a satisfying consummation; that innumerable British readers consider him, during these current months, but as an uneasy interruption to their ways of thought and digestion, not without a certain irritancy and even spoken invective. For which, as for other mercies, ought he not to thank the Upper Powers? To one and all of you, O irritated readers, he, with outstretched arms and open heart, will wave a kind farewell. Thou too, miraculous Entity, that namest thyself YORKE and OLIVER, and with thy vivacities and genialities, with thy all-too Irish mirth and madness, and odour of palled punch, makest such strange work, farewell; long as thou canst, fare-*well!* Have we not, in the course of eternity, travelled some months of our Life-journey in partial sight of one another; have we not lived* together, though in a state of quarrel!

* * *

APPENDIX I

CARLYLE'S ACCOUNT OF *SARTOR RESARTUS* TO JAMES FRASER, 27 MAY 1833

FRASER, publisher of *Fraser's Magazine* from its inception in February 1830 until his death in 1841, included a translation by Carlyle in its first number. Thereafter, Carlyle was a regular contributor. In November 1830 he began complex negotiations with Fraser over the serial publication of *Sartor Resartus*. For over a year these negotiations had been broken off. The letter to Fraser printed here, with the omission of opening and concluding paragraphs on other matters, reintroduces the possibility of serial publication, and contains Carlyle's fullest account of the manuscript to date.

Most probably you recollect the Manuscript *Book* I had with me in London; and how during that Reform hurlyburly,* which unluckily still continues and is like to continue, I failed to make any bargain about it. The Manuscript still lies in my drawer; and now after long deliberation I have determined to slit it up into stripes, and send it forth in the Periodical way; for which in any case it was perhaps better adapted. The pains I took with the composition of it, truly, were greater than even I might have thought necessary, had this been foreseen: but what then? Care of that sort is never altogether thrown away; far better too much than too little. I reckon that it will be easy for the Magazine Printer to save me some thirty or forty complete Copies, as he prints it; these can then be bound up and distributed among my Friends likely to profit thereby; and in the end of all we can *re*print it into a Book proper, if that seem good. Your Magazine is the first I think of for this object; and I must have got a distinct negative from you before I go any farther. Listen to me, then, and judge.

The Book is at present named "Thoughts on Clothes; or Life and Opinions of Herr D. Teufelsdröckh D.U.J."; but perhaps we might see right to alter the title a little;* for the rest, some brief Introduction could fit it handsomely enough into its new destination: it is already divided into three "Books," and farther into very short "Chapters," capable in all ways of subdivision. Nay some tell me, what perhaps is true, that taking a few chapters at a time is really the profitablest way of reading it. There may be in all some Eight sheets of *Fraser*.* It is put together in the fashion of a Didactic Novel; but indeed properly *like* nothing yet extant. I used to characterize it briefly as a kind of "Satirical Extravaganza on Things in General"; it contains more of my opinions on Art, Politics, Religion, Heaven Earth and Air, than all the things I have yet written. The Creed promulgated on all these things, as you may judge, is *mine,* and firmly *believed:* for the rest, the main Actor in the business ("Editor of these sheets" as he often calls himself) assumes a kind of Conservative (tho' Antiquack) character; and would suit *Fraser* perhaps better than any other Magazine. The ultimate result, however, I need hardly premise, is a deep religious speculative-radicalism (so I call it for want of a better name), with which you are already well enough acquainted in me.

There are only five persons* that have yet read this Manuscript: of whom two have expressed themselves (I mean convinced me that they *are*) considerably interested and gratified; two quite *struck,* "over-whelmed with astonishment and new hope" (this is the result I aimed at for souls worthy of hope); and one in secret discontented and displeased. William Fraser is a sixth reader,* or rather half-reader; for I think he had only got half-way or so; and I never learned his opinion. With him, if you like, at this stage of the business you can consult freely about it. My own conjecture is that *Teufelsdröckh,* whenever published, will astonish most that read it, be wholly understood by very few; but to the astonishment of some will add touches of (almost the deepest) spiritual interest, with others quite the opposite feeling. I think I can practically prophecy that for some six or eight months (for it must be published without interruption), it would be apt at least to *keep the eyes* of the Public on you.

Such is all the description I can give you, in these limits: now what say you to it? Let me hear as soon as you can; for the time seems come to set these little bits of Doctrine forth; and, as I said, till your *finale* arrive, I can do nothing. Would you like to see the *Ms.* yourself? It can come, and return, by Coach for a few shillings, if you think of that: it will of course want the Introduction, and various other "O. Y.'s"* that will perhaps be useful. I need not remind you that about shewing it to any third party (as I have learned by experience) there is a certain delicacy to be observed: I shall like to hear from you first. Write to me, therefore, with the same openness as I have done to you; we shall then soon see how it lies between us.

APPENDIX II

WILLIAM MAGINN'S PORTRAIT OF CARLYLE, JUNE 1833

THE description of Carlyle printed here, written in 'imitative Carlylese', is by William Maginn (1793–1842), editor of *Fraser's Magazine* from 1830 to 1836. Printed in the June 1833 issue, five months before the first instalment of *Sartor Resartus*, it was number 37 of Maginn's 'Gallery of Literary Characters'; other subjects included Coleridge, Hazlitt, Scott, and Disraeli.

Maginn's portraits were accompanied by pen-and-ink sketches by the Irish painter Daniel Maclise (c.1806–70), using the pseudonym Alfred Croquis. Carlyle termed his sketch 'a very considerable likeness. Done from life in Fraser's back-parlour in about twenty minutes' (*Collected Letters*, vi. 125 n. 16.). He was less enthusiastic about the piece by Maginn, 'a mad rattling Irishman', which he found 'hardly intelligible . . . but complimentary enough' (ibid. vi. 406).

Here hast thou, O Reader! the-from stone-printed effigies of Thomas Carlyle, the thunderwordoversetter of Herr Johann Wolfgang von Goethe. These fingers, now in listless occupation supporting his head, or clutching that outward integument which with the head holds so singular a relation, that those who philosophically examine, and with a fire-glance penetrate into the contents of the great majority of the orb-shaped knobs which form the upper extremity of man, know not with assured critic-craft to decide whether the hat was made to cover the head, or the head erected as a peg to hang the hat upon;—yea, these fingers have transferred some of the most harmonious and mystic passages,—to the initiated, mild-shining, inaudible-light instinct—and to the uninitiated, dark and untransparent as the shadows of Eleusis— of those forty volumes of musical wisdom which are commonly known by the title of *Goethe's Werke,* from the Fatherlandish dialect of High-Dutch to the Allgemeine-Mid-Lothianish of Auld Reekie. Over-set Goethe hath Carlyle, not in the ordinary manner of language-turners, who content themselves with giving, according to the capacity of knowingness or honesty within them, the meaning or the idea (if any there be) of the original book-fashioner, on whom their secondhand-penmongery is employed; but with reverential thought, word-worshipping even the articulable clothing wherein the clear and ethereal harmony of Goethe is invested, Carlyle hath bestowed upon us the *Wilhelm Meister,* and other works, so Teutonical in raiment, in the structure of sentence, the modulation of phrase, and the round-about, hubble-bubble, rumfustianish (*hübble-bübblen, rümfüstianischen*), roly-poly growlery of style, so Germanically set forth, that it is with difficulty we can recognise them to be translations at all.

Come, come, some reader will impatiently exclaim,—quite enough of this! A whole page of imitative Carlylese would be as bad as the influenza. In human English, then, Thomas Carlyle,—like Dionysius, of Syracuse, among the ancients, and Milton and Johnson among the moderns,—formerly instilled the prima stamina of knowledge into the minds of ingenuous youth; but for some years past has retired from what Oppian calls, or is supposed to call (see Bayle *in voce*),* feeding the sheep of the muses, to the rural occupations of a Dumfriesshire laird, in a place rejoicing in the melodious title of Craigenputtock, an appellation which must have delighted his ear, from its similarity in harmonious sound to the poetical effusions of the bards he loves. Here he occupies his leisure hours in translating Goethe, or in corresponding with the *Edinburgh Review*, or *Fraser's Magazine*, the *Morning Post*, or the *Examiner*,—in all, donner-und-blitzenizing* it like a north-wester. To his credit be it spoken, he gave a Christian and an honourable tone to the articles of the *Edinburgh;* but he came too late. The concern was worn out and gone, and not even Carlyle could keep it from destruction, particularly when he was associated with Thomas Babble-tongue Macaulay, whose articles would swamp a seventy-four.* He has a more congenial soil in *Regina,** where he expounds, in the most approved fashion of the Cimbri and the Teutones, his opinions on men and things, greatly to the edification of our readers. Of his contributions to the forty-eight feet of diurnal or septimanal literature which are set before the industrious eyes of the readers of newspapers, we know nothing.

He is an honourable and worthy man, and talks the most unques-tionable High Fifeshire. Of our German scholars, he is clearly the first; and it is generally suspected that he has an idea that he understands the meaning of the books which he is continually reading, which really is a merit of no small magnitude, particularly when we consider that nobody ever thinks of publishing a translation from the German without prefixing thereto a preface, proving in general in the most satisfactory manner that his predecessors in the work of translation made as many blunders as there were lines in the book, and that of the spirit of the original they were perfectly ignorant. Even-handed justice is sure to bring back the chalice to his own lips, and he receives the same compliment from his successor.

APPENDIX III

CARLYLE'S ACCOUNT OF *SARTOR RESARTUS* TO RALPH WALDO EMERSON, 12 AUGUST 1834

EMERSON (1803–82) first wrote to Carlyle in May 1834, having read the first four instalments of *Sartor Resartus* in *Fraser's Magazine*. Carlyle's reply, of which a long paragraph on *Sartor Resartus* is printed here, begins his side of a correspondence that lasted for almost forty years. Because of Emerson's advocacy, *Sartor Resartus* was published in book form first in America and subsequently in England; his preface to the first American edition concludes the 'Testimonies of Authors' in Appendix V below. With his letter, Carlyle sent Emerson four copies of the privately issued volume of *Sartor Resartus* (1834); see Note on the Text, above.

You thank me for *Teufelsdröckh:* how much more ought I to thank you for your hearty, genuine tho' extravagant acknowledgement of it! Blessed is the voice that amid dispiritment stupidity and contradiction proclaims to us: *Euge* [well done]! Nothing ever was more ungenial than the soil that poor Teufelsdröckhish seedcorn has been thrown on here; none cries, Good speed to it; the sorriest nettle or hemlock seed, one would think, had been more welcome. For indeed our British periodical critics, and especially the public of Fraser's Magazine (which I believe I have now done with) exceed all speech; require not even contempt, only oblivion. Poor Teufelsdröckh! Creature of mischance, miscalculation, and thousandfold obstruction! Here nevertheless he is, as you see; has struggled across the Stygian marshes, and now, as a stitched Pamphlet "for Friends," cannot be *burnt,* or lost—before his time. I send you one copy for your own behoof; three others you yourself can perhaps find fit readers for: as you spoke in the plural number, I thought there might be three; more would rather surprise me. From the British side of the water, I have met simply *one* intelligent response; clear, true, tho' almost enthusiastic as your own: my British Friend too is utterly a stranger, whose very name I know not, who did not print, but only write and to an *unknown* third party.* Shall I say then: "In the mouth of *two* witnesses"? In any case, God be thanked, I am done with it; can wash my hands of it, and send it forth; sure that the Devil will get his full share of it, and not a whit *more,* clutch as he may. But as for you, my Transoceanic Brothers, read this earnestly, for it *was* earnestly meant and written, and contains no *voluntary* falsehood of mine. For the rest if you dislike it, say that I wrote it four years ago, and could not now so write it, and on the whole (as Fritz the Only* said) "will do better another time." — With regard to style and so forth, what you call your "saucy" objections are not only most intelligible to me, but welcome and instructive. You say well that I take up that attitude because I have no known public, am *alone* under the Heavens, speaking into friendly or unfriendly Space; add only that I will not defend such attitude, that I call it questionable, tentative, and only the best that I in these mad times could conveniently hit upon. For you are to know, my view is that now at last we have lived to see all manner of Poetics and Rhetorics and Sermonics, and one may say generally all manner of *Pulpits* for addressing mankind from, as good as broken and abolished: alas, yes; if you have any earnest meaning, which demands to be not only listened to, but *believed* and *done*, you cannot (at least I cannot) utter it *there,* but the sound sticks in my throat, as when a Solemnity were *felt* to have become a Mummery; and so one leaves the pasteboard coulisses, and three Unities, and Blair[']s Lectures,* quite behind; and feels only that there is *nothing sacred,* then, but the *Speech of Man* to believing Men! *This,* come what will, was, is and forever must be *sacred:* and will one day doubtless anew environ itself with fit Modes, with Solemnities that are *not* Mummeries. Meanwhile, however, is it not pitiable? For tho' Teufelsdröckh exclaims: "Pulpit! Canst thou not *make* a pulpit, by simply *inverting the nearest tub";* yet alas he does not sufficiently reflect that it is still only a *tub,* that the most inspired utterance will come from *it,* inconceivable, misconceivable to the million; questionable (not of *ascertained* significance) even to the few. Pity us therefore; and with your just shake of the head join a sympathetic even a hopeful smile. Since I saw you, I have been trying, am still trying, other methods, and shall surely get nearer the truth, as I honestly strive for it. Meanwhile I know no method of much consequence, except that of *believing,* of being *sincere:* from *Homer* and the *Bible* down to the poorest Burns's *Song* I find no other *Art* that promises to be perennial.

APPENDIX IV

CARLYLE'S DEFENCE OF *SARTOR RESARTUS* TO JOHN STERLING, 4 JUNE 1835

JOHN STERLING (1806–44) was a member of the Apostles during his undergraduate years at Cambridge and subsequently came under the spell of Coleridge, who influenced his decision to become an Anglican clergyman. At the time he first met Carlyle in February 1835, Sterling was in the process of withdrawing from his clerical commitment as a curate because of ill health and religious misgivings. His intimate friendship with Carlyle was cut short by his premature death. In his *Life of John Sterling*, published in 1851, Carlyle argued that his friend's religious beliefs had been less orthodox and less certain than others had claimed.

On 29 May 1835 Sterling wrote Carlyle a voluminous letter criticising *Sartor Resartus*; this was subsequently printed, with omissions, in Carlyle's *Life*. The letter printed here, with the omission of a concluding paragraph on other matters, is Carlyle's defence against two of Sterling's charges: that the style of *Sartor* is inaccurate, and that the work does not uphold the Christian faith. Several days before receiving Carlyle's reply Sterling renewed his criticisms of the style of *Sartor*, in a letter which Carlyle 'made into matches' (*Collected Letters*, viii. 134 n. 1).

I said to Mill* the other day that your Name was HOPEFUL; of which truth surely this copious refreshing shower of really kind and genial criticism you have bestowed on the hardened, kiln-burnt, altogether contradictory Professor Teufelsdröckh, is new proof. Greater faith I have not found in Israel! Neither here shall faith and hope wholly fail: know, my Friend that your shower does not fall as on mere barren bricks, like water spilt on the ground; that I take it hopefully in, with great desire (knowing what spirit it is of) to *assimilate* such portion of it as the nature of things will allow. So much, on this sheet, I must announce to you, were it at full gallop, and in the most imperfect words.

Your objections as to phraseology and style have good grounds to stand on; many of them indeed are considerations to which I myself was not blind; which there (unluckily) were no means of doing more than nodding to as one passed. A man has but a certain strength; imperfections cling to him, which if he wait till he have brushed off entirely, he will spin forever on his axis, advancing nowhither. Know thy thought, *believe* it; front Heaven and Earth with it,—in whatsoever *words* Nature and Art have made readiest for thee! If one has thoughts not hitherto uttered in English Books, I see nothing for it but that you must use words not found there, must *make* words,—with moderation and discretion, of course. That I have not always done it *so*, proves only that I was not strong enough; an accusation to which I for one will never plead not guilty. For the rest, pray that I may have more and more strength! Surely too, as I said, all these *coal-marks** of yours shall be duly considered, for the first and even for the second time, and help me on my way. With unspeakable cheerfulness I give up *"Talented":** indeed, but for the plain statement you make, I could have sworn such word had never, excepted for parodistic ironical purposes, risen from my inkhorn, or passed my lips. Too much evil can hardly be said of *it:* while speech of it at all is necessary.—But finally do you reckon this really a time for Purism of Style; or that Style (mere dictionary style) has much to do with the worth or unworth of a Book? I do not: with whole ragged battallions of Scott's-Novel Scotch, with Irish, German, French and even Newspaper Cockney (when "Literature" is little other than a Newspaper) storming in on us, and the whole structure of our Johnsonian English breaking up from its foundations,—revolution *there* as visible as anywhere else!

You ask, How it comes that none of the "leading minds" of this country (if one knew where to find them) have given the Clothes-Philosophy any response? Why, my good friend, not one of them has had the happiness of seeing it! It issued thro' one of the main *cloacas* of Periodical Literature, where no leading mind, I fancy, looks, if he can help it: the poor Book cannot be destroyed by fire or other violence now, but solely by the *general* law of Destiny; and *I* have nothing more to do with it henceforth. How it chanced that no Bookseller would print it (in an epoch when Satan Montgomery runs or seems to run thro' thirteen editions),* and the Morning Papers (on its issuing thro' the *cloaca*) sang together in mere discord over such a Creation: this truly is a question, but a different one. Meanwhile, do not suppose the poor Book has *not* been responded to; for the historical fact is, I could show very curious response to it here; not ungratifying, and fully three times as much as I counted on, as the wretched farrago itself deserved.

You say finally, as the Key to the whole mystery, that Teufels-dröckh does not believe in a "personal God." It is frankly said, with a friendly honesty for which I love you. A grave charge nevertheless, an *awful* charge: to which, if I mistake not, the Professor laying his hand on his heart will reply with some gesture expressing the solemnest *denial*. In gesture, rather than in speech; for "the Highest *cannot* be spoken of in words." *"Personal,"* "impersonal." One, Three, *what* meaning can any mortal (after all) attach to them in reference to *such* an object? *Wer darf ihn* NENNEN [Who dares name him]? I dare not, and do not. That you dare and do (to some greater extent) is a matter I am far from taking offence at: nay, with all sincerity, I can rejoice that you have a creed of that kind, which gives you happy thoughts, nerves you for good actions, brings you into readier communion with many good men; my true wish is that such creed may long hold compactly together in you, and be "a covert from the heat, a shelter from the storm, as the shadow of a great rock in a weary land." Well is it if we have a printed Litany to pray from; and yet not ill if we *can* pray even in *Silence,* for Silence too is audible *there*. Finally assure yourself I am neither Pagan nor Turk, nor circumcised Jew, but an unfortunate Christian individual resident at Chelsea in *this* year of Grace; neither Pantheist nor Pottheist, nor any Theist or *ist* whatsoever; having the most decided contem[pt] for all manner of System-builders and Sectfounders—as far as contempt may be com[patible] with so mild a nature; feeling well beforehand (taught by long experience) that all such are and even must be *wrong*. By God's blessing, one has got two eyes to look with; also a mind capable of knowing, of believing: that is all the creed I will at this time insist on. And now may I beg one thing: that wherever in my thoughts or your own you fall on any dogma that tends to estrange you from me, pray believe *that* to be *false;*—false as Beelzebub, till you get clearer evidence.

However, descending from the Empyrean to London pavements, let me tell you that I am actually bestirring myself to try whether the people will give me any employment in this matter of National Education. Mill and some others undertake to help me, but have not reported yet. It is a confused business; out of which darkness is rayed forth on me hitherto. If we fail in it, there is some likelihood I may cross the Atlantic soon.* The Book-Trade seems to me *done* here: a man must go where his work lies, where they will keep him in existence for his work.

APPENDIX V

CARLYLE'S SUPPLEMENTARY MATERIAL TO THE 1869 EDITION OF *SARTOR RESARTUS*

FOUR items were appended to the 1869 edition of *Sartor Resartus*, volume one of the collected Library Edition of Carlyle's works, of which three are printed here. The first, an 'Author's Note', points out that the second item, 'Testimonies of Authors', had previously been included in the first English edition of 1838. They provide, Carlyle wrote to his brother John on 14 July 1838, 'covertly a history of the poor Manuscript & publication', embracing 'the wisest and stupidest, the worst and best, that can be said of it' (*Collected Letters*, x. 122). The 'Bookseller's Taster', whose note to the publisher John Murray is given verbatim, is the Rev. Henry Hart Milman. 'Bookseller to Editor' is a revised version of a letter from Murray to Carlyle, dated by Carlyle 17 September 1831 but apparently written on 6 October (see *Collected Letters*, vi. 6 n. 1). The excerpts from reviews in the *Sun*, a London newspaper, and the *North American Review*, a Boston magazine, are correctly dated; both were published anonymously, but the latter has been attributed to the review's editor, Alexander H. Everett. The last, and much the most important, of the four 'Testimonies' is by Emerson, the 'New-England Editor', originally prefaced to the first and second American editions of *Sartor Resartus*, 1836 and 1837.

The third item added by Carlyle to the 1869 edition is a 'Summary' of *Sartor Resartus*. Many later editions insert these abstracts at the head of each chapter, making the work less of a prose fiction and more of an argumentative treatise. Carlyle's index, not included here, is also designed to present *Sartor* as prose of thought and to conceal its fictitiousness.

This questionable little Book was undoubtedly written among the mountain solitudes, in 1831; but, owing to impediments natural and accidental, could not, for seven years more, appear as a Volume in England;—and had at last to clip itself in pieces, and be content to struggle out, bit by bit, in some courageous *Magazine* that offered. Whereby now, to certain idly curious readers, and even to myself till I make study, the insignificant but at last irritating question, What its real history and chronology are, is, if not insoluble, considerably involved in haze.

To the first English Edition, 1838, which an American, or two American had now opened the way for, there was slightingly prefixed, under the title '*Testimonies of Authors*,' some straggle of real documents, which, now that I find it again, sets the matter into clear light and sequence;—and shall here, for removal of idle stumbling-blocks and nugatory guessings from the path of every reader, be reprinted as it stood. (*Author's Note, of* 1868.)

TESTIMONIES OF AUTHORS

1. HIGHEST CLASS, BOOKSELLER'S TASTER

Taster to Bookseller.—"The Author of *Teufelsdröckh* is a person of talent; his work displays here and there some felicity of thought and expression, considerable fancy and knowledge: but whether or not it would take with the public seems doubtful. For a *jeu d'esprit* of that kind it is too long; it would have suited better as an essay or article than as a volume. The Author has no great tact; his wit is frequently heavy; and reminds one of the German Baron who took to leaping on tables, and answered that he was learning to be lively. *Is* the work a translation?"

Bookseller to Editor.—"Allow me to say that such a writer requires only a little more tact to produce a popular as well as an able work. Directly on receiving your permission, I sent your *Ms.* to a gentleman in the highest class of men of letters, and an accomplished German scholar: I now enclose you his opinion, which, you may rely upon it, is a just one; and I have too high an opinion of your good sense to" &c. &c.— *Ms.* (*penes nos*),* London, 17*th September* 1831.

2. CRITIC OF THE SUN

"*Fraser's Magazine* exhibits the usual brilliancy, and also the" &c.* "*Sartor Resartus* is what old Dennis used to call 'a heap of clotted nonsense,'* mixed however, here and there, with passages marked by thought and striking poetic vigour. But what does the writer mean by 'Baphometic fire-baptism'? Why cannot he lay aside his pedantry, and write so as to make himself generally intelligible? We quote by way of curiosity a sentence from the *Sartor Resartus;* which may be read either backwards or forwards, for it is equally intelligible either way: indeed, by beginning at the tail, and so working up to the head, we think the reader will stand the fairest chance of getting at its meaning: 'The fire-baptised soul, long so scathed and thunder-riven, here feels its own freedom; which feeling is its Baphometic baptism: the citadel of its whole kingdom it has thus gained by assault, and will keep inexpugnable; outwards from which the remaining dominions, not indeed without hard battering, will doubtless by degrees be conquered and pacificated.' Here is a"—*. . . —*Sun Newspaper, 1st April* 1834.

3. NORTH-AMERICAN REVIEWER

. . . "After* a careful survey of the whole ground, our belief is that no such persons as Professor Teufelsdröckh or Counsellor Heuschrecke ever existed; that the six paper-bags, with their China-ink inscriptions and multifarious contents, are a mere figment of the brain; that the 'present Editor' is the only person who has ever written upon the Philosophy of Clothes; and that the *Sartor Resartus* is the only treatise that has yet appeared upon that subject;—in short, that the whole account of the origin of the work before us, which the supposed Editor relates with so much gravity, and of which we have given a brief abstract, is, in plain English, a *hum*.*

"Without troubling our readers at any great length with our reasons for entertaining these suspicions, we may remark, that the absence of all other information on the subject, except what is contained in the work, is itself a fact of a most significant character. The whole German press, as well as the particular one where the work purports to have been printed, seems to be under the control of *Stillschweigen & Co.*—Silence and Company. If the Clothes-Philosophy and its author are making so great a sensation throughout Germany as is pretended, how happens it that the only notice we have of the fact is contained in a few numbers of a monthly Magazine published at London? How happens it that no intelligence about the matter has come out directly to this country? We pique ourselves here in New England upon knowing at least as much of what is going on in the literary way in the old Dutch Mother-Land as our brethren of the fast-anchored Isle; but thus far we have no tidings whatever of the 'extensive close-printed close-meditated volume,' which forms the subject of this pretended commentary. Again, we would respectfully inquire of the 'present Editor' upon what part of the map of Germany we are to look for the city of *Weissnichtwo*—'Know-not-where'—at which place the work is supposed to have been printed, and the Author to have resided. It has been our fortune to visit several portions of the German territory, and to examine pretty carefully, at different times and for various purposes, maps of the whole; but we have no recollection of any such place. We suspect that the city of *Know-not-where* might be called, with at least as much propriety, *Nobody-knows-where*, and is to be found in the kingdom of *Nowhere*. Again, the village of *Entepfuhl*—'Duck-pond'—where the supposed Author of the work is said to have passed his youth, and that of *Hinterschlag,* where he had his education, are equally foreign to our geography. Duck-ponds enough there undoubtedly are in almost every village in Germany, as the traveller in that country knows too well to his cost, but any particular village denominated Duck-pond is to us altogether *terra incognita.* The names of the personages are not less singular than those of the places. Who can refrain from a smile at the yoking together of such a pair of appellatives as Diogenes Teufelsdröckh? The supposed bearer of this strange title is represented as admitting, in his pretended autobiography, that 'he had searched to no purpose through all the Heralds' books in and without the German empire, and through all manner of Subscribers'-lists, Militia-rolls, and other Name-catalogues,' but had nowhere been able to find 'the name Teufelsdröckh, except as appended to his own person.' We can readily believe this, and we doubt very much whether any Christian parent would think of condemning a son to carry through life the burden of so unpleasant a title. That of Counsellor Heuschrecke—'Grasshop-per'—though not offensive, looks much more like a piece of fancy work than a 'fair business transaction.' The same may be said of *Blumine*—'Flower-Goddess'—the heroine of the fable; and so of the rest.

"In short, our private opinion is, as we have remarked, that the whole story of a correspondence with Germany, a university of Nobody-knows-where, a Professor of Things in General, a Counsellor Grasshopper, a Flower-Goddess Blumine, and so forth, has about as much foundation in truth as the late entertaining account of Sir John Herschel's discoveries in the moon. Fictions of this kind are, however, not uncommon, and ought not, perhaps, to be condemned with too much severity; but we are not sure that we can exercise the same indulgence in regard to the attempt, which seems to be made to mislead the public as to the substance of the work before us, and its pretended German original. Both purport, as we have seen, to be upon the subject of Clothes, or dress. *Clothes, their Origin and Influence,* is the title of the supposed German treatise of Professor Teufelsdröckh, and the rather odd name of *Sartor Resartus*—the Tailor Patched— which the present Editor has affixed to his pretended commentary, seems to look the same way. But though there is a good deal of remark throughout the work in a half-serious, half-comic style upon dress, it seems to be in reality a treatise upon the great science of Things in General, which Teufelsdröckh is supposed to have professed at the university of Nobody-knows-where. Now, without intending to adopt a too rigid standard of morals, we own that we doubt a little the propriety of offering to the public a treatise on Things in General, under the name and in the form of an Essay on Dress. For ourselves, advanced as we unfortunately are in the journey of life, far beyond the period when dress is practically a matter of interest, we have no hesitation in saying, that the real subject of the work is to us more attractive than the ostensible one. But this is probably not the case with the mass of readers. To the younger portion of the community, which constitutes everywhere the very great majority, the subject of dress is one of intense and paramount importance. An author who treats it appeals, like the poet, to the young men and maidens— *virginibus puerisque*—and calls upon them, by all the motives which habitually operate most strongly upon their feelings, to buy his book. When, after opening their purses for this purpose, they have carried home the work in triumph, expecting to find in it some particular instruction in regard to the tying of their neckcloths, or the cut of their corsets, and meet with nothing better than a dissertation on Things in General, they will—to use the mildest term—not be in very good humour. If the last improvements in legislation, which we have made in this country, should have found their way to England, the author, we think, would stand some chance of being *Lynched*. Whether his object in this piece of *supercherie** be merely pecuniary profit, or whether he takes a malicious pleasure in quizzing the Dandies, we shall not undertake to say. In the latter part of the work, he devotes a separate chapter to this class of persons, from the tenour of which we should be disposed to conclude, that he would consider any mode of divesting them of their property very much in the nature of a spoiling of the Egyptians.

"The only thing about the work, tending to prove that it is what it purports to be, a commentary on a real German treatise, is the style, which is a sort of Babylonish dialect, not destitute, it is true, of richness, vigour, and at times a sort of singular felicity of expression, but very strongly tinged throughout with the peculiar idiom of the German language. This quality in the style, however, may be a mere result of a great familiarity with German literature; and we cannot, therefore, look upon it as in itself decisive, still less as outweighing so much evidence of an opposite character."*—*North-American Review*, No. 89, *October* 1835.

4. New-England Editors

"The Editors have been induced, by the expressed desire of many persons, to collect the following sheets out of the ephemeral pamphlets† in which they first appeared, under the conviction that they contain in themselves the assurance of a longer date.

"The Editors have no expectation that this little Work will have sudden and general popularity. They will not undertake, as there is no need, to justify the gay costume in which the Author delights to dress his thoughts, or the German idioms with which he has sportively sprinkled his pages. It is his humour to advance the gravest speculations upon the gravest topics in a quaint and burlesque style. If his masquerade offend any of his audience, to that degree that they will not hear what he has to say, it may chance to draw others to listen to his wisdom; and what work of imagination can hope to please all? But we will venture to remark that the distaste excited by these peculiarities in some readers is greatest at first, and is soon forgotten; and that the foreign dress and aspect of the Work are quite superficial, and cover a genuine Saxon heart. We believe, no book has been published for many years, written in a more sincere style of idiomatic English, or which discovers an equal mastery over all the riches of the language. The Author makes ample amends for the occasional eccentricity of his genius, not only by frequent bursts of pure splendour, but by the wit and sense which never fail him.

"But what will chiefly commend the Book to the discerning reader is the manifest design of the work, which is, a Criticism upon the Spirit of the Age—we had almost said, of the hour—in which we live; exhibiting in the most just and novel light the present aspects of Religion, Politics, Literature, Arts, and Social Life. Under all his gaiety the Writer has an earnest meaning, and discovers an insight into the manifold wants and tendencies of human nature, which is very rare among our popular authors. The philanthropy and the purity of moral sentiment, which inspire the work, will find their way to the heart of every lover of virtue."—*Preface to Sartor Resartus: Boston, 1835,** 1837.*

SUNT, FUERUNT VEL FUERE.*

London, 30th June 1838.

† *Fraser's* (London) *Magazine, 1833–4.*

SUMMARY

BOOK I

Chapter 1: Preliminary

No Philosophy of Clothes yet, notwithstanding all our Science. Strangely forgotten that Man is by nature a *naked* animal. The English mind all-too practically absorbed for any such inquiry. Not so, deep-thinking Germany. Advantage of Speculation having free course. Editor receives from Professor Teufelsdröckh his new Work on Clothes.

Chapter 2: Editorial Difficulties

How to make known Teufelsdröckh and his Book to English readers; especially *such* a book? Editor receives from the Hofrath Heuschrecke a letter promising Biographic Documents. Negotiations with Oliver Yorke. *Sartor Resartus* conceived. Editor's assurances and advice to his British reader.

Chapter 3: Reminiscences

Teufelsdröckh at Weissnichtwo. Professor of Things in General at the University there: Outward aspect and character; memorable coffee-house utterances; domicile and watch-tower: Sights thence of City-Life by day and by night; with reflections thereon. Old 'Liza and her ways. Character of Hofrath Heuschrecke, and his relation to Teufelsdröckh.

Chapter 4: Characteristics

Teufelsdröckh and his Work on Clothes: Strange freedom of speech; transcendentalism; force of insight and expression; multifarious learning: Style poetic, uncouth: Comprehensiveness of his humour and moral feeling. How the Editor once saw him laugh. Different kinds of Laughter and their significance.

Chapter 5: The World in Clothes

Futile cause-and-effect Philosophies. Teufelsdröckh's Orbis Vestitus. Clothes first invented for the sake of Ornament. Picture of our progenitor, the Aboriginal Savage. Wonders of growth and progress in mankind's history. Man defined as a Tool-using Animal.

Chapter 6: Aprons

Divers Aprons in the world with divers uses. The Military and Police Establishment Society's working Apron. The Episcopal Apron with its corner tucked in. The Laystall. Journalists now our only Kings and Clergy.

Chapter 7: Miscellaneous-Historical

How Men and Fashions come and go. German Costume in the fifteenth century. By what strange chances do we live in History! The costume of Bolivar's Cavalry.

Chapter 8: The World out of Clothes

Teufelsdröckh's Theorem, "Society founded upon Cloth;" his Method, Intuition quickened by Experience.—The mysterious question, Who am I? Philosophic systems all at fault: A deeper meditation has always taught, here and there an individual, that all visible things are appearances only; but also emblems and revelations of God. Teufelsdröckh first comes upon the question of Clothes: Baseness to which Clothing may bring us.

Chapter 9: Adamitism

The universal utility of Clothes, and their higher mystic virtue, illustrated. Conception of Mankind stripped naked; and immediate consequent dissolution of civilised Society.

Chapter 10: Pure Reason

A Naked World possible, nay actually exists, under the clothed one. Man, in the eye of Pure Reason, a visible God's Presence. The beginning of all wisdom, to look fixedly on Clothes till they become transparent. Wonder, the basis of Worship: Perennial in man. Modern Sciolists who cannot wonder: Teufelsdröckh's contempt for, and advice to them.

CHAPTER 11: PROSPECTIVE

Nature not an Aggregate, but a Whole. All visible things are emblems, Clothes; and exist for a time only. The grand scope of the Philosophy of Clothes.—Biographic Documents arrive. Letter from Heuschrecke on the importance of Biography. Heterogeneous character of the documents: Editor sorely perplexed; but desperately grapples with his work.

BOOK II

CHAPTER 1: GENESIS

Old Andreas Futteral and Gretchen his wife: their quiet home. Advent of a mysterious stranger, who deposits with them a young infant, the future Herr Diogenes Teufelsdröckh. After-yearnings of the youth for his unknown Father. Sovereign power of Names and Naming. Diogenes a flourishing Infant.

CHAPTER 2: IDYLLIC

Happy Childhood! Entepfuhl: Sights, hearings and experiences of the boy Teufelsdröckh; their manifold teaching. Education; what it can do, what cannot. Obedience our universal duty and destiny. Gneschen sees the good Gretchen pray.

CHAPTER 3: PEDAGOGY

Teufelsdröckh's School. His Education. How the ever-flowing Kuhbach speaks of Time and Eternity. The Hinterschlag Gymnasium: rude Boys; and pedant Professors. The need of true Teachers, and their due recognition. Father Andreas dies; and Teufelsdröckh learns the secret of his birth: His reflections thereon. The Nameless University. Statistics of Imposture much wanted. Bitter fruits of Rationalism: Teufelsdröckh's religious difficulties. The young Englishman Herr Towgood. Modern Friendship.

CHAPTER 4: GETTING UNDER WAY

The grand thaumaturgic Art of Thought. Difficulty in fitting Capability to Opportunity, or of getting under way. The advantage of Hunger and Bread-Studies. Teufelsdröckh has to enact the stern monodrama of *No object and no rest*. Sufferings as Auscultator. Given up as a man of genius. Zähdarm House. Intolerable presumption of young men. Irony and its consequences. Teufelsdröckh's Epitaph on Count Zähdarm.

CHAPTER 5: ROMANCE

Teufelsdröckh gives up his Profession. The heavenly mystery of Love. Teufelsdröckh's feeling of worship towards women. First and only love. Blumine. Happy hearts and free tongues. The infinite nature of Fantasy. Love's joyful progress; sudden dissolution; and final catastrophe.

CHAPTER 6: SORROWS OF TEUFELSDRÖCKH

Teufelsdröckh's demeanour thereupon. Turns pilgrim. A last wistful look on native Entepfuhl: Sunset amongst primitive Mountains. Basilisk-glance of the Barouche-and-four. Thoughts on View-hunting. Wanderings and Sorrowings.

CHAPTER 7: THE EVERLASTING NO

Loss of Hope, and of Belief. Profit-and-Loss Philosophy. Teufelsdröckh in his darkness and despair still clings to Truth and follows Duty. Inexpressible pains and fears of Unbelief. Fever-crisis: Protest against the Everlasting No: Baphometic Fire-baptism.

CHAPTER 8: CENTRE OF INDIFFERENCE

Teufelsdröckh turns now outwardly to the *Not-me;* and finds wholesomer food. Ancient Cities: Mystery of their origin and growth: Invisible inheritances and possessions. Power and virtue of a true Book. Wagram Battlefield: War. Great Scenes beheld by the Pilgrim: Great Events, and Great Men. Napoleon, a divine missionary, preaching *La carrière ouverte aux talens.* Teufelsdröckh at the North Cape: Modern means of self-defence. Gunpowder and Duelling. The Pilgrim, despising his miseries, reaches the Centre of Indifference.

Chapter 9: The Everlasting Yea

Temptations in the Wilderness: Victory over the Tempter. Annihilation of Self. Belief in God, and love to Man. The Origin of Evil, a problem ever requiring to be solved anew: Teufelsdröckh's solution. Love of Happiness a vain whim: A Higher in man than Love of Happiness. The Everlasting Yea. Worship of Sorrow. Voltaire: his task now finished. Conviction worthless, impossible, without Conduct. The true Ideal, the Actual: Up and work!

Chapter 10: Pause

Conversion; a spiritual attainment peculiar to the modern Era. Teufelsdröckh accepts Authorship as his divine calling. The scope of the command *Thou shalt not steal.*—Editor begins to suspect the authenticity of the Biographical documents; and abandons them for the great Clothes volume. Result of the preceding ten Chapters: Insight into the character of Teufelsdröckh: His fundamental beliefs, and how he was forced to seek and find them.

BOOK III

Chapter 1: Incident in Modern History

Story of George Fox the Quaker; and his perennial suit of Leather. A man God-possessed, witnessing for spiritual freedom and manhood.

Chapter 2: Church-Clothes

Church-Clothes defined; the Forms under which the Religious Principle is temporarily embodied. Outward Religion originates by Society: Society becomes possible by Religion. The condition of Church-Clothes in our time.

Chapter 3: Symbols

The benignant efficacies of Silence and Secrecy. Symbols; revelations of the Infinite in the Finite: Man everywhere encompassed by them; lives and works by them. Theory of Motive-millwrights, a false account of human nature. Symbols of an extrinsic value; as Banners, Standards: Of intrinsic value; as Works of Art, Lives and Deaths of Heroic men. Religious Symbols; Christianity. Symbols hallowed by

Time; but finally defaced and desecrated. Many superannuated Symbols in our time, needing removal.

CHAPTER 4: HELOTAGE

Heuschrecke's Malthusian Tract, and Teufelsdröckh's marginal notes thereon. The true workman, for daily bread, or spiritual bread, to be honoured; and no other. The real privation of the Poor not poverty or toil, but ignorance. Over-population: With a world like ours and wide as ours, can there be too many men? Emigration.

CHAPTER 5: THE PHŒNIX

Teufelsdröckh considers Society as *dead;* its soul (Religion) gone, its body (existing Institutions) going. Utilitarianism, needing little farther preaching, is now in full activity of destruction.—Teufelsdröckh would yield to the Inevitable, accounting that the best: Assurance of a fairer Living Society, arising, Phœnix-like, out of the ruins of the old dead one. Before that Phœnix death-birth is accomplished, long time, struggle, and suffering must intervene.

CHAPTER 6: OLD CLOTHES

Courtesy due from all men to all men: The Body of Man a Revelation in the Flesh. Teufelsdröckh's respect for Old Clothes, as the "Ghosts of Life." Walk in Monmouth Street, and meditations there.

CHAPTER 7: ORGANIC FILAMENTS

Destruction and Creation ever proceed together; and organic filaments of the Future are even now spinning. Wonderful connection of each man with all men; and of each generation with all generations, before and after: Mankind is One. Sequence and progress of all human work, whether of creation or destruction, from age to age.—Titles, hitherto derived from Fighting, must give way to others. Kings will remain and their title. Political Freedom, not to be attained by any mechanical contrivance. Hero-worship, perennial amongst men; the cornerstone of polities in the Future. Organic filaments of the New Religion: Newspapers and Literature. Let the faithful soul take courage!

Chapter 8: Natural Supernaturalism

Deep significance of Miracles. Littleness of human Science: Divine incomprehensibility of Nature. Custom blinds us to the miraculousness of daily-recurring miracles; so do Names. Space and Time, appearances only; forms of human Thought: A glimpse of Immortality. How Space hides from us the wondrousness of our commonest powers; and Time, the divinely miraculous course of human history.

Chapter 9: Circumspective

Recapitulation. Editor congratulates the few British readers who have accompanied Teufelsdröckh through all his speculations. The true use of the *Sartor Resartus*, to exhibit the Wonder of daily life and common things; and to show that all Forms are but Clothes, and temporary. Practical inferences enough will follow.

Chapter 10: The Dandiacal Body

The Dandy defined. The Dandiacal Sect a new modification of the primeval superstition Self-Worship: How to be distinguished. Their Sacred Books (Fashionable Novels) unreadable. Dandyism's Articles of Faith.—Brotherhood of Poor-Slaves; vowed to perpetual Poverty; worshippers of Earth; distinguished by peculiar costume and diet. Picture of a Poor-Slave Household; and of a Dandiacal. Teufelsdröckh fears these two Sects may spread, till they part all England between them, and then frightfully collide.

Chapter 11: Tailors

Injustice done to Tailors, actual and metaphorical. Their rights and great services will one day be duly recognised.

Chapter 12: Farewell

Teufelsdröckh's strange manner of speech, but resolute, truthful character: His purpose seemingly to proselytise, to unite the wakeful earnest in these dark times. Letter from Hofrath Heuschrecke announcing that Teufelsdröckh has disappeared from Weissnichtwo. Editor guesses he will appear again. Friendly Farewell.

EXPLANATORY NOTES

AN exhaustively annotated edition of *Sartor Resartus*, with its vast vocabulary and dense allusiveness, would require thousands of notes. To keep the notes to this edition within reasonable bounds we have, in general, annotated words only if not found in the *Concise Oxford Dictionary*; foreign terms only if not already translated in the text; and allusions only when the context calls attention to them. We have also noted the more significant revisions made in editions of *Sartor* after the *Fraser's Magazine* version; see the Note on the Text, above. A separate glossary of people and places is designed to reduce the number of annotations required.

We are much indebted to several previous editors of *Sartor Resartus*: Archibald MacMechan (1896), J. A. S. Barrett (1897), P. C. Parr (1913), Clark S. Northup (1921), William Savage Johnson (1924), and Charles Frederick Harrold (1937).

BOOK I

1 *Mein Vermächtniss . . . die Zeit*: one of the epigraphs to Goethe's *Wilhelm Meister's Travels* (1821–9); in one of Carlyle's translations: 'My inheritance, how wide and fair! / Time is my estate; to Time I'm heir.'

3 *How the apples were got in*: allusion to John Wolcot's satirical poem on George III, 'The Apple Dumplings and a King' (*The Works of Peter Pindar* [1812]); unable to find any seam in a dumpling, the monarch asks, 'How, how the devil got the Apple in?'

Social Contract . . . Standard of Taste: Rousseau's *Social Contract* appeared in 1762; Hume's *Of the Standard of Taste* in 1757. The other subjects mentioned here had also been treated in various 'disquisitions'.

4 *Shakespeare says*: *Hamlet*, IV. iv. 37.

Catholic Emancipations, and Rotten Boroughs, and Revolts of Paris: three political *causes célèbres* of the late 1820s and early 1830s. A bill to remove civil disabilities from Catholics was passed by Parliament in 1829. The Reform Bill of 1832 largely abolished rotten boroughs, that is, electoral districts which had come to contain very few voters but which continued to send representatives to Parliament. The Revolt of Paris refers to the three-day revolution of July 1830, which overthrew Charles X.

Höret ihr Herren und lasset's Euch sagen: 'Listen, gentlemen, and let it be told you'; the first line of a folk-song, supposed to be uttered by the bellman on his nightly rounds.

5 *Our Humorist . . . pots of ale*: Samuel Butler, *Hudibras* (1663–78), I. i. 121–2.

vigorously enough: 'vigorously' in later editions.

Many shall run . . . increased: Daniel 12: 4.

stinted: 'stunted' in later editions.

6 *Professor Teufelsdröckh of Weissnichtwo*: 'Professor Devil's-excrement of Know-not-where.'

von Diog. . . . Weissnichtwo, 1833: 'by Diogenes Teufelsdröckh [Born-of-God Devil's-excrement], Juris Utriusque Doctor [Doctor of Civil and Canon Law], etc., Silence and Co., Know-not-where, 1833.' In later editions, 1833 is changed to 1831.

Weissnichtwo'sche Anzeiger: 'Weissnichtwo Advertiser.'

7 *Möchte es . . . auch im Brittischen Boden gedeihen*: 'May it also thrive on British soil.'

8 *whose seedfield . . . is Time*: adapted from a phrase ('mein Acker ist die Zeit') in one of the epigraphs to Goethe's *Wilhelm Meister's Travels*. See above, note to the epigraph on *Sartor*.

the whole Parties of: 'all party-divisions in' in later editions.

9 *Waterloo-Crackers*: large fire-crackers made to celebrate the British victory over France in 1815. *Fraser's Magazine* was noted for its irreverence and satirical pyrotechnics.

Hofrath Heuschrecke: 'Councillor Grasshopper.'

the Family, the National: both these publications were typical of a number of 'libraries', encyclopaedic or periodical in character, some of which were published under the auspices of the Society for the Diffusion of Useful Knowledge.

10 *Oliver Yorke*: pseudonym of William Maginn (1793–1842), editor of *Fraser's Magazine*. But footnotes signed 'O. Y.' are presumably by Carlyle himself.

11 *wear*: weir.

Amicus Plato, magis amica veritas: 'Plato is a friend, but truth is a greater friend.'

12 *Zum Grünen Ganse*: 'The Green Goose'; changed to 'Zur Grünen Gans' in later editions.

13 *Bleibt doch ein echter Spass- und Galgen-vogel*: 'He will always be a true joker and a gallows-bird.'

   Wo steckt der Schalk?: 'Where is the rascal hiding?' In later editions, 'Wo steckt doch' (Where on earth).

   Sansculottism: philosophical radicalism; literally, 'without breeches'. During the French Revolution the term was used to describe radical republicans among the Paris poor who gave up the knee-breeches associated with the *ancien régime* and adopted trousers as a symbol of the new era.

14 *Wandering Jew*: legendary figure; having refused Christ permission to rest at his house while carrying the Cross, he was condemned to wander until Judgement Day.

   Allgemeine Zeitung: 'Universal Gazette.'

16 *Wahngasse*: 'Fantasy-lane.'

   Orte . . . Airts: points of the compass.

   speculum or watch-tower: presumably an error. *Speculum* is Latin for mirror; *specula* for watch-tower.

   Schlosskirche: 'Castle church.'

17 *Ach, mein Lieber*: 'Ah, my dear sir.'

   Boötes . . . Hunting Dogs: northern constellations; *Boötes*: a man with a crook.

   coverlid: 'coverlet' in later editions.

18 *Rouge-et-Noir*: a card game played at a table with red and black compartments.

   Rabenstein: raven's stone; the gallows.

   mein Werther: literary for 'my good friend'; after Goethe's *The Sorrows of Young Werther* (1774).

19 *Blücher Boots*: half-boots named after the Prussian general Gebhard von Blücher.

   Erdbebungen: literally 'earth-vibrations'; changed to the standard 'Erdbeben' in later editions.

21 *Das glaub' ich*: 'I believe that.'

   Pedro Garcia's . . . Bag of Doubloons: in an anecdote told in the preface to Lesage's *Gil Blas* (1715–35), two students chance upon a stone bearing the inscription 'Here lies interred the soul of . . .

Pedro Garcia'. One of them laughs at what he takes to be a joke. The other digs beneath the stone and finds a bag containing a hundred pieces of gold and a card appointing the finder the heir of Pedro Garcia. Lesage advises the reader to keep this story in mind in reading the adventures of Gil Blas and not to miss the moral concealed beneath the surface of the narrative.

23 *Baptist . . . wild honey*: John the Baptist; Matthew 3: 4.

25 *remote echo*: 'echo' in later editions.

Chancery suitors: those petitioning the court of the Lord Chancellor, until 1873 the second highest court in England.

Seven Sleepers: seven Christian youths of Ephesus who were said to have slept in a cave for nearly two hundred years, thus escaping the persecutions of the third and fourth centuries.

28 *Esprit des Lois . . . Esprit de Coutumes . . . Esprit de Costumes*: 'Spirit of the Laws . . . Spirit of Customs . . . Spirit of Costumes.'

Cause-and-effect Philosophy: allusion to British empirical thought of the seventeenth and eighteenth centuries.

29 *Adam-Kadmon*: 'the first man', a cabbalistic term.

Nifl and Muspel . . . of the antique North: i.e. of Scandinavian mythology.

30 *Orbis Pictus*: 'The World in Pictures', an illustrated school-book by Amos Comenius, was published in Nuremberg in 1658; *Orbis Vestitus*: 'The World in Clothes'.

King Nibelung: hero of a German epic of the Middle Ages; twelve days should be four.

chlamides . . . philibegs . . . Gallia Braccata . . . fardingales: short cloaks worn by Greek soldiers; kilts; Gauls wearing breeches; farthingales (hooped petticoats).

33 *Liverpool Steam-carriages*: the second English railway, between Liverpool and Manchester, had been opened in 1830.

38 *Teusinke*: a bell-shaped girdle.

41 *Faust's Mantle*: in Goethe's *Faust*, part I (1808), Faust is carried through the air on a mantle provided by Mephistopheles (scene iv).

the Apostle's Dream: Acts 10: 9–18.

42 *too, must we*: 'also, we have to' in later editions.

Fortunate Islands: in Greek mythology, islands to which heroes passed without suffering death.

Cogito ergo sum: 'I think, therefore I am'; the famous phrase of René Descartes, in his *Discours de la méthode* (1637).

43 *Moscow Retreats*: Napoleon's disastrous retreat from Moscow in 1812.

the Sphinx's secret: the Sphinx, a fabulous monster, put to death all who could not answer her riddle: 'what animal walks on four legs in the morning, two at noon, and three in the evening?' When Oedipus gave the correct answer—man—the Sphinx killed herself.

44 *the Living*: 'Living' in later editions.

In Being's floods . . . seest Him by: Goethe's *Faust*, I. i. 501–9.

45 *a forked straddling animal with bandy legs*: *The Memoirs of Martinus Scriblerus* (1741), ch. 11; by Swift and his fellow Scriblerians.

46 *a Buck, or Blood, or Macaroni, or Incroyable, or Dandy*: as used here, more or less synonymous terms for modish young men.

49 *Haupt- und Staats-Action . . . Pickleherring-Farce*: stock German tragedy and comedy of the seventeenth century.

the tables . . . are dissolved: Horace, *Satires*, II. i. 86.

infandum! infandum!: 'unspeakable, unspeakable.'

Bed of Justice: the *Lit de Justice* was the throne upon which the King of France sat when he attended Parliament, at which time he would compel the registration of his edicts.

benefit of clergy: the right of the clergy to be tried by an ecclesiastical court; later extended to anyone who could read.

Yorick Sterne's words: words in Laurence Sterne's *Tristram Shandy* (1760–7), v. vii.

51 *Descendentalism*: a coinage, to express the antithesis of Transcendentalism.

Shekinah: Talmudic name for the symbol of the divine presence.

52 *Charlemagne-Mantle*: the magnificent robe of the Emperor Charlemagne (*c*.742–814), said to be preserved at St Peter's, Rome.

the wisest of this age: Goethe; the quotation is from *Wilhelm Meister's Travels*, ch. x.

53 *in partibus infidelium*: 'in the country of the unbelievers.'

the Arabian Tale: 'The Greek King and Douban the Physician', in the *Arabian Nights*.

the Mechanics' Institute: college for working-men, founded in Glasgow (1823) and in London (1824).

Old-Roman geese: the alarm given by disturbed geese is said to have saved the Capitol from capture when attacked by the Gauls in 390 BC.

Armer Teufel: 'Poor devil'.

55 *Hebrew Psalmist . . . God is there*: Psalms 139: 9–10.

too: 'thyself' in later editions.

57 *Attention a Stretching-to*: the literal meaning of the Latin verb *attendere* is 'to stretch [the neck] towards'.

59 *Goethe . . . remarked*: in *Wilhelm Meister's Apprenticeship* (1795–6), II. iv.

Old-Clothes Jewry: humorous allusion to the Old Jewry, a street in London, formerly a ghetto.

60 *sympathetic-ink*: invisible ink, made visible by heating.

verehrtester Herr Herausgeber: 'most esteemed Mr. Editor.'

stand: 'will stand' in later editions.

cursiv-schrift: running handwriting in which the characters are joined.

Sibylline leaves: in Virgil's *Aeneid*, the Cumaean sibyl writes her oracles on leaves to be blown to the wind and thus lost.

61 *P. P. Clerk of this Parish*: an allusion to Pope and Gay's *Memoirs of P. P. Clerk of this Parish* (1728), which parodies self-important memoirs such as Bishop Burnet's *History of his Own Time*.

BOOK II

63 *Entepfuhl*: duck-pond.

64 *Desdemona . . . Othello*: Othello, I. iii. 128–68.

least: 'heart' in later editions.

camisade: night attack.

65 *Pitt Diamond*: brought from India by Thomas Pitt, it was sold to the French Regent in 1817, becoming one of the crown jewels of France.

Friedrichs: Prussian gold coins.

67 *Walter Shandy . . . Names*: the pet theory of Walter Shandy, Tristram's father; *Tristram Shandy*, I. xix.

68 *Gneschen*: 'little Diogenes'; a diminutive formed from the last syllable of Diogenes' name.

70 *Arnauld . . . rest in*: remark made by Antoine Arnauld (1612–94), French philosopher and theologian, in response to a friend who had expressed a desire for tranquillity.

71 *Kuhbach*: Cow-brook.

pengun: pop-gun, formed from the barrel of a quill pen.

73 *double-barrelled Game-preserver*: ironic term for the aristocracy, with their love of game-shooting; cf. the epitaph at the end of II. iv.

Incredible: 'Incalculable' in later editions.

74 *Schiller's Wilhelm Tell . . . the World*: from Tell's soliloquy as he awaits the Austrian Tyrant Gessler, whom he has resolved to kill; *Wilhelm Tell* (1804), IV. iii. 58.

75 *Prospero's Island*: in Shakespeare's *The Tempest*.

78 *Hindoo character*: i.e. meditative, contemplative, patient, etc.

79 *Gymnasium*: grammar school, at which classics and literature are taught.

80 *Hinterschlag*: 'Slap-behind.'

82 *boundless*: 'bottomless' in later editions.

84 *nowise*: 'never or seldom' in later editions.

90 *Zähdarm*: 'Tough-gut.'

Frisch zu, Bruder: 'Get on with it, brother.'

91 *Soul . . . Stomach*: the suggestion that 'soul' and 'stomach' are related in Finnish is a hoax.

92 *Scottish Brassmith's Idea*: the steam-engine, invented by a Scot, James Watt (1736–1819).

94 *gin-horse*: horse used for working a gin, a machine for raising ore in a mine.

words of Ancient Pistol: in Shakespeare's *Merry Wives of Windsor*, II. ii. 2.

95 *Examen Rigorosum . . . Auscultator*: final law examination in a German university; *Auscultator*: a student lawyer, who has passed his first examination.

96 *ever Life for the Living*: 'always life for a living one' in later editions.

97 *Herr Teufelsdröckh . . . eingeladen*: 'Mr Teufelsdröckh is cordially invited by the Countess on Thursday to an aesthetic tea.'

98 *unison*: 'harmony' in later editions.

Bübchen: 'small boys', not 'young gentlemen'.

99 *Holy Alliance of Sovereigns*: league formed by the sovereigns of Russia, Austria, and Prussia in 1815.

100 *Sir Hudibras's sword . . . hack*: *Hudibras*, I. i. 361–2.

102 *Hic Jacet . . . sub dato*: 'Here lies Philip Zähdarm, surnamed the Great, Count of Zähdarm, of the Imperial Council, Knight of the Golden Fleece, the Anklet, and the Black Vulture. Who during his sublunary existence destroyed with lead five thousand partridges and openly turned into dung, through himself and his servants, quadrupeds and bipeds, not without tumult in the process, ten thousand million pounds of assorted food. He now rests from labour, his works following him. If you seek his monument, look at the dung-heap. He made his first kill on earth [date]; his last [date].' The penultimate sentence alludes to the inscription on the tomb at St Paul's Cathedral, London, of its architect, Sir Christopher Wren: 'Si monumentum requiris, circumspice' (If you seek his monument, look around you).

103 *herring-busses*: small boats used in the herring-fishery.

Calypso-Island: the nymph Calypso detained Ulysses for seven years on the island of Ogygia; *Odyssey*, I. v.

106 *St. Martin's Summer*: fine weather in November; St Martin's day is 11 November.

Petrarchan and Werterean: in the style of the Italian poet Petrarch (1304–74), famous for his love lyrics; and of Goethe's sentimental novel, *The Sorrows of Young Werther*.

107 *Waldschloss . . . absolved . . . Relatio ex Actis*: 'Forest-castle'; 'graduated'; 'official reports'.

108 *ahnungsvoll*: 'full of foreboding.' In later editions this is mistakenly changed to *ahndungsvoll* (full of revenge).

111 *Archimedes-lever*: alluding to the famous saying on leverage by Archimedes (287–212 BC), Greek mathematician: 'Give me a place to stand and I will move the world.'

114 *Satanic Poetry*: term used by Southey in 1821 to characterize the poetry of Byron, Shelley, and others.

117 *suit*: 'suit thee' in later editions.

118 *Du Himmel*: 'Good Heavens.'

Richter's words . . . Night: passage from the end of Richter's *Quintus Fixlein* (1796).

119 *Fortunatus' Hat*: legendary folk hero, whose wishing hat transports him wherever he desires.

Lover's Leap: a cliff in western Greece, from which Sappho is said to have plunged to her death for love of Phaon.

120 *The end of Man . . . Thought*: adapted from Aristotle's *Ethics*, I. iii.

rugged . . . names her: Philoctetes, l. 391.

123 *new*: 'mad' in later editions.

124 *Profit-and-Loss Philosophy*: Utilitarianism.

Prometheus Vinctus: Prometheus Bound, the title of a play by Aeschylus. In Greek mythology Prometheus, having endowed mankind with the gift of fire stolen from heaven, was punished by Zeus, who chained him to a rock and sent a vulture to chew his liver.

even: 'ever' in later editions.

125 *recks*: 'boots' in later editions.

Siècle de Louis Quinze: the century of Louis XV, King of France from 1715 to 1774, the age of rationalism and scepticism.

Lubberland: 'land of sluggards'; a favourite word of Carlyle's.

126 *Milton says . . . misery*: Paradise Lost, I. 57.

128 *have often*: 'often' in later editions.

Faust's Deathsong: Goethe's *Faust*, I. iv. 1573.

Rue Saint Thomas de l'Enfer: 'St Thomas Hell Street.'

129 *Baphometic Fire-baptism*: a phrase of uncertain meaning; perhaps 'baptism of wisdom'. Baphomet is the idol that the medieval Knights Templars were accused of worshipping.

130 *Centre of Indifference*: literally, the point midway between the two poles of a magnet, at which the attractive force is stable; see the final sentence of this chapter.

131 *required*: 'acquired' in later editions.

Armida's Palace: in Tasso's *Jerusalem Delivered* (1580–1), book 16, the palace of an enchantress.

133 *Dumdrudge*: Carlyle's invention, from 'dumb drudgery'.

131 *fiction of the English Smollett*: Tobias Smollett's *The Adventures of Ferdinand Count Fathom* (1753), ch. xli.

135 *Berlin-and-Milan Customhouse-officers*: alluding to Napoleon's Berlin and Milan decrees of 1806–7, ordering the seizure of British exports, which the kings of Europe were obliged to enforce.

136 *La carrière ouverte aux talens*: literally, the career open to those with talent.

138 *caput-mortuum*: 'death's-head.' An old chemical term denoting the residuum after distillation or sublimation; here, a worthless residue.

141 *Apage Satanas*: 'Get thee hence, Satan' (Matthew 4: 10).

145 *Hochheimer . . . Ophiuchus*: Rhine wine from Hochheim near Mainz; the throat of the serpent borne by *Ophiuchus* the Serpent Bearer, one of the constellations.

 Wisest of our time . . . begin: Goethe in *Wilhelm Meister's Travels*, ch. xiv.

146 *opened*: 'founded' in later editions.

148 *Fichte's Wissenschaftslehre*: 'The Theory of Knowledge' (1794) by Johann Gottlieb Fichte.

 Whole Duty of Man: an anonymous devotional work (1659).

 a wise man . . . Action: Goethe in *Wilhelm Meister's Apprenticeship* (v. xvi).

 Do the Duty . . . nearest thee: *Wilhelm Meister's Apprenticeship* (VII. i).

 Lothario . . . nowhere: *Wilhelm Meister's Apprenticeship* (VII. iii).

150 *Ecce Homo . . . Choice of Hercules*: 'Behold the man' (i.e. Christ), John 19: 5; proverbial choice between Virtue and Vice.

152 *Code Napoléon*: compilation of the laws of France, drawn up under Napoleon in 1802–8, which still forms the basis of the French legal system.

 deliration: delirium.

BOOK III

158 *Diet of Worms . . . Peterloo*: at the Diet of Worms, Austria, in 1521, Luther was summoned (but refused) to retract his heresies. At the battles of Austerlitz and Waterloo, 1805 and 1815, Napoleon won his greatest victory and suffered his final defeat. At St Peter's

Field, Manchester, ironically named 'Peterloo' after Waterloo, an assembly of protesting workers was attacked by the military in 1819.

Thirdborough in his Hundred: constable in his district.

161 *Fancy-Bazaar . . . Day and Martin*: the Soho bazaar in London; manufacturers of blacking.

163 *man*: 'men' in later editions.

165 *the Frenchman . . . Thought*: Voltaire, *Dialogue* xiv.

166 *right hand . . . left hand*: 'left hand . . . right hand' in later editions, as in Matthew 6: 3.

Shame: 'Shame (*Schaam*)' in later editions; the only occasion on which a German word has been added to the text.

167 *Motive-Millwrights*: Utilitarians.

long-eared enough: the sophism known as Buridan's Ass; if an ass stands between two equally attractive bundles of hay and chooses one, it has free will. If we deny the existence of free will, the ass must starve.

Marseillese Hymns, and Reigns of Terror: i.e. the French Revolutionary marching song 'La Marseillaise', and the climax of bloodshed during the Revolution, 1793–4.

168 *groschen*: German coin of small value.

Peasants' War: uprising of the peasants in Germany, 1524–5; their symbol was a 'clouted Shoe'.

170 *Wau-Wau*: corrected in later editions to 'pawaw' (i.e. powow), the medicine man of North American Indians.

Ancient Pistol . . . little price: *Henry V*, III. vi. 47.

Champion of England: coronation official who appears in full armour to challenge anyone who might dispute the sovereign's right of succession. At the coronation of George IV in 1821, the aged Champion mounted his horse with difficulty.

Now last but one—Ed.: 'That of George IV' in later editions.

172 *Helotage*: Carlyle's coinage for helotism; the system of serfdom in ancient Sparta. The Helots, slaves of the Spartans, were periodically murdered to reduce their numbers.

174 *Indignation*: 'Indignation bear him company' in later editions.

united: 'our united' in later editions.

177 *dogleech*: veterinary surgeon for dogs, or medical quack.

178 *Job's news*: i.e. bad news.

179 *sic-vos-non-vobis*: 'thus you labour not for yourselves' (Virgil); i.e. a state of unfairness.

180 *we find*: 'we to find' in later editions.

Doctor Utriusque Juris: Doctor of Civil and Canon Law.

183 *Spartan broth*: served to the hardy Spartans as a guard against luxury.

called: 'men call' in later editions.

Mirza's Hill: in Addison's 'Vision of Mirza'; *Spectator* 159 (1 September 1711).

184 *Whispering-gallery*: gallery running round the dome of St Paul's Cathedral, London, with an unusual capacity to carry sound.

185 *with even*: 'within' in later editions.

187 *Hebrew Lawgiver . . . Apostle of the Gentiles*: Moses and Paul.

188 *Herzog . . . Marshall*: *Herzog* and *Dux*, German and Latin for duke; *Jarl*, Danish for nobleman; 'Marshall' ('Marshal' in later editions) from Danish *Marskal*, horse-servant.

Popinjay: see Scott's *Old Mortality* (1816), ch. iv.

189 *Ballot-Box*: demanded by the Chartists, but not introduced until 1872.

Peace Society: founded by the Society of Friends (Quakers) in London in 1816.

190 *Paris and Voltaire*: after an absence of twenty-eight years, Voltaire returned to Paris in triumph in 1778, three months before his death.

Hortus Siccus . . . Italian Gumflowers: 'dry garden', i.e. a collection of dried plants for study; artificial flowers.

192 *Miserere*: have mercy; from the fifty-first Psalm, 'Have mercy upon me, O God'.

193 *Diogenes the First*: when a tedious lecture was ending, Diogenes reputedly said: 'Courage friends! I see land.'

Dutch King of Siam: in his *Essay Concerning Human Understanding* (1690), Locke describes a Dutch ambassador telling the King of Siam about the thick ice formed in winter in Holland; the incredulous King is sure that the ambassador is lying (IV. xv).

196 *wise*: 'manner' in later editions.

197 *Luther's Picture of the Devil*: Luther reputedly flung his inkstand at

the Devil who appeared to him while he was translating the Psalms.

198 *imagings (not imaginings)*: 'imagings or imaginings' in later editions.

199 *Orpheus*: 'Orpheus or Amphion' in later editions. Amphion, son of Zeus, made stones move of their own accord during the building of the walls of Thebes. Orpheus, less relevantly, tamed wild beasts with his lyre.

   Steinbruch: quarry.

   truth: 'true' in later editions.

200 *English Johnson . . . Cock Lane*: the 'Cock Lane Ghost' was an imposture, produced by a girl living in Cock Lane, London. Samuel Johnson visited the girl's house in 1762, but declared the ghost to be a fraud.

202 *We are such stuff . . . sleep*: The Tempest, IV. i. 156–8.

203 *And like . . . behind*: The Tempest, IV. i. 151–6.

204 *Horn-gate*: in the Aeneid, vi. 893 ff., the gate of sleep that produces true dreams, opposed to the 'Ivory-gate' that produces false dreams.

205 *Magna Charta . . . measures*: the celebrated charter of the liberties of England was signed by King John in 1215. Sir Robert Cotton (1571–1631), collector of manuscripts, reputedly rescued it from his tailor.

   Thirty-nine Articles: the doctrinal tenets of the Church of England.

207 *Worth*: 'World' in later editions.

   Clotha Virumque cano: 'Clothes and the man I sing', parodying the opening line of the Aeneid, 'Arms and the man I sing'.

208 *Lord Herringbone*: i.e. a typical dandy, named after the herringbone stitch.

209 *Zerdusht, Quangfoutchee, Mohamed*: Zoroaster, Confucius, and Mohammed; respective founders of the Parsee, Confucian, and Islamic religions.

210 *Menadic . . . Eleusinian or Cabiric*: the Maenads were inspired female worshippers of Bacchus, the god of wine; the Eleusinians worshipped Ceres, the goddess of agriculture; the Cabiri were deities worshipped in Greece and Egypt.

Magnetic Sleep: from 'animal magnetism', an early term for hypnotism.

deliquium: melting or liquefaction.

Fire-balls . . . Alien: balls of fire which reputedly prevented Julian the Apostate's attempt to rebuild the Jewish Temple at Jerusalem, in defiance of the Christians.

211 *Stillschweigen'sche Buchhandlung*: 'Silence Bookshop.'

Mohamedan reverence even for waste paper: because, according to the *Spectator*, no. 85, it 'may contain some piece of their Alcoran'.

Pelham: a novel by Bulwer Lytton, published in 1828. The seven 'Articles of Faith' that follow are based on passages in *Pelham* which were omitted or altered in later editions.

212 *Hallanshakers*: Scotch for beggars.

Bogtrotters, Redshanks, Ribbonmen, Cottiers, Peep-of-day Boys, Babes of the Wood, Rockites: Irish terms for, respectively, peasants, the bare-legged, members of the Catholic Ribbon Society (opponents of the Protestant Orangemen), cottage dwellers, Protestant insurgents, outlaws, and revolutionaries of 1812, signing their notices 'Captain Rock'.

213 *irrevocably enough*: 'irrevocably' in later editions.

seemed indescribable: 'did not seem describable' in later editions.

214 *Brahminical feeling*: Brahmins oppose the killing of animals.

Potatoes-and-Point: i.e. nothing but potatoes, from the Irish joke of eating potatoes while pointing to something else saved for a future meal.

The late John Bernard: English actor and writer (1756–1828), whose *Retrospections of the Stage* was published posthumously in 1830. The excerpt 'from the original' is from I. xi. 349–50.

215 *original*: in later editions, the heading 'Poor-Slave Household' is here inserted.

abode: in later editions, the heading 'Dandiacal Household' is here inserted.

A Dressing-room . . . Apron: the passage is from Bulwer Lytton's Introduction to *The Disowned* (1828).

216 *Potwallopers*: i.e. householders; those who boiled their own pots.

218 *Pelion on Ossa*: the mythological Titans attempted to reach heaven by piling Mount Pelion on Mount Ossa (*Odyssey*, xi. 305 ff.).

Hans Sachs . . . Schneider mit dem Panier: German poet (1494–1576), one of whose songs is entitled 'The Tailor with the Banner'.

Taming of the Shrew: an anonymous tailor appears in IV. iii.

219 *sartorius*: thigh muscle used to produce the tailor's cross-legged sitting position.

Swift . . . Divinity: referring to the tailor-worshipping sect in Swift's *A Tale of a Tub* (1704), sec. ii.

Franklin . . . Kings: the words quoted are inscribed in Latin on a bust of Benjamin Franklin (1706–90), American statesman and author, who discovered that lightning was an electric charge.

greatest living Guild-Brother: Goethe; the quotation is from *Wilhelm Meister's Apprenticeship* (II. ii).

220 *Sic itur ad astra*: 'This is the way to the stars' (*Aeneid*, xi. 641).

221 *being*: 'having' in later editions.

222 *brush*: 'sponge' in later editions.

223 *Gowle*: ghoul; 'gowl' in later editions.

Ew. Wohlgeboren: 'Your Honour.'

225 *it*: 'this' in later editions.

lived: 'existed' in later editions.

APPENDIX I

227 *Reform hurlyburly*: agitation leading to the Reform Bill of 1832.

title: Carlyle first refers to the work as *Sartor Resartus* in a letter of 18 July 1833 to John Stuart Mill.

Eight sheets of Fraser: Carlyle's estimate proved correct; the work was published in eight instalments.

228 *five persons*: the five readers cannot be precisely identified, but probably include William Glen, John Stuart Mill, and Henry Inglis. The sixth, William Fraser, was James Fraser's brother and editor of the *Foreign Review*.

"*O. Y.'s*": notes spuriously attributed to 'Oliver Yorke', pseudonym of William Maginn, the editor of *Fraser's Magazine*.

APPENDIX II

230 *Bayle in voce*: the reader is referred to Pierre Bayle's *Dictionnaire*

historique et critique (1695–7), *sub voce* (under the heading) Oppian, the name of two Greek poets of the second century A D.

donner-und-blitzenizing: thundering and lightning.

a seventy-four: a large ship, with seventy-four guns.

Regina: *Fraser's* was popularly dubbed *Regina*, Queen of the Magazines. The Cimbri and Teutones were ancient Teutonic tribes.

APPENDIX III

231 *British Friend . . . party*: Father O'Shea, an Irish priest of Cork, who wrote to Fraser commending *Sartor Resartus*; Carlyle finally met him in 1849.

232 *Fritz the Only*: Frederick the Great; see *Sartor Resartus*, p. 63 above.

Blair's Lectures: Hugh Blair's *Lectures on Rhetoric and Belles Lettres* (1783).

APPENDIX IV

233 *Mill*: John Stuart Mill.

234 *coal-marks*: black marks of censure.

"Talented": one of the many words in *Sartor* to which Sterling objected.

Satan Montgomery: Robert Montgomery's religious poem *Satan* (1830) had been widely praised and frequently reprinted.

235 *cross the Atlantic*: *Sartor Resartus* was published in Boston nine months later, in March 1836; see Note on the Text, above.

APPENDIX V

237 *penes nos*: in our possession.

Fraser's . . . &c.: this sentence is not in the review of *Fraser's Magazine* in the *Sun*, 1 April 1834, from which the rest of the excerpt is taken.

old Dennis: John Dennis (1657–1734), dramatist and critic, known for the vigour of his criticism.

238 *Here is a "*—: the omitted sentence continues: 'bray worthy of the

most sonorous animal that ever chewed the thistle.' The reviewer goes on to compare Carlyle's sentence with another by an 'eminent transcendental philosopher of the day', concluding: 'These two scribes should be harnessed together in a donkey cart. They have both an equal length of ear.'

. . . *"After*: the omission is a brief discussion of the 'Editorial Difficulties' chapter, Book I.

hum: humbug or hoax.

240 *supercherie*: hoax or fraud.

. . . *character."*: the remainder of the review, omitted by Carlyle, gives an outline of *Sartor*, provides copious extracts, and identifies Carlyle as the author.

241 *1835*: Carlyle's error; should be 1836.

Sunt, Fuerunt vel Fuere: 'That's the way they are, that's the way they have been.'

GLOSSARY OF PEOPLE AND PLACES

Aaron, brother of Moses; his rod performed many miracles.

Adamites, second-century heretical sect, whose efforts to return to a pre-lapsarian innocence included the discarding of clothes.

Agora, market-place in Greek cities.

Alaric (*c.*376–410), King of the Goths, who captured and plundered Rome in 410.

Alexander the Great (356–323 BC), King of Macedon, who conquered much of the ancient world.

Almack's, fashionable London assembly-room, founded by William Almack in 1765.

Ammon, principal Egyptian deity, with a temple and oracle in an oasis of the Libyan desert.

Amur, principal river of Eastern Asia.

Angelo, Michelangelo (1475–1564).

Arachne, Lydian maiden who challenged Athena to a weaving contest; after losing she was turned into a spider.

Arbela, town in ancient Assyria, where Alexander the Great defeated the Persians in 331 BC.

Arkwright, Sir Richard (1732–92), inventor of the spinning-jenny.

Athos, Holy Mountain in Macedonia; site of numerous monasteries.

Baliol, John (1249–1315), King of Scotland 1292–6; his nickname 'Toomtabard' is Scotch for 'empty gown'.

Bardili, Christoph Gottfried (1761–1808), German philosopher.

Bazard-Enfantin, Armand Bazard (1791–1832) and Barthélemy Prosper Enfantin (1796–1864); two French followers of Saint-Simon.

Bichat, Marie François Xavier (1771–1802), French physiologist and anatomist.

Bivar, Rodrigo Diaz de (*c.*1040–99), Spanish national hero.

Boileau-Despréaux, Nicolas (1636–1711), French poet and critic. According to Helvétius, his coldness and severity were owing to a bizarre childhood injury: 'a turkey gave him several blows of the beak on a very delicate part.'

Bolívar, Simón (1783–1830), South American statesman and liberator.

Buchan-Buller, whirlpool on the coast of Buchan, Scotland, formed by a cauldron-like well in the rocks.

Büsching, Anton Friedrich

(1724–93), German geographer; author of *A New Description of the Earth* (1754–9).

Caaba, sanctuary in the Great Mosque at Mecca, containing a sacred black stone.

Cadmus, legendary founder of Thebes and introducer of the alphabet into Greece.

Caesar, Julius (102–44 BC), according to Plutarch's *Lives*, when Caesar leapt into the sea to escape from the Egyptians after the battle of Pharos, he swam with one hand and kept his papers dry with the other.

Cain, the first farmer and first city-dweller, as well as the first murderer.

Callot, Jacques (1592–1635), French painter and engraver.

Campus Martius, 'Field of Mars'; assembly place in ancient Rome.

Cassini, Giovanni Domenico (1625–1712), Italian astronomer and director of the Paris observatory; author of *Règles de l'Astronomie Siamoise.*

Chronos, Greek god of Time; confused with Kronos, the father of Zeus. Kronos devoured his children, but Zeus escaped this fate and overthrew his father.

Chrysostom, St John (347–407), early Greek father of the Christian Church.

Cicero, Marcus Tullius (106–43 BC), Roman orator and exemplar of wisdom.

Cid (from *Seid* or Lord), see **Bivar.**

Cincinnatus, Lucius Quintius, Roman hero called from farming to the Dictatorship (458 BC); he returned to farming after only a few days.

Congreve, Sir William (1772–1828), inventor of a powerful rocket enclosed in a metallic case, named after him.

Cousin, Victor (1792–1867), French philosopher.

Crim Tartary, part of the Crimea inhabited by Tartars.

Curragh of Kildare, plain in county Kildare, Ireland.

D'Alembert, Jean (1717–83), French mathematician, philosopher, and encyclopaedist.

Darnley, Henry (1545–67), second husband of Mary Queen of Scots; she is said to have been attracted to him because of his figure.

Diogenes, Greek Cynic philosopher of the fifth century BC, celebrated for his sharp wit; he was reputed to live in a tub.

Dionysius' Ear, cave by means of which Dionysius the Elder, Tyrant of Syracuse (c.432–367 BC), could overhear his prisoners.

Donau, the River Danube.

Downing Street, London street containing Government offices and the official residence of the Prime Minister.

Elizabeth of Hungary (1207–31), on one occasion St Elizabeth disobeyed her husband by bringing a basket of food to the poor at her gates. On being intercepted by her husband, she hid the basket under her apron. When uncovered, the food was found to have been miraculously transformed into roses.

Epictetus, first-century Stoic philosopher. The *Enchiridion*, or handbook, of Epictetus was compiled by his pupil Arrianus.

Ernulphus, Bishop of Rochester (1040–1124) who wrote a celebrated curse, the full text of which is given in Sterne's *Tristram Shandy* (III. xi).

Eros, principal god in Greek myth, born from the cosmic egg produced by Chaos (or Night).

Erostratus, in 356 BC he set fire to the temple of Diana at Ephesus in order to be remembered in history.

Estrapades, the *Place de l'Estrapade* in Paris, named after the torturing of Protestants by the 'strappado' or rope used to dislocate the arms.

Eurotas, principal river of Laconia in ancient Greece, near Sparta.

Faust (or Fust), Johann (*c.*1400–66), partner of Johann Gutenberg in Mainz; originator of movable type in printing.

Field Lane, notorious in Carlyle's time for its shops dealing in stolen goods.

Fox, George (1624–91), founder of the Society of Friends (Quakers) and known as 'the man in leather breeches'.

Frederick the Great (1712–86), Frederick II, King of Prussia.

Fritz the Only, see **Frederick the Great.**

Gao (or Gaváh), legendary Persian blacksmith who led a successful rebellion, using his leather apron as a standard.

Gehenna, valley of Hinnom near Jerusalem, where children were sacrificed to Moloch; hence a prototype of Hell.

Gibeonites, biblical inhabitants of Gibeon, condemned by Joshua to be hewers of wood and drawers of water for having deceived him.

Golgotha, place of skulls; Calvary.

Graham, Dr James (1745–94), founder of a Temple of Health in London and inventor of a Celestial Bed, designed to cure sterility.

Hadrian (76–138), Roman Emperor who held that a ruler should, like the sun, visit every part of his dominions.

Hannibal (247–183 BC), at the age of 9, the Carthaginian general swore an oath of life-long enmity to Rome.

Hebron, residence of King David and burial place of the patriarchs.

Hegel, Georg Wilhelm Friedrich (1770–1831), German idealist philosopher.

Helvétius, Claude Adrien (1715–71), French philosopher and author.

Hengst and Horsa, leaders of

the Germanic invaders of Britain during the fifth century.

Henry the Fowler (876–936), Henry I, King of Germany.

Herschel, Sir William (1738–1822), English astronomer of German birth, who attempted to count the stars of the Northern Hemisphere.

Hertha (or Nerthus), ancient Teutonic earth-goddess of fertility.

Hochkirch, town in Saxony where Frederick the Great was defeated by the Austrians in 1758.

Humboldt, Alexander von (1769–1859), German naturalist and explorer.

Hutton, James (1726–97), Scottish geologist.

Ishmael, Abraham's son, left in the desert as a child; his cry for help was heard by God, who gave him his name ('I have heard').

Issus, town in Cilicia, where Alexander the Great defeated the Persians in 333 BC.

Jean Paul, see **Richter**.

Jenner, Edward (1749–1823), English physician and discoverer of vaccination.

Johnson, Samuel (1709–84), man of letters; his respect for Church dignitaries is recorded in Boswell's *Life of Johnson* (1791).

Joseph II (1741–90), Emperor of Austria, who outraged Hungarians by ordering the Hungarian crown to be sent to Vienna.

Justinian (483–565), Emperor of Constantinople, who supervised the compilation of a Pandect, or Digest, of the commentaries of jurists on Roman laws.

Kepler, Johann (1571–1630), German astronomer.

Knox, Elizabeth, youngest daughter of John Knox, the sixteenth-century Scottish reformer. After the exile of her husband, John Welch, she pleaded for his pardon, which King James promised to grant only if Welch would acknowledge the authority of the bishops.

Kunersdorf, Prussian village where Frederick the Great was defeated by the Russians and Austrians in 1759.

Lagrange, Joseph Louis, Comte (1736–1813), French mathematician and astronomer; author of *Mécanique analytique* (1788).

Landgravine Elizabeth, see **Elizabeth of Hungary**.

Laplace, Pierre Simon, Marquis de (1749–1827), French mathematician and astronomer; author of *Mécanique céleste* (1799–1825).

Lawrence, Sir William (1783–1867), English surgeon and physiologist.

Lilis (or Lilith), Adam's first wife, according to the Talmud.

Lingard, John (1771–1851), Roman Catholic historian of England.

Loretto-shrine, small Italian town containing the reputed house of the Virgin Mary, said to have been conveyed there from Nazareth by angels.

Luther, Martin (1483–1546), German religious reformer, who in 1520 publicly burned the papal bull by which he was excommunicated. His German translation of the Bible appeared in 1534.

Lycurgus, Spartan lawgiver of the ninth century BC.

Maesogothic Ulfila, see **Ulfila**.

Magendie, François (1783–1855), French physiologist, noted for his research on the nervous system.

Maggiore, Lago, large lake in northern Italy.

Mahmoud, Sultan (1785–1839), Mahmoud II, Sultan of Turkey 1808–39.

Majendie, see **Magendie**.

Malines, Belgian town, famous for its lace.

Malthus, Thomas Robert (1766–1834), English political economist and author of the *Essay on the Principle of Population* (1798), which advocates restraints on population growth through limiting the number of births.

Malzleins, Malzlein, a suburb of Vienna.

Marchfeld, plain near Vienna where Ottokar, King of Bohemia, was slain by Rudolph ('Rodolf') of Hapsburg at the battle of Stillfried in 1278, and where Napoleon defeated Francis I ('Kaiser Franz') of Austria in 1809.

Melchizedek, biblical priest-king of mysterious origin.

Memnon, Ethiopian hero, son of Eos, or Aurora, the dawn. His statue at Thebes was supposed to emit a sound like that of a breaking chord when struck by the first rays of the sun.

Merrick, see **Meyrick**.

Meyrick, Samuel Rush (1783–1848), his *Critical Inquiry into Ancient Armour* was published in 1824.

Milo, athlete of Crotona during the sixth century BC. Said to have carried a 4-year-old bullock around the stadium at Olympia and afterwards to have eaten it all in a single day.

Minerva, Latin name for Athena, goddess of wisdom and war, who was said to have sprung, fully armed, from the head of Zeus.

Monmouth Street, noted in the eighteenth century for its old-clothes shops run largely by Jews.

Montesquieu, Charles Louis, Baron de (1689–1755), French philosopher and historian; his *Esprit des Lois* appeared in 1748.

Montgolfier, hot-air balloon, first raised in 1783, named after the French inventors Stephen and Joseph Montgolfier.

Nebuchadnezzar, biblical king of Babylon, who attempted to burn his foes in a fiery furnace.

New Holland, Australia.

Newton, Sir Isaac (1642–1727), English mathematician and astronomer, who continued the work of Johann Kepler.

Novalis (1722–1801), pseudonym of Friedrich von Hardenberg, German poet and idealist.

Oken, Lorenz (1779–1851), German naturalist and philosopher, real name Ockenfuss, founded the controversial journal *Isis* in 1818.

Ormuz, Persian island, with a large, wealthy market in the late Middle Ages.

Otaheitean, Tahitian.

Otto, Kaiser, Otto I of Germany (912–73), who welcomed scholars to his court.

Palais Bourbon, Chamber of Deputies (French Parliament) in Paris.

Papin, Denis (1647–1712), French physicist and inventor of a 'steam digester' for raising the temperature of boiling water.

Paullini, Christian Franz (1643–1712), German compiler, author of *Zeit-Kürzende erbauliche Lust* ('Time-Shortening Uplifting Pleasure', 1695–1725).

Paullinus, see **Paullini**.

Philip, King, Philip II of Spain (1527–98), whose introduction of the Inquisition into the Netherlands was opposed by a group calling themselves the *Gueux* (beggars).

Pierre-Pertuis, 'Pierced Rock'; a natural passage through a large rock in the Bernese Alps, Switzerland.

Pisgah, biblical mountain from which the Lord showed Moses the Promised Land.

Pius VII (1742–1823), Pope from 1800 to 1823.

Pyrrhus (318–272 BC), King of Epirus, who twice defeated but was finally conquered by the Romans.

Richter, Johann Paul Friedrich (1763–1825), German Romantic humorist, who wrote under the name 'Jean Paul'.

Rosa, Salvator (1615–73), Italian painter of the Neapolitan school.

Rossbach, town in Saxony where Frederick the Great defeated the French in 1757.

Royer-Collard, Pierre (1763–1845), French philosopher.

Saint-Simon, Claude-Henri, Comte de (1760–1825), philosopher and founder of socialism in France.

St Sophia, Mosque of Holy Wisdom at Constantinople.

St Stephen's, i.e. the House of Commons in Westminster.

Salamanca University, Spanish University, famous from the fifteenth to the seventeenth century.

Samarcand, town in Turkestan; an important seat of learning in the fifteenth century.

Sanconiathon, legendary Phoenician sage.

Saturn, Roman god of agriculture; mistakenly identified with the Greek gods Kronos and Chronos.

Schonbrünn, Imperial castle near Vienna, where important treaties were concluded during the Napoleonic Wars.

Schreckhorn, 'peak of terror'; a principal summit of the Bernese Alps in Switzerland.

Schwartz, Berthold, German monk who discovered the process of granulating gunpowder early in the fourteenth century.

Seneca, Lucius Annaeus (c. 4 BC–AD 65), Roman Stoic philosopher and dramatist.

Shinar, site of the tower of Babel.

Siloa (or Siloam), river and pool near Jerusalem.

Solon (c.638–559 BC), Athenian lawgiver.

Stewart, Dugald (1753–1828), Scottish philosopher and professor at the University of Edinburgh.

Sybaris, Greek city in Southern Italy, famous for its luxury (hence 'sybarite').

Tadmor (or Palmyra), Syrian city, destroyed in 273 but leaving splendid ruins.

Tarakwang, Emperor (1781–1850), Tao Kuang, Emperor of China 1820–50. The 'White Water-roses' or Water Lily faction was active during the early part of his reign.

Tattersall, London horse-market.

Teniers, David (1582–1649), Dutch painter, as was his son and namesake (1610–90).

Themistocles, Athenian statesman of the fifth century BC.

Tiber, river in Italy, by Rome.

Tombuctoo, Timbuctoo: a town on the edge of the Sahara desert, the subject of Tennyson's poem *Timbuctoo* (1829).

Treisnitz, Triesnitz; a town near Jena, in Germany, where Schiller and Goethe sometimes met, beginning in 1789.

Trimberg, Hugo von (1260–1309), German author and Meistersinger.

Trismegistus, Hermes, 'thrice-greatest'; name given by the Greeks to Thoth, Egyptian god of speech and letters.

Tubalcain, the first metalworker, according to Genesis.

Ude, Louis Eustache (1769–1846), famous French cook, chef to Louis XVI.

Ulfila (or Ulfilas) (c.311–83), Bishop of the Goths, who translated the Bible into Gothic; the oldest extant writing in the Germanic languages.

Vaucluse, French village near Avignon; home of Petrarch.

Wagram, village near Vienna, where Napoleon defeated the Austrians in 1809.

Werner, Abraham Gottlob (1750–1817), father of German geology.

Wesley, Charles (1708–88), brother of John Wesley; writer of well-known hymns.

Wesley, John (1703–91), founder of the Methodists.

William the Silent (1533–84), Prince of Orange and Count of Nassau, founder of the Dutch Republic; known for his diplomatic silences.

Winnipic, Lake, Lake Winnipeg in Manitoba.

Zeno, Greek philosopher of the third century BC; founder of the Stoic school.

Zinzendorf, Nikolaus Ludwig, Count von (1700–60), German religious reformer; reviver of the Moravian Church.

MORE ABOUT | **OXFORD WORLD'S CLASSICS**

The Oxford World's Classics Website

www.worldsclassics.co.uk

- Information about new titles
- Explore the full range of Oxford World's Classics
- Links to other literary sites and the main OUP webpage
- Imaginative competitions, with bookish prizes
- Peruse the Oxford World's Classics Magazine
- Articles by editors
- Extracts from Introductions
- A forum for discussion and feedback on the series
- Special information for teachers and lecturers

www.worldsclassics.co.uk

American Literature

British and Irish Literature

Children's Literature

Classics and Ancient Literature

Colonial Literature

Eastern Literature

European Literature

History

Medieval Literature

Oxford English Drama

Poetry

Philosophy

Politics

Religion

The Oxford Shakespeare

A complete list of Oxford Paperbacks, including Oxford World's Classics, Oxford Shakespeare, Oxford Drama, and Oxford Paperback Reference, is available in the UK from the Academic Division Publicity Department, Oxford University Press, Great Clarendon Street, Oxford OX2 6DP.

In the USA, complete lists are available from the Paperbacks Marketing Manager, Oxford University Press, 198 Madison Avenue, New York, NY 10016.

Oxford Paperbacks are available from all good bookshops. In case of difficulty, customers in the UK can order direct from Oxford University Press Bookshop, Freepost, 116 High Street, Oxford OX1 4BR, enclosing full payment. Please add 10 per cent of published price for postage and packing.